A Novel

by

Gerald D. Otis

Dedication

*To all those who have served their
nation by their military service.*

Acknowledgments

The author wishes to thank Dr. Michael Napoliello (author of *189th and Washington: Stories from a Wonderful Bronx Neighborhood*) for his thorough scrutiny of an earlier version of this manuscript and for making many valuable corrections, additions, subtractions and suggestions. Credit is also due to Eric Larsen, fellow Northfielder, retired college professor and accomplished author (*A Book of Reading, A Nation Gone Blind* and the award winning *An American Memory*), for his astute criticisms and recommendations to improve my story telling. A special thank you goes to Dr. John R. Graham (author of *Sea Change*), longtime friend and colleague, for his reflections on working in a total institution and especially for his contribution to the summary description of *Vetlandia*. Gratitude is also due to Lynda Southworth (yet another Northfielder), grammarian, spelling error sleuth, and woman with an ear for dialogue, for her work on the very first versions of early chapters as they were completed.

CHAPTER 1

ON THE ROAD

Tom hoisted one eyelid, peering out on an incoherent world. There was a buzzing sensation in the back of his head as if a dentist were using a course bit to furiously drill away at a diseased tooth. His tongue felt like a marshmallow, making it hard to swallow. Each strand of hair on his head was vibrating in competition for his attention. The sunlight pouring in the window felt like a million needles poking into his one exposed retina. His leg muscles burned as if he had been running in a marathon. Aches all over his body made him feel like he had fallen off a truck and bumped along the roadway.

Sitting on the edge of the bed, Tom surveyed the room but seemed unable to comprehend what he was seeing. What is this place? What am I doing here? Nothing came to mind. His failure to generate the coordinates of himself in time and space was pushing him to the edge of panic. Am I dead? Is this purgatory? Am I destined for hell?

Climbing into the pants and shirt piled on a nearby chair, then sliding into a pair of loafers, he tentatively poked his head out the door, retracting like a startled cat at the first hint of sound or movement. Stumbling outside where cars were whizzing by on the busy street, he walked down the sidewalk to the corner and squinted at the street signs. Dodge and Speedway. The names didn't evoke any meaning. Nor did the blinking white sign with the stick figure drawing on it. What town is this? What the fuck is going on? This is really eerie, he thought.

Tom sat down on a bench at a bus stop to see if the mental fog would go away. Slowly, it began to register that a green light meant "Go" and a red light meant "Stop" for motorists. He walked a few blocks down Speedway and saw a building that stirred some sort of vague recognition as if he had seen it somewhere long ago. He decided to go into the Quick Print business on the ground floor.

"Hi Tom," said the attractive young woman at the counter with blond curls cascading down below her shoulders. "Where have you been?"

Incredulous at being recognized but hoping it would turn out they were lovers, Tom asked, "Do you know me?"

"Oh, come on Tom, you're pulling my leg. Don't try to tell me you don't remember that you work here. That's not going to get you out of explaining where you have been for the last two days. Tom Ward, the amnesiac! The boss is really going to like that one! What did you do, go out and tie one on with your buddies over at Cochise?"

"Oh, yeah," said Tom as if he had been suddenly jogged back into a semblance of normal consciousness. He remembered being in college but things were still vague and strange.

"No, I wasn't out drinking. I just seem to have lost a couple of days. Just another instance of the Ward Curse, I guess."

Skeptically she asked, "And I suppose you don't remember anything during that time?"

"No. The last thing I remember is going home from English class on Wednesday night. I can't remember what the lecture was about, though. Hope I took some notes," he said with a wry smile directed toward Jill. She grinned in return.

Jill Endersby liked Tom – his sense of humor, sensitivity, and compassion, and had thought about getting romantically involved with him at one time. But she had decided to maintain her distance. She knew he was an English major and that he liked history. She knew he had been discharged from the army and that he came from California. But he hesitated to say much about his past. He was too guarded and reserved. And now this. He was just too weird.

A tall rotund man in his mid-forties appeared from one of the back rooms. "Hey, Tom. We've missed you around here the last couple of days. Where have you been and why didn't you call and let us know you were not going to be at work?"

"I'm sorry. I guess I seem to have passed out or slept the last two days away. I woke up about an hour ago. I am now finally getting my bearings. I would have called but I was completely out of it."

"That's too bad," his boss said with more than a trace of sarcasm. "The quality of your work has been outstanding and you get a lot accomplished when you are here. And you get along very well with the customers. But, you know, this is a business and our employees are supposed to be here. We can't put things on hold waiting for you to show up. I had to spend most of my time for the last two days filling in for you. So, I guess I'm going to have to let you go. I'll give you two weeks pay and I'll write a letter of recommendation if you want. I'm sorry, but that is the way it is going to have to be."

Dejected but not surprised, Tom walked out of the store and headed back to his room. Oh, shit. What am I going to do now? His mind was now fully alert and he began to think of his options now that he would not have an income. By the time Tom got home he had decided to drop out of school. Without a job, he couldn't afford it and besides, he did not do well in some courses that were required for graduation, like the sciences. But he got good grades in those courses he was enthusiastic about. He surveyed his meager belongings and decided it wouldn't take long to pack.

Tom decided to check in with Dave Bowlby, his former army buddy, who had urged him to come to Tucson to live and further his education. Dave was nearing completion of his PhD in psychophysiology and trying to decide where he wanted to start his career. The last time Tom had talked with him he was considering possibilities in the west since he didn't care for the claustrophobic corn belt or the high-octane lifestyle of the east coast.

Maybe I can get some tips on where to relocate from Dave, he thought to himself as he made a salami sandwich for his lunch. To use the time until he knew Dave would be back from school, he started arranging things for packing then walked to the bus stop.

Getting off the bus at Speedway and Second, Tom made his way past the pomegranate bushes that grew along the alley, and up the stairs to Dave's apartment on the second floor of a guesthouse. It was a one-bedroom place that had been inhabited by university students for decades. The bathroom still harbored the black wall and purple toilet seat bestowed upon it by some previous residents.

Dave came to the door and invited Tom in. "Haven't seen you in a while, Tom. Where have you been and what's happening? Can I get you a beer or some coffee?"

"A beer would be nice, thanks," said Tom. "I just got fired from my job, and I'm thinking about dropping out of Cochise and moving someplace else."

"Why'd you get fired? I thought you were doing well at that printing place."

"I was, but I had another seizure and ended up missing two days of work. I was really out of it and must have spent the whole time in bed. At least, I hope that's where I was. When I came to, I didn't know where I was and couldn't make any sense out of anything. I forgot where I worked until I walked down the street and thought a building looked familiar. So I walked in and got fired. The job wasn't that great but I liked being around Jill and it paid my bills."

Dave was present when Tom was doing repair work on a missile launcher in Germany. Another soldier had jumped into the driver's seat and decided to move it, not bothering to tell anyone. Tom fell off, his head striking a tree on the way down. He was unconscious for about 30 minutes and had his first seizure at that time.

The army hospital he was sent to in Germany was unable to get his seizures under control so they sent him to a second one. When that also failed, he was airlifted back to the US and during that flight, he was on a continuous IV and nearly died a couple of times. At Letterman General Hospital they managed to get his seizures controlled but, oddly, the head injury also caused him to develop diabetes. And his seizure medications would affect his diabetes medication so that one or the other condition was frequently uncontrolled.

After many months, the physicians managed to achieve a fragile balance, and Tom was discharged from both the hospital and the army. The VA gave him a 40% service-connected disability, but that did not fairly reflect the degree to which his condition affected his life. He could go for months without having an episode. Then something would tilt his blood sugars out of bounds, and he might have a full-blown seizure.

"Oh, God!" exclaimed Dave. "That bump on the head has really messed you up. I remember early on when we were in the army. You were all gung-ho to do well and make rank. You were smart and enthusiastic and you would have made it, if that accident hadn't occurred."

"Yeah, a lot of my get-up-and-go got up and left after that. Some things I just can't do nearly as well as I used to, but others I'm still pretty good at. I met some guys in the hospital that had it a lot worse than I did. One guy, a tank driver, was waiting in line to be placed on a railroad car to be sent to another place in Germany. Some goofy guy in the tank behind him loaded his cannon and fired right into this guy's tank. Two guys inside were killed immediately and there was a terrible fire, but he and another guy were able to get out through the bottom escape hatch. He was burned all over and had to have a whole slug of skin grafts. He used to complain most about when they would peel the dead skin off, which was really painful. He told me everyone in that unit could hear the screams of the skin graft patients. So I guess I could have had a worse fate."

"That may be true," said Dave. "There is always someone in the world who has had it worse than you. Maybe that gives a person some kind of relief by comparison, but that does not diminish the more-than-usual amount of suffering you have had yourself, Tom. Don't deny it. Your injury is not like a bullet wound that can heal or a lost limb that can be replaced with an artificial one, which may not be like the original, but can still function pretty well. There is no prosthetic for an injured brain. It will always be getting in the way of what you want to do."

Dave was a good friend and Tom knew it. He appreciated that Dave would always tell him the unvarnished truth. It helped him get a clear fix on his problems rather than fuzzifying them like the denial and minimizing he would get from people, even doctors, trying to cheer him up or distract him.

"Yeah. I think I should drop out of college. I have problems remembering things in class unless I write it all down and I have a hard time with math. Sometimes I just draw a blank with some computation that I used to know well. Or I will get the order of things scrambled, even in English classes where I ordinarily do well. Some nights I will study and have things down pretty well and by the time I wake up the next day, a lot of it will be gone. It's very frustrating."

Tom paused, looking out the window, and said, "And then there is my social life. I was never real outgoing, but I used to have friends and girlfriends. Now I hesitate to get involved with anyone because about that time, I'll have a seizure that will scare them off. The last time I went to a party with a girl, I had a seizure and pissed all over myself. That was the end of that. She didn't even let me take her home."

"Yeah," said Dave. "People still discriminate against those with epilepsy. I guess it seems mysterious and scares them. Major seizures are pretty dramatic events to witness. Some patients have seizures that those around them don't even notice. And people don't usually know enough about it to know what to do, so they feel helpless too. Yet it is a frequent enough condition that the average person is bound to run into people who suffer from it. The problem probably could be diminished substantially by a little public education."

"I doubt that will happen in my lifetime," said Tom. "Anyway, I've got to find someplace where I can make a living and have options if my seizures cause me to be fired again. I can't go to a regular college because they expect you to follow a schedule and they don't accommodate us misfits very well. I'm thinking it has to be a place with a much more thriving economy than we have here in Tucson."

"I've been told that Las Vegas has a booming economy right now," said Dave. They have all those casinos that bring in a ton of visitors every year, all year around. They need lots of employees to service the needs of all those tourists and gamblers – dealers, slot machine guys, bouncers, accountants, restaurant employees, hotel people, gas station attendants, and mechanics. And all those employees need some place to live, so there is a construction boom going on there too. The casinos provide lots of buffet meals that are of decent quality and relatively cheap too. Of course, the economy is heavily dependent on the gambler-tourist-entertainment sector, but that doesn't seem like it is going to dry up any time soon."

"Hmm," said Tom as he thought about the prospect of moving to Las Vegas. "I could work in one of those casinos. I don't gamble and that might be a plus for me in one of those places. If worse came to worst, I could always work in a restaurant or do something on a construction crew."

"You have to get a certificate from the gaming board if you work in one of the casinos, and they would probably have to do a background check."

"No problem. I've never been arrested and don't have any outstanding debts."

"Why don't we go over to Caruso's for dinner," said Dave. "My treat since you are going to need your funds for transportation if you move."

Tom gave himself a shot of insulin in anticipation of an onslaught of calories. Then the pair climbed aboard Dave's motorcycle, a late model Honda, and quickly traversed the few blocks over to 6th St. and 4th Avenue. Under the benign influence of good Italian food, a nice atmosphere, and a fine red wine, they continued to discuss the pros and cons of Tom moving to Las Vegas. By the end of the evening, when he bid Dave adieu, Tom was convinced that Nevada would be his next home.

In the morning Tom packed those few belongings he was unable to accommodate in his duffel bag into two cardboard boxes. He lugged the parcels down to Speedway and made his way to the Greyhound Bus Depot where he arranged for them to be sent to Las Vegas and held until his arrival. Then it was back to his apartment for some final cleaning up and settling of accounts. On the way, he stopped to close his bank account. He had advised his landlord before he took his parcels to Greyhound that he was going to leave the next day and that any mail that might arrive could be forwarded to General Delivery in Las Vegas. He obtained his rental deposit and added it to his funds from the bank and his final check from Quick Print. The total was not impressive considering he would need some funds to get settled in Nevada, so he decided he would hitch rides to save money. He made a small cardboard sign that said, "North to Vegas."

Tom got up early to find a ride going north on Interstate 10. He ate most of what remained in his refrigerator, packed a sandwich and some snacks in his duffel bag, and threw the rest in the garbage. Then he took the bus down Speedway to Oracle Road and west on Miracle Mile to the snack food distribution center off Romero Road. He figured he would be able to hitch a ride with one of the truckers as they left the building and were traveling slowly to get on the freeway. After several vehicles passed him by, he simply sat on a post and held out his sign as trucks approached. Finally, one stopped and the driver beckoned him to climb aboard.

"Thanks for stopping," said Tom as he tried to unobtrusively survey his middle-aged benefactor while the driver took his measure of the thin, young man who had become his traveling companion.

"Christian Atkins is the name. Call me Chris. I can use someone to keep me entertained and awake on the road," said the driver.

"I'm Tom Ward. I sure hope I can keep you awake or else we're both in trouble," Tom joked.

"So you're headed for Lost Wages. Why the hell do you want to go to that god-awful den of iniquity?"

"Looking for work," said Tom. "I'm hoping to get a job in one of the casinos. I've been told that business is booming up there."

"That it is," said the driver. "That it is. By the way, I'm not going all the way up there but I can get you part of the way."

"How far are you going?"

"I'm heading straight north to Phoenix on I10 and then north on I17. I turn east at Flagstaff. I can let you off at a truck stop up there and you can catch a ride going west on I-40.

The driver eased the Freightliner through eight of its ten gears as he gained speed and left the access road, entering the ramp to the freeway. Soon they were leaving Saguaro National Park on the left and Oro Valley on the right.

"Ironwood Forest is over there on the left," said the driver, trying to get a conversation going. "You ever been over there?"

"No, replied Tom. "I never got a chance to see much of the countryside. Since I got here I have always been in school or working and I don't have a car."

The driver shifted into ninth and finally tenth gear as they escaped from the dense traffic of the city.

"Those ironwood trees can live for 800 years, really dense wood, almost like ebony but with a reddish brown color. The Seri Indians down in Sonora are famous for carving it into small sculptures of animals and birds, polishing them up using wet and dry sandpaper so that they almost look like stone. A guy named Jose Astoga got the art going back in the '50s to sell to tourists. In the '70s the Mexican government started promoting it. Now, about half the Seri population is involved in ironwood carving. A whole family will work on pieces together, some members carving, some sanding, some finishing. There are only about 650 of them left."

As they traversed the bare countryside, the driver observed, "We're in Hohokam country now. There's a forest area up to around Casa Grande and Coolidge where they lived from about 600 AD. I guess the area has been inhabited since the time of Christ. Hohokam means 'those who have gone before' and their descendants are the Papago and Pima Indians, although those names were given to them by Spanish colonizers.

"They used to make knives out of volcanic rock they mined there. The Hohokam had stable agricultural communities and grew cotton, tobacco, maize, beans and squash, and especially agave, using some pretty sophisticated irrigation systems. The villages had a courtyard with common areas for ball games and ceremonies and communal ovens. They traded with the Mogollon to the east and south and the Anasazi — the ancient pueblos — to the north, way up into what is now Utah and Colorado. They made nice turquoise mosaic jewelry and developed fired polychrome pottery too. Then, about the middle of the 14th century the villages were abandoned, probably due to drought or to heavy rain that destroyed the irrigation canals. An army camp was established near the remains of the largest village, Snaketown, in 1865. A couple years later, using the old canals as a basis, a retired soldier started the Swilling Irrigating and Canal Company and the settlement that grew up in its wake was called Phoenix."

"Jeez, you sound like a tour guide. You must know a lot about this area."

The driver laughed. "Not really. I'm just a tourist who likes to learn about places I go. I was over in Albuquerque one time and I saw these paintings by Helen Hardin, a Santa Clara artist, and her mother who is also an artist although they have very different styles. It was in an Indian Art gallery up on Central operated by this old guy who used to have a trading post over on the Navajo reservation, or just off it. Both women did these paintings using Hohokam figures and I was fascinated by them, so I looked up where these ancient people came from and found that it was from over here."

"So you've got an interest in art too? That's cool," said Tom. "I liked the Indian art and jewelry I saw in Tucson. I went to Ted de Grazia's place once. He did paintings of Indian subjects, but he wasn't really an Indian himself. He was actually an Italian-American born in Arizona. He did all sorts of other creative things too – sculptures, lithographs, jewelry. He even did some composing, acting and directing. I like people like that, that can do a variety of different things."

"Yeah, me too although I don't have those kinds of talents. I understand that de Grazia apprenticed with Diego Rivera down in Mexico back in the '40s. He was more of a rebel than Rivera – didn't like the way education was being controlled by politics and corporations. He did a mural over at the University of Arizona that roused the ire of the powers that be, so they whitewashed right over it, destroyed it. So much for freedom of expression! Seems like a lot of artists turn out to be rebels of one sort or another."

"Wow, I didn't know that about de Grazia, "said Tom.

They passed Picacho Peak on the left and soon, on the right, they saw the exit to Coolidge. The driver, continuing in his tour guide role, noted that there were the ruins of a large great house and some smaller structures created by the Hohokam near Coolidge. "Interesting place," he said. "They had a thriving community out here in the middle of nowhere and traded with other Indian tribes from quite far away. Shells from the coast of California have been found in some of their jewelry."

Passing around the town of Casa Grande, Tom looked out the window to see palm trees and grass surrounding many apartment buildings and motels. He spotted a lowered 1950s model Chevrolet pick-up truck parked at a restaurant and wondered what life was like in a small desert city back in those days.

The driver, following Tom's gaze, announced, "It's a bedroom community to Tucson and Phoenix now. It used to be an agricultural area and there are still some cotton fields around. But a lot of snow-birds decided to move out here permanently and they wanted to bring their lawns with them. Not like the Indians who knew how to live in the desert and not abuse nature and limited resources like water."

"We don't seem to learn much from previous generations, do we?" said, Tom.

"No, modern man, or at least a lot of them, just specialize in screwing things up," said the driver. Glancing at Tom, he said, "So you aren't from Tucson?"

"No, sir. A friend of mine from the army suggested I come to Tucson to work and go to school. He said it was a nice town, not too big, not too small, and the weather was great most of the year. So I did and it was going OK until I lost my job."

"How did you lose your job? Company go belly up or get moved off shore?"

"No, nothing like that. When I was in the army I fell off a tow-missile carrier and hit my head. Ever since then I have had seizures, off and on. Well this time I had one and was out of it for two days. My boss couldn't handle that and he fired me. I think he was really pissed because he had to fill in for me. I can understand why. Just wish it hadn't happened. But you never know what may come to pass. Maybe it will turn out to be a good thing."

"That's too bad. It's hard to get along when you don't have a job. I've had some periods like that myself. When I got back from Vietnam after serving in the Marine Corp, I used to work for General Dynamics. Worked my way up to being a foreman building guided missiles. I had a hundred men that I was responsible for. I was a Mason too, and got up to the 33rd degree. Worked my ass off and ended up having a heart attack. So then everybody was afraid of hiring me – seemed to think I was going to have another heart attack and croak at any moment. I had a wife and a daughter in graduate school – molecular biology – so I had to have an income. I decided to get my commercial drivers license and drive my own truck. That was before I started contracting for this company."

"How did you end up in Tucson?" asked Tom.

"Well, that's kind of a long story, young fella," said Chris. He gazed at some spot on the highway about a quarter mile ahead and paused in his account. Tom thought he didn't want to talk about it, but he waited without saying anything.

"My daughter was killed down near San Diego by a drunk driver going the wrong way – a head-on accident, killed her instantly. She had a research scholarship and would have graduated that year. Then her mother caught cancer. We didn't have any insurance so I had to mortgage the house and sell my rig in order to pay the medical bills. Then she died anyway. God, I loved that woman."

He was silent for a time and then said, "We had a house overlooking the ocean with a pool and I would have had it all paid off in just a few years if she hadn't gotten sick."

Tom glanced over and saw the driver gulp as a tear ran down his cheek. He was feeling uncomfortable as if he had opened up a Pandora's box of grief that threatened to flood the cab of the truck.

"I'm sorry," said Tom. "I didn't mean to pry."

"No, it's OK kid. Don't worry. I've worked it through pretty well. 'Course I wasn't doing too great right after it happened. Well, then I decided to get away from everybody and go work on a ranch in Nevada out in the middle of nowhere for a friend of mine. I liked the physical work – I was like a cowboy and general roustabout – and I lived in a bunkhouse with the rest of the crew. But I had diabetes and ran out of insulin, so I had to go into town to get my prescription refilled. Well, the foreman decided I couldn't go, even though I told him I'd get into real trouble and die without it. He thought I was faking it, I guess. So I told him, 'Fuck you, I'm out of here' and I took off.

"After I got my medication, I took my truck to a car wash to get it cleaned up. I went into the waiting area and waited for them to call me when it was ready. I waited and waited and no one called my name so I went up and asked where my vehicle was and they said it wasn't there — even claimed I had never brought it in! But I was able to show them the ticket and that convinced them. Lost everything I had. At that point I really lost it. I threw a fit in the waiting room and scared the shit out of everyone. They called the police but by the time they got there I had run out of steam and was just depressed as hell and ready to check out of this world."

Tom was dumbfounded that a person could have that many bad things happen to him all in a row without being cursed. What are the chances of that, he asked himself. But he still felt a kind of kinship with the man that he couldn't explain. He wanted to say something to him that would make him feel better but everything he could think of sounded idiotic. Instead, he asked, "What did you do?"

"Well, I didn't do anything really. The police took me to the VA hospital and they fed me some drugs that didn't do a damn thing except give me bad dreams and make me want to knock myself off. I was there for about three weeks and didn't get any better so they sent me off to this place in Oregon. It used to be an army camp back in WWII. They ran two divisions of recruits through there before the war ended. After that, the place was turned into a long-term care facility for vets.

"When I was there they ran about a thousand vets through a year. A lot of them didn't get very good treatment. Most of them were addicted to drugs or alcohol and would relapse every so often. The treatment teams didn't know how to deal with that except to throw them back out on the street when they relapsed. Then they would let them back in after they cooled their heels for a year or so in homeless shelters or jails or slept in those big cement culverts down by The 909 — that was a bar that was about a half mile from the place. A lot of the staff thought that treatment was like breaking a horse: make life uncomfortable enough, break their spirit and they would become compliant and do as they were told."

"Doesn't sound like a very good facility to me," said Tom.

"It was pretty good for me because I didn't have any alcohol or drug problems. I had a doctor who took good care of my medical problems. I got to see a psychologist once a week. He was one of the few that actually did any psychotherapy in the place. I think I probably drove him crazy the first few months I saw him. I wouldn't say how I felt about anything. I'm not sure I even knew at that point and I sure as hell didn't want to talk about it. It hurt too much to even think about it. Every time he would start nosing around about something that would make me anxious or sad, I'd change the subject or ask him some question as if I were really curious about it. He was not one of these guys that would avoid your questions or give you a bunch of bullshit – he always answered them directly and made sure you understood the answer.

"But then what he did was to just start talking about my work history and what I liked about it and what challenges I faced. He never pushed me to say or do anything, not a thing, but would ask a lot of questions about what I liked to do and how I went about solving problems. He gave me a test that identified what kind of personality I have, which turned out to be pretty interesting. He showed me how I had a different perspective and different talents than other people and how that might cause problems or maybe even be helpful, depending on the other person and the task at hand. It was kind of amazing how it fits me. We did that for a long time and then I gradually told him about my family and all the losses I experienced and how puzzled I was that all this happened to me. And how mad I was. I was really pissed at God for letting this happen when I had done all the right things. I had been a diligent worker, a responsible father, and a pretty good husband. Why did He let this happen to me?

"This guy seemed to grasp it all. I don't know, he must have seen a lot of guys like me in that place. A lot of the vets had really sad stories to tell. He even got me to understand the way my emotions work. I always thought that was some kind of mystical thing but he showed me how there was a pattern to what would set off different emotions and how there was a kind of purpose in the way we react. Within a few months, I was getting involved in activities around the place and talking with people, smiling for the first time since all this shit started to take place, and having some hope.

"Well, the last day I was there I came into his office all dressed up in a suit and tie and clean shaven. The secretary didn't even recognize me and I had been coming there every week for six months. The doc, he just about fell off his chair! He was all smiles and it was obvious he was happy I was feeling better. I went back home, bought a used rig, and started contracting with various distributors, like this one. It's not like I forgot everything that happened, but I can live with it now and accept that it happened to me and it wasn't my fault."

Tom was silent for a long while, letting what he had heard sink in.

The big truck rolled along to Phoenix, skirting the west side of the city until it turned onto Interstate 17 toward Flagstaff. The driver focused on navigating the heavy traffic while Tom stared out the window at the shopping malls, motels, and residential areas of Arizona's largest city. Rock lawns and cinder block walls contained the mostly low buildings, with sage, Spanish broom, and pyracantha bushes punctuated by mesquite trees and the occasional palm to mitigate the pale desert landscape. The scenery became more interesting as they moved out of the suburbs to see in the distance expansive vistas, buttes, and mountains worn down by the elements and large groupings of pinon trees.

Tom broke the silence by saying, "You said you were in Vietnam. What part of the country were you in?"

"I was in the Marine Corps, a 155 millimeter gun battery supporting the 1st Marine Division. We were stationed just below the DMZ east of the Phu Bai airfield which was just south of Hue about eleven miles."

"Lot of fighting?"

"Yeah, we saw our share. We were in the Battle of Hue City which lasted for 26 days. Our firing battery managed to hit all of our assigned targets, but it was a bloody fight. We destroyed what was once a beautiful old city."

"Sounds gruesome. I guess that is what you have to do in a war – destroy things."

"Yeah, that's the name of the game. One time we got overrun. A group of sappers got in through the outer and inner wire running around our fire base. We had six guns, some engineers, an LZ, a Tactical Operations Center, an aide station with medics, a communications bunker and a bunch of infantry that was supposed to protect us. Well, a group of VC armed with AK-47s, Rocket Propelled Grenades, satchel charges and hand grenades got through. We had a partially dug down bunker made of sandbags and wood from old ammo crates. They threw grenades in through our vents. Killed a bunch of sleeping guys outright. Shit!"

"God damn! What did you do?"

"I was scared shitless! I couldn't see from all the smoke and debris in the air, I couldn't breathe, I couldn't hear from the blast ringing in my ears, but I finally made it to the entrance of the bunker with my rifle. I managed to pull one guy out and then I began to run like hell, shooting at the gooks and trying to make it to a safe place over by our howitzer. I ran out of ammo and picked up an AK-47 from one of the dead VC. I think I got a few of them. I don't remember a lot about it, I was just operating on instinct and adrenaline. My leg was bleeding. I could hardly walk. Finally, the other guys in the battery pushed the VC out and I was taken to the aide station. They gave me a Bronze Star and wrote me up in Stars and Stripes. Big deal! I was sent to a hospital for a short time and was back at it in just a few days. That's when we went up to Hue."

"That's incredible! I don't know how you managed to come through it."

"Oh, well. That was just The Nam. That was the way it was in those days and in that place."

"My dad was over there stationed at some secret base in Thailand. It was mainly a secret to the American public, I guess. Udorn, I think was the name of it."

"Udorn was up in the north, just south and west of the Laotian border. The Air Force had helicopter bases and bases for B-52s all over Thailand. They had an agreement with Thailand that they would be considered Royal Thai Airbases under the command of Thai officers, even though they were really US bases. The US had all sorts of combat aircraft flying out of those bases, B52s making bombing raids on North Vietnam, F-4s flying escort, Stratotankers for refueling, some other planes used for recon before and after attacks, others used to jam radar. And the Laotians flew some T-28 fighter-bombers out of those bases too. They were all trying to stop supplies from coming down from North Vietnam on the Ho-Chi-Minh Trail. The choppers and another type of plane, the STOLs or Short Take Off and Landing aircraft, were used to fetch pilots shot down over Laos. The STOLs used little landing strips the Hmong had carved out of the forest for that purpose. The Hmong were mountain people. They were also called Montagnards in Vietnam and Cambodia."

"My dad was in Special Forces and worked with MACV at some point. I don't know exactly what he did."

"Special Forces. Hmm." The driver was trying to recover some dim memories from long ago. He said, "That wasn't my area of operations, but I remember reading that the CIA had an operation going on in Laos since the early sixties and a lot of it was controlled out of Thailand, but it was all kept hush-hush because we were not supposed to have any troops in Laos according to a UN agreement. 'Course, the North had organized, equipped and led their own group in Laos too. They weren't supposed to be there either, according to the UN, so neither side spoke publicly about the fighting and bombing that was going on there. The only people in the dark about it were the civilians in the good old US of A."

Feeling safe and comfortable with this straight-talking veteran, Tom confessed, "My dad died when he came home on leave in December of 1970."

The driver hesitated briefly before answering. "I'm sorry to hear that. Was he injured during the war or did he get sick over there? How old was he?"

"He was 39 years old and he was neither injured nor sick. I was eight at the time. They said he died from an overdose of drugs and brandy. They said it was a suicide. But my mother and his friends claimed he never drank brandy and they didn't believe he wanted to or would have even considered committing suicide. He had planned to go to some kind of veterans meeting in January but he never made it."

"Hmm," Chris said again. He was silent for a long time, trying to remember the tumultuous events that occurred during those years. He remembered the disgust he felt when he attended the big Vietnam Veterans Against the War meeting – the Winter Soldier Investigation – that took place in Detroit in January of 1971.

Over 100 honorably discharged veterans had gathered to spill the beans about atrocities committed in that southeast Asian country, implying that it was pervasive and condoned by superior officers. The meeting came just after the conviction of Lt. William Calley for his part in the massacre at My Lai. These ex-soldiers and marines reported on the torture and murder of suspects and prisoners of war captured by Americans and South Vietnamese forces, the wanton killing of innocent, unarmed civilians, the brutalization and rape of Vietnamese women in the villages, military policies that enabled indiscriminate bombing and the random firing of artillery into villages that resulted in the burning to death of women, children, and old people, the widespread defoliation of lands and forests, the use of various types of gases, the mutilation of enemy bodies, and the like.

Mark O. Hatfield, the senator from Oregon, entered the whole record of the testimony at the Winter Soldier Investigations into the Congressional Record for all to see. He emphasized that such actions appeared to be the consequence of policy adopted by our military commanders and that the knowledge of incidents resulting from these policies was widely shared. And he noted that such actions if substantiated, would place the United States in violation of the Geneva Convention and other international agreements relating to the conduct of war that had been ratified by the U. S. Government. He urged Congress to conduct hearings and a special commission be formed to investigate these matters and their moral implications.

John Kerry, a Vietnam veteran and one of the leaders of the anti-war campaign, commented at the time, "Someone has to die so that President Nixon won't be the first President to lose a war." He questioned the administration's strategy of gradually pulling out US troops and turning the war over to the South Vietnamese military. "How do you ask a man to be the last man to die in Vietnam? How do you ask a man to be the last man to die for a mistake?"

The most powerful antiwar demonstration held up until that time — dubbed Dewey Canyon III — triggered a series of major demonstrations that made it clear that the American people wanted the US out of Indochina. It was followed by the May Day demonstration when 35,000 protesters camped out in Potomac Park and planned their actions while listening to rock music. The government intended to disrupt the demonstration by using low-flying helicopters to disperse the crowd but that move was thwarted by the release of huge numbers of helium-filled balloons tethered to the ground by cables.

The Nixon administration canceled the protester's permit and had police dressed in riot gear move in phalanxes through the camp, firing tear gas and knocking down tents. Yuppies engaged in hit-and-run tactics throughout the city, trying to disrupt traffic and cause chaos in the streets. Politicians were harassed by protesters and Nixon, who was in California at the time, refused to give federal employees the day off, further disrupting traffic in the city. Police, using tear and emetic gases, some of them dropped from helicopters, roamed through the city arresting anyone who looked like a demonstrator, including construction workers who had come out to support the administration.

Most of those arrested were released without charges but 79 were eventually convicted. A class action suit brought by thousands of detained protesters and supported by the ACLU eventually convinced the US Congress to recognize the illegal nature of the arrests because of a violation of the constitutional right of free assembly and agreed to pay a settlement to those arrested.

Chris sighed, looked at Tom, and said, "Those were bad days. The government did some terrible things and wouldn't own up to them. The vets tried to make people aware and get them involved in changing things but, in those days, they couldn't do so. The whole thing was very disappointing."

Tom, feeling uneasy about asking more questions, simply accepted the man's summary judgment about that era.

"Yeah," he said. "That's what I have heard."

It was dusk when the truck entered the outskirts of Flagstaff. Chris took the exit to get onto Interstate 40 going east and then pulled off on East Butler, coming to a stop at the truck stop near the Little America Travel Center. There were about 25 trucks parked in the lot and it looked to be a quite busy place.

"There's a restaurant over there that has pretty good grub and a lot of truckers eat there. I'll buy you dinner and then you can see if you can hitch a ride going west from here on I40."

Tom gobbled down the Swiss steak and mashed potatoes special like he hadn't eaten in ages. He thanked Chris profusely for the ride and the meal and his benefactor shook his hand and wished him well in Vegas.

∞

Tom started soliciting a new ride, walking past the truckers seated at the counter and announcing his need. Many glanced at the young man and looked back at their plates. Some appraised him to see if he posed any kind of threat, should they offer him a ride. Finally, a man sitting alone in a booth waved his hand and said, "Hey, kid. Come on over here."

"So, you're looking for a ride to Las Vegas?"

"Yeah, said Tom. You going that way?"

"All the way," said the man with rough facial features and a few days' growth of beard. "Why should I give you a ride?"

"I can help out along the way, wash your windshield and pump gas, or whatever you need."

"Uh-huh, whatever I need." said the man with an off-kilter grin resembling a smirk on his face. He looked Tom over carefully. "You ever been in trouble with the law? Why are you hitching?"

"Nope! Don't even have a parking ticket," said Tom. "I lost my job and had to drop out of college so I'm going to Vegas to see if I can get a job. Need to save my money to get a place to stay once I get there."

"OK. I'll take a chance on ya but ya better not give me any trouble. We'll saddle up in a few minutes after I finish my coffee and hit the head. I'm Billy Joe and my truck is the red Mack with the tanker on the back that says Great Western on it."

"My name's Tom Ward," said Tom as he offered to shake his benefactor's hand.

"OK, little Tommy," Billy Joe responded as he clasped Tom's hand in both of his. We's going to have a great time on the road. Meet you out there in 15 minutes."

Tom went out, found the truck, and sat on the running board, waiting for the driver to appear. When he did, they pulled up to the diesel pump and Billy Joe began the slow process of filling his tank with fuel. Tom retrieved a washer-squeegee with a long handle and cleaned the windshield on both sides. He wanted the driver to think he was an asset to have along, not just some bum looking for cheap transportation.

Soon they were on the road, heading toward Kingman, Arizona. Tom tried to break the ice with some small talk. "Do you like being a truck driver," he asked.

The trucker looked at him like he was an idiot but then said, "I guess it's OK. Better than being on the clean-up crew in a whore house!"

Tom cracked a polite smile. "Yeah, I guess it would be better than that."

"Say, how was the snatch at the college you went to? All that pussy running around shaking it in your face." He poked Tom in the shoulder like he was some buddy from high school. "Must have had a perpetual hard-on. I'll bet it was like to burst at the seams and spout a fountain of cum all over the place."

Tom was getting a little uncomfortable about the direction the conversation was going. This guy was a little creepy. Not that he felt ill at ease talking about sex, but this seemed to be rather gross and too soon to be discussing such things with a virtual stranger.

"I didn't get much of a chance to sample the offerings at school. I was too busy studying and besides I've got this medical condition that has kept me from having any long-term relationships with girls since I got out of the army."

"What's wrong with you? Did you get your pecker shot off in the war?" The driver guffawed.

Tom laughed. "No, not that. I fell off a missile launcher and hit my head and ended up having seizures."

"So you fall down, pass out, and shake and piss all over yourself. Must make fucking girls difficult, I suppose. Does your equipment still work?"

"Sometimes I have the kind of seizures you're thinking of, but usually I get short episodes where I am just out of it for a while – no falling down or convulsions. And, yes, my equipment still works."

"You ever try anything besides girls?"

Tom swiveled toward the passenger-side door as the driver patted him on the left thigh, lingering longer than expected for just a chummy poke.

Seeking to shift the conversation, Tom ventured, "Where are you from?"

"Where am I from? Why, I'm a good 'ol redneck from down Texas way. Grew up with my mama and an older sister. Never knew my dad. Sis taught me how to fuck. Used to give a pretty good blow job too. Mama liked to sit in a chair next to the bed and watch. Kept it all in the family until Betty Joe got all cut up by a guy down the road and bled out like a stuck hog. She was only 14 when that happened."

Tom took a long quizzical gaze at the driver and said, "You gotta be shitting me?"

"Naw," he laughed. "Guess we had a kinda different family, growing up. 'Course when the school or the county sent inspectors around mama made sure we didn't say anything about the fucking. She said they just wouldn't understand our way of doing things. We managed pretty well, though. Mama had a few boyfriends and they kicked in some money to help put food on the table. After Betty Joe died we took in some run-away teens that needed a home. Mama liked to say we were running our own social service agency. She taught them how to go out and pander for their keep. They kinda took Betty Joe's place and kept me busy."

Oh, my god. This guy is a fucking nut job, thought Tom but he said, "That's interesting. When did you start driving a truck?"

"After I got out of prison. Served eight years. Twelve year old girl claimed I raped her. Didn't do no such thing. She wanted it, I could tell. It was consexual. She was like a bitch dog rubbing her cunt up and down my leg. I slammed it to her and she loved it, made her cry with joy. Then she ran home and told her mother."

"That's too bad," said Tom, wondering how he was going to get away from this leftover from *Deliverance*. He couldn't just jump out of the truck. They were going too fast and he would kill himself for sure. I'll wait until we stop for gas and tell him I'm sick and need to go see a doctor. He fell silent, lost in thought as the driver reached over and turned on the radio.

Tom looked out the window, watching the white lines go by in a hypnotic succession as the soft music played. After being up for 20 hours, he suddenly felt very tired. He drifted off into a light sleep and dreamed about a large Campbell Tomato Soup can keeping him blocked from a door. He felt like he was suffocating and in his twilight state, he thought maybe his T-shirt had somehow gotten wrapped up around his neck. He reached up to loosen it when he realized there was a rope around his neck. He bolted upright, wide awake. Billy Joe pulled him out of the cab and threw the rope up over the round steel bead running over the top of the tanker. He tied Tom's hands together, pulled the rope from around his neck, and bound it to his hands. Then he pulled Tom up by his bound hands so that only the toes of his feet could touch the ground.

"What the fuck are you doing," screamed Tom? "Let go of me. Put me down from this thing, you pathetic no-good son-of-a-bitch. You ding-a-ling fucker, you bastard, you shit-head."

The screams and invective only seemed to excite the truck driver more. He had that shit-eating grin on his face that Tom remembered from the truck stop. Why didn't I take that as a warning? Billy Joe loosened Tom's belt and lowered his pants and undershorts. Tom thrashed about like a beheaded chicken, trying to get away from the touch of this madman. "Oh, shit, shit shit," exclaimed Tom as panic overwhelmed him.

Billy Joe began to massage Tom's genitals. Tom was frozen with fear. "Whassa matter, college boy, doesn't that excite you a little bit? Let me try something else to help you get it up." Taking out a buck knife, he began to make slow shallow incisions on Tom's legs, watching the blood spiral down his exposed limbs as Tom screamed in pain. He placed the side of the blade on Tom's penis and continued his taunting. "Now wouldn't it be a shame if I slipped and cut it off? Oops, almost did it," he said as he let the knife slip a little. He laughed at Tom's frantic reaction to his sick joke.

The torture continued for quite some time with the truck driver mumbling incomprehensible things about his mother before he tired of it and retrieved a jar of Vaseline from the truck cab. Taking a goodly amount of the salve on two fingers, he slathered it between Tom's cheeks. He inserted his rigid member into Tom as his victim squirmed, cried, and screamed in pain. When it was over, Tom hung from the rope like a cadaver from a lynching. The truck driver brought out a gas can and a shovel.

"Go ahead and kill me. I don't have anything to live for now," said Tom when he surmised what the guy had in mind. Billy Joe began to dig a shallow grave, whistling and singing "Whistle while you work" and laughing to himself. "What do you think of this little adventure, mother?" he said to no one in sight.

When he had the grave prepared, Billy Joe cut Tom down and let him drop to the ground. He cut his rope loose from Tom's hands and rolled it up, placing it back in the cab of his truck. Tom lay there, too weak and dispirited to make a move. Shivers washed over his body.

About that time, a pair of headlights appeared far down the road they had taken to get off the freeway. Billy Joe breathed an "oh, oh" and picked up the shovel swinging it and hitting Tom on the head and body three or four times. Tom didn't lose consciousness but thought it best to play dead if he was going to have any chance of survival. The truck driver dragged him to the grave and tossed him in, his pants still tangled around his legs. Tom managed to get his right hand in front of his mouth as he landed, creating a small air-space as he felt the dirt being thrown on his back and head. He waited for what seemed like an eternity, taking little sips of air from the space below his hand before he heard the truck leave.

Gerald D. Otis

CHAPTER 2
The Sons of Liberty

Just after daybreak, Mortimer Kilpatrick drove his Hummer a half mile up a dirt road from the main highway to a remote, wooded site south of Grants Pass, land made available by a farmer sympathetic to the cause. Wolfgang Gunnar and Whitey Green were already there, dressed in camo clothing with high-laced boots, rifles slung over their shoulders on leather slings. Several women, similarly attired in camo clothing, were setting up folding benches and chairs, percolating coffee, and preparing to fry strips of bacon with eggs and grilled toast. Soon more vehicles arrived, parking along both sides of the entry road and disgorging men of various ages carrying diverse weapons and boxes of equipment. A sign with an arrow directed the newcomers to a registration table where they received their assignments for the day. New arrivals were encouraged to have breakfast, talk with their peers, and then pitch in to get the training camp ready for the activities that were to follow.

North of the breakfast area, a shooting range was being set up with silhouettes of enemy soldiers or government agents pointing firearms in the direction of the shooting line. To the east of the breakfast area, a section was being readied to practice hand-to-hand combat and wilderness survival techniques. Further east men hoisted barricades, dropped ropes from trees, and erected dummies to be pounded, speared, or shot with arrows. On the northeast corner of the property, furthest away from the breakfast area, men were arranging natural cover for recruits to place low-yield explosive charges. A first-aid station occupied a small tent between the breakfast area and the hand-to-hand section. It was staffed by a registered nurse and two aides she had trained to treat the kinds of injuries usually seen at the camp.

The Sons of Liberty were preparing themselves for what they regarded as threats to their desired way of life, indeed, to their very existence. Standing in opposition to broad left-wing government authority, they decried the overreach of federal agencies. They considered themselves to be "nationalists," the last line of defense against invading foreign immigrants and radical liberals. Many of them believed that a secret group, global in scope, intended to create a worldwide socialist government that would undermine the rights that American citizens enjoyed, especially the right to bear arms. Some of the economic and political elite, especially those who had Jewish-sounding surnames, were seen as playing a major role in the takeover of traditional American institutions and imposing their will on ordinary citizens.

Mortimer Kilpatrick sauntered over to greet Wolfgang Gunnar and Whitey Green. The three of them moved to the table holding the coffee pot, prevailing upon one of the women to pour them their first cup of the morning. Sipping the hot brew, the three men strolled about the different parts of the camp, at times chatting with the men setting up the area, making suggestions, or answering questions. Gunnar was occasionally saluted as the officer of a superior rank, with Green as his adjutant and Kilpatrick as just "some guy tagging along."

To his companions, Kilpatrick said, "You know, guys, we have to start going beyond this self-protection and survival thing. We've got the recruitment part down pretty well. We'll have over two hundred men out here today. But, looking forward, what we need are some new tactics where we take the initiative, especially in the urban environment, like using fireworks, making chemical-filled bottles that can be thrown, using paintball guns and pepper spray."

"And taking hostages to use as bargaining chips," Gunnar volunteered.

"There are circumstances where that would be appropriate, Wolfgang, that's true" conceded Kilpatrick. "But before that, we're going to be organizing and mobilizing demonstrations for people and policies we like and counter-demonstrations against those on the other side. We need to start practicing how to influence people's attitudes."

"You mean kind of like a public relations or propaganda arm?" asked Green.

"Yeah, that's it, Whitey. We can offer security for groups of people that are expressing our views or complaining about the government. We'll play the role of protector for the disenfranchised or downtrodden. We can also develop some friends in law enforcement by offering to supplement their forces when they are overwhelmed."

"We have been a secret organization for a number of years now, boss," said Green. "How are we going to keep the law from cracking down on us?"

"I've been talking with a couple of our congressmen who share our concerns. The son of one of them is even a member of our organization. These are the kinds of people who have connections and can provide cover for us if we become more public. They can claim we are just upright citizens asking for our rights guaranteed under the constitution. And they can provide cash, directly and indirectly, for our organization and ourselves. Of course they expect something in return. You know, launching demonstrations that attack their rivals, attacking symbols of the other guy's power, mounting efforts to disrupt the plans of those they are running against. You remember Nixon's Dirty Tricks Gang, don't you?"

Whitey Green chortled, "We can make them look pretty tame by comparison."

"What about the things we have going on over at the other place?" interjected Wolfgang Gunnar. "We've got a lot of irons in the fire and we don't want to get ourselves over-extended. We're pulling in some heavy green for our, eh, employment services," he said, emitting a little laugh, "and I, for one, don't want to put that in jeopardy."

"Don't worry, Wolfgang. We are going to take it slow and won't imperil our employment services. I'm just looking ahead, looking at what's happening in other parts of the country. You have to be ready to take advantage of opportunities as they arise, before they are overtaken by other events and cease to exist."

Mortimer Michael Kilpatrick had been coached in "seizing the moment" from a young age. His father, Melor or Mel, was operating a small appliance repair business with two teenage boys as assistants in 1944 when President Franklin Delano Roosevelt signed the GI Bill that allowed millions of soldiers returning from World War II to enroll in college or job-training programs and gave them access to low-interest loans to buy homes. In the five years that followed enactment of the legislation, the total number of private for-profit vocational schools in the United States tripled, with more veterans attending these schools than were enrolled at public and nonprofit colleges.

Mel, seeing an upsurge in the appearance of new trade schools and always on the lookout for opportunities to better his lot, quickly latched onto the chance to expand his business at government expense. He filed for and received authorization to offer job training to 20 veterans in his newly created corporation, the Appliance Repair Institute of America. He hired high school teachers to teach courses for extra money and sometimes had his students work unpaid "internships" at his other businesses.

The way the GI Bill was written, funds were distributed directly to the school owners without any provisions designed to hold them accountable to taxpayers. Banks and lending institutions saw a person running a federally funded school as a good risk and made it easy for the owners to get expansion loans. And that is exactly what the enterprising Mr. Kilpatrick did. He created more corporations with names like American School of Shoe Repair, Academy of TV Repair, Foundation of Home Inspectors, and The National College of Chick-Sexing, filling them all with veteran students. He even offered correspondence courses awarding actual "diplomas" for automotive repair and carpentry.

To attract veterans, he advertised in newspapers, magazines, and on the radio, often making misleading offers with extravagant and unjustifiable claims. Since there were no loans involved, a veteran had no reason to care if he just attended a few classes and dropped out. He might still get a free TV set that was offered as an incentive for enrolling. The owner, for his part, had no reason to care if he lost students when they dropped out since he already had, in hand, the money the government had allocated for their education and then he had space for new students.

The money just continued to roll in. Mel thought he had found the golden goose. He bought fancy cars for himself and his family members, bought houses in several states, belonged to the best social clubs and golf courses, went on extravagant vacations, and sent his spoiled son, Mortimer, to the best private schools. He proudly proclaimed that he was a "self-made man" and complained about the taxes he had to pay to his true benefactor, Uncle Sam.

But it was not to last. The report of a special investigative commission came out that found some kind of irregularity or questionable practice in 1,237 schools identified by the VA as receiving funds under the GI Bill and seventy-eight percent of them were in for-profit schools. More than ninety percent of the 329 schools that had lost their accreditation were also for-profit schools. Many veterans were trained for occupations for which they were unsuited or occupations for which they were unable to find jobs once they finished training. Proprietary schools were accused of overcharging, using misleading advertising, and engaging in promotional scams. Only 20% of the veterans in proprietary schools ever completed their courses. Schools and their executives were convicted of fraud in many cases.

Even now, decades later, many colleges and institutions carry on the same tradition by engaging in different forms of fraud against the government. They falsify that the institution is "accredited" though it is not or they lie to an accrediting body that the school has met criteria when it hasn't. They pay commissions or provide other incentives to people who recruit students to enroll in the school or encourage students to fake their academic records to obtain federal funding.

Congress got into action, under the leadership of the chairman of the House Select Committee, when they barred payment for non-accredited, non-degree courses at the for-profit schools if more than 85% of their students were veterans. The proprietary school's golden goose was cooked when the Korean War GI Bill made monthly tuition payments directly to veterans instead of to the schools. A few years later, when the country was concerned about lagging behind the Soviets in the space race, Eisenhower signed the National Defense Student Loan Program, restricting funding to public and nonprofit colleges.

Mel's little empire collapsed. He was tried and found guilty of fraud, had to go to prison for a year, and was on probation for five years. No more lavish parties, foreign vacations, or fancy cars. He had to sell all of his houses except one. Mortimer was still in high school at the time and all his classmates knew about it. He was embarrassed by the media attention and crushed by his loss of status. He had to give up his fancy sports car and get a part-time job in order to go to public universities rather than the Ivy League ones he had been eyeing.

Even though father Mel had been tried under a Republican administration, he railed against government overreach, the weakening of capitalism, the lack of incentive for free enterprise, and about foreign cultural values being forced upon true Americans. He claimed that policies enacted by the Democratic Party had ruined small businesses and were empowering criminals. He often used an example he saw in the newspaper of a new policy that was developed when two teens were shot by police after the teens ran from the scene of a crime. Both teens had weapons, were out in the middle of the night, had criminal records, ran from the cops, and raised their guns just before they were shot.

"What the fuck! These Democratic politicians think the cops should just sit around and wait to get shot before shooting back. That's crazy as a loon!"

Once he was out of prison, Mel began secretly associating with people who adopted a rather inconsistent and fanciful narrative about American history, one that thought the federal income tax and even the federal government itself was illegitimate. He felt his rights were being unfairly denied and, in bolstering his argument, he embraced legal theories that reinterpreted the Constitution and merged disparate ideas from the Articles of Confederation and the Bible.

Ignoring the fact that the Constitution is the law of the land and that the Supreme Court is the ultimate interpreter, they enthroned the county sheriff as the top law enforcement officer with powers greater than any elected official, whether local, state, or federal. They believed that the federal government was not a genuine "state" but instead a "corporation," illegally controlling the republic through a territorial government in Washington, DC.

This illegitimate government, it was argued, was simply using its citizens as collateral to be held against foreign debt, thereby making them slaves of the state. According to this logic, the currently prevailing law was based on principles of international commerce (admiralty or maritime law as symbolized by the gold fringes on the flags displayed in courtrooms) and not on "God's law" (common law based on custom or court decisions) that the Founding Fathers intended. Therefore, US judges and lawyers were de facto agents of a foreign power and the validity of the legal system could be challenged.

Using pseudo-legal arguments, members of this group frequently violated laws they considered illegitimate, such as purchasing license plates, obtaining driver's licenses, registering their vehicles, and paying taxes. They used fake bonds to avoid taxes and sometimes even managed to get refunds. They reneged on debts and mortgages, writing "Accepted for value" on bills and collection papers. They squatted in vacant homes, claiming ownership or filed false liens on someone's property, thereby causing a "clouded" title that affected the other person's credit and ability to get loans. They used signatures and thumbprints in red ink or blood, to signify that they were canceling the connection between the flesh and blood person and the legal persona they called a "straw man."

Eventually, members of the group set up militias of self-appointed "sheriffs," as well as "common law courts" to handle matters regarding movement members. While their courts were devoid of any real legal authority, they were used to formalize the "declarations of sovereignty" of movement members, in a process known as "asseveration," an emphatic declaration that some things were just "self-evident," as if no supporting evidence were necessary. These sovereign citizens would sometimes put enemies, such as public officials, on trial in absentia and sentence them to death for "treason".

"Mort," as he was called, had been close to Mel as he was growing up and worshiped him for having bestowed riches upon the family and climbing the social ladder. Now that it was all gone, he heard and believed his father's account of how their fall from grace had taken place, that it was unjust and the fault of a corrupt and illegitimate government. His anger and resentment grew, fueled by his loss of status among his peers and the rhetoric of his father and his militia friends.

Mort joined the militia but kept his membership hidden as he went through college. Although his grades were not outstanding due to his frequent partying, he applied to medical school and was accepted after his father prevailed upon one of his old associates who had become an administrator in a large medical school and didn't want his previous participation in fraudulent activities to become known.

Somehow, perhaps through cheating and hiring a double to take tests, Mort managed to make it through medical school and pass the National Boards. He was drinking quite heavily by then and knew he couldn't just slip by in a difficult internship and residency, so he opted to specialize in Physical Medicine and Rehabilitation.

His parents' marital problems added another layer of resentment to Mort's umbrage. His mother did not buy into his father's rationalizations and, after years of degradation, finally decided to strike out on her own, freeing herself of this embarrassing, ungrateful, and domineering man. In doing so, her crafty lawyer managed to help her take the majority of the couple's assets, leaving Mel in dire straights. In a drunken fit of rage, he tried to run over his ex-wife with his car but missed and drove straight into a concrete wall. Although the incident was labeled a probable suicide by the police, Mort felt his mother's actions had precipitated his father's untimely death.

Mort Kilpatrick lost his first job due to frequent drunkenness and eventually had his medical license suspended, pending treatment for his alcoholism. Finding it difficult to be considered for good jobs, he applied to the Veterans Administration, which always had a problem recruiting and retaining qualified physicians because of low pay, insufferable red tape, and requirements imposed by various levels of administration. Although he still had occasional relapses, he managed to hold on to his job.

After a couple of years of regular employment, he realized he was a talented bullshitter — he had a good gift of gab and could persuade people to the point of view he was espousing. He took advantage of the VA's in-house training opportunities for administrative positions. This program was much like the in-house training program General Motors used that turned out executives with the same old tired ideas of their predecessors, and eventually contributed to the undoing of the company as foreign auto-makers gained ground.

Mort ascended the VA administrative hierarchy by moving from institution to institution as positions became available, and before he could be exposed as a know-nothing. He developed his skills at detecting improprieties of his superiors, such as secret love affairs, misuse of funds, or other violations of the rules, and used this knowledge to extract glowing letters of recommendation from them, they being happy to rid themselves of someone who could tarnish their records.

Mort eventually became an administrative assistant and then assistant director at small rural outposts in the VA system. When the then-current Chief of Staff (COS) at what was known as "Vetlandia" was removed for embezzlement, he was right on top of it and submitted his application to replace him.

Mort was now positioned to make the government pay for the injustices they imposed on his father and his own thwarted ambitions, and at the government's expense, no less! As his tenure and grade in the VA had grown, his status in the right-wing militia also grew. But he and his superiors knew that he could not assume a publicly visible role without endangering his valuable position in the VA. All agreed that he should be "the power behind the throne" of the state chapter of the Sons of Liberty with someone less prominent being the nominal head. Mort found this straw person to be Clarence Youngblood, an outspoken and ambitious young man, who had joined the ranks of the militia at 18 years of age, along with his father. Then he could not be exposed when the militia expressed their views or took public actions. Besides, a brilliant idea began to form in his mind. Why not use his position to recruit new members of the militia who were already trained by the military?

Many (although still a minority) of the veterans who sought admission to Vetlandia had flexible consciences, had been in prison, had drug or alcohol addictions, or were down on their luck for one reason or another. If he, as COS, could get some key VA positions filled with people loyal to him, he might be able to offer these recruits "assistance" in getting service-connected disabilities or other financial benefits. He might be able to get them into college or help them obtain jobs through VA-sponsored training programs. He could provide them with a reference identity group in his militia that would build their confidence and reinvigorate their dreams about adventure, playing with guns, and blowing things up.

In exchange, these recruits could kick back a certain percentage of their gains to help build the weaponry and gear of his militia. Using the rationale of the militia for justifying illegal acts, they might even be willing to participate in some extra-curricular activities like transporting drugs to dealers or driving illegal aliens to employment at farms, ranches, and slaughterhouses around the country. The latter was especially appealing as it could generate revenue from both sides: the aliens would pay him for guaranteed jobs and the employers would pay him for supplying a cheap labor pool.

Now he had to figure out how to pull it off. To get veterans through the disability system, he would have to have one or more physicians to certify claimed physical problems, a psychologist to substantiate psychological problems, and a social worker to help complete forms and coach subjects on how to answer the typical questions asked by disability interviewers. A disability determiner at the regional office might be coaxed into the fold by offering financial incentives (bribes) or threats of exposure of whatever they had to hide. All of these people would have to be trained on how to identify the desired characteristics veterans should possess for recruitment into the militia and exclude the "do-gooders" who might expose the operation to authorities. To get selected veterans into training programs where they could be useful to the militia, it would be desirable to have a compliant vocational counselor on board.

It was a big job but the thought of sticking it to the government he so despised and the weak-kneed liberals who kept them in power, inspired him to take it on. He started by getting to know the staff members who were already at Vetlandia. An examination of the resumes of the current batch of physicians was a first step.

He quickly discovered that Dr. Wolfgang Gunnar was a kindred spirit after reading of his frequent bouts with the law for drunken driving, reckless flying of his private airplane, and beating up his wife. When Dr. Gunnar was charged with attempted murder and managed to get his judge friend to have the case moved to a different county, he was convinced he had a partner in crime. He called him in for a chat where he could further assess his attitudes and any hint of regret. Finding none, he invited him over to his residence where they could have a drink and discuss their future projects at the facility. He didn't disclose the whole panorama of his vision but he did get Dr. Gunnar's assent to provide his imprimatur of disability on any veterans the COS might send his way. That was a start and once the psychiatrist indulged in the dark side, the COS knew he could persuade him to extend his illicit activities and help recruit others to the enterprise. In exchange, Kilpatrick would consider him to be his right-hand man at work with all the power and privileges that might afford.

During each of the section addictions treatment groups that he led, to which section psychologists, social workers, vocational counselors, and chaplains were "invited" to attend, the COS was able to determine which staff members had the kind of attitude he was looking for. He would pose dilemmas that addicts might face and encourage the onlooking staff to answer what they might do or had done in such situations. It was a slow process since he did not want to appear too eager for particular kinds of answers, but he was eventually able to compile a list of potential collaborators to whom additional persuasive measures could be applied.

Most staff members were not eligible for the kinds of activities he had in mind. For example, the head of the Psychology Service, Dr. James Holbrook, was known to have reported Dr. Gunnar to his superior for having struck a patient and had supported Dr. Oldman, an experienced staff psychologist, in his attempt to expose unethical behavior at the facility. He would have to keep his eyes peeled for opportunities to get rid of such individuals or to force them into compliance with his desires. But there were enough staff members that had that tough-minded, hardhearted, unscrupulous, or opportunistic attitude he desired.

The other avenue for gaining membership in Mort's club was through new hires. He made it known to the heads of the various services that he wanted to interview any candidates for vacant positions and have his judgment be given weight in the hiring decision. Thus, when the Medicine Department wanted to add a new section doctor, Mort was able to recommend the candidate with the poorest record, someone who had been a captain in the army for 20 years yet never received a promotion, was often disciplined for abusive or disrespectful behavior toward patients, and had what was deemed an "obnoxious, hostile and whiny" personality. That's the kind of guy who would need to hold onto his job since it was unlikely that he would be offered any others, someone who could be pushed or enticed to do whatever his superiors wanted him to do.

He knew, from Dr. Gunnar, that the head of the Psychology Service and several of his section psychologists were unlikely to go along with any of his illegal schemes, so when a potential opening came up, he helped an attractive female member of his militia, Carole Harding, to become a "ringer" candidate for the position. Knowing that credentials were seldom checked for veracity in hiring decisions, he found the name of a deceased psychologist from a large Midwestern university, requested academic records from both graduate and undergraduate colleges, and identified individuals working at the places the deceased psychologist worked, for whom he created letters of reference, to be submitted to the Chief of Psychology as part of her application package. Her references being deceased, she did not have to worry that they would respond that they never heard of her. After refining her resume and a bit of coaching as to the kinds of answers to interview questions that would stand her in good stead, she appeared for her job interview with the members of the Psychology Service.

Mort would have to keep his organization within an organization hidden from the Director of the facility. The Chief of Staff is responsible for supervising the staff and ensuring the quality of care for veterans staying at the facility. He works with the Director to implement policies and procedures for the programs of care while facilitating continuity of care for residents. Importantly, the COS manages the schedule, logistics and communications of the Office of the Director, thereby giving him a degree of control over the latter in spite of having a narrower scope of responsibilities.

The Director, on the other hand, is the nominal leader of the whole facility who is the go-between with higher levels of administration and with local community organizations. Although he presides at celebrations and official events, it is rare for a patient to interact with him at all. His most important real work is to oversee the budget, try to extract resources from Central Office, and implement the policies and procedures emanating from that Washington-based agency.

The Director of Vetlandia, Alfred Horton, had graduated from the same in-house administrative training program that Mort had attended. Not the brightest bulb in the pack, Alfred was nevertheless ambitious and managed to work himself up from employment in the food service sector to head of Vetlandia. He was not confident of his skills and was relieved to be able to rely on the older, more educated Mort Fitzpatrick for direction and advice. He was often embarrassed by making some stupid remark, while within earshot of other staff or patients, that revealed his lack of understanding of the people or activities he was engaged in. In manner, he reminded one of a certain Vice President who misspelled the word "potato" at a children's spelling bee, thought that it was "very wasteful" not to have a mind, and that he "had made good judgments in the future." Horton knew enough to not further display his ignorance by making an issue of his gaffes. Mort was delighted that Alfred was his Director, played to his vanity, offered false praise and reassurance, and guided him in the directions that were most useful for his own objectives.

∞

The trio, Mort Kilpatrick, Wolfgang Gunnar, and Whitey Green, walked back to the breakfast area where a podium had been erected for Youngblood to give an inspirational message. The voice on the loudspeaker instructed all members of the militia to assemble in the breakfast area for an address by their nominal leader. Youngblood, having memorized the speech that Mort had written for him, ascended the podium and took the microphone in hand.

"Gentlemen, we are gathered here today to get ready. To get ready for the conflict we all know is coming – the conflict between us real Americans, we who believe and are willing to die for the country our Founding Fathers left us, and those heinous, weak-kneed, left-wing radicals who want to tear down our country and force us to yield to the dark forces, that want us to live in a country devoid of freedom, of self-determination, of religious virtue, and of tax fairness.

"The typical citizen out there is sleepwalking, lost in the void of space and time, ignorant of the impending disasters about to befall us. We patriots have to wake them up and resist the Democrats' plan to have us passively descend into that madness. Our elected officials will not keep us safe. We have to take up arms to defend our families and our homes, to resist government overreach. We have that right written into the Constitution! We are the bulwark to restrain these evil forces that emanate from the deep state and the worldwide conspiracy to make us all slaves to an all-seeing, all-powerful, New World Order.

"Today we are going to practice survival and self-defense. We are going to learn how to protect ourselves in hand-to-hand combat and with primitive weapons, to master the use of our firearms, to use explosives to keep from having our positions overrun. Soon, we are going to adopt methods to go on the offensive, to carry the battle to the enemy. You will be informed more about that as we continue in our struggle for justice and the way of life enjoyed by those who came before us.

"For today, I want you all to know that you are the true champions of the American Way, the defenders of the homeland, the stalwart loyalists to God's Law. Be safe out there and keep the faith!"

A round of applause arose from the gathering while Clarence Youngblood looked to Mort Kilpatrick, his mentor, for a nod of approval.

CHAPTER 3
Welcome to Vetlandia

It was fortunate that the grave was shallow and the soil was mostly sand as Tom only had to displace about six inches of it to be free. First, he used his right arm like a lever, pounding his elbow upward until he felt no resistance. Straightening out his arm so that it was free, he began scraping the dirt away from his head. Once he had removed enough dirt so he could breathe, he rested before removing more dirt and wiggling the rest of his body from his would-be tomb.

He was weakened from the ordeal but now felt a renewed interest in living. He removed his dirt-filled pants, shook them off as best he could, and put them back on. In the distance, he saw a stationary light and began to make his way toward it, stumbling frequently and stopping many times to rest. The blood on his legs had mixed with the dirt from the grave, which seemed to stem the flow of fresh blood. His head and back ached from the shovel blows, he couldn't see well, and he felt a buzzing in his head, but he was determined to reach his goal.

The light turned out to be on the porch of a farmhouse about a mile away and when he knocked on the door, the couple who lived there was hesitant to let their bloody, dirty visitor in. He provided, through his tears, an abbreviated explanation of what happened and how he got there. Finally, his desperate pleading for help caused them to relent. He was barely able to crawl through the doorway before he collapsed on the floor. The husband took a long measured look at Tom, suspecting what else had happened, and went to a cabinet in the corner of the room, returning with a large glass of brandy. "Here, drink this. God damn," he said, "You can't trust anyone anymore. What is this world coming to?"

The farmer called the police and told them to bring an ambulance. He went to his bedroom, returning with some underwear, a pair of his old pants, and a shirt. He asked Tom if he was strong enough to sit in a plastic chair in the shower to get the blood and dirt off his body and Tom agreed. After a warm shower, the farmer wrapped him up in a large beach towel and his wife applied antiseptic and bandages to many of the cuts on his legs and the abrasion on his head. Tom was grateful for their nurturance but was still shaking from his ordeal. He knew what happened but at the same time found it hard to fully appreciate that it was not merely a dream, something he read about long ago or a movie he had seen.

The police and ambulance arrived in about an hour and a half. Tom told them what happened and described the truck and the driver insofar as his mind would allow him, but he wasn't able to remember the name written on the tanker's body. They dutifully took his report and the medics checked him over for injuries: two broken ribs, a concussion, lacerations on both legs, his head, and his back, and traumatic stress. The ambulance driver asked if he had insurance and Tom said no but that he was a service-connected veteran. "I guess we'll take you to the VA Hospital in Las Vegas then. It'll take about ninety minutes to get there."

Tom fell asleep on the ambulance gurney under the watchful eyes of one of the EMTs who helped him aboard. He was disoriented when he was awakened after arriving at the hospital, not being sure whether he was still in the grave and dreaming or if he was actually in a safe place. Within a few minutes, he was wide awake and responding to inquiries from hospital staff about the status of his sensory nerves, if he had pain here and there, if he was able to move this and that, if he felt nauseous or dizzy, if he had any preexisting medical problems, if he was on any current medications, if he had any medication allergies, and so on. They took his vital signs, took blood samples, checked his oxygen level and his airways, inspected and cleaned his wounds, and bandaged them, as necessary. Due to loss of blood and dehydration, he was given a transfusion and an IV of fluids and electrolytes. They told him he didn't appear to have any life-threatening injuries but they would run several other tests in the next few days to make sure. Tom was then moved to a hospital room where he again fell fast asleep.

Of course, nurses did not allow him to sleep uninterruptedly, feeling it their duty to awaken him for measurements, shots, and pills every few hours. Tom filled the time in between with dreams of being cut and sexually abused by the truck driver, struggling to get out of the grave, and scenes from his childhood. When morning finally came around, he awakened with a start, quickly surveying his surroundings to make sure he was in a safe place and that his visual images were not elements of a dream. The pains in his side from his broken ribs helped convince him that the terrors of the previous night had, indeed, occurred. A kind nurse brought him some broth and toast. Then he was placed in a wheelchair and taken to an appointment with his doctor.

Dr. Lufkin glanced up as Tom was wheeled in, quickly returning to reading notes from Tom's electronic medical record. "Hmm. Looks like you got pretty badly beaten up yesterday. Two broken ribs, some cuts and bruises and a whack on the head. Were you drunk at the time?" Without waiting for an answer, he commented, "Don't know why you guys can't behave yourselves."

Tom started to explain his recent experience but the doctor didn't seem to have any interest in it. "Yeah, yeah. I've heard enough. I don't need to know any more details. It's not like you are unique. We get cases like yours all the time. We'll get you patched up and out of here in a few days. Then you can go back to your drinking and carousing until the next time you get into a fight. No drugs for you for pain but you can take Tylenol. Any questions? You can take them up with the social worker."

Tom was nonplussed. "I...I...," he uttered as a flash of anger flushed his face but he knew he had best not express it for fear of reprisals. He wanted to talk with the doctor about his sexual assault and how he was buried alive but this white coat had zero bedside manner and didn't seem amenable to learning the facts of the matter. He had seen this kind of doctor before when he was recovering from his head injury. He was just another doctor who practiced presumptive medicine, assuming he already knew what it was necessary to know about his case. To hell with what the patient has to say about his circumstances. The lab tests and "objective" observations tell the whole story. The orderly moved him back to his room with Tom still shaking his head in disbelief.

Tom did not see his doctor again until his discharge examination. He spent his time watching TV, walking the grounds, and talking with other vets. A few days before he was to be discharged, he was able to talk with the social worker and tell him about the events with the truck driver. The social worker was surprised to find that there was nothing about the traumatic event in the patient's records, but then he had seen poor records on many vets he had worked with and shrugged it off as "one of those things." However, he did believe that Tom was subjected to severe trauma and required extended care that the hospital could not provide. He wanted to send him to a place in Oregon that did not have the restrictions on the length of stay that hospitals did and he heard they had recently started a program for the treatment of post-traumatic stress. Tom wondered if it was the same place where the first truck driver was treated. The social worker made a call to the Oregon facility and made arrangements to have Tom transferred there in the next couple of days.

∞

Leaving the desert of Nevada and riding the bus through the lush green mountains and countryside of southern Oregon lifted Tom's spirits some. It was like a new beginning, a shedding of all the emotional baggage attached to his recent past or so he thought. The bus dropped him off at the depot in the nearest town where a friendly outreach social worker named Jan Burke greeted him and provided a ride to the facility a few miles outside of town. Besides getting new transfers to the facility, Jan was assigned the task of coaxing homeless vets to leave their sleeping quarters in parks, under bridges or in the large concrete culverts a sympathetic construction company allowed them to inhabit.

Jan wanted her "rescues" to succeed in the facility that she knew was far from a perfect institution. The "Irish mafia" that was in charge of the place was not reluctant to wield power in arbitrary ways if it would make them look good to their superiors or hide some impropriety on their part. Many of the physicians held the vets in contempt for their use of alcohol or drugs to manage their disjunctive emotions and would withhold appropriate treatment until the patient jumped through what they considered proper hoops. Some would practice presumptive medicine, assuming the patient must be guilty of something, no matter what story he told.

Some of the nonprofessional facility assistants would surround themselves with "pet" patients to carry out "incentive therapy" assignments in their domain and take advantage of various opportunities to get rid of patients who challenged their authority or those that they didn't like. It was not always easy for naive patients to successfully wend their way through this maze of interpersonal relations and group dynamics. Of course, some street-wise patients could recognize their guileless colleagues and take advantage of their credulity to achieve nefarious goals. Or they could use the staff's "games" to their advantage, playing one off against another to come off a "winner."

Jan explained to Tom that the facility was organized into five sections, each with its treatment team composed of a doctor, a nurse, a psychologist, a social worker, a nutritionist, an occupational therapist, an alcohol and drug treatment representative, and a section facility coordinator. She pointed out that some teams were better in some respects than others, mostly dependent on the training, professionalism, and especially the attitude of the team members.

The physician was the nominal leader of the team and thus had the most influence in determining what happened to patients. But some physicians were more receptive to input from other team members than other physicians. Some suggestions from team members were more oriented toward functional improvement in patients while other suggestions targeted punishment or premature discharge. Some team members would doze off during meetings without being roused by their peers.

After a series of intake interviews, patients would come before their treatment team and work out a treatment plan. Often this would turn into a contentious meeting as patients and team members would have different ideas about ethical goals, how to achieve them, and the duration of treatment. More often than not, the patient's ideas were not given serious consideration.

Jan Burke advised Tom that he should be careful and get to know the "lay of the land" before he decided to place a great amount of trust in what anyone told him, whether a patient or staff member. "Take your time and ask several patients what they think about the competence and reliability of staff or other patients," she said.

Tom asked, "What should I do if I need some help in working out personal problems?"

Jan hesitated before she answered. "Be careful what you say if you see the chief psychiatrist. He has a reputation for belittling patients and sometimes worse. Some of the psychologists and social workers are okay but others mostly try to avoid seeing patients except for initial interviews, which they are required to do. It all depends on the section you get assigned to and you have no control over that. Sections three and five are pretty good."

Jan emphasized that the use of street drugs or alcohol was the major no-no in the facility and that frequent urine screens and breathalyzer tests, if positive, could lead to immediate discharge. "Once you get kicked out," she said, "it might be a year before you can get readmitted."

Tom experienced some trepidation after receiving this precautionary advice and when he saw the old WWII-era brick buildings as they came into view. The grounds were very well manicured through the efforts of patients with Incentive Therapy positions and the buildings appeared well cared for despite their age. All had ramps going up to sliding glass doors that were activated when someone came within range. Jan noted that, while convenient for patients in wheelchairs, it also allowed a young black bear to recently gain entrance and run down the hallway from one end of the building to the other as patients leaped for cover into the nearest rooms with doors that could be closed.

"Bears! You have bears in this area, right on the campus?" asked a skeptical Tom.

"Don't worry," said Jan. No one was hurt and it doesn't happen very often. We are not far from the wild here. We do have the occasional bear or cougar that comes visiting and you can walk down to the river and fish for salmon. Some of the doctors even do that during their lunch break."

Jan dropped Tom off at the admissions building. The first thing he noticed when he entered was the shining tiled floors, looking almost like a mirrored surface. Glancing down the hall, he noted a veteran dressed in an orange smock operating a huge buffing machine. Seeing the Walkman connected to his ears, Tom waved to the man as he went by. The man looked up and nodded his head in response. When he arrived at the room serving incoming patients, the others waiting in the ante-room pointed him to a vacant chair.

The muscular man sitting next to him had both arms covered with tattoos, wore a headband and a vest with a Harley-Davidson emblem on it, and sported short gloves with the fingertips cut off. He stuck out his hand, introduced himself as Kent Lewis, and asked if this was Tom's first time at the facility.

"First time," said Tom. "I was sent from the Las Vegas VA. How about you?"

"This is my third time here. Been in a lot of other VAs. Haven't been able to get my act together since Vietnam. I was in the Army. Went over from Korea with a Republic of Korea outfit." He watched the younger man's face for any sign that he recognized the significance of this fact, but saw none. "I was in the Vegas VA once. Had a bit of a problem there so they sent me to a private hospital on their dime."

"What happened?," inquired Tom innocently.

"Well...," said Kent as he hesitated telling the story for fear of alienating his new acquaintance. "You see, I go really haywire sometimes and can get pretty violent. Can't control my temper once it gets set off. This time I was freaking out in downtown Vegas and called the VA to come get me. They gave me a bunch of shit over the phone and I got really mad. Rode over there on my motorcycle and walked in the door with a sawed-off shotgun in one hand and a revolver in the other. Told everyone to get on the floor. Asked them what it took to get any treatment there. Everybody scattered, diving behind desks and running into offices. They called the police and a SWAT team arrived. Negotiated with them for about an hour before I calmed down and gave up. They put me in cuffs and shot me full of Thorazine. Everyone there was scared to deal with me so they sent me to a private hospital for a few days and then they sent me here for the first time."

"Holy shit" exclaimed Tom. He wanted to ask what was the nature of Kent's involvement in Vietnam but thought that might be too sensitive a topic for casual conversation.

"I've cooled down quite a bit since then. I got a handle on my alcohol and drug use the first time around and tried to stay away from situations that would set me off. I couldn't sleep inside with other people except in the hospital – was afraid I might wake up from a nightmare and start killing or hurting someone. So I spent a whole year sleeping under a truck and built me a trailer with a bed and overhead on it so I could sleep outside. The second time I was here, I saw a psychologist who helped me cope with the civilians and tame my PTSD some. Still have it but I'm not running around like a crazy man anymore – mostly. Just need a little tune-up now. I've had some tough months lately."

"Wow! So I guess a person can get some help here then?"

"You have to watch your backside though. There are people here who get off on making life difficult for us vets. But there are also some very helpful folks too. Keep a low profile until you know who to trust and how things work." Kent was called for his initial interview and wished Tom well as he sauntered off.

Eventually, Tom's number came up for the intake procedure to begin. He was assigned to Section 3 and told he would have a roommate in his lodging in building 201. Meals were to be in the dining hall or the canteen. He was given a map of the facility and a list of rules he had to comply with during his stay. Again, he was warned about alcohol or drug usage and the consequences. He was given a list of appointments with his treatment team members, the first being with the section facility assistant immediately following provision of his DD-214 and signing of various forms.

Nearly all of the many buildings were connected by long main hallways. Tom tried to figure out his current location and headed for the Section 3 office in Building 201. When he got there, he gave his slip with his name and room assignment to the veteran Incentive Therapy worker who put a set of linens, towels, and toiletries on a cart and lead him to his new home.

Tom entered the room behind the IT worker who introduced him to Tony Napoliello, his roommate, commenting that they were both from California. He placed the bedding and supplies on the vacant bed in the room and departed with a "Welcome to Vetlandia" sign-off. "Vetlandia" was not the real name of the facility but was so designated by the veterans themselves and everyone, both staff and patients, used it in everyday discourse although not in official correspondence.

Tony was a thin guy of average height, clean-shaven and neatly dressed in khakis and a long-sleeved shirt who appeared to be in his 50s. He was a calm, deliberative individual, pausing a sufficient time to think before proceeding with an utterance. Tom surmised that he had various intellectual interests and was broadly knowledgeable about many things.

Tony pointed out his domain in the room and indicated the area Tom could call his own. He cautioned that he did not sleep well in total darkness and preferred to have a small light on at night. Otherwise, he didn't volunteer information about himself. But he seemed to be friendly and courteous and Tom felt he could relate to him without fear he would be shamed or intimidated in the process.

Searching for commonalities, Tony asked, "Where did you grow up in California?"

"In the northern Bay area outside of San Francisco. I have a brother and sister that still live there," Tom responded.

Tony continued, "I'm from the Los Angeles area, large Italian family in the construction trades, for the most part. What did you do in the service?"

"I was in the Army, mobile missile launcher crew, stationed in Germany. I got knocked off the top of one of the missiles when I was working on it and hit my head on the way down. Spent a lot of time in hospitals. That ended my military career right quick."

"Damn, that's a bummer," said Tony.

"Yeah, I've been trying to put my life back together ever since. Things haven't worked out very well. The head injury gave me seizures and, for some reason, diabetes, and now the medications for one seem to throw off the medications for the other. Hard to get and keep a job when you go off the beam unexpectedly."

As he made his bed and put away his belongings, Tom inquired about Tony's military experience.

"I worked in Army Intelligence and, yeah, I know, lots of people say that is an oxymoron, but that's what I did," he laughed. "Served three tours in Vietnam. In fact, I was one of the last people to go into and out of Saigon in 1975. We did some nasty things interrogating prisoners back in the day so now I have a touch of PTSD. After the war we kept tabs on some Soviet agents in Washington, DC. That was interesting. We sent them a Christmas card, just to let them know we knew about them and were watching their activities." He laughed again. "One time I went to South America and posed as a bible salesman. Almost got caught but managed to talk myself out of it."

Tom commented, "My dad was over in Vietnam on some special mission in Thailand and Laos, in Special Forces. Don't know exactly what he did. He was home on leave in 1970 when he died. They said it was a suicide. I guess, at the funeral, his buddies told my mother they thought there was something fishy about the coroner's report, but I never found out what it was."

"That's a shame, kid. There were a lot of bizarre things that happened in those days. Do you know much about the Vietnam War?"

"I've read some novels and seen a lot of movies about it, but I haven't really studied it like in academic accounts. All I knew was that we went over there to stop the spread of communism, and it turned into a quagmire. Nobody in my family wanted to talk about it because it brought back painful memories of my father. Then I got all involved in my own career in the Army before I got hurt. From there, it just kind of faded into the background for me."

Tony suggested "You might want to read *The Elephant and the Tiger* by Wilbur Morrison. It gives the whole bloody history of that mess over there from the time when the French were fighting the Vietminh. A good novel is *The 13th Valley* by John Del Vecchio. He was there, felt the pain and sorrow, the senselessness and futility of it all. There were a few moments of joy and laughter too, but damn few."

His natural curiosity aroused by the suicide story but with some apprehension for fear of insulting or embarrassing the kid, Tony asked, "You don't suppose your dad was involved in something he shouldn't have been, do you?"

"I've had my suspicions that I've been cursed," Tom laughed, "but I've got nothing to go on, really. My life changed quite rapidly back then."

Tom paused, as images from that era popped into consciousness before he quickly pushed them out of his mind.

"I've wondered over the years about what might have happened and what might have led up to it, but I haven't had any evidence to go on other than that he didn't drink brandy like the coroner claimed, and that his friends and my mom found it hard to believe that he would commit suicide. They were suspicious about what he was doing over there too but didn't tell me what they thought might have happened. Probably because I was so young at the time. You know, you hear a lot of stories about what guys saw over there and what they did. It's easy to imagine all sorts of horrible things that may have taken place."

"Yeah," agreed Tony, "that was not our most virtuous war, that's for sure. Most of the CIA's plans over in Laos were carried out by a Hmong general – Vang Pao was his name. He was one tough son-of-a-bitch, who got shot several times leading his troops on missions against the Pathet Lao and the North Vietnamese. He was in plane crashes, people tried to assassinate him, and he even survived a carpet bombing. He was wounded so many times that he was held together with a lot of wires and pins. But he just kept on going. He was fiercely loyal to his mountain people and, even while he managed an army, he started many social, medical, and educational programs to lift his people out of poverty.

"He did a good job for his CIA handlers too, particularly Col. Bill Lair, the station chief. And the CIA loved him because he did whatever it took to accomplish their objectives. That included hauling opium crops to market in Thailand and Vietnam using Air America airplanes. That is, until the CIA got scared of being found out. Then they gave Vang a bunch of planes that he used to form his own private airline. That separation from the CIA made it possible for the Agency to deny that they had any involvement in the drug trade!"

"What the hell was he doing getting involved in helping with opium transport? For the money, I suppose?"

"Well, he got personally rich," Tony maintained, "but he also did it to persuade the different Hmong groups to sign their young men up in his army. Some of these kids were barely teenagers and about a third of them got killed, so the age of the recruits kept getting younger and younger. You see, the Hmong were not just one ethnic group but rather a conglomerate of different tribes, each with a different leader and social networks. They resented being derisively called the "Meo" people and were looked down upon by the low-land Laotians because their needs were being ignored.

"Vang Pao was a skilled politician in being able to use their indigenous beliefs to get Hmong groups that were often in conflict with each other to work with him to carry out CIA missions. Mainly he used the exchange principal, you know, 'I'll get this for you if you do this for me.' He'd get money from the CIA to make pay-offs to people of influence in the particular tribe as well as to pay the young enlistees and their families. Opium was a basic cash crop over there and agreeing to get their raw opium transported to places where it could be converted into heroin was part of his deal. He also did not hesitate to use the stick as well as the carrot to get his way — he would kill people who objected too much or didn't act reasonably to his requests. So he was both feared and respected."

"He must have been quite a character! What happened to him? Did he survive the war?"

"He survived alright and came to the US along with about 200,000 of his followers. There are some large Hmong settlements in California around Fresno, in St. Paul, Minnesota and in Wausau, Wisconsin. He still is their leader and is known as The Moses of the Hmong. He continues to advocate for education of the Hmong in this country. He has pushed to get Hmong to vote and run for political office and he created the Lao Family non-profit to help adapt his countrymen to life in this country. Of course it has been a long time since the end of the war and the younger generation of Hmong don't have much interest in going back to their native land. But Vang Pao is still pretty impressive for a reformed drug-runner and guerrilla fighter!"

"I'll say," said Tom.

Tony Napoliello fell silent again for quite a spell. The suspiciousness and distrust he felt after getting out of the army were starting to kick in again. What if this kid's father was planning on going to one of the demonstrations and reporting about our involvement in Laos? Hell, he might have worked with Tony Poe, the guy that was used as a model for the Marlon Brando character in the movie *Apocalypse Now*, who used to drop severed heads onto Laotian villages from airplanes to intimidate them into going along with the CIA's plans. The kid's father could have been involved in some shit like that, he thought. Maybe some of his comrades wanted to take him out before he could say anything that would implicate them in war crimes. Or maybe it was some of Vang Pao's men who were ordered to silence a potential troublemaker.

Tony knew, from his intelligence work, that Special Forces were often involved in the training of South Vietnamese soldiers and he didn't see why they might not also be involved in the training of Hmong recruits. Maybe there were more sinister forces at play, trying to keep the Nixon administration from looking bad. He remembered reading that Nixon's White House considered John Kerry a threat, an articulate guy with a bunch of war medals who looked and sounded too much like a Kennedy for them to sit complacently by and let him gain ascendance. So Nixon set out to discredit him and infiltrate his organization with the help of his aide, Charles Colson. It would be not much of a stretch to think they would want to get rid of another troublemaker before he shot his mouth off.

This whole thing could be hard for this young man to figure out. On the other hand, maybe he didn't need to figure it out. He decided to drop the conversation before he got himself too pumped up. Tom had finished putting his things away so Tony asked him, "You want to go down to the Canteen and grab a cup of coffee?"

"Sure," said Tom.

As they traversed about half a mile of hallways, Tony identified various parts of the facility: the library, the chapel, the gym, the pharmacy, the infirmary, and the auditorium. Pointing out one of the windows, he indicated the golf course and the fishing pond with ducks floating around on it. "Every now and then they have to clean out the pond because the bottom gets filled up with duck shit. Foul-smelling stuff!"

Arriving at the canteen, they got in line to get coffee and a snack. Tony paid and they found an empty booth to sit in. Soon, a tall man with a definite limp, younger than most of the men, came up to say hello. "This your new roomie, Tony?"

"Yeah, Buster, this is Tom Ward. Army missile crew. Tom, this here is Buster Rollins, Air Force. Been here a few years." The introductions specifying service unit as reference group was *de rigueur* for the facility, offering the opportunity to establish commonalities if there were any. The added reference to the duration of Buster's stay was intended to alert Tom that there was something odd about Buster.

"Welcome to Vetlandia, Tom," said Buster. Moving directly to his area of interest, he asked, "Are you a Christian?"

Tom felt uncomfortable, not knowing what he would be letting himself in for if he answered the question. Tony intervened, commenting "Buster likes to argue about religion."

"I don't like to argue about it," said Buster with a pout. "I just like to discuss religious issues to get different perspectives on them. Sometimes they turn into arguments when people don't like my challenges to their beliefs."

"Well, I don't have any strong religious beliefs, so I don't think I would be a very good person for you to discuss them with," said Tom, deflecting the request for additional interaction with this individual.

"Maybe you'll change your mind after you've been here a while," said Buster as he ambled off to another table.

Tony whispered to Tom, "He's harmless most of the time and isn't bad to talk to if you can stay away from religion. He lost his leg in an auto accident. Before he came here, he got into some big vocal fights with a couple of priests, got thrown out of the church. He's had several squabbles with people here about religion, including the chaplains."

Tony spotted a friend coming off the coffee line and waved. The guy with a missing front tooth, self-extracted with a pair of pliers when the dentist put him off too long, smiled broadly and came over to their booth. He asked, "Mind if I join you?"

"Not at all," said Tony, motioning him to sit on his side of the table. "Jerry, this here is my new roommate, Tom Ward. Army missile crew. Tom, this is Jerry McCall, Navy Riverine Force. He's on Section 3 too."

"Riverine Force, hmm. Were you one of the guys who went up the rivers in Vietnam?" asked Tom.

"Yeah, we did that. Mekong Delta – III Corp and IV Corp. We ran Armored Troop Carriers up and down the rivers chasing Charlie. Three miserable years after the Navy lied to me about what my duties would be. I spent nine years in the Navy. Got my head all screwed up over there and got my lungs ruined with asbestos working on submarines at Marc Island afterwards. But I'm working at getting squared away," he said, with a wry smile.

"I'm going to college, aiming for a degree in English or maybe Journalism."

"You can do that here?" asked Tom.

"Yeah," Jerry replied. "If you are on the right section and have the right case manager. Otherwise they're likely to make you immediately get a job and discharge you after you save enough money for a rental deposit and first month's expenses."

"Any word on your service connection yet?" asked Tony.

"No," Jerry grumbled. "I'll probably get denied again, but I got all the paper work submitted. Those guys take every opportunity to stall your claim, try to save the government some money. How's your claim coming?"

"I got 50% but I'm going for an upgrade — have to get more documentation about my condition and substantiate that I was where I said I was and did what I said I did. Same 'ol shit! I started this process about three years ago," Tony said with exasperation.

"Ray, the Marine, finally got his after five years – gave him $150,000 plus 100%," said Jerry. "Guess they finally believed him about being a POW. The scars all over his body weren't good enough. Plans on going back to Arizona to start his own construction business. Lucky bastard!"

Turning his attention to Tom, Jerry asked "Where you from, Tom?"

"Well I was working and going to school in Tucson before I came here. When I was in the Army I got knocked off a mobile missile launcher in Germany, hit my head coming down. Have had seizures, off and on, ever since. That made me lose my job. I couldn't afford to go to school. And then I had some more problems on the road, so I came here. I'm originally from the San Francisco area."

Jerry McCall made eye contact with Tony who met his gaze and quickly turned his attention to his coffee cup. Jerry concluded that Tom's vagueness about "problems on the road" signaled it was a sensitive area and not to be asked about.

"So I guess we are all from California," he said. "I was living in a tent in the mountains after the Gulf War started. Then the earthquake hit. I was having all sorts of flashbacks and bad dreams, so I checked into the VA and they sent me here. Good thing too. Have you seen Doc Oldman yet?"

"No. I just got here. Who is Doc Oldman?"

"Oh, he's the psychologist on our section. You'll see him for an intake. You probably will like him. He's one of the good ones around here. I think of him as a kind of leprechaun. You'll see what I mean."

Hank Burns came over to the table, a tall muscular black man and another member of Section 3. "What are you guys plotting over here?" he said with a smile.

"We're hatching a revolution, going to take over the place and have a big party – free beer for everybody," rejoined Tony.

"Have a seat and join the conspiracy, Hank," said Jerry.

"This is my new roommate, Tom Ward," said Tony. "Tom was in the Army – mobile missile launch crew. Tom, Hank Burns here was in the 173rd Airborne Light Infantry Brigade. Charlie wasn't able to kill this old sack of shit no matter how hard they tried, even put a bounty on his head" he said laughing.

"They sure tried though," said Hank. "When they failed, our side tried to get us too. What a bunch of fuck-ups!"

"Dare I ask what happened," asked Tom, sheepishly.

"Hill 875 near Dak To was all full of tunnels and the enemy shot at us through slots in the ground. We pushed up to the top of the hill, shooting into the ground on full automatic all the way. Killed a lot of those little guys at close range. It was brutal and bloody. There was a triple canopy so the Air Force couldn't see what was below. Well, we got to the top of the fucking hill and they dropped a 500-pounder on us. Killed a bunch of us that the enemy spared. Then we had to sit there with all the bodies stinking to high heaven in the heat and humidity. You could hardly breathe, had to just take small sips of air at a time," he said, demonstrating the action, "or the smell would make you puke."

Tom could see that Hank still had a lot of anger connected to that event and thought he may have overstepped some boundaries. "I didn't mean to..."

"Don't worry about it, kid. I get mad all over again every time I think about it. But I don't go off on innocent bystanders any more like I used to. Well, most of the time I don't." And then he smiled at Tom.

"That must have been tough," said Tom. My dad was over there with Special Forces. Don't know what he did but he was in Thailand most of the time. He died when he was home on furlough."

The three older vets exchanged questioning glances and Tony surreptitiously put his forefinger in front of his lips, signaling the other two not to inquire further.

∞

The stocky Chief of Staff with the prematurely weathered face, Mort Kilpatrick, walked into the office of the chief of psychiatry, Dr. Wolfgang Gunnar, without knocking. Addressing the surprised patient in the room, he said, "Run along now. I've got something important to discuss with the doctor. Schedule another appointment with the receptionist on your way out." Turning to Dr. Gunnar, he asked "Are you taking care of that problem we talked about the other day?

"Yeah, I'm on top of it, boss."

Mort snapped, "That sonofabitch has all sorts of information about our little enterprise here and if that gets out, we'll be finished. I've jumped through hoops trying to keep that bastard alive but the stubborn fucker won't give an inch. He's wanted to take you down too ever since you first interviewed him and now he wants to come after me."

"Yeah, don't worry, boss. I arranged for a couple of the boys to make him turn up on that little island in the river. They are going to make it look like a drunken accident. As far as the cops will ever know, the guy just got snockered, fell into the river, and drowned. The police will find a couple of empty whiskey bottles and some marijuana in his pocket."

The object of this lethal plotting was Scott Parks. Scott's "fuck you" attitude started when he was in high school. He refused to obey a teacher's demand that he stop complaining about the teacher's treatment of a fellow student from a minority group. Scott took the teacher to court and won his case. His dad, being a decorated WWII vet, tried to get Scott to keep a lower profile and demonstrate a modicum of conformity. But the elder Parks's tendency to shove improprieties under the rug alienated his son even further, causing him to drop out of school and run away from home. Scott was drafted into the Marine Corps despite being married and the father of two young children. That pissed him off too and he vowed to get even.

When he got to Vietnam, Scott discovered a conspiracy in the accounting for military equipment. If they had more radios than showed up on the records, they simply made the books balance by digging a hole, dropping the excess equipment into it, and filling it with dirt. Food supplies were being sold off to local distributors and the "use" records were adjusted accordingly. When Scott tried to expose the fraud, his superiors sent him to a front-line combat unit for his efforts. There, Scott felt a fallen comrade's skull disintegrate in his hands as he tried to resuscitate him after he was shot by the enemy. That experience had a profound effect on the idealistic and tenderhearted conscript, intensifying his already simmering anger toward those in charge, whom he believed had allowed this injustice to take place.

Scott was wounded in combat and the evacuation helicopter used in the "dust off" was shot down, resulting in his sustaining a severe back injury. In a coma for two months, he woke up in a naval hospital in the US where he had to learn how to walk again. After that ordeal, the Marine Corps placed him in a psychiatric ward before unceremoniously discharging him to the street.

Scott joined the Vietnam Veterans Against the War and participated in many protests and demonstrations, getting arrested and beaten several times. His wife, unimpressed by his moral zeal, decided he was a deadbeat dad and divorced him. He met a philosophically compatible woman on a hike, they became lovers, and together they moved into a forest on the Canadian west coast, building their own home and living as far apart from society as possible. After a few years of frontier life, his second wife tired of the experiment and went back to school, without Scott.

Depressed and disillusioned, Scott checked into Vetlandia, where he was soon inspired to continue his crusading. He had a run-in with Dr. Gunnar, who was despised by most other vets, and Scott managed to gather dozens of written complaints against him, submitting them to the district office. District sent the packet of complaints back to the Chief of Staff at Vetlandia and told him "make the problem go away." When the District Office did not respond with an investigation, Scott managed to get a secret address for the Secretary of Veterans Affairs and sent the whole package of affidavits and legal records to him. At that point, he suddenly became a real threat to local officials and, therefore, someone who had to be discredited or eliminated.

First, they claimed that Scott was crazy and his words should not be considered valid. But he had the testimony of dozens of other vets affirming that the same kinds of things had happened to them. His case manager, Dr. Oldman, determined by psychological testing that Scott was not psychotic and was above average in intelligence, so the "crazy ploy" turned out to be a bad argument.

Next, they tried to catch him using drugs or alcohol and discharge him for violating facility policy. But Scott was too clever to fall into that trap, staying away from the facility if he used alcohol and taking a dietary supplement to disguise any marijuana use. Of course, they could have planted prohibited items in his room and "discover" them on an impromptu room inspection but that might be difficult if his roommate was present and saw them hiding false evidence.

Would they dare resort to more drastic measures? Some residents and staff thought that was a possibility. They knew there were a few despicable people who wanted to hold onto their power at Vetlandia and those individuals could recruit some even nastier people, from those who came to the facility as patients, to carry out their wicked intentions. Some of the down-and-outers would do almost anything if it meant they would get special treatment or favors from the staff. It was known for a fact that one patient served as a spy for Dr. Wolfgang Gunnar. If the spy heard some gossip that could be useful for the shrink, he would immediately run off to tell him about it. Then Gunnar would take it out on the target in some way – either by withholding pain medication, dosing him with high levels of anti-psychotics, making snide entries about him in his chart, or telling made-up stories about him to other staff.

"There's no way that any of this can be tied to us, is there?" the COS inquired from Dr. Gunnar. "I know that Oldman is sympathetic to Scott's complaints and that could get messy."

"No. The FBI might come snooping around since they investigate unnatural deaths of VA inpatients. But we get a thousand patients coming through here every year and a lot of them are suicidal. We have a suicide attempt nearly every week. Who is to say that Parks is not one of those poor bastards that decided to end it all?"

"Yeah, that'll be our story line. The FBI will start with Director Horton and he'll be shitting bricks thinking he will lose his job. He already knows Parks has been a trouble maker from the reports he got back from Regional. I'll fill him in on Parks's history of psychiatric problems and calm his nerves about any repercussions for him."

CHAPTER 4
The Lay of the Land

For the next few days, Tom Ward had a flurry of appointments with his treatment team. Most interviewers treated him with respect and oriented themselves to identifying Tom's goals and developing a plan to meet them. The drug and alcohol specialist appeared more suspicious than the others, challenging Tom on the frequency, magnitude, and duration of his usage of various substances. The hidden agenda of others, to shorten the stay of the patient as much as possible while not too obviously violating government regulations and professional ethics, was visible in the options they presented and the degree to which they considered patient desires. The vocational therapist seemed to consider only paths to immediate employment and used limited educational or training possibilities as an excuse unless the patient's illness was connected with his military service and could be funded by a disability claim. The social worker appeared somewhat compulsive in writing down all of the details of Tom's life, even those Tom found hard to remember or considered of little importance.

Doctor Whitey Green wrote orders for the usual lab tests even though Tom had them only a few weeks earlier. He lectured Tom about alcohol and drug usage and refused any medication for the back pain Tom still experienced from being hit with a shovel. He was critical of Tom's efforts to keep his blood glucose at acceptable levels and disparaged Tom's claim that it was connected to his use of Dilantin.

"Dilantin has nothing to do with it. Those seizures of yours are not *real* seizures. They are what we call pseudo-seizures. They are due to your psychological problems, not to any real physical injury. You may have talked somebody into giving you a service connection on that basis, but I'm not buying it. So what I am going to do is reduce the amount of Dilantin you are taking, effective immediately."

"But, but the doctors at Walter Reed..."

Tom's objection was cut off in mid-stream with a snippy remark that betrayed the doctor's hypersensitivity to criticism and penchant for intimidation.

"And who do you think is the doctor in this room?" growled Dr. Green.

"Well, I...," began Tom.

"And don't you forget it, you fucking ass-wipe. I had to deal with enough of you fuck-ups when I was in the Army. I won't let you get away with your shit here!" said Green menacingly.

Tom just looked at him with wide eyes, said not a word, and left quickly.

When Tom went for his first meeting with the psychologist, Dr. Oldman, he was greeted warmly by the secretary who explained that the doctor was in session but would be with him shortly. He took a seat in one of the chairs that lined the hallway spanning five offices. Another relatively young veteran who was waiting asked, "Are you one of Oldman's boys?"

Tom asked, "What's an Oldman's boy? I'm new here."

"He sees a lot of the guys on our section that are fucked-up in the head. Usually one hour a week. Most of us like coming here. It helps."

"What does he do?" asked Tom.

"Well, that is kind of hard to answer," said the vet. "He does different things with different people. But you can expect that he will ask you a lot of questions, at least at first, and he'll give you a personality test that can really peg the way you're inclined to look at things. He'll do some other things to make sure the test results are accurate. And then he'll ask you more questions to get you to consider different ways of looking at things and deciding what to do. He never tells you what to do, but he will help you think of alternatives and how to evaluate them. It's interesting."

Soon Dr. Oldman and a patient emerged from his office. The doctor made a bee-line down to the end of the building, past the toilets, the testing room, and the biofeedback office, outside to the cement stoop where he smoked a cigarette. Five minutes later, he was back, asked if he was Tom Ward, introduced himself, and ushered Tom into his room.

In order to get a quick assessment of the patient's state of mind so that he could decide whether to proceed with the standard intake interview or if he had to make a diversion to deal with any matters that couldn't wait, the doctor asked, "How are you feeling today?"

"Not too bad. I'm still getting used to the place," said Tom, not wanting to be too revealing before he knew how he was being regarded.

"OK then. What I am going to do is ask you a bunch of questions and give you some short tasks. Be as accurate as you can be. Let's start with your past medical history. I see by your records that you were seen at the hospital in Las Vegas. It says you were the victim of an assault. Can you tell me a little more about that?"

Tom related the complete story of the assault, sexual molestation, and being buried alive by the truck driver. The doctor did not intrude on his narrative other than to ask for some clarifying information. Tom noticed only a widening of the eyes and a wince on the face of the doctor as he told certain parts of his story.

After Tom finished his account, the doctor exclaimed, "Holy shit! That must have been a terrifying experience."

Tom acknowledged that it was and indicated that he had nightmares of the incident ever since, was easily startled, and was "kind of paranoid."

"What do you mean by that," asked the psychologist.

"Well, I'm cautious about what people are up to when they approach me. Always wondering if they have some nefarious purpose in mind. Try to stay away from people I don't know."

"That isn't technically paranoia," said Dr. Oldman. "But it is a natural reaction to the kind of experience you have had. It might take quite a while to get over but we can work on it here if you want. For right now, however, we need to get through the rest of this intake interview. Tell me about the injury you sustained while in the Army."

Tom went through the whole series of events, hospitalizations, the fight to get his seizures under control, the development of diabetes, and the complications caused by taking Dilantin and insulin at the same time. Tom told him about the article he read that considered that very complication.

"I didn't know that," said the doctor. "Certainly seems possible though."

Dr. Oldman then asked a series of questions about current medical and psychological symptoms and how they affected Tom's ability to work and engage in social life, any periods of time that he was without symptoms, and any treatments that seemed to help or make matters worse. He inquired about any sleep disturbance, impulse control problems, suicidal or homicidal ideation, delusions, hallucinations, obsessive behavior, depression, and panic attacks

Then he switched pace and gave Tom three things to remember. He asked him to repeat them and then told him that he would ask him to recall them again in a few minutes. Next, he had Tom repeat a series of numbers, increasing the length of the series by one each time until Tom failed the trial twice. The following tasks involved subtracting numbers by seven from 100, naming the last few presidents, explaining the meaning of some proverbs, and telling how two items were alike.

By the time they had gotten through the psychological screening tests, over an hour had passed without getting to Tom's family and occupational history. So Dr. Oldman told Tom they would have another session the following day to complete the intake.

Tom felt somewhat exhilarated following the interview. He felt that he had been listened to and believed, that the doctor knew what he was doing, was thorough in his examination, and would not slap him with some hair-brained diagnosis. Tom was hoping he would be able to obtain psychotherapy as part of his treatment plan.

The next day the secretary greeted Tom by his first name and engaged in some short chit-chat with him, which made him feel like a real person, not just another in an endless stream of vets. The doctor invited him into his office with a big smile and again asked how he was doing, to which Tom responded, "I'm doing pretty good today, thank you."

"Fine. What we have left to do is go through your family and occupational history. Is your father still living?"

"No. He died in 1970."

Dr. Oldman looked up from his writing pad and raised an eyebrow."What did he die from?"

Tom went on to relate the circumstances of his father's death and the questions that his mother and his father's friends raised about it.

The doctor furrowed his brow so that a dozen wrinkles appeared on his forehead. "Hmm. That does seem to be one of the most unusual methods of committing suicide I've ever heard of. Do you know what he did in the Army?"

"No, only that he was on some assignment to a secret base in Thailand. I was so young at the time, eight years old, that they never bothered to tell me, probably didn't think I would understand it anyway. You probably know that a lot of guys over there participated in atrocities of one sort or another. Well, I sometimes wonder if my dad was involved in any of that and if all the crap that I call my life isn't some kind of retribution for things my father did – the Ward Curse."

"I see," said the psychologist as he remembered a former patient who believed he was being tortured in his nightmares by ghosts of the relatives of the innocent checkpoint guard he had impulsively murdered in order to protect a girlfriend who was smuggling drugs.

"Kind of like the sins of the father being visited upon the son. I'm not inclined to believe in ghosts other than in a metaphorical sense but you may have developed some kind of a psychological connection there. Let's leave that for a later discussion, shall we?"

"Sure," Tom nodded his assent.

"How about your mother. Is she still alive?"

"No, she died about a year after my father."

The doctor straightened up in his chair and a puzzled look appeared on his face. "Oh, no! How did she die?"

"She committed suicide. Started up the car in the garage and closed all the windows. My older sister rushed in and tried to get her out of the car, but couldn't and backed the car right out of the garage, broke the door. But it was too late. I ran and hid behind the pool house."

Dr. Oldman was nonplussed, at a loss as to what to say or even think. He learned that there was even more.

"My mom had a hard time after my father died. She was depressed and drank a lot. One time she took all of us kids into the kitchen and fed us a lunch of Campbell's Tomato Soup. She turned on the gas in the oven and said she would meet us again in a better place. I woke up being carried away by a fireman."

"Wow! What happened then?"

"She was taken away for an evaluation and we stayed with her parents while she was in the hospital. When she got out, we went back to live with her but she wasn't well – never was. After she died, we went back to live with her parents again. They didn't want us there and always used to criticize me and belittle me. I thought it was because I didn't do anything to stop mom from killing herself. I ran away and went to live with an aunt and uncle but they were both alcoholics and didn't seem to want me around either. I lived with my sister after that until I graduated from high school. Then I joined the Army."

Dr. Oldman was quiet for several moments, reflecting on what he had just heard. "You have an amazing amount of resilience, given all that has happened to you from a young age. Most people telling a story like that would be completely bonkers. Yet you are very coherent, are interested in a lot of things, and still want to go on and make something of your life.

"Well, I'm not all that well put-together! I'm a nervous wreck, I have bad dreams, my head doesn't work right, I've got a lot of guilt and depression, I pull my hair out and I have a bunch of compulsive habits. And I don't know what I want to do or what I can do."

"Oh, yeah, I recognize all of that," nodded Dr. Oldman. "We can work on that here and maybe get it under control. What I meant was that you have had a lot of very severe traumas that could be overwhelming to most people if they had experienced them. In other words, you're in good shape given everything you have been through."

"Thanks a lot!" said Tom, laughing. "I'm in good shape for the shape I'm in!"

Dr. Oldman laughed too. "What I would recommend, if it is agreeable to you, is that you see me once a week for psychotherapy and maybe attend one of my PTSD groups."

"Aren't the guys in those PTSD groups all combat veterans? I haven't been in combat."

"Yeah, but many of the traumas they experienced were not during combat itself and most of the didactic information applies to any kind of trauma, not just combat. The psychological processes in different kinds of traumatic stress are very similar. The men are generally a good bunch of guys who I think would be accepting of your attendance."

"OK. Sounds good to me," agreed Tom.

"I also want to do some further testing to see how your head injury has affected your mental abilities. I'll see if I can get you in in the next few days."

Two days later Dr. Oldman administered a series of psychological tests and had Tom wait while he scored and interpreted them. Then he explained the results.

"Tom, the results look like those we usually obtain in cases of brain injury. Your capacity for organizing and putting together different pieces of information in order to solve a problem have fallen off some. You didn't do well on tasks requiring rapid perception and integration of what it is that a situation requires and then taking action to achieve a goal. You can still do it, but it takes a lot of effort to stick with the process. You can't easily switch from one task to another and you may have some difficulty learning new information. You may have a problem with keeping your attention on the task at hand and telling the difference between essential and nonessential details. Does that sound about right as you see it?"

"Wow! Those are areas in which I have problems, that's for sure," said Tom. "I'm easily distracted and can't remember shit. I often have to sit and look at a problem for a long time before I can start working on it. My math skills suck."

"You do best on tasks requiring the use of verbal information that you learned in the past, using common-sense judgment and applying it in social situations," Oldman continued. "It looks like your overall intellectual functioning has been reduced quite a bit from what it was prior to the injury. I estimate your pre-injury level of functioning to have been in the superior range, but now it is just in the above average range. And even though most of your areas of functioning are still above average, that is not like being a person who has never had a brain injury."

"What does all this mean for me going to school or getting a job?"

"It depends on a lot of things: what courses you have to take, how the material is taught, how much leeway you have as to time to complete course work, how much frustration you are able to tolerate. Now, as I said, you still have many abilities that are well above average." Encouragingly, he added, "If you can find a course of study that favors those, you may do very well."

"Yeah, hmm..."

"I would stay away from the hard sciences and complicated technical areas. But fields where you are able to work with people and use your common-sense judgment would probably be a good choice. We can explore this as we go along. In addition, you can also work with the vocational counselor to narrow down your options. Furthermore, you should also seek to have your service connection upgraded," Dr Oldman continued.

"I was reduced to ten percent when I didn't show up for an interview a few years ago. I thought I would be able to get a job and not need it," Tom added.

"The ten percent you currently have is not appropriate for the degree of impairment you suffered from your injury in the service. See Sam, the social worker, about getting all the papers you need to fill out and expect it to take a while."

About a week later, after Tom had completed all his assessments, he appeared in front of the treatment team to formalize his treatment plan. Dr. Oldman was in charge of that part of the meeting and integrated suggestions from other team members into the plan. Tom was to get an incentive therapy job in the library. He would follow the recommendations of the dietitian regarding his diabetes and general nutrition. He must participate in recreational and physical therapy activities for general conditioning. He had to work with the vocational counselor to develop a plan for training or finding employment. He was required to take his medications as prescribed plus he would see Dr. Oldman at least weekly. If there were any indications that emerged during his stay that he had a substance abuse problem, he was obliged to work with the counselor to develop a plan to maintain abstinence.

On the first day of his IT assignment, Tom met the chief librarian, Mrs. Conklin, a tenderhearted divorcee of 60 years who, after some disheartening experiences, put on a gruff, tough-minded, cynical front in order to protect herself from manipulation by crafty patients. At first, this presentation put Tom off but he soon began to see through it as he worked with her in the library. In turn, she became more impressed with Tom as she observed the quality of his work and the respect he showed other veterans while remaining aloof from the scheming ones.

She inquired about his background and Tom provided the broad outlines leaving out the gory details. They discussed various problems in the library and the facility in general convincing Mrs. Conklin that she liked the way Tom thought about things. She also admired the way he could handle difficult, demanding veterans without losing his cool. With some of her other employees, reactions to loud verbally abusive patients could escalate into major conflicts requiring assistance from the facility police department.

Tom took a shine to the physical therapist who treated him as if he were a genuine person and to Bennie Foster, a blue-eyed, bald-headed patient assistant with a winning smile who was quite large in circumference, but a barrel of laughs as he told stories from his efforts as a vacuum cleaner salesman and later as a casino employee. His humor was self-deprecating, centering on how he bamboozled unsuspecting customers, but ended up losing everything to his shady employers. He had joined the Coast Guard thinking he would avoid getting sent to Vietnam. However he ended up serving on a Point-class cutter in Coast Guard Squadron One, providing gunfire support to friendlies and disrupting enemy supply lines around the Mekong Delta.

His cutter took a lot of enemy fire from the shoreline. What's more, there was an incident of friendly fire when the Air Force mistook his ship for an enemy target. Bennie had been awarded a Bronze Star and a Presidential Unit Citation, but never talked about the circumstances leading to the awards. He was much more comfortable cracking jokes than talking about his war experiences.

Tom decided to take up leather craft as a hobby. An occupational therapist was in charge of all the different leisure time pursuits while the actual instruction was provided by another patient who obtained the position as an Incentive Therapy job because of his obvious talent in that area. The only problem with Terry Wells, the instructor, was that he would sometimes explode in anger if an interlocutor did not treat him with respect. After one such episode in which Terry and a truly obnoxious patient were close to coming to blows, Terry disappeared for about an hour. Tom later learned that Dr. Oldman had instructed Terry to come to his office when he was about to vent his rage and they would review the exciting circumstances, what he wanted to accomplish by expressing his anger, how this episode was like previous episodes, what his options were in the situation and what consequences he could expect if he acted on his first impulse. Then he would coach Terry on what factors to take into consideration in making a judgment as to whether or not the satisfaction he might experience by expressing his anger was worth having done so.

When Terry returned to the leather shop, he was much subdued, apologized for losing his cool, and told Tom how he had had difficulties controlling his anger all his life. He said he must have been in 2000 physical altercations over the years, typically winning the fight but getting fired from his job or just walking off and getting drunk. And he lost many girlfriends because of his temper outbursts. Yet with Tom, Terry was always friendly and helpful in sharing his knowledge and skills as a leather worker. Terry thought his coaching sessions with Dr. Oldman during the heat of the moment were helping him think about what he was doing rather than rashly lashing out at the source of his anger. Terry reminded Tom of his motorcycle-riding friend, Hal, who used to fly into a fit of rage when frustrated by some simple thing, like a mechanical problem with his Zundapp, yet be as calm and friendly as if nothing had happened five minutes later.

Having been forewarned about Dr. Wolfgang Gunnar, the chief psychiatrist, Tom was cautious on their first encounter. Dr. Gunnar reviewed Tom's medications and voiced his skepticism about his patient's seizure diagnosis, agreeing with Dr. Green that it was not a genuine seizure disorder. He even implied that Tom was feigning the condition in order to get special treatment.

Tom asked, "What special treatment is that?"

Dr. Gunnar reacted with a tirade of invective. "You young punk! Who the hell do you think you are, questioning my judgment? I aught to knock you head off, you flaky faggot!" as he made a foreshortened swing at the hapless patient in front of him.

Caught by surprise at the psychiatrist's vehemence, Tom stuttered back, "I....I didn't mean to offend you. I don't think I have gotten any special treatment since I had this head injury."

"Crap! You're just trying to angle some kind of service connected compensation for a made-up condition, like the rest of these bums that come in here. You're all alike, trying to live off the taxpayer. If I had my way, they'd throw all of you bastards out on the street. Go work for a living! See how you like getting up every day and putting in eight hours. You're just a drain on society!"

Tom sat silent, trying to think of some way to excuse himself. Dr. Gunnar calmed down, realizing that his yelling had carried out into the waiting room, and potentially earned a reprimand for his hostile display by higher-ups in the medical establishment of the facility. He shifted to another focus of his interest and continued, "You see that psychologist Dr. Oldman on Section 3?"

Tom hesitated, not knowing where this was going. "Yeah."

"What do you think of him? What's he doing with you?"

"I don't know. I just started seeing him. He gave me some tests to identify my loss of function due to my head injury."

"And I suppose he is trying to get you to file for compensation too? And trying to fill your head with all that Jungian bull shit?"

Trying to claim ignorance, Tom said, "I don't know about any of that. I'm just trying to be compliant with what I am asked to do."

"Ha!" said Gunnar, derisively. "How about you report to me what he says to you? I could probably prescribe some pills that would make you feel good if you could keep me informed."

"I don't think I could do that," said Tom. "I would never make a very good spy."

"Then fuck you, you little bitch. Get the hell out of this office and don't come back."

Tom quickly took his leave, glad that he was out of the presence of such a contemptible person. Back in his room, he related the encounter to his roommate, Tony Napoliello.

"Yeah, that sounds like him," said Tony. "He is a pure slime ball. He was trying to intimidate you and recruit you to be one of his tattletales. He tries to gather information about other staff members he doesn't like in order to use against them when it suits his purposes. You can't trust him about anything. Do you know Herb Sims? he's one of them."

"No I don't know him."

"And Georgie Cramden? He's another Gunnar informant. He also has a child-porn racket he is running, pulls stuff off the internet and sells it to whoever he can. Another slime ball! Don't talk to either of these two jerks. They'll take it directly to Gunnar."

The next time Tom saw Dr. Oldman, he mentioned that Dr. Gunnar seemed to have an interest in him.

"Yeah, I imagine he does," said Oldman, smiling. "We're not close friends."

Tom was about to discuss some disturbing feelings he had since the event with the truck driver when, all of a sudden, he fluttered his eyelids and began to slide off the overstuffed chair in which he was sitting. Dr. Oldman didn't understand what was happening at first and yelled "Tom, are you OK?".

When Tom started to straighten out in a rigid position and quiver and twist his arms, Dr. Oldman knew it was a seizure. He knelt down next to the unconscious Tom, trying to figure out how to put something between his teeth so he wouldn't bite his tongue. About that time, his superior, who had the office next door, burst in, quickly assessed the situation and sent out a "Man Down" alert to the Infirmary staff. They arrived within 5 minutes and carted Tom off on a stretcher to the infirmary. Dr. Oldman, sweating and a bit shook by the event, commented to his boss, "Well I guess that settles the question of whether or not Tom has a seizure disorder!".

But, of course, it did not. Whitey Green and Wolfgang Gunnar continued to assert Tom had "pseudo-seizures" in spite of the fact that two PhD psychologists personally observed a grand mal seizure as it occurred. The two MDs did not relent and re-institute Tom's Dilantin until Dr. Oldman threatened to make a formal complaint to the Regional Office. That threat meant that Dr. Oldman was the target for more retaliatory actions whenever they could be enacted without connecting them to the Doctors Gunnar and Green.

Tom continued to see Dr. Oldman on a weekly basis. The doctor allowed Tom to direct the course of the interview. If Tom didn't know what he wanted, the goal became to establish what was important to Tom. Dr. Oldman then would ask ambiguous questions to stimulate Tom's thinking, would ask him how he felt when various events occurred and would reflect back on what Tom had just said, but in a slightly different way that made him ponder his own mental processes.

The first problem they worked on was Tom's guilt at not having done anything to save his mother when she gassed herself in the garage. He had run off and hid in the pool shed while his sister struggled to get her mother out of the car.

Dr. Oldman asked Tom what he thought he could have done. After thinking for a few moments, Tom could not come up with anything specific, but was sure there was something he should have done.

"Could you have lifted her out of the car?"

"No, she was too heavy and wedged in behind the steering wheel. My sister couldn't budge her either which is why she just put the car in reverse and let it crash through the door," admitted Tom.

Dr. Oldman confronted Tom with another possibility, "Could you have performed CPR on her?"

"No, I didn't know about CPR then. I was only eight years old."

Dr. Oldman listed all the possibilities, "Oh, you were only eight years old and couldn't get her out of the car and didn't know about CPR?"

"Yeah," and then it dawned on Tom. "Oh, I guess I'm judging myself from the perspective of an adult and not that of a frightened child. "

"I guess so, stated Dr. Oldman. "Doesn't seem really fair, does it?"

Sometimes Dr. Oldman would help Tom interpret the meaning of a dream, such as the one he had that involved being confronted with a huge raving madman who was trying to harm him when he opened the door to his room.

"Am I picking up on something about my roommate, Tony? He has told me about some of the things they did to prisoners in Vietnam."

"Does he have any characteristics like the creature you confronted in your dream?" asked Dr. Oldman.

"No. He is actually pretty mellow, doesn't try to be domineering, and has never done anything to scare me."

"Then it probably isn't about him. Tell me more about this creature," Dr. Oldman queried.

"Well, he was really mad, like he was ready to kill somebody. I was scared and tried to close the door, but he was too strong! I couldn't hold the door any longer. That's when I woke up."

"Let's assume for the time being, the dream is about you or some problem you are dealing with at the present time. Is there anything that is making you so angry you would want to destroy the object of your anger?" Dr. Oldman questioned.

"Well, there is something. Remember I told you about that thing that happened to me when I was hitchhiking?" asserted Tom strongly.

"Yes. I remember – getting sexually assaulted and buried alive."

"Yeah, well I was really frightened! It still scares me when I think about it which is why I push it out of mind as soon as I can – think of something else, look for some kind of distraction. But recently, as I get further away from the incident, there is another feeling that keeps cropping up."

"What's that, Tom?"

"I'd really like to kill that son-of-a-bitch! I have fantasies of beating him to a pulp with a baseball bat and cutting him up with his own fucking knife! Then I think what would happen if I did it, and I can imagine myself sitting in jail for the rest of my life. Then I shut it all down by pushing it out of mind."

"So what does the madman in your dream represent?" posed Dr. Oldman.

"I guess it's my anger. And I'm afraid I won't be able to control it."

"Sounds like a good fit to me. A dream is usually just a metaphorical way of thinking about a problem."

∞

Tony introduced Tom to another one of his friends, Dave Brody. Dave was a tall, lanky individual who didn't talk much, a LRRP in Vietnam, (Long Range Reconnaissance Patrol, pronounced "Lerp"). LRRPs would sometimes be dropped in each of the corners of a one-mile square section and move in toward the center of the square, trying to rouse the enemy and kill them. Or they might go out as a small unit, engage the enemy and then retreat, setting up an ambush for the pursuing NVA (North Vietnamese Army) soldiers. Dave was such a cool customer that he once took a lunch break in the middle of a firefight because it went on for so long. After the war, he used his experience with munitions to get a job blowing up old smokestacks. "I always liked to blow up stuff," he said. Unfortunately, his erratic behavior lost him good jobs. Finally, he decided it would be best if his wife and daughter didn't have to put up with him, so one day he didn't return home.

Tony told Tom that Dave had been slated to go to a full-time PTSD program but freaked out on the bus going to the hospital and got in a fight with the driver. After being expelled from the bus, Dave called Dr. Oldman saying he was of the mind to blow up the nearest small town. "It'll make Rambo looked like a kindergartner," he claimed in his frenzied state of mind. Dr. Oldman talked him down and managed to get a veteran's representative to pick him up and return him to Vetlandia.

"Wow! Sounds like he really freaked out," said Tom, imagining himself becoming similarly disturbed. He knew that his own feeling of having been "cursed," possibly because of something his father had done in Southeast Asia, might sound equally bizarre and didn't want Dr. Oldman to think he was psychotic. He was not yet confident enough to explore the superstitious belief with Dr. Oldman.

CHAPTER 5
Implacable Memories

"You a vet? Want to come in out of the cold?"

Jan Burke walked along the ends of the culvert sections, all dispersed in neat rows on the property, yelling out to the shadowy figures inhabiting them. She was making her usual Monday morning rounds of the homeless camps around town, checking on her flock of potential veterans for those who might be appropriate for admission to Vetlandia. First on her list was the huge precast concrete box culverts used for things like storm drains, utility tunnels, and water diversion channels under roads and railways. The kindhearted manufacturer had allowed homeless veterans to camp out overnight in these ten-foot diameter sections as long as they hauled their trash away, didn't defecate on the property, and were gone by eight o'clock in the morning.

Arriving before the daily eviction deadline, Jan was loaded down with her briefcase of VA documents, her purse containing a cellphone, a vial of pepper spray, and an extendable baton in the event she encountered some crazy person looking to cause her trouble.

Most of the culvert denizens just ignored her or made some sarcastic comment, but when she came to the next to last culvert, the occupant, dressed in insulated canvas pants and a heavy flannel shirt was stuffing his belongings into a backpack. He grunted a reply, "Think they'll let me back in, ma'am?"

"You've been there before, have ya?" Jan countered with a question of her own.

"Yeah. About three years ago. Didn't leave under the best of circumstances, I'm afraid."

"What happened?" Jan inquired.

"I got mad and cussed out a nurse and then went out and got drunk. So they threw me out. I've got an anger problem, I guess. Had it for years. It comes on me so fast, I can't control it."

Jan had been around long enough to know the signs. She asked, "You a Vietnam vet?"

"Yeah. I was over there for 26 months. Seven years in the army. Haven't been quite right ever since."

"Yeah, I know it has been difficult for a lot of the guys to get back to a normal life after being over there. Think you can stay sober long enough to give it another try?"

"It's either that or I off myself and get it over with. I can't stand this shit much longer. I'll bet they'll just tell me to get lost. I've managed to alienate everyone that's tried to help me on Section Five."

"Feeling pretty discouraged, huh?" She paused, not expecting a response, and tried to make eye contact, which he avoided.

"Maybe we can get you in on another section. What's your name? You got a DD214?"

"Daniel Hanson." He began searching in his backpack for his military records, finding them in a waterproof pouch. He pulled out his DD214 and handed it to her.

Jan jotted down some numbers and notes. Glancing at his MOS, she asked, "You were a corpsman?"

"Yeah. Started out as a corpsman, spent some time working in an army hospital in Japan. I joined a Ranger group for a while, then spent some time in a hole in the ground. Ended up in Graves Registration."

"A hole in the ground?"

"It was a Technical Operations Center sixteen feet underground. I operated a field radio monitoring requests for extractions and artillery support and made up casualty lists."

"Hmm," Jan had never heard of such duty and tried to imagine what it must have been like. "What have you been doing since you were last at Vetlandia?"

"Hanging out in the mountains in Wyoming, doing some ranch work. Not much else."

"You know that maintaining your sobriety is a big deal at this facility. That's what your readmission is going to depend on. How often and how much have you had to drink over the last six months?"

"I drank a lot for about seven years because of my chest pains. I thought I was having heart attacks. But I spent $1600 of my own money having it checked out and was told I was 'One stressed-out son-of-a-bitch.' I have been sober for 10 of the last 17 years and I've only had about one beer a month for the last year."

"Hmm. Well, let me go run this by the admissions people and see what they think. You gonna be here tomorrow if I stop by?"

"Got no place else to go," said Daniel. "I'm at the end of my rope."

When Jan got back to her office, she pulled up the VA records for Daniel Hanson on her computer and learned that he had been treated at five other facilities since 1976, had several serious medical problems, including thrombophlebitis, as well as two suicide attempts, and two arrests for assault. She surmised that he probably was downplaying the role alcohol played in his difficulties.

When she discussed Daniel with the admitting physician, she made the case that Daniel Hanson needed both medical and psychological treatment, but acknowledged there were risks involved, that he might act out, relapse, or commit suicide. She opined that he appeared to be suffering a great deal. It made her think he should be given another chance for humanitarian reasons.

For good measure to sway the doctor's decision, she commented, "You know sure as blazes that there will be hell to pay if he kills himself in the community after being denied admission to the VA. The newspapers and TV will have a field day with that kind of story."

The physician trusted Jan's judgment more than his own in such matters and went along with her recommendation that Daniel be admitted. The next day, Jan notified Daniel to make his way to the facility admissions office for processing, that he was expected and would be housed in Section 2.

After getting settled into his room and chatting with his new roommates, Daniel began his round of routine intake interviews. He admitted to members of the treatment team that he used alcohol excessively for a time to ease the pains in his chest that started when he was in Vietnam. Although he minimized his more recent problems with alcohol, records told a different story. On an earlier admission, he stated to the section social worker that alcohol was his principal problem and admitted to experiencing DTs and blackouts. He had agreed to a treatment program to address these issues but took an irregular discharge before making much progress.

Daniel Hanson acknowledged many psychological and psychophysiological symptoms common to patients with Post Traumatic Stress Disorder — PTSD. He tried to kill himself twice by combining drugs with alcohol. Besides the stress-induced chest pains, he complained of chronic anxiety with occasional panic attacks, nightmares, flashbacks, disturbed sleep, and thoughts and memories that came to him unbidden. He had explosive and easily triggered anger, amnesias, paranoia, a morbid preoccupation with death, and what sounded like dissociative states. Hopeless, sad, and uncertain of himself, he couldn't get close to anyone, tended to be a loner, and had periods of overwhelming guilt and shame.

His high anxiety, betrayed by the rapid bouncing of his right foot, was noted by several people who interviewed him. Others noted his exaggerated response when startled and extreme expressions of anger toward family and authority figures. He cried and blew his nose throughout several interviews and had occasional lapses of attention where he seemed to be "someplace else."

Psychological testing revealed severe anxiety and agitation, fear of making emotional attachments, depression, and preoccupation with morbid material. He was overly suspicious and hypersensitive to criticism and was inclined to criticize and blame others.

Daniel began treatment for his numerous physical problems and started psychotherapy with Dr. Magnuson who asked about his childhood relationship with his father.

"The first image that comes to mind is when I pulled some neighbor kid out of the lake. The poor kid was damn near drowning. He was exhausted and scared and thrashing about. When I told my dad about it, I was expecting him to be proud. I thought I'd get some small token of commendation from him. But, no, instead he tore into me like I had committed some cardinal sin. Thwack, thwack, thwack! Even now, I can hear and feel his doubled-over razor strop as it tore into my back."

Dr. Magnuson could see Daniel flinch several times in a row as he related the incident. "Goodness," he said, "did he explain why he was doing it?"

"Explain, oh yeah, he explained alright. He said, 'You dumb shithead! You could have drowned and left me short-handed and then I'd have to pay for your fucking funeral. You scared the bejesus out of your mother, and she'll blame me for that too. I'll teach you a lesson you won't soon forget, you little bastard!'"

Daniel's alcoholic father was a combat veteran of the Pacific Campaign during WWII and, as he told it, was proud of having faced adversity without faltering. Daniel wondered, at the time, if he could ever live up to his father's expectations. Try as he might to shoulder his share of work on the farm and at his mom's store, it was never good enough. He might as well be dead.

His four brothers and three sisters didn't fare much better, but Daniel seemed to be the one singled out for derision and humiliation. As he matured, he developed a good deal of anger toward his father, not only for the way he was treated, but also for his father's physical abuse of his mother and his sexual assault of his sisters. The anger seemed to act as a kind of insulation from even more devastating feelings. Anger became his friend and protector. His mother did not try to resist or intervene, just turned a blind eye to her husband's madness and focused her attention on succeeding in her business ventures.

Daniel was an average student in school but he excelled in classes that interested him. He surpassed his peers in sports, as a tenor soloist in a choir, and drama club. After graduation, he volunteered for military service at his father's urging to keep up the reputation of the family as being staunchly patriotic. He chose the Army because he had three brothers in different branches of the service at the time and thought it would be neat if they represented the whole spectrum of choices.

After basic training, his first assignment was as a medical corpsman at a military hospital in Japan for which he received his father's scorn because he was safely tucked away from the "real action." The hospital averaged 1000 patients, but about five or six patients died during every shift. Daniel felt quite upset by his impotence in stemming the tide of loss of life. Parents were flown in to see their sons, but about 90% of the time their sons were dead when their relatives arrived. The place was replete with drug dealing, physician and nurse incompetence, and patient neglect.

"Is that why you left that assignment?" asked Dr. Magnuson.

"No. That was really disgusting, but the reason I left was that I felt I was avoiding the real fighting that my patients went through. I thought I was a coward just like my dad said. So I volunteered for hazardous duty to prove to myself that I could do it." He laughed at his naivete. "I was an idiot!"

Daniel thought he might be more effective and earn his father's respect by volunteering for a combat role. Consequently, he was transferred to Okinawa for three weeks of live-fire training and then to Vietnam where he was assigned for ten and a half months to an ARVN Ranger Group. He was wounded by shrapnel in his right thigh and knee and was in a coma for three days from a head injury.

After five months in a field hospital, he was transferred to a Technical Operations Center near Pleiku, located sixteen feet below ground. His job was to operate a field radio receiving requests for either artillery support or evacuations of the troops involved and to prepare casualty lists.

"I can still hear the screaming and pleading for help on the radio from some group that needed support. If their location was within half a kilometer from a red pin on a fire control grid map, they were shit out of luck. Their request was likely to be denied by the commanding officer. The excuse he gave me for the denials — it may have all been bullshit — was that it was needed to reduce destruction of friendly villages as a part of the

Pacification Program. After one incident where many people were killed, I was so outraged that I blew up at the colonel in charge. After that, they removed me from the facility."

About a week later, Daniel Hanson was approached by his commander and First Sergeant and taken to II Corp where he met with two individuals dressed in sports jackets, who he later learned were counter-intelligence operatives (CID). They recruited him into the drug interdiction program to work undercover at a Graves Registration collection point. His cover job was to put MIAs into a new computer system and to do "recovery." The procedure involved joining an ARVN (Army of the Republic of Vietnam) unit, going to the site of a battle, called a "forensic area," and picking up bones and other objects for identification purposes. There were twenty collection points and two morgues in Vietnam, one in Da Nang and the other near Saigon at Tan Son Nhut Airbase. Daniel started at a collection point near Pleiku and later was transferred to the mortuary in Saigon.

A collection-point team was the first to receive the dead from the battlefield. Besides the bodies, they were supposed to gather all information that might be used to identify the dead, such as dog tags, names that were supposed to be on boots and clothing, but often weren't, unit identification, fingerprints, footprints, teeth, body marks, scars, tattoos, anything that might help. The bodies or body parts and identifying information were placed in green rubber body bags, loaded into two-and-a-half-ton trucks, and brought to the collection point.

The deceased men arrived just as they were found on the field. Everything in the soldier's pockets, usually only a wallet and some military scrip (the "money" troops were paid with in Vietnam), were inventoried. All clothing was removed using big scissors to cut bootlaces and uniforms. Anything that might prove to be disturbing to the family was removed. Then it was all burned.

The bodies were placed on concrete slabs and washed and cleaned, as much as it was possible, using soapy water and huge sponges. Afterward, the nude bodies were carefully zipped into clean body bags along with the men's belongings for the trip to the Saigon Army mortuary. There they were embalmed, dressed in new uniforms, and sealed in airtight aluminum caskets for the flight home to their families.

"We were taught to treat the bodies with respect, as if they were members of our own families," said Daniel. "But dealing with those dead and mutilated bodies did a number on your mind. You'd think about these guys having mothers and girlfriends and how they prayed for their safe return just like your own mother or girlfriend did. Why were they the chosen ones rather than you? What justice was there in that? A lot of guys couldn't handle it and asked to be reassigned."

As the war progressed and the number of casualties increased, the collection points and the morgues got overwhelmed and the refrigeration units could not keep up with the demand, so bodies that were recovered from wet areas and swamps deteriorated rapidly in the tropical heat.

But other things concerned CID and that became Daniel's undercover job. He observed bodies being cut open and drugs being sewn into them before being resealed and marked so that affiliates back in the United States could identify the cadavers containing drugs and remove the contents. Heroin was being purchased for $1700 per kilo in the war zone and resold in the US for $20,000. This was when one of his superiors at the morgue in Saigon held a pistol to his head to ensure that he realized this was a big operation with operatives all over the military and civilian life who would know if he ever spoke of these matters.

"He said that if I ever mentioned anything to anyone, I would be hunted down and killed as would all members of my family. Every time I think of what these assholes did, the anger just bubbles up in me and I want to strike out."

"Did you ever mention it to anyone?" asked Dr. Magnuson.

Daniel snorted. "Yeah, I did. That's how they recruited me into the drug interdiction program in the first place. Then my ass was really in a jam! They wanted me to play along with these bastards and report to them which body bags or coffins contained drugs so they could track down who else was involved. It was nerve-wracking, believe me. I couldn't betray my disgust with the fuckers or they'd kill me for sure and I had to transmit my information without arousing suspicion. I ended up being a nervous wreck! I'm still a nervous wreck!"

"I can see why," said Dr. Magnuson.

Daniel departed Vietnam when his immediate supervisor, an Air Force Captain, came up to him and told him his cover had been blown and that he was to go with two men he had along with him. They quickly filled out the necessary administrative papers and he was taken by Jeep to the airport where he boarded a plane for home. Everyone on the plane was jubilant but he was feeling like a mouse in a cage, waiting for execution. He was the only Army person on the plane, all the others being Air Force, so he figured he had been pegged by one of the sinister operators in Graves Registration and they had sent someone to "take care of the rat."

Daniel Hanson spent 26 months in-country before returning to the states and was discharged three years later. One of his brothers picked him up at the airport and drove him to the family home 12 miles outside of the nearest small town. He looked battle-worn and weighed only 117 pounds. His father thought he was using drugs and ordered him out of the house but later relented. They often ended up arguing about something. His brothers and sisters thought he was "all fucked up" and kept asking him what was wrong. They could not understand why he couldn't stay in one place, why he changed jobs four or five times every year, and why he wouldn't greet or talk with people at family gatherings.

"These people were supposed to be my kin, but I didn't feel like I knew them at all. I felt like there was a kind of invisible wall between us."

Although he was married for seven years and fathered three children, he only spent three years living with his family. He could not stand the doctrine propagated by his wife's church and the demand that they attend services five times every week. He felt uncertain of his feelings toward her and lost all of his sexual desire.

"I'd take off to the woods for months at a time, and she would never know when or if I would return. I guess I didn't make life easy for her."

∞

Two days after Daniel met with Dr. Magnuson for the second time, he missed the regular bed check. Cindy Cox, the section assistant, formed a small search patrol and found him wandering among the bushes on the golf course.

"What are you doing out here?" she asked.

"I don't know," replied Daniel. "What time is it? What day is it?"

"It's eleven o'clock. Tuesday. What do you last remember?"

"Last I can remember, it was just after dinner. I was having chest pains. I pissed on myself, so I got into the shower, but then I fell down and couldn't get up. I think I blacked out after that."

The next day Daniel mentioned the episode to Dr. Short who asked if he had any periods where he seemed to lose track of time before.

"Yeah, back in Vietnam. I used to space out a lot after I got hit and was in the hospital. I often didn't know what day it was. Got chewed out for it a few times."

Dr. Short suspected a possible seizure disorder and referred Daniel for a sleep-deprived EEG to be carried out at the VA hospital in Portland.

Daniel showed up at the infirmary, apparently believing he was at an evac hospital and looking for a friend. A breathalyzer produced a BA of 0.227, the cutoff for "official" inebriation being 0.08, so he was given a dose of inapsine and placed in seclusion. The addictions therapist, uncharacteristically, rejected the usual punitive discharge and recommended Daniel be retained and treated for both alcohol abuse and PTSD. The treatment team expressed its displeasure by placing him on two weeks restriction, requiring his medication be taken on the mortifying pill line which was usually populated by psychotics and the severely impaired, and moving him to a different room, all of which placed Daniel in ill humor.

He missed two bed checks and, intoxicated, turned on all the lights when he entered his new room and threatened his roommates. In the morning, a nurse removed him from the facility bus going to Portland but he refused to accompany her to the infirmary, knowing he would be in for disciplinary action of some sort. A short time later he showed up at the sick call window yelling that he had been "dragged around" by the nurse and demanding that he be allowed to go to Portland for his EEG. He disappeared before the police arrived, but they caught up with him after he was talked down from his excited state of mind by Cindy. Fearing that Daniel might attempt suicide and might have a seizure disorder, the section social worker helped him to fill out applications for PTSD programs but the effort was abandoned when he decided that Daniel was too fragile to be able to even complete a program.

About a month later, Daniel experienced an "anniversary reaction" related to when a friend standing right next to him was shot in Vietnam.

"Why didn't I warn him about the dangers of standing out in the open? He was brand new and didn't know anything."

He feared going crazy because he couldn't block out the feelings of loss, sadness, outrage, fear, and shame associated with this event and with other things he did and didn't do while in Vietnam. He got drunk, walked into the infirmary hollering in Vietnamese, made threatening movements toward staff, and used the finger-in-the-ear, thumb-as-revolver-hammer gesture to imply suicidal intent. The physician on duty, angered by the hostile display, deemed Daniel to be a danger to himself and the staff. Daniel, now even more angry and upset than before by the hostile and controlling reaction he precipitated, asked for a discharge and it was granted "forthwith on an irregular basis."

After three months back in the culverts, those who had worked with Daniel most closely and felt sympathetically inclined toward him despite his difficult behavior relented and gave him another chance. Shortly after doing so, he wandered into the infirmary in a confused state with dilated pupils and unsteady on his feet. His blood-alcohol level or BA was 0.000, that is, he was stone-cold sober. He remained in the infirmary overnight, responding with verbal hostility when he believed one of the male nurses was harboring ill will toward him. The next day, after becoming angry and argumentative in a medical education class, he was brought to the treatment room in a wheelchair by a fireman. He had become lightheaded and fell on the lawn after smelling a sweet odor and seeing a face. He had taken two nitroglycerin tablets for chest pains at the time.

Two weeks later the facility police found Daniel wandering about the golf course. He knew who he was but could not give the current year. At the infirmary, his BA was again 0.000 and Dr. Short thought Daniel had a complex partial seizure. Daniel did not correct Dr. Short's misinterpretation of his smelling experience but when he saw Dr. Magnuson he related that he knew the sweet odor he had smelled was one of fresh blood. He connected it to an incident when he was in the underground Tech Op Center and 59 people were killed after their request for evacuation was denied. That was the incident that had so enraged Daniel that he blew his stack at his CO, the person who denied the request and subsequently cast Daniel into the arms of CID.

An infirmary nurse said she had been talking with Daniel when, all of a sudden, "He looked past me, put out his hand and said 'Wait!' At the same time he pushed his bedside table out of the way and moved to the middle of the next bed toward the door. At that point he limped back to bed and stared past me and then at the floor. He had broken into a sweat and his eyes were dilated. I called his name, but it was five or ten minutes before he could answer. He didn't remember heading toward the door and said he heard and smelled something, but did not elaborate any further."

These occasions of strange behavior that could definitely not be attributed to alcohol use seemed to precipitate more positive and supportive sentiments toward Daniel in team members and fostered a greater willingness to work with him. They focused their treatment efforts on Daniel's isolation and sensitivity to rejection, his sleep disturbance and nightmares, his intrusive morbid thoughts of death, and his anger and anxiety levels. They tried to change these states by giving feedback to him about their sentiments toward him, giving him psychoactive medications, interpreting his dreams, and providing psychotherapy aimed at increasing his level of understanding of the role of his thought processes in recovery. They tried to raise his awareness of the dynamics of anger, anxiety, and PTSD. Optimistically, they anticipated significant progress could be made in one year and expected him to discharge within two years.

Daniel participated in the team meetings and was open about his experience.

"You have no idea how much the team meeting inspired me," Daniel remarked after one such meeting.

Dr. Magnuson noted during this session that Daniel did not bounce his leg and was, for the first time since admission, able to emit a spontaneous burst of genuine laughter. The more positive sentiments toward Daniel were echoed in progress notes by both doctor and nurse the next day. Other staff noted his reduced level of anger and reassured him when he expressed fears that staff were mad at him and might discharge him. An unexplained change in what he expected — a medication change or an error in his food tray — could still elicit angry comments toward staff but this was not allowed to slide. After one of these episodes, he apologized and revealed to the section nurse that he was trying to clean up his act and was concerned about how he was being perceived by others.

Daniel saw two different psychiatrists and related some of his wartime experiences to them but subsequently thought he had revealed too much and began to believe that staff was thinking "hate thoughts" toward him. He became surly with them, even though they tried to respond to his inquires and calm his fears. To Dr. Magnuson, he expressed his ambivalence about beginning to like, trust and care about the staff while relinquishing the security provided by his anger. He made a successful attempt to explain to the nurse the military experiences that conditioned his cantankerous coping methods, in fact eliciting a good deal of empathy for his plight.

∞

At one point, Daniel and Tom shared a room in the infirmary at the same time. Daniel was there to evaluate a possible thrombosis in his leg, and Tom was there to have his Dilantin adjusted after he had another seizure. Both were critical of the medical care they were receiving, although Daniel was more likely to voice his complaints directly to the staff while Tom was more discreet. Both were temperamentally alike in being thoughtful, reflective characters, so they liked each other almost immediately and talked frequently.

Both were outraged and furious with staff when a young veteran committed suicide right in the infirmary while they were there. The victim, a young man with a penchant to care about others, was separated from his wife and daughter, whom he loved deeply. He was an indecisive person, fearing to assume responsibility. His low self-esteem and cynicism undermined his devotion to his family. A closet cross-dresser even though his sexual orientation was heterosexual, he refused to admit that certain of his behaviors were self-defeating and had to be changed. He hanged himself the day after his wife decided to divorce him and restrict his ability to see his daughter.

Tom Ward and Daniel Hanson confronted the staff, demanding to know why he wasn't watched more closely, why materials he used in the suicide were allowed in his room, why he wasn't given anti-anxiety medications, and so on. Other patients rallied behind them. The staff was hurt and angered by the criticism they were receiving from patients and became defensive. Some staff members were also critical but most were silent, knowing that next time it might happen to them. Of course, the on-duty staff were chagrined to have this happen on their watch, and they knew they would be subject to an investigation. Their defensiveness further riled the patients with what was claimed to be their indifference to the value of veterans' lives.

Tom worked through his feelings about the suicide with Dr. Oldman. and Daniel discussed it with Dr. Magnuson. Daniel recalled the "human errors" by staff that had so infuriated him when he worked in the hospital in Japan, including one of his own that he feared might have led to the death of a patient. He had missed an infection that was developing in one of his patients and when he finally discovered it, the patient had to be rushed into surgery where everything went wrong and the patient died. Since that time, he confessed, he had become very intolerant of errors on the part of others as well as himself.

Dr. Magnuson remarked to Daniel that it was best not to make errors, but that only gods were completely error-free. If one did not allow forgiveness, one could never be redeemed. Daniel was not convinced.

"You've never been in war. Horrible things happen, and some things are just not eligible for forgiveness."

By and large, Daniel was sharing his feelings and perceptions with staff during this period and his combativeness with staff decreased. He began warning staff about an upcoming Vietnam anniversary that could result in him exhibiting peculiar behavior or anger. There was one brief dissociative episode when he was found crouching in the corner of his room, did not respond to questions, and reported having a few bad nights, but there were no angry behaviors directed toward staff.

Daniel was found to have a blood clot behind his left knee and was transferred to Portland VAMC for about a week before returning to the infirmary in Vetlandia. He voiced his concern about his blood clots to the section nurse two days later and said he was "stressed to the max." He became loud and demanding with one of the nurses who suggested he talk with Dr. Magnuson. The latter thought that his angry manner was related to anxiety about the possibility of dying just as he was developing some hope. Daniel continued to alternate irritability with cooperation until he was discharged from the infirmary to go back to his section after the Doppler ultrasound showed a complete clearing of the thrombus from his leg.

Dr. Magnuson left no ambiguity when he stated the requirement that Daniel had to change his confrontational behavior toward staff to remain at the facility.

"So you're leaving me no options, but to stuff my anger, is that it?" Daniel complained.

While agreeing with Dr. Magnuson that involvement in anger management and grief and loss groups might be beneficial, given the nature of his triggers, Daniel had doubts that it would work for him.

"I was mad as hell at Dr. Whitey Green the other day and walked away. But then I couldn't sleep that night and obsessed about it for the next two days. How is that any better?"

When Dr. Magnuson tried to coach him to interrupt the obsession and transform the affect, Daniel expressed doubts that he would be able to imagine transforming his anger into anything else.

Switching tactics, the therapist tried to get Daniel to consider the idea that he might be creating and maintaining his anger for some purpose he wasn't aware of.

"My belief system was shredded back in Vietnam and now it's impossible for me to put it together again. My anger just happens without any deliberateness about it. The same thing happens when I go out and drink. I'm not trying to be a jerk for some hidden reason or just for the hell of it. It just happens."

In the next few days, Daniel felt depressed over the news that Portland had nothing to offer for his back and testicular pain. He had an increase in flashbacks, nightmares, sleep problems, night sweats, depression, and intrusive thoughts. He began reflecting on a scene, perhaps a screen memory foreshadowing unconscious attempts to punish himself — or have the staff do it for him. It took place on a gravel road in Vietnam.

"I was bound with bamboo, gagged with something like a small NVA flag and bleeding. I was kicked off the truck, a North Vietnamese Army truck, and somehow I got taken to a hospital."

After this terse account of the experience, without further elaboration, Daniel abruptly left the office.

Thoughts of suicide had become more comforting for Daniel lately. He started dropping hints about what he considered his failure of courage in Vietnam. One day a jackhammer, sounding like a machine gun, occurred outside Dr. Magnuson's office and

Daniel appeared to be thrown into one of his dissociative states, talked of walking into a ravine, sensing that something was not right, but being unable to warn others of the danger. The dire consequences that ensued, the image Daniel relived, was of a parent and her children being blown up by a mortar round. Afterward, he continued to get little sleep and had violent dreams.

Daniel had obtained an IT job in the facility police department, but several "man down" incidents had stressed him out, and he feared making a fatal error. He reported to Dr. Magnuson that there was some kind of disaster in the field in Vietnam that led to shame and guilt. At that time and ever since, he felt he had to redeem himself. He had become quite intolerant of human errors, including his own, and he had decided that dying was the way to go after four unrelated incidents — two more "man down" calls to IT dispatch, looking in a field for a patient who was reported to have hurt himself badly, and being unable to obtain ultrasound treatment through Medicaid.

At about 10:15 that evening, the Acting Officer of the Day was contacted by a Vetlandia police officer who found a suicide note in Daniel's room saying goodbye to his children. A complete search was conducted inside and outside by the housekeeping assistants and the police. Two nurses did a pill count and found 84 Tylenol #3s were missing from those dispensed earlier.

At noon the next day, Daniel reported to Dr. Magnuson that after their last session, he experienced a flashback.

"Everything became Vietnam, complete with the smells. I called my brother and said good-bye. I was going to walk into traffic, but then I thought I needed to go to town to get drunk so I could get the courage to pull it off. I had been building up to it for about a month. When the moment of truth came, I chickened out."

Daniel was subsequently found by the facility police and brought to the infirmary where he admitted to Dr. Poole that he had been drinking and taking multiple medications in an attempted suicide. He had three abraded areas on his arms that appeared to be bite marks.

"Yeah, I got bit by some family members," he volunteered. "What's it to ya? I don't think they were rabid. I probably won't die from them, but if I do, what's the big deal? You incompetent, mother-fucking assholes would be happy to see that, wouldn't ya?"

Daniel was sent to Providence Hospital where his stomach was lavaged. When he got back, he continued his verbal attacks against staff, liberally laced with obscene language, and began to stalk, bait, and provoke those who were nearby. Police and fire departments were called in for a show of force. They physically subdued him and a nurse injected him with inapsine. Then he was placed in seclusion, all the while continuing to upbraid the staff for their incompetence and arbitrariness.

The physician on duty was so outraged by Daniel's behavior that he considered discharging him to the street, calling the sheriff, or having him transported to a locked facility. The treatment team decided to discharge Daniel by the close of business the following day. Dr. Poole cited Daniel's inability to follow Vetlandia rules and contracts and added that, if he acted out in any way, his discharge would be immediate. The era of rapprochement between Daniel and the treatment team had ended.

CHAPTER 6
On Thin Ice

The next day a meeting of the Disturbed and Violent Behavior Committee or DVBC was called. This committee was composed of representatives from psychology, medicine, nursing, administration, facility operations, and others, as needed. Their purpose was to assess a patient for his infringement of the rules and arrive at a majority decision regarding conditions of discharge or retention. Although there was usually a bias against the patient already, the committee went through the motions of a "fair trial" so they couldn't be accused of malfeasance later. Anyone wanting to speak on behalf of the patient was allowed to speak first. The others then chimed in with counter-examples designed to discredit the patient or his supporters. After the "charges" against Daniel were listed by the physician chairman of the committee, Dr. Magnuson was invited to speak on the patient's behalf.

"I know that Daniel Hanson has put you all through a lot and that he has been difficult to deal with because of his easily elicited and openly expressed anger, because of his extreme fearfulness, and because not discharging him when he drank provided a mixed message to the rest of the section. But you need to appreciate his suffering and the horrors that he has been through. He may be seeking rejection or punishment, and thus redemption for what he regards as sins that he committed during his military duty. He has learned to use alcohol and anger to cope with the traumatic events he experienced in Vietnam and the continuing feelings that overwhelm him at times. He was making progress in dealing with staff and understanding his angry behavior until his physical problems got in the mix and complicated everything. Recently, I realized that the talking cure was not working fast enough to keep pace with the team's growing resentment, and I tried to get a jump-start by seeking resources for eye-movement desensitization."

Dr. Magnuson tried to cast the dilemma into a problem-solving context, considering Daniel as the raw material to which the team was supposed to apply their professional skills to mold him into an acceptable, functioning adult.

"I think it is our job to help him in spite of himself, in spite of the difficulties he presents us, calling us names and impugning our competence. I cannot abandon a patient without violating my professional ethics. Now, I think if we continue to work on his fearfulness, guilt and shame, we can undercut both his desire to use alcohol and his explosive outbursts of anger."

As logical as Dr. Magnuson's approach appeared, asking the team members to just do their jobs was met with a wall of resistance.

"You're just buying into his bullshit," said the substance abuse counselor in a challenging tone of voice. "He's an alcoholic, plain and simple, and he won't get better until he accepts that fact and works a 12-step program."

"I don't think he wants to get better," said the section assistant. "He could do it all himself if he stayed sober and wanted to. His so-called PTSD symptoms are merely part of his image, the way he presents himself in order to appear to be a big shot and to get out of things. Without it he would be a nobody, he wouldn't have a life."

The social worker, himself a Vietnam vet, volunteered that Daniel was "a Vietnam Vet With PTSD" and that without that identity, he might collapse.

"He uses Vietnam to get attention," the vocational therapist claimed. "He's a very needy person, very fearful, and he tries to control things by invoking some event from the war. We don't know if any of the things he says actually happened over there or that they happened to him. There are so many stories like that going around this place, he could have picked it up and used it from anybody."

"I agree. I think he uses those stories and his symptoms opportunistically to get whatever advantage there is to gain at the moment," voiced the recreational therapist. "He tries to gain attention so as to feel important, elicit sympathy and forgiveness, emphasize his suffering so as to get his care givers to try harder, deflect condemnation for his drinking violations, on and on. He could even be faking his symptoms too, for Christ's sake."

Countering this armchair psychologizing, the section nurse disagreed. "If you were there and witnessed his behavior when he was in one of those dissociative states, like I have, you wouldn't doubt that he has PTSD. His physiological responsiveness — sweating, dilated pupils and the way he is transfixed by whatever he is visualizing — that can't be faked."

Dr. Short agreed with the nurse and shifted the argument to practical considerations rather than psychological dynamics.

"Yeah, I saw it too. He really gets freaked out. There's no doubt he has PTSD and that he's afraid and goes into dissociative states, or he drinks and acts out. But the problem I have is that I don't have the time to spend talking with Daniel trying to calm him down. I know he has to do that to improve, but it takes too much time. I have other patients waiting. I can't be wasting so much time on one patient. I'm even hesitant to spend any more time on this committee dealing with it."

"And he'll squeal like hell if you don't spend the time with him," offered the dietitian.

Dr. Magnuson objected to the assertion that too much time and too many resources were being spent with Daniel.

"I still see all my other patients. Daniel doesn't get all my attention. Most of the time being spent is in the form of socioemotional support being delivered in the context of other functions, such as when a nurse attends to his physical needs. Don't you think that is part of your job?"

Dr. Short defended himself against the implied criticism of Dr. Magnuson's comment by saying "I really like Daniel and feel sorry for him. But the team simply spends too much time with him."

The nurse expressed her frustration by listing off three or four patients that also required lots of attention for their medical problems, problems that would ordinarily be treated in a hospital setting. Perhaps out of disappointment with his repeated failures to stay sober, she impugned Daniel's motives.

"In hindsight, we wanted to give Dan the benefit of the doubt, to give him options. We bent over backward for him. We tried the hard-nosed approach, the poor Daniel method. We did everything possible and it didn't work. He wants to be taken care of and blames others when things don't go his way. Either he should be locked in a room or he should be kicked into the street."

The psychologist, Dr. Magnuson, acknowledged additional institutional barriers to adequate patient treatment.

"We get a large number of mail-in patients with a known history of major problems. Do we have to tell them 'We can't take care of you?' We've become a dumping ground for the penal system as well as for other facilities experiencing cutbacks and shortened lengths of stay. The administration wants to keep the beds full to maintain our funding but that undercuts any screening function during the admissions process. Facilities for patients requiring intensive long-term inpatient care are nearly non-existent. Hospitals provide only short-term treatment for any patient and that is not sufficient for the needs of 'difficult patients,' as they are called. The conundrum is, we can't ethically just throw a sick patient out on the streets, but maybe we can't treat them here either."

The Patient Representative added, "It's true, we're not a secure psychiatric facility and yet we are asked to treat severely disturbed patients that are not okay to be flung out onto the streets. Everyone is functioning at or near their maximum levels. More than that and there will be a degradation in the quality of their performance. Since the self-esteem of most professionals depends upon doing their jobs well, they have in mind a certain acceptable quality in the work they produce, not just in its quantity. Difficult patients can easily push demands on care givers to unacceptable levels resulting in intra-personal conflict, poor judgment, distortions of perception, burn out, acting out, staff conflicts, and other things that can have adverse consequences for the system as a whole. Treating difficult patients is labor intensive and requires sufficient human resources so that the system can maintain its integrity."

The treatment team was well acquainted with Daniel Hanson and felt they had made extraordinary efforts to try to help him overcome his problems, even after repeated violations of facility rules. Again and again, allowances were made for his degree of severity and his apparent need. But Daniel either did not perceive these as concessions, did not see interpersonal transactions as necessarily reciprocal, could not process the information, or believed he could continue to run on credit.

After his last detox, the mood turned surly toward both Daniel and Dr. Magnuson. The team didn't want to put up with Daniel in defiance of his therapist's protestations that this was not a professional way to handle the situation. In any event, his debt became too great for his caregivers to bear and sentiments mounted to terminate his stay at Vetlandia.

Manifestations of these sentiments in staff behavior served as positive feedback to help spiral the system out of control. After Daniel exhibited one exceptionally distasteful display of venomous vitriol, one group was mobilized in as passionate a way to toss him out on his ear without regard for patient welfare, ethical deliberation or liability considerations.

Fortunately, a cooler head prevailed. The patient representative convinced the chief of staff that this case could draw unwanted attention to the facility administration and that the patient should remain in the infirmary until after his surgery. Upon his return, a decision would be made regarding recovery time and discharge date.

∞

"How ya doing, Daniel? I hear you got the powers that be all in a snit the other day? They giving you a bad time, are they?"

Learning of the high-octane hubbub over at the infirmary, Tom was paying a visit to the friend and fellow protester he had made during the infirmary suicide incident.

"I'm on thin ice here, Tom. I think they're going to toss me out as soon as they can. Seems they aren't too fond of my style of self expression. 'Course I wasn't too diplomatic in presenting my criticisms of their job performance."

He laughed at his understatement and Tom smiled in response.

"I don't suppose the alcohol alarm bell helped much either," chided Tom. "You need to chill out, step away from the fray a bit. Dr. Oldman tells me that diplomacy and having a cool head has its place if you want to be effective."

"Yeah, I suppose he's right," said Daniel. "I get so torqued-off at the stupidity, lack of compassion, and arbitrariness of some of these jerk-offs that I blast off and say to hell with the effects. I got some other problems I try to control with booze that feeds right into it and then I go all haywire and fuck everything up."

"That's easy enough to do. I've tried that method myself a few times. Didn't work out very well for me. But I can sympathize with your feelings about a lot of the staff around here. Not all of them, mind you, but a lot of them. I'm probably on thin ice here too. They don't seem to care for my criticisms of medical care for veterans any more than they do yours."

The difference between the two was that Tom couldn't simply be written off as a drunk or a mentally ill wacko and that made him dangerous, like the now-deceased Scott. He could cite facts and authorities from different institutions, and he could present a good argument in writing. He was liked and respected by a lot of the non-medical staff at Vetlandia, most notably the liberal snowflakes who were prone to resist the administration's autocratic rule.

"Do you think the problem is only overblown egos or is there something else going on?" asked Daniel.

"What else could be going on?" asked Tom.

"I don't know but I've been thinking a lot recently about Scott Parks, the guy they just found dead on the island in the river. Did you ever meet him?" Daniel inquired.

"No, but I heard some of the guys talking about him. He tried to expose the head headshrinker for patient abuse, didn't he?" questioned Tom.

"Head headshrinker, that's good!" Daniel laughed. "Yeah, that's right. The administration is sweeping it all under the rug — nothing will ever come of it. Well, I may be showing my paranoia, but I'm thinking that a bruised ego and a slap on the wrists from Regional Office aren't really enough reason to knock off a guy. Do you?" said Daniel with a question on his face.

"Some people do awfully nasty things out of embarrassment or humiliation," opined Tom, "but, no, I think in order to take such a drastic action would require something more to be at stake. "

"That's what I think. I wonder if Scott turned up something that might be even more of a problem for some of these yo-yos. I saw a lot of shit going down in Vietnam – drug smuggling, trafficking military script, stealing supplies, sometimes even disappearing whole two-and-a-half-ton trucks, murdering civilians. You name it, it was probably going on over there," said Daniel.

"A lot of Vietnam vets say the war was complete chaos and all sorts of civilized norms didn't seem to apply. But here? What could they be up to in a federal health care facility? Seems a bit far-fetched, don't you think?" Tom offered.

"Yeah, maybe you're right," Daniel replied. "Maybe it's us rabble rousing misfits that's the problem. I see lots of vets that just zip in, get their medical problems taken care of, get a job or get disability compensation, and then make a life for themselves in the community. The powers that be seem to favor the hidebound, flag-waving, traditional types around here. Maybe we should stick to trying to get our own acts together, get what help we can out of this place, then get the hell out. Still, I wouldn't put it past some of these bastards to line their own pockets at our expense, if they could."

"Tell you what, Daniel. While you're cooling your heels in here, I'll look around, ask around, see if I can turn anything up."

∞

When Tom returned to his room, he asked his roommate, Tony Napoliello, to tell him what he knew about Scott Parks.

"Well, Scott had a run-in with Dr. Gunnar and began to check around with other vets to see what kind of experience they had with him. Turned out they were either in a furious rage or were deeply depressed after seeing him, usually wanting to kill either him or themselves, depending upon the strength of their ego and whether they were inclined to direct their anger outward toward the target that instigated it or inward toward themselves. They complained about being treated with contempt, being degraded and humiliated, and having their concerns minimized or considered a manipulation, often with the doctor using vulgar language and ordering them out of his office.

"Scott became so enraged by the behavior of Dr. Wolfgang Gunnar toward patients that he sent a letter to Regional Office accusing him of patient abuse. He went a little overboard, assuming that Gunnar had lost his license because of the charges against him, so he accused him of practicing without a license too. And he accused the COS of being an active alcoholic and conspiring with the former Director to protect Gunnar. The former Director had himself been removed from his position due to improper conduct. The errors and unsupported allegations Scott had allowed to slip into his complaint undermined its effectiveness. Dr. Oldman cautioned him to make sure, in the future, that he had his facts straight before he made any accusations or put anything in writing," added Tony.

"Did anything come of it?" asked Tom

"You may have guessed by now that complaints by patients against doctors are routinely ignored around here, whether they are made through the patient representative or made directly to the regional office. The patient representative works under the direction of the COS and follows his orders, which are usually to come up with a plausible excuse to get rid of the offending patient. If the complaint is sent to the regional office, they simply bounce it back to the COS to take care of it. If the complaint is made to a congressman, one of his office staff will send an inquiry to the Director, who will then write a response to the congressman characterizing the patient as mentally impaired and claiming the charges are groundless. The congressman will typically accept whatever he or she is told without investigating further.

"Sometimes, the influence flows in the opposite direction," Tony continued. On one occasion that I know of, the alcoholic brother of a US senator was threatened with discharge after several instances of drunkenness, but a letter from his sister to the Director quickly quashed the discharge and earned an 'I owe you one' invisible token in return. Such debts come in handy when the question of appropriations comes around."

Regional Office sent Scott's letter back to the Director who gave it to the COS. The COS broke into Dr. Oldman's office in a rage, waving the letter in his hand. Infuriated, he bellowed out, "What the fuck is this? I am no longer drinking and Dr. Gunnar didn't lose his god-damned license to practice. Who the hell is this Parks guy anyway? Is he some kind of nut job or just another troublemaker? What's his diagnosis?" Kilpatrick demanded.

Dr. Oldman only revealed that Scott was a Vietnam veteran who, in the past, had been a political activist with liberal views. When he asked the COS if he wanted to meet with him, Mort paused for a moment, no doubt calculating the implications of such a confrontation. Then he said, "No, I don't want to meet with him. Just find out what he wants or what will placate him."

Scott Parks had made some allies in his patient abuse campaign against Dr. Gunnar. Both Dr. Oldman and his colleague, Fred Bojorquez, the section social worker, were sympathetic to and unofficially supported his efforts. The wife of Fred Bojorquez had been a court stenographer and suggested that Scott look in a particular place and present his requests in a particular way to obtain any court transcripts regarding Dr. Gunnar.

The effort proved very productive. They learned that Wolfgang Gunnar had been arrested for attempted murder in connection with a shooting incident. Two young men had driven onto his rural foothill property, and he fired a handgun at them striking the cab of their truck. He had been drinking with a friend and business partner in an exotic animal hunting resort east of town. His friend happened to be a judge and, with his assistance, Gunnar managed to move the trial to a different county where the charges were reduced to a misdemeanor. He was convicted, but he was only sentenced to a period of probation, did not lose his license to practice medicine in the state, and he continued to work at Vetlandia. He was required to get psychiatric treatment. However, the treatment was provided by his friend, another local psychiatrist.

The courthouse documents also included several DUIs, two restraining orders filed by his wife for holding her against her will and breaking her arm, a malpractice suit that was settled out of court, a violation of airport regulations when he flew his private airplane in for a landing during a blinding fog, and two charges in another county. Scott also obtained evidence of collusion and perjury by the psychiatrist who was presumably treating Dr. Gunnar.

"So Scott sent the documentation to the Regional Office," Tony continued, "asking for an investigation, and they, again, sent the material back to the COS. The COS called Scott into his office where there were several other people present who he did not know. In spite of this apparent attempt at intimidation, Scott laid out his indictment of Gunnar and asserted that he was unfit to treat veterans."

Shortly thereafter, there was a bizarre incident in which Scott was rounded up by Vetlandia police and brought to the infirmary presumably to determine his dangerousness. Dr. Oldman arrived while another psychologist was talking with Scott. There were two men present that Scott thought were there to see if they could court-commit him to a state hospital. They didn't get away with that because the psychologist could find no evidence of his dangerousness and so they released him to go back to his normal activities in the section.

"Now you really have to give it to old Scott, he didn't give up. No sir, he managed to get the private address for the Secretary of Veterans Affairs from a former staff member who had successfully sued Vetlandia for violation of the Americans with Disabilities Act. He copied the 110-page documentation of his charges, added complaints by other patients who felt abused by Gunnar, and sent the material by certified mail to the Secretary of the whole damn VA. Scott continued to send signed letters from other patients to the private address for the Secretary as they were produced, but never received an acknowledgment that any action would be taken.

"Finding the VA system totally unresponsive, Scott connected with a couple of journalists who, he said, were working on a story about the abuses at Vetlandia. I didn't talk with him after that, and now they found Scott's body over on that island in the river. I wonder if he left any records of what he had found. He was usually pretty careful that way. He had the 'good paranoia' of an intelligence officer. It wouldn't surprise me if he salted away copies of what he had someplace or gave them to somebody he could trust."

"That's an incredible story," said Tom. "It's hard to believe that they would kill him to shelter Gunnar as far as his activities at Vetlandia go. Patient abuse doesn't rise to the level where it captures the attention of any of the higher-ups in the administration. If anyone at Vetlandia had anything to do with Scott's death, it would only make sense if he had evidence of some crime that was less susceptible to debate than patient abuse. Who might know what dirt Scott Parks had on anyone beside Wolfgang Gunnar?"

"Hard to say," Tony responded. "Could be one of his close friends, like Ernie, or it might be one of the staff he got to know and trust, like Oldman or Fred Bojorquez or Veronica Ramsey — she's one of the decent substance abuse counselors. No one has come forward to say anything about it, so far. They might be scared they could end up having the same fate as poor Scott."

Tom tried to imagine what actions he might take if he had incriminating information on people who could do him harm. Take out a safe-deposit box? Send a letter to himself so that it would appear in his in-mail? Copy it to a computer disk or storage device? Send it to a relative? He decided to ask around to see if he could drum up any leads.

In the canteen or on the golf course or sitting around waiting for appointments across the street at the cafe frequented by many vets, Tom would strike a pose as a new patient who didn't know how things worked at Vetlandia, allowing him to ask a lot of questions without sounding like he was looking for anything in particular.

He found that many inhabitants observed that certain of their fellows had a surprisingly easy time of it in Vetlandia, compared to what they, themselves, had experienced. These guys had their medical problems taken care of without having to hassle their caregivers, got into truck driving school without a lot of bother, and were quickly employed by one particular local trucking firm. Others obtained service connection for a disability on their first try without having to scrounge for ancient records and reapply over and over again before a determination was made. Some obtained employment at the facility itself or were allowed to attend the local college for extended periods without being required to save money for room and board or threatened with discharge.

What did they have in common? Tom received a variety of responses to that question. Some called them brown-nosing bull-shitters. Others thought they were straight-laced patriotic types, not a bunch of fuck-ups. Some said they had the traditional tough-minded military mentality. Some called them "pricks" and others called them "lucky as shit." Hmm. Not a lot to go on there, Tom thought, but I'll keep it in the back of my mind for future reference.

At his IT job in the library, Tom ran into a lot of different vets and a few staff members who wanted to learn something other than what was provided by drug reps. As they checked out books, periodicals, or documents, he would strike up a casual conversation and make very general inquires as to what they thought about various problems or happenings in the facility that many complained about, what they thought was the cause of it or what they thought was going on "behind the scenes," who was involved, and so on – just a general fishing expedition with his ears attuned to any connection with Scott Parks or any other kind of impropriety.

Veronica came by Tom's desk to ask if the library had a particular journal she was interested in. He found it for her, and she expressed her appreciation.

"Thanks, Tom. I have a hard time finding things in this place."

"No problem," said Tom. "By the way, you knew Scott Parks didn't you?"

"Yes, I knew him. Why do you ask?"

"Don't you think it was rather suspicious that he turned up dead after complaining about Gunnar?"

"When I saw that in the paper," answered Veronica, "I figured it would become a topic of speculation among you guys, even though a cause of death hasn't been determined yet. Yes, the circumstances make you wonder, I'll grant you that. There are a lot of odd things that happen around here, but I can't talk about specific patients, even if they are dead. Thanks again for the help."

As the next vet in line, Andrew Hammons, came up to Tom's desk to check out a book. It was obvious he overheard the previous conversation.

"She may not be able to talk to you about what some of the guys go through around here, but I can give you an earful about what these assholes did to my ex-roommate. They really fucked him over! He's probably laying dead somewhere right now, the poor sonofabitch! And here he was, one of the good guys routing out the drug dealers the staff claim to hate."

"What?" said Tom, caught by surprise. "Come again?"

"I don't want to go into it right now, not here," said Andrew. "You never know who might be listening. Stop by my room one of these nights and I'll give you the run-down on good old Gene Lofgren."

CHAPTER 7
The Fickle Finger of Fate

It was the end of a day-long meeting in which staff members were being trained on how to safely and effectively take down unruly patients using the "hanging" technique," a procedure whereby one staff member would hang on each of the patient's arms with their full dead-weight while another would approach from behind and hug the patient while applying resistance to forward movement. Dr. Gunnar signaled the COS, Mort Kilpatrick, by a prearranged hand gesture that he would like to speak with him.

"What's up?" asked the COS.

"One of my informants came to me late yesterday with news that an FBI agent was wandering around the grounds with one of the patients. Don't have any other information but thought you might like to know."

"I don't like the sound of that," said the COS. "Find out who he was and who the patient is. Read the patient record and intake sheet and jot down anything we should be concerned about. Get back to me right away on that."

Wolfgang Gunnar spoke again with the COS the next day. "Looks like the patient, one Eugene Lofgren, has a legitimate reason for being here – lots of medical problems and he was one of the victims in a robbery and murder down in San Francisco. The FBI agent appears to have been just a friend that came to visit him after he was admitted here. But listen to this! The progress notes from Dr. Oldman indicate that the two of them, Lofgren and the FBI agent, worked together trying to catch drug dealers at that free clinic down there where all the murders took place. Sounds like Lofgren has been a troublemaker for a long time and now he's talking with that troublemaker of our own, Oldman, on a regular basis. We don't know what he knows about this place and if he is still working with that FBI guy. I don't like it."

"I don't like it either," said the COS. "I think it would be best if it can be arranged that Lofgren has a short stay here at Vetlandia. Get together with Green and help him form a plan to usher him out of here, not too gradual like. And see what you can find out about the FBI agent from our friends down in the Bay area."

"Gotcha, boss. I'm on it," replied Gunnar.

∞

Gene Lofgren was a large man – six foot two and 245 pounds – somewhat disheveled in appearance with a full beard, long hair, and glasses. He was one of those gentle giant guys, big enough to break a man in half but a pussycat underneath. Kind and helpful to those in need, he nevertheless had a backbone and was able to act courageously to right what he considered a wrong or injustice, to persist in the face of threats and intimidation.

His early life was not an easy one. His mother was hurt in an industrial accident and couldn't support Gene and his younger brother, so she signed them over to the state where they were placed in an orphanage in a rough area of town. The institution split the two of them up, which made Gene feel even more abandoned. A lot of bad things routinely happened there, including physical and sexual abuse. Children's bodies were dug up from unmarked graves on the grounds after the place was shut down by the state. Gene developed a lung ailment at the orphanage and was placed in the ward of a hospital where he thought he would be left to die, like his impoverished roommates who also had no one to look out for their best interests. But then the big roulette table in the sky smiled down on him. He was chosen for a trial of a new medical procedure at Yale University and he survived. This was the beginning of his feeling that it was just "dumb luck" that he had been selected to live while many of his friends were dished out "bad luck" for no rhyme or reason. One of them committed suicide, one overdosed on drugs, and one died a few feet from Gene when he tried a foolhardy stunt, jumping off a building. He felt he had let them down in some unspecified way and was obliged to make up for this unfair twist of fate by helping the less fortunate.

Notwithstanding many obstacles along the way, Gene did well in school, spent four years in the Air Force, and was the first one from his orphanage to go to college. He was a humanities major at UConn and then a research assistant in sociology while he did postgraduate work.

Gene was working as a research planner for a poverty program when he got a phone call from Jackie, a girlfriend who had traveled to South Africa to experience a different culture. She had become strung out on drugs, managed to get pregnant, and was associating with unsavory characters. Feeling that he had to rush to the rescue of the damsel in distress, he finished up an urgent part of the project he was working on, took a leave of absence, and flew to Africa. But he was too late. She had already died from an overdose. As if the universe was sending him a message, Eugene was late getting to the airport for his return flight, only to learn that the plane had been bombed and all onboard, including some important representatives from the United Nations, were lost. Lady Luck had spared him again. This was at a time when demonstrations for and against the Vietnam War were going on all over the country.

Back in the US, Gene was still mourning the loss of his girlfriend when he saw tanks driving up the street outside his office window. He felt like the world had gone crazy and that life had lost all meaning. He decided to drop out of graduate school, obtaining a job for the state welfare department. He initiated two drug treatment programs in Hartford but, adding to his melancholy, drug dealers managed to kill another one of his close friends. Finding he couldn't tolerate the lack of merit with which fate was dispensed, he decided to chuck it all and relocate to California.

For the next 20 years, he devoted himself to doing what he could to halt the scourge of drug addiction. That's what gave his life meaning after all the losses he had experienced due to drugs. He volunteered at the Berkeley Free Clinic and obtained paid employment as a program planner, evaluating drug programs for the city of Berkeley. In exchange for a rent-free apartment, he worked as a clerk at the Hotel Berkeley Inn on Telegraph Avenue. Eventually, the Free Clinic gave him a paying job coordinating crisis services, writing grants, sitting on regional boards, and providing services to the many victims of street drugs.

As Gene's fate would have it, he ended up knee-deep amid a territorial drug war. When he tried to get a meth dealer into the Witness Protection Program so that he could testify, the man was murdered. A woman friend who was going to testify before the state legislature about the murder of a prominent educational reformer by members of a revolutionary group was murdered by drug dealers too. Many radical groups were roaming all over the Bay area at the time and Gene Lofgren held them all in contempt because they weren't interested in treating drug-related health problems, as they maintained, but just in starting a self-aggrandizing revolution. He discovered that one of these groups was involved in the operation of the Free Clinic where he worked and tried to expose it. The clinic directors seemed unconcerned about drug-using employees and, for all his efforts, Gene was beaten several times and three other employees who tried to help him were murdered.

Finally, an FBI agent, Frank Celiberti, took notice of Gene's efforts when he made comments at a public hearing. They became good friends and Gene supplied him with observations of activities around the Free Clinic while the agent showed Gene pictures of people to be on the lookout for and report who were their associates. Frank visited Gene in the hospital when he was beaten by drug dealers and later, when he suffered a heart attack and had bypass surgery. He appreciated the older man's guts and perseverance in pursuit of his idealistic goals despite threats, intimidation and physical injuries.

After his heart attack, Gene Lofgren was forced to live on Social Security Disability and received discounted rental rates in his apartment building by being a contact person, someone who relayed messages and answered questions from tenants. He continued to volunteer at the Free Clinic, giving lectures to staff and anyone interested in disrupting the scourge of drug addiction. But then the ownership of his apartment building changed. This time, not because of the fickle finger of fate but because of corporate greed, he lost his discount and was forced to borrow money from friends to cover unexpected expenses for going to and from medical appointments.

Gene Lofgren and Frank Celiberti were having dinner at a Sizzler restaurant in San Francisco when fate dealt them another bad hand — they were held hostage during a robbery. The manager was tortured and eventually murdered. Gene was forced to lie face down on the floor with the other patrons who were present while one of the criminals held a shotgun to his head, threatening to blow his brains out if he made a move. He was lying on the floor close to the exit and the bandit with the shotgun moved back and forth, nervously checking to see if the police were coming. He kept threatening Gene as he shoved the barrel of the shotgun into his neck. Periodically, he would yell directions to his accomplice in the back of the store on how to torture the store manager to get him to reveal the whereabouts of the key to the cash box. Gene could hear the screams and pleading of the store manager as he was being tortured and knew in his gut that the man was going to be killed.

Afterward, Gene worked with the local police to identify the culprits. The larger man of the two had been apprehended but the other one was still free. The police told him that the one at liberty was the more dangerous of the two because his MO was to find a not-too-bright person to do the actual killing and dump him later. The police said that he had killed other witnesses in similar robberies.

One of the other hostages and a potential witness had started to live in his car. The mouthpiece for the apprehended killer had already visited him and that meant the information about his residence could get back to the killer and then to the other bandit who was still on the loose. He was petrified with fear that the killer would find him.

Gene was scared too that he might be found and eliminated, but he continued to work with the police because he believed it was his duty. The hapless victim started having chest pains and difficulty breathing during the robbery and these problems continued for the next few months, causing him to freak out even more. He had nightmares, was afraid of being outside his apartment, and thought he was going to be killed. He was trying to hold it all together but a number of things ganged up on him.

While Gene was on the floor in the restaurant, he clenched his jaw so hard that he broke some teeth. He wanted to do part-time teaching in the future, so he didn't want to look like a bum. He applied for and received dental care through the Crisis Victims Act in Oakland. His FBI friend suggested he sue the restaurant chain for negligence since they had been told to have a guard at that time of night due to crimes in the area, but they didn't do it. Gene thought he might be able to recover what he had lost as a result of being in the restaurant that night by pursuing that claim. He broke two more teeth by clenching his jaw, he couldn't concentrate or think straight, and, on the anniversary of the robbery and murder, he woke up with a painful pinched nerve in his neck. He checked into the local VA Psychiatric Clinic where it was arranged for him to be sent to Vetlandia for PTSD treatment and monitoring of his deteriorated physical condition. His court case was still being litigated when he arrived at Vetlandia, and, while he was a patient, he traveled back and forth to California by bus every month or so to get his dental care and meet with his lawyer.

Gene saw Dr. Oldman every week and the doctor referred him for biofeedback to help control his anxiety and blood pressure. Oldman tried to get him to join one of his PTSD groups but he declined because he was too distrustful of others. The doctor did his usual psychological things, helped Gene interpret his dreams, and explored his thought processes and emotions. And he had him read a book called *Shattered Assumptions* that helped him make sense of his symptoms. He still felt vulnerable and lacking in resilience, continued to break his teeth, and had to urinate all the time. He was afraid of the upcoming trial and the prospect of facing the criminal mastermind of the robbery and murder. When he went for an interview with the psychiatrist hired by the restaurant, he was so upset that, when he later saw his dentist, he vomited into the rinse basin and the work was delayed.

Veronica Ramsey, one of the better substance abuse counselors, after watching a teaching video that Gene made at the Free Clinic, recognized his knowledge and skill in the addictions field and asked him to participate in one of her groups as an expert. But he refused, thinking it required making a total commitment, and, now feeling weak and unsure, feared the responsibility and the prospect of making errors. She considered him to be overly conscientious and loyal, plagued by guilt over not being able to save his friends. She wondered if perhaps he believed that he dragged them into "his thing" and they perished as a result. Maybe he still thought himself invincible and that he should be able to pull the fat out of the fire no matter what the circumstances.

As the new year dawned, Gene was brought to a team meeting where the nurse presented a plan for him to start an office job and save $100/month in preparation for his discharge. There was no mention of his medical problems or of being treated for PTSD using psychotherapy and biofeedback since Dr. Oldman had been banned by Dr. Whitey Green from attending that portion of the meeting.

Gene thought the patients were being exploited and forced to work for low wages. Looking at it from a labor union perspective, he considered working for 70 cents an hour to be unethical and feared that the patients would take their resentment out on him because he would represent the authority of the section office, where it was proposed that he take an IT job. He thought the administration's attempt to promote the work requirement as "therapy" was too reminiscent of the Nazis' notion of "Arbeit macht frei." Gene would rather volunteer to work for free than accept a pittance and cast it as if it were real employment, so he didn't pursue obtaining an IT assignment. When he saw his nurse supervisor again, she noted his objection to participation but disregarded it, setting a start date some three weeks hence.

It wasn't much longer before Gene came back to his room complaining that he had no energy and had to lie down. A doctor diagnosed him as having early bilateral Carpal tunnel syndrome that could require surgery if symptoms got worse. His biofeedback technician told him that stress from "extraneous factors" was being reflected in his biofeedback data.

Then his 80-year-old mother, who lived alone in northern Maine, broke her arm. He wanted to visit her but, he learned, the VA was going to bill him for the costs of his medical treatment from his presumed assets, the paltry settlement he expected to receive from his lawsuit against Sizzler. Dr. Whitey Green had tipped off the cost-recovery minions in the financial office, who salivated at the prospect of being credited with contributing to VA coffers. All the money Gene was going to use to pay off the loans that he received from friends and make the trip to see his ailing mother would be gobbled up by the voracious administration.

By the end of the month, Gene was at loggerheads with his nurse and Dr. Green regarding his IT assignment. In a huff, the nurse proclaimed that the window of opportunity for taking an IT job had passed and he would be discharged. She claimed she had brought the patient to a core team meeting where it was unanimously agreed to discharge him due to so-called "non-compliance." Yet Dr. Oldman was not informed of the meeting and even one of the core members indicated that she had never been asked what she thought about the matter.

Gene appealed the decision to the Disciplinary Appeals Board the same day and subsequently approached Dr. Oldman in a very distraught state. Oldman called the psychologist on another section, Dr. Anderson, who attended the DAB meeting, to get his perceptions of what happened. Anderson said he had mentioned Gene's cognitive and depressive impairments at that time and suggested three alternative ways of resolving the conflict, including seeing the acting COS and patient representative about moving to another section. All of his suggestions were ignored. The physician who recorded the results of the DAB meeting and who had read none of the voluminous progress notes specifying his health conditions, financial circumstances, and homelessness, claimed Gene had participated in a helpful therapeutic program but now, all of a sudden, seemed to be simply using the facility for room and board. No matter that it was the case that almost all of the homeless inpatients were using the place as temporary room and board.

She further claimed that Gene had refused to take prophylactic INH therapy as recommended by the VA TB Clinic because of a recent TB test. He had disputed the results of the VA skin test and had gone to the local public health clinic where he obtained a negative assessment of his TB status. She falsely asserted that Dr. Oldman had been very supportive of the need for Gene to take an IT assignment, blithely omitting the part that it was intended as a *test* of his stamina, a test that he did not pass. Angered by another challenge to his authority, Dr. Green got into it with Dr. Oldman, who had recruited Dr. Anderson and their Service Chief, Dr. James Holbrook, to stand up for Gene and the rule of rationality in decision-making about his case.

Continuing with her blatant lies, the nurse, maintained that Gene was unable to describe why he was not actively participating in any treatment or therapeutic program or showing any desire to change. Ignoring the concerns expressed by several staff members, she held that Gene was medically stable and should be discharged so that he might be able to continue to receive outpatient medical, psychiatric, and psychological care at the California Soldier's Home. What's that? He's medically stable but he needs treatment?

Gene continued his appeal, seeing the administrative assistant to the COS who, after consulting with Dr. Anderson, overturned the discharge, deeming it unsupportable given the documented facts and exposing them to the possibility of charges of malpractice. A doctor from another section, no doubt sympathetic to Dr. Green, agreed to accept the patient but he imposed impossible conditions. First, that Gene obtain a full-time eight-hour-per-day IT job before being transferred as opposed to the two to four hours per day that was originally proposed. Second, he had to save 75% of the money he earned and place it in a patient account. Third, he had to work with a social worker on a discharge plan and discharge within 3 months. Fourth, all treatment had to be provided by the new section staff. Continuity of care, which used to be a major tenant of medical ethics, was jettisoned altogether. Having no other place to go besides living on the street and knowing he needed medical care, Gene agreed to the terms and immediately obtained an IT job in the facility kitchen.

It was obvious that the plan was designed to punish Gene Lofgren for his impudence in questioning his medical care, stress him beyond his level of tolerance, and force him out of the facility on an irregular basis once he broke, at the same time claiming they had acted according to a plan that he had agreed upon.

Within days, an IT supervisor reported that Gene complained of leg and chest pains. The sympathetic addictions specialist, Veronica Ramsey, recorded Gene's pain complaints and history of not being able to stand more than three hours per day for several years. She suggested Gene be allowed to find another IT job and noted that there were both physical and mental reasons for him not to be discharged. On the same day, Dr. Whitey Green claimed he had talked with the nurse, another doctor, and the COS assistant and they felt Gene should be discharged immediately for non-compliance. He claimed to have talked with several members of the two treatment teams and that the consensus was that Gene be discharged by COB that day.

The section assistant brought Gene to his office to have him explain the reason for walking off his job. Gene stated he was sick and had gone to a civilian doctor in town for help, another slap in the face for Dr. Green. Again riled by the questioning of his judgment and authority, Whitey Green declared that "Mr. Lofgren should be given an irregular discharge this very day."

Gene brought a letter he received from Providence Hospital indicating that he had pneumonia to Dr. Anderson. The latter said he did not understand the impending discharge since the patient was complying with the requirements. He thought Gene was very anxious and should be given some leeway because of his illness.

When Dr. Green was informed that Gene had pneumonia, he smirked as if placing the term in quotation marks. He complained that Gene had not informed anyone of that fact and ordered that he be retained in section until Green, himself, determined that he was sufficiently recovered so he could be discharged. Covering his backside, he acknowledged that Gene complained of fatigue, night sweats, and lack of energy, but did not state that he actually had them. He gave Gene some kind of medication and told him he would *not* be transferred to another section and would be discharged as soon as he recovered from his pneumonia. The toady nurse told Gene's social worker to furnish the patient with a packet of information about temporary and long-term housing.

The Chief of Psychology Service, Dr. Holbrook, said Gene was unable to attend his biofeedback appointments because he was exhausted, had confused affect, was nauseated, and was vomiting. Commenting about the lack of a discharge plan despite the impending discharge two days hence, he expressed grave concerns regarding the wisdom of the planned action. As a result of an appeal to the acting COS to intervene in the matter, Gene was sent to Roseburg VAMC, some 90 miles away.

When he was discharged from that hospital, he returned to Vetlandia and sought readmission but learned that his discharge had been deemed irregular even though he had been sent to a treatment facility. His name had also been placed on a "Do Not Readmit" list maintained on a computer by one of the admissions physicians, apparently at the behest of Dr. Green. According to a lawyer who was told of the procedure, maintaining such a list would be considered illegal if there were no specific criteria and actual assessment of the individuals who were placed on it.

∞

Tom was a little jittery as he knocked on Andrew's door. Why was this guy so cagey about saying anything in the library where others could overhear? Is he some kind of a nut trying to pose as if he is "in on the know" so he'll look important? Is there, indeed, something evil going on at Vetlandia or is it just the everyday paranoia of down-and-out vets? Should I be scared? Should I keep my mouth shut and mind my own business?

Andrew opened the door with a frown on his face, melting into a smile when he recognized it was Tom visiting him.

"You decided to show up. I wasn't sure how serious you were about looking into things that are going on here. Come on in and have a cup of coffee."

Tom entered a room much like his own with two windows on one wall, two beds, a table with three chairs, and a couple easy chairs. Surveying the wall decor he spotted a picture of an aircraft carrier, a picture that he presumed was his one-time base of operations and another of what looked like a high-tech cubicle in the innards of the ship. On an easel next to the table was a well-done very detailed pencil sketch of an eagle.

"You the artist?" asked Tom.

"Yeah, that's my anti-anxiety medication. It may show my obsessive-compulsive side but it doesn't have any side effects like the chemical shit they toss at all the vets that they think need it."

"I think you've got some talent there. Ever try to sell them?"

"Naw, I just do it for my own entertainment. It relaxes me. I worked for the post office for 25 years and no, I didn't go postal, not once." He laughed. "I even bought one of their old delivery trucks and fixed it up so it's air-tight and runs like a champ."

"Yeah, I've seen you driving by in it. Looks really sharp. I gather from the picture that you were in the navy?" asked Tom.

"Yeah. Navy intelligence. I was on that carrier during the Iran hostage crisis in 1980. We knew the rescue attempt would fail the day before because the planes and choppers were not in good shape. They were leaking oil and couldn't handle the sand without some major changes. But the politicians were raring to go and had their way. They went in spite of what we in intelligence had to say. It was a total disaster. I don't know how the politicians can just nonchalantly place young men in danger and the military brass just go along with it."

Andrew's secondary duties were in fire control and they had a major fire after a plane crashed on the deck. He lifted the hatch from below deck and saw only a wall of fire that he and the others in his crew were expected to walk into and suppress. He well remembered the struggle to breathe as he wielded the fire suppression equipment. There were a lot of injuries, the memories of which caused him, even now, to wince.

He had wanted to make the Navy a career but when he got home, he was too spaced out from PTSD to remain in the service. His family didn't understand his depression and his attempts to seek a solution to a problem where the source of the difficulty was in his assumptions and, therefore, invisible to his rational thinking. He was sent to various hospitals while still in the navy and made some kind of "example" in front of a large audience of fledgling doctors, which he didn't appreciate at all. At Vetlandia, he first was seen by the man-hating female psychologist, Carole Harding. Deserted by her husband, she operated chronically in her inferior function and didn't provide any understanding, let alone sympathy to her patients.

Andrew poured them each a cup of coffee and they sat down at the table. "So what got you interested in Scott Parks?"

"Well, I heard he turned up dead out on that island in the river after he complained about the way Gunnar was treating patients, or at least some patients. People have been claiming the two are related, that someone had him offed because of that. But it doesn't make much sense to me that anyone would go to such an extreme when the VA doesn't do anything about patient complaints anyway. What's the point? Why not just ride it out until the complainer gets discharged?"

"Good question – the same one I have about my ex-roommate, Eugene Lofgren. What happened to him doesn't make any sense to me either. He was a stand-up guy and what they did to him was just plain cruel and stupid. They drove him out of Vetlandia when he was sick and had no resources to speak of. Eugene Lofgren was a decent kind of guy, a crusader against drug pushers and drug addiction. Even though he lived frugally, a step away from homelessness, he still tried to make this a better world as much as he could. You would think they would want to help a guy like him in a place like this that draws all sorts of vets who have succumbed to the lure of drugs, but that doesn't seem to be the case."

"Yeah, you would think so," opined Tom.

"He began to see Dr. Oldman in order to help him deal with all the traumas he had. I don't know what they all were but I know his luck wasn't any better when he was a kid. He had all sorts of medical problems – heart, arteries, diabetes. He had a hard time walking these long hallways and oftentimes became fatigued from the heat.

"When I first saw him, Gene seemed confused and he couldn't express his feelings or ideas very well. He was jumpy, down in the dumps, wary of everybody, and couldn't last a full hour with Dr. Oldman. He always had to sleep with a light on and any noise in the hallway would give him a start. He had to wear a bite guard at night because of his jaw-clenching and breathing problems. He woke me up with his nightmares on many an occasion, and he didn't like to talk or even think about that Sizzler robbery where he was held hostage."

Andrew filled Tom in on the facts of the robbery and murder, as he understood them.

"Did he say what his nightmares were about?"

"Just that his friends were always getting killed and, in one, his mother was killed by the criminals who had followed him to her residence. You have to remember that this was a very responsible guy who expected a lot from himself. He said that Dr. Oldman kept reminding him that humility was a virtue."

"I hadn't thought about it before," said Tom, "but I guess you can expect too much of yourself, so much that you drive yourself crazy."

"Exactly," said Andrew. "Eventually, Gene talked more, experienced less anxiety, had fewer disturbing dreams and was able to walk with more confidence. Toward the end of the year, the section nurse, who was his treatment manager, asked Dr. Oldman if he thought Gene was ready for a three to four hour Incentive Therapy assignment. He agreed it might be a good time for Eugene to *test* his abilities and stamina. He did not mean they should see how much it would take to overwhelm them."

"And, of course, that is what they did," Tom said in anticipation of Andrew's explanation.

"You're catching on, my friend." Andrew related what he knew about the efforts of Dr. Green and his nurse to run Eugene out of Vetlandia.

Thinking out loud, Tom remarked, "They must have had it out for this guy for some other reason, but why? What did they have to gain? Or were they afraid of some threat he posed to them? What possible threat could an old, beaten down, and physically ill vet present to them?"

"The same questions I asked myself at the time and ever since. They had some reasons they offered up as a kind of diversion but nothing with any substance to it."

Tom opined, "They were going to drum this disabled vet out of the facility for having been disabled, both physically and mentally. That is criminal, it is pure craziness and cruelty!"

"My sentiments, completely," said Andrew.

"Whew!," exclaimed Tom. That is incredible. What a story of abuse and, on the other hand, of a man's dedication to a principle. Do you know what happened to him?"

"No, I haven't heard from him since they refused to readmit him from the hospital. I'm afraid he is laying dead somewhere. Maybe he was murdered by the Sizzler bandits, or by some drug dealers. Maybe he is camped out on the streets, living in a cardboard box. Who knows? I do know he was dealt a shitty hand by the assholes who work in this place, who didn't recognize him for the kind of man he was."

"Maybe they did know the kind of person he was and that's why they got rid of him," ventured Tom. "I mean look at his case and then look at the case of my friend, Daniel Hanson. I'll tell you about him another time, but he got the same kind of shitty treatment that Eugene got by the same cast of characters. Both were victims of abuse at the hands of VA staff. Now I know a lot of doctors have a lofty notion of their importance, their intelligence, their so-called 'station in life,' and when a patient comes along and punctures their balloon, they can get all bent out of shape about it and retaliate. They can get away with murder."

"You can say that again," said Andrew.

"But this is just too much!" continued Tom. "Too much spite and concerted effort to get rid of the little troublemakers, too much to be accounted for by a few ruffled egos. I ask myself, 'What else do they have in common?' Both were fighting the drug traffickers, both could figure out when something didn't smell right and they both were willing to risk their lives to speak out about it. And what about Scott, the guy they found dead down on the river? He called them out to their faces, followed all the proper channels for reporting abuse, but nothing came of it. He began nosing around, looking for other things they may have been involved in, and ends up face down in the mud of the mighty Rogue. I'll bet he found something else on these bastards, something clearly illegal. I am beginning to wonder if there is a drug connection in all three cases?"

"There has to be something else," said Andrew. "Gene had a friend who visited him here at Vetlandia. I met him. He was an FBI agent, Frank Celiberti. I thought it was all bullshit until he showed me his badge and his identification card from the agency. He said that Gene and he used to work together back in the San Francisco-Oakland area. He expressed a lot of admiration for Gene but Gene just brushed it off, embarrassed by the attention being placed on him. He eventually told me about some of the things they were involved in and some of the things that happened. It was some pretty deep shit, I'll tell ya — people getting murdered, Gene getting beat up more than once."

"Do you know if anyone else at Vetlandia knew this friend was an FBI agent?"

"I don't know for sure. Gene took him down to the canteen for lunch and you know how that place is. Could easily have come up what with the kind of prodding for personal information that we get from some of the yahoos around here. Or it could have been overheard by someone nearby."

CHAPTER 8
Flight of the Raven

Tom first met Peter Steele in a day room at Vetlandia where several patients were watching a TV special about the OJ Simpson robbery trial that occurred after his famous murder trial. Pete came to be known as "Cowboy" at Vetlandia because he first rode into the facility on a horse, a means of conveyance that could not be stored at the facility except for overnight as he arranged for admittance.

Cowboy was a wild and rebellious type who grew up on a ranch in Montana. His father was a diplomat whose wife often went with him overseas, leaving the boys in the care of ranch hands who were wont to discipline the boss's kids. Cowboy and his brothers raised themselves and had a lot of freedom. They learned to ride horses, wrangle cattle, shoot rifles and pistols, and hunt early in life. They worked on the ranch, learned to fly a small airplane, and got into a lot of scrapes for hell-raising in the nearby small town.

Cowboy went through ROTC in college and joined the Air Force right after graduating. He was sent to Vietnam as a Forward Air Controller. Flying in a slow unarmed light aircraft much like the one he had learned to fly as a teenager, his job was to search for enemy convoys and troop concentrations and mark them with special smoke-producing rockets that told fighter pilots where to aim when they came flying through like bats out of hell in their jets. The controllers had to stick around an enemy area, often taking ground fire, while waiting for approval from several layers of higher-ups to mark the targets, and then standing by until the fighters arrived. They had a high casualty rate and were known as brave but somewhat crazy bird-men.

With all of his experience flying small planes, Cowboy was good at his job, but he bristled at all the bureaucratic oversight while his life and the lives of friendlies on the ground were in danger. The rules of engagement required that they fly at a relatively high altitude to avoid small arms fire but then they couldn't clearly see what was happening on the ground and might accidentally endanger civilians or friendly forces. And if they dropped down for a closer look, they could get court-martialed because the generals and politicians had to cover their backside from accusations of unnecessarily endangering pilots or making mistakes causing civilian lives.

All the pilots were drilled on the new rules, so if a mistake was made and there were civilian casualties, it could be blamed on the actions of a rogue pilot. That was not the image of a flier Cowboy had in mind when he heard stories about WWII pilots battling it out with the Luftwaffe or Japanese Zeros. Cowboy was prone to speak his mind, often without tact or sensitivity. He wanted to make his own decisions and trust his perceptions and skills, unencumbered by some desk jockey far away from the scene of action.

Undercover operatives noticed Cowboy's discontent with standard Air Force operations and recruited him into a covert air program, named after the Steve Canyon TV program of the late 50s, that was part of the secret war in Laos. The campaign was not openly talked about by civilians because the terms of the Geneva Accords, signed between the United States and North Vietnam in 1962, guaranteed the neutrality of the Kingdom of Laos with the provision that all foreign military forces had to leave the country. Nevertheless, both sides knew the war was going on and each had forces in Laos.

Operating under the call sign Ravens, a small group of forward air controllers, scrubbed of their military identity and disguised as civilian forest rangers or agricultural advisers working for the US Agency for International Development, AID, operated with minimal resources but a lot less administrative oversight to use unconventional methods to disrupt the flow of troops and supplies along the part of the Ho Chi Minh Trail from North Vietnam to South Vietnam that ran through Laos. These forward air controllers were daredevil nonconformists, flying their small, slow aircraft on three or four missions a day, sometimes at night, over the jungles and around the mountains of Laos, spotting targets, and radioing in airstrikes from US Air Force and Laotian aircraft based in Udorn, Thailand that carried heavier ordnance. Once the cavalry arrived, the Ravens would fire white phosphorus or "Willy Pete" rockets at the targets to identify them for the more heavily armed aircraft. It was dangerous duty — 16% of them lost their lives.

The Ravens used intelligence supplied by the CIA, received air support from the US and Laotian Air Forces and, in theory, worked under the American ambassador. They would have a briefing every day or two, and the ambassador would establish the limits on where they could go and what they could do. Having been appraised of their targets, they would attend an evening briefing between Laotian troops and the local CIA where they would modify whatever the ambassador said to fit the circumstances as they knew them. The CIA and the Hmong, the local guys, knew what they wanted to get done. The pilots themselves would get together in the morning and decide who was going where then troll around in the air seeing what they could find.

The United States, through the CIA and Special Forces, had been training Hmong tribesmen to fight the North Vietnamese in Laos since the early 1960s. A socially skillful young Hmong with a magnetic personality named Vang Pao assumed the role as their leader, later to become an almost mythical hero, a Laotian Moses who used a ruthless guerrilla army to avenge the depredations visited on his people by the North Vietnamese and their local affiliate, the Pathet Lao, at the same time addressing Hmong educational, economic and social needs.

Born in 1929, Vang Pao was one of twelve children of subsistence farmer parents who traded goods grown on their mountainous farmlands with the more economically advantaged lowland communities. When he was 13 years old, he was humiliated when his people would come down from the mountains in their bare feet, get treated like underlings of menial status by the storekeepers in the towns, and taunted with the derogatory term Meo, making him feel that he was just another inferior animal in the world. That, he said, was when he dedicated his life to loving and improving life for the Hmong people.

For the next 20 years, he devoted himself to excelling in the military forces of the French and Lao governments. When the US began looking for Laotian leaders to primp for attaining their objectives, he was at the top of the list. One official gushed that he was the personification of Genghis Khan. Vang Pao was already well established as one of the most respected military commanders in the country when he met with Bill Lair of the CIA in 1961. The North Vietnamese and the Pathet Lao were killing his people, and he had no qualms about allying with the Americans to reverse the fortunes of war.

To join the Ravens, Cowboy flew to Thailand where his military record was placed in a top-secret intelligence file and he was "sheep-dipped." His identity was completely erased, and he turned over all personal items that indicated he was an American soldier: dog tags, uniform, and all ID cards. He was sent to Vientiane, Laos where he received a Laotian driver's license, a nickname, and a cover story tagging him as an agricultural adviser. Finally, he was sent to Long Tieng, the second-largest town in Laos even though no maps divulged its existence. Elaborate CIA telecommunications antennas existed next to primitive native dwellings and the locals sauntered down dirt roads with their mules, passing stacks of newly-minted bombs.

The casually attired CIA operatives were given monikers like Black Jack, Showboat, and Borax. The flamboyant pilots had all been a bunch of fuck-ups in the regular Air Force but here they were regarded as being "colorful characters." Rank was largely disregarded as was most of the military protocol. Cowboy loved the place and fit in well with the other off-beat personalities populating the town. He let his hair and beard grow, affected an aggressive, overly-confident stride, and sported a Stetson hat that he tipped with great flourish whenever he encountered an attractive woman. He liked setting the US Air Force pilots stationed at Udorn, who flew T-28s (a radial-engine counter-insurgency aircraft), straight about what was what on the ground in Laos and wouldn't hesitate to dress them down if they claimed authority or prestige that they did not deserve. However, he was supportive and encouraging to the Hmong T-28 pilots who had overcome prejudices and obstacles to arrive at their current positions.

Cowboy's aircraft was a single-engine Cessna L-19/O-1 "Bird Dog" with a top speed of 130 miles per hour — a descendant of the Cessna 170 civilian light airplane produced between 1948 and 1956. Johnny Carson's sidekick, Ed McMahon, flew 85 missions in one during the Korean Conflict, earning six air medals in the process. The characteristics of the plane allowed it to fly low, slow, and close to the battlefield while the pilot observed the enemy and located exploding shells, adjusting the artillery fire using his radio, in the manner of a bird dog used by pheasant hunters. Though his O-1 gathered a lot of bullet holes, he preferred it to the tame duty in Vietnam where he called in many fewer air strikes. He carried a Ka-bar knife, a 0.45 automatic, and enough valuables to bribe someone if need be. In the event of impending capture and torture by hostile forces, he had a vial of quick-acting poison available to avoid a prolonged and painful death.

Cowboy and the other Ravens regarded General Vang Pao as their de facto leader despite the official chain of command. Vang was both fearsome and diplomatic. He had himself been shot up so badly that Cowboy likened him to the old equipment on his ranch, held together with baling wire and duct tape. Vang was able to get contentious tribes with different values and customs to work together toward a common goal. He would show respect toward his brave troops and express grief when they were lost. Yet he could kill anyone disloyal ruthlessly with no qualms or regrets. He rejected Ravens who didn't perform up to his standards and sent them back to Vietnam. He sent the men in his army who were in the best fighting shape into brutal high-risk situations, resulting in a high casualty rate. Of the remainder, about 60% were youngsters between 10 and 16 years of age. The rest were over 45 years old. As his army decreased in size and effectiveness, Vang placed more and more demands and responsibility on the American air controllers under his command, increasing their casualty rate also.

One time Cowboy figured out the location of a Pathet Lao installation that was responsible for killing many Ravens. He fired a white phosphorus rocket at the site and the responding F-4 pilots from an aircraft carrier hit the white smoke from his rocket. When he returned to base, he learned that the targeted site and the 37 mm anti-aircraft gun alongside it had both been destroyed but they were on the off-limits list of the American Embassy. He had broken one of the infrangible rules. The ambassador was all bent out of shape and ordered the air attache to investigate. Cowboy was in hot water.

But General Vang Pao intervened, arguing that the idea of "rules of war" was an oxymoron and should be relaxed since there was no such thing as humane treatment when the enemy was trying to kill you. According to one of their newspapers, the Pathet Lao wanted to eliminate all the Hmong, every last vestige of them. Vang Pao and his soldiers were fighting ruthlessly and desperately because they were in an existential battle. If they did not prevail, there would be no Hmong.

The more they associated with him, the more Cowboy and the other Ravens began to think highly of Vang Pao and his band of crusaders. Vang, in turn, learned to respect the gutsiness of the rag-tag group of air controllers. As their small planes got shot full of holes, he saw them as dedicated and like-minded warriors in the battle for freedom.

But Air Force officers based in Udorn, Thailand weren't pleased with not being in control of the obstreperous Ravens, who were using US air power as they pleased, even wrecking expensive equipment with abandon and disregarding official reconnaissance photos as useless. They began to complain and put restrictions on when the Ravens could fly, forcing them to stay on the ground more than they wanted.

As Vang's army shrunk in size and age, they didn't have the number of troops on the ground to take over and hold areas pinpointed by the Ravens and destroyed by Air Force firepower. The Ravens decided to augment their usual targeting function and fly three planes in formation with two crewmen in each plane. The pilot with the greatest skill in maneuvering through the mountains during heavy cloud cover would take the lead.

The Ravens in the backseats of the aircraft, armed with an assortment of bombs, grenades, and machine guns from a secret stockpile, would fire out the window at the North Vietnamese troops below. The whole idea was a bit insane and quite illegal. The air attache wanted to court-martial the lot of them, but, again, Vang Pao came to the rescue, convincing the powers-that-be that his band of fighters was still of value to US interests, especially now when their war was not going well. He even managed to have medals awarded to most of the Ravens, much to the consternation of the officers from Udorn.

∞

After his tour of duty, Cowboy returned to the ranch in Montana. His father died, his mother moved into town, and his oldest brother assumed management of the operation. He thought he might get the same sense of excitement that he experienced in Laos by trying a job using some of his military skills — blowing up smokestacks and old buildings. It was fun for a while blowing up stuff but it had no significant purpose to it. Nothing could match the emotional intensity of flying with the Ravens, where you lived by your wits, fought the good fight, and didn't have to be at the beck and call of some idiot supervisor.

He didn't much care for the mood of the country, what with all the war protests and complaints about atrocities committed by American troops, the blaming and denials. This will never do, he thought. I've got to see if I can lead a normal life without running around like some kind of a nut, chasing the next adrenaline rush. I need some solitary time to clear my head of all the chatter, the conflicting voices, the exciting but haunting memories of Laos, and all the friends I left buried in the mountains.

Cowboy started dating an old girlfriend, Lois, the daughter of another rancher. Lois loved animals, nature, and the free and independent life that existed in earlier days on the range. She could ride and rope and throw small steers, just like Cowboy, and she didn't need any thrills other than those that were run-of-the-mill in that context. When one of the feed suppliers for the ranch invited Cowboy to make a bid on driving a small herd of horses across two counties to another ranch, he jumped at the chance and asked Lois if she would accompany him. Together they plotted the route, got the required permissions from property owners, obtained the necessary health certifications from veterinarians, calculated the supplies they would need for themselves and the horses to make the journey, arranged to have what couldn't be carried brought to them by truck along the way, and estimated costs plus a reasonable profit.

The adventure turned out to be a great success and lots of fun for the couple that would soon marry. They camped out under the stars, ate, drank, and sang around a campfire, and made a good return on the investment of their time. Soon known as "the drover duet," the go-to resource for moving domestic herds of horses, cattle, or sheep from one place to another over land, they began getting more requests for their services. When they had a large herd to move, they would recruit local ranch hands to assist and they would add more Australian Shepherds or Blue Healers to their canine workforce. At times, they would cross state boundaries, and once they even herded a group of steers from Mexico to a feedlot in southern Arizona.

Between jobs the drover duet would hang out in small towns near their last destination, keeping in touch by telephone with their base at the family ranch near Deer River. It was in one of those small towns that Cowboy developed a passion for frontier justice. A ten-year-old girl had been kidnapped, raped, and murdered, and the prime suspect was an itinerant farm laborer from south of the border. There was a long trial during which the state could marshal only circumstantial evidence and the defense claimed prejudicial attitudes on the part of the prosecution and possibly the jury as well. The judge declared it a mistrial and the prosecution decided not to expend the funds necessary to ask for a retrial, so the defendant went free.

A small group of old cowpokes and ranchers were so outraged that such an abhorrent crime should go unavenged that they formed a vigilante organization to see what they could do to bring about justice. They were convinced that the former defendant had committed the crime and that he had gotten away with it only because he had a slick, unscrupulous lawyer who was able to unfairly take advantage of defects in the justice system.

Cowboy, hearkening back to his days with the Ravens and Vang Pao, decided there was an expedient way to determine the truth and dispense a more appropriate decree. They would simply abduct the accused and grill him in such a way that he would voluntarily confess to having committed the crime. They did so, and when the frightened roustabout lived up to their expectations by describing in detail what he had done with the young girl, details that matched the physical evidence in the case, they were again overcome with revulsion and unanimously and quickly dispensed their verdict. Cowboy pulled the trigger. He had no misgivings about what he had done, certain that it was what the little girl would have wanted, had she lived. No doubts, that is, until people reading about the death of the former defendant in the newspapers began to question the wisdom of citizens taking the law into their own hands.

Cowboy and his wife continued with this throwback style of life for 20 years. But the rugged demands of his work — the hours in the saddle, sleeping on the hard cold ground, wrestling stubborn animals, the less than balanced diet – took their toll on Cowboy. He had chronic back pain and he developed a limp that wasn't assuaged by shots of red-eye. Their last delivery of a herd of horses to a new guest ranch left them in Eagle Point, Oregon. It was at a local bar that he learned about Vetlandia and decided to ride over and see if they could do anything about his medical problems.

∞

In a flashback to the famous murder trial, the TV screen shows the white Bronco driving along the Los Angeles freeway with supporters holding up signs cheering OJ on. A chorus of boos is heard from the patients watching in the Vetlandia day room. The scene on the screen shifts to the jury listening to tape recordings of Mark Furman making racial slurs and bragging about his tough approach to law enforcement. Soon, Johnnie

Cochran is seen, holding up a leather glove and delivering the oft-repeated phrase. "If it doesn't fit, you must acquit." The veterans were all transfixed by what they were watching on the TV screen, occasionally blurting out snide remarks about the bias of the majority black jury and the incompetence of the prosecution lawyers and their witnesses.

A cacophony arose in the viewing audience when the verdict was read. "That sonofabitch got away with murder. Now he's on trial for robbery. What's wrong with our fucking courts anyway?"

"That's just not right. Something has to be done about it."

Cowboy watched the reactions of the viewers, trying to assess if any of the onlookers had the degree of commitment to do something about it. The veteran sitting next to him appeared to be somewhat agitated by the program and the reactions of the veterans.

"Do you think we have a miscarriage of justice in this case, young fella?" Cowboy softly posed the question to Tom Ward.

"God, I don't know," said Tom. "The physical evidence and the motive all seem to point toward him but there weren't any eye-witnesses except maybe the dog and he can't testify. I know there's somebody I'd like to kill," he chuckled, "but I wouldn't have the balls to pull it off and I sure as hell couldn't afford a team of lawyers like OJ."

"Oh, so you're identifying with the perp rather than the victim, then?" questioned Cowboy, innocently.

"I wasn't thinking about it that way," said Tom. "I guess I could identify with both the victim and the aggressor. I was a victim and I'd like to get even for what happened to me, so that makes me an aggressor, I guess."

"I see," said Cowboy. "Don't suppose you'd like to tell me what happened?"

"No. I don't want to talk about it. I just had some trouble on the road and I'd...," he paused, "I'd just like to forget about it. It's over and done."

"Yeah, I gotcha," said Cowboy in a comforting manner. "I've had some of those times too. Say, I'm Pete, by the way, Pete

Steele." He stuck out his hand. "They've taken to calling me Cowboy since I got here."

"Tom Ward," came the reply, shaking the offered hand. "Cowboy? Is that what you do?"

"Well, I'm a drover. Me and my wife we herd horses, cattle and sheep cross-country. Been doing it ever since I got back from Vietnam, well Laos actually."

"Laos? My dad was stationed in Thailand, at a secret base they called Udorn."

"Udorn? I've been there many times. I was with the Ravens in Laos. We were flying light spotter planes and would call in air strikes for the US and Laotian Air Forces stationed in Udorn, sometimes the Navy planes on carriers off the coast. Was your dad with the Air Force?"

"No, he was with Army Special Forces."

"Did he make it back?"

"No. He died when he was home on leave under unusual circumstances, I guess.

"Hmm, yeah, unusual circumstances. What branch of the service were you in?"

"I was in the army, a mobile missile crew. Got injured over in Germany when some asshole decided to move the missile when I was on top, doing some maintenance. Hit my head on a tree on the way down and have had trouble ever since."

"Is that the guy you want to bump off?"

"Huh? No. Oh, that was someone else. Did you ever hear of a guy named Vang Pao over there?"

"Hear of him? Shit, he was my boss. Not my Air Force boss but he was the guy that us Ravens answered to over there. The General was one tough son of a gun as long as you didn't cross him and then he could be ruthless. He always treated us well and we respected his bravery and courage. He did a lot for his people, still does I'm told. He lives down in California. There are Hmong refugees down there and in Minnesota and Wisconsin."

"Do you know if he had anything to do with the Special Forces in Thailand?"

"I don't know but I probably can find out for you. I still have contact with a couple of the Hmong Ravens that came over. Wondering what your dad did over there, huh?"

"Yeah. I'd like to know if he was involved in anything over there that would make him want to kill himself. I know it's been a long time but I'd kinda like to know and put it to rest in my mind."

"What was your dad's name?"

"John Thomas Ward"

"And he was in Special Forces at Udorn. Is that right?" Cowboy asked as he wrote down the information.

"Yeah, that's it. I'd really appreciate it if you can find anything out. I'm on Section 3 and I work over in the library most days."

CHAPTER 9
The Trial

Mindful of his promise to find out any information he could about the activities of Tom's father in Thailand, Cowboy made a call to an old friend, a former T28 pilot and member of the Hmong community in the Fresno area. After exchanging pleasantries and reminiscing about their time together in Laos, he got to the point of his call.

"Hey, my friend, do you think there is any way I could talk with the General for a few minutes? I'm trying to find out some information about a guy that worked with Special Forces over in Udorn, Thailand. He died back in 1970 under strange circumstances while at home on leave and his son is wondering what he may have been involved in over there."

"You haven't heard the news, have you?"

"News. What news? I'm sitting in a VA facility up in Oregon."

"The General's been arrested!"

"What! What the hell for?"

"For violation of the Neutrality Act and trying to overthrow a sovereign government. That's what the feds claim, anyway."

"Holy shit! I know he has been auguring to go back over there for years but I thought he gave all that up when his attempt at negotiating a deal for the Hmong with the Laos government failed."

Indeed, the US government had arrested Vang Pao along with Lt. Colonel Harrison Ullrich Jack, a respected West Point graduate, member of the California National Guard, and former Ranger during the Vietnam war, who had been working with Vang Pao to help Hmong refugees. Several other members of the Hmong community were arrested and all were charged with a supposed plot to overthrow the communist government of Laos.

The purported conspiracy began with the remnants of Vang Pao's army that remained in Laos after the war. The lowland Lao along with the Vietnamese communist government was attempting to systematically eliminate all Hmong who collaborated with the imperialist invading Americans, killing some 10,000 of them. About 300,000 fled to Thailand and half that many resettled in the United States. The remainder of those abandoned by the US government constituted small bands of CIA-trained fighters, the largest being the Ethnic Liberation Organization of Laos with a few hundred members who carried out small-scale operations. Mostly, they lived on the run with their families in the jungle, surviving on wild plants and trying to evade being killed by the Laotian security forces.

Ullrich Jack and Vang Pao had talked about getting 500 AK-47s to give to the insurgents so they could protect themselves while making their way to relative safety in Thailand. Jack approached one of his contacts, presumably a defense contractor, about making the purchase and the guy immediately went to the Bureau of Alcohol, Tobacco, Firearms and Explosives (ATF) and reported the conversation.

The next person to appear on the scene, unbidden, was an ambitious undercover ATF agent who called Jack and told him he could provide weapons for the Hmong to defend themselves and that it did not involve taking over the country or hurting people. He secretly recorded a conversation with the 12 people involved in the plot at a Thai restaurant and then walked them over to an RV filled with machine guns, antitank rockets, grenade launchers, land mines, and other weapons. He convinced Jack to brainstorm with him on the problem of what was needed to effectively carry out the plan. The participants were duly impressed with what the two of them came up with and what the fake arms dealer had to offer (including obtaining trained mercenaries). They suspected or, more accurately, hoped that the "arms dealer" actually worked for the CIA. They didn't come up with the ideas, but they liked what they heard being proposed.

The agent suggested they write up a 90-day plan for how they would accomplish their goals, which they subsequently called

Operation Popcorn (Political Opposition Party's Coup Operation to Rescue the Nation). Dang Vang, an unemployed 48-year-old business proposal writer, was paid $5000 for composing the document that outlined a plan with a $28 million budget. It detailed the costs for weapons ($10 million), hiring local mercenaries and 1000 men to provide security, paying off coup leaders, political and military consultants, and buying office supplies. They would recruit former special forces soldiers to fight in their militia and train Hmong-Americans through the California Highway Patrol (CHP) for security operations, the graduates later being asked to abandon CHP and move to Laos for law enforcement jobs.

About 200 law-enforcement agents in California launched the sensational bust, arresting eight former Laotians and the former army colonel, and claiming they were involved in a plot to overthrow the government of Laos. The ATF took pride in stopping a humongous attack on the Lao government, disregarding the fact that the Hmong that remained in Laos were distributed too sparsely and were too battered to carry out a coup, and that the Hmong-Americans trying to supply them were simply too muddled and inefficient to provide the necessary wherewithal. The government's case was weakened by the undercover ATF agent's role in ginning up the plot and his offer to obtain fantastic weapons and American-trained mercenaries but the defendants were jailed, nevertheless.

"Yeah, we are in quite an uproar around here and I can't help with your request right now," continued the voice on the phone. "We're setting up protest rallies and getting organized to fight the assholes trying to paint all us Hmong as terrorists. Tell ya what, though, I can give you the name of someone that might be able to help you. His name is Russel "Rusty" Neil but we always used to call him Rusty Nail. He used to be a Master Sergeant in Special Forces stationed at Udorn. He knows Harrison Jack and even lives in the same town. Tell him I'll vouch for you You got something to write down his phone number?"

Cowboy scrambled to find a pen and paper and then said, "Yeah, go ahead." After repeating the number back to him for confirmation, Cowboy expressed his gratitude and offered encouraging words to his friend in his efforts to free the general.

The next day, Cowboy dialed the number and stated to the voice on the other end that he was referred to him by his friend, that he had been with the Ravens in Laos and was now acting on behalf of a younger veteran who wanted to find out about his father's activities during the war.

"You were with the Ravens, huh? Who was your superior officer?

"We were required to report to the ambassador but Vang Pao was the commander who made the operational decisions."

"Yeah. What was the kid's father's name again?

"John Thomas Ward"

"Sounds vaguely familiar. I think I may have known him. Give me a few days and let me check in some of my old records. Give me your name, address and a phone number where I can get back to you."

Cowboy knew the delay was in order for Rusty to check out his legitimacy and he expected it. You could never be too cautious when an unknown person comes asking for information about one of your associates.

Four days later, Cowboy's Motorola Razr V3 came to life while he was walking down the hall and headed toward his room. He stepped up his pace when he realized who was calling him back.

"Yeah, Rusty Neil here. Sorry about the delay but I had to check you out and then dig into some old shit I haven't looked at in decades. I think I may have something that could be of interest to the young man you mentioned last time we talked. His father and I crossed paths a few times over there."

"Just a second. Let me get some paper and a pen to take notes," said Cowboy. "OK, go ahead." He listened attentively, asked a few questions, and dutifully jotted down the relevant information. At the end of the conversation, Cowboy thanked Neil profusely and offered to return the favor if he could.

"Tell the young man that he can call me anytime if he has more questions. You still flying?" asked Neil.

"Once in a while, enough to keep my license alive. Mostly, I ride horses now. My wife and I make a living as drovers, heard livestock over open ground."

"Wow, that's quite a change from what you used to do. Sounds like you've had an interesting life. You should come down here and visit sometime. We can drink a few beers and swap war stories."

"I'd like that. Maybe after I get my body repaired."

Cowboy rushed over to Tom's room, notes in hand.

"I've got some information about your father," he blurted out as Tom welcomed him inside. Tony was there and offered to leave if they wanted privacy, but Tom insisted he should stay, that he trusted Tony to be discrete about any shocking details that might emerge and could provide moral support if he freaked out.

Cowboy began to recite what Neil had told him. "Seems that your dad and Rusty Neil both were involved in training Vang Pao's army. Rusty was a weapons expert and taught the new recruits how to shoot rifles and pistols, place explosive charges, and use Claymores and Rocket Propelled Grenades. Your dad taught small unit tactics, survival, close combat, and first aid. Rusty said your dad was a decent kind of guy and was good at what he did but, after about three years of seeing the trainees get younger and younger and the death toll mount for these child soldiers, he started to get burned out. The deaths of these young boys that he had worked so closely with really bothered him. It tore at his heart.

"He started saying that he thought the world should know what was going on in Laos, that maybe then the government would commit some ground troops to the effort and spare these Hmong children. He had heard about the anti-war demonstrations back home by Vietnam vets and, while he didn't think the war should be abandoned, he started threatening to divulge to the public the sacrifice of these young lives. His superiors told him to keep his mouth shut and decided he needed a break, so they sent him home on leave. That's when he died."

"Did he know about my dad's supposed suicide?"

"Yes, he did and he didn't think it made any more sense than did your dad's friends and your mom. He doubted that it was a real suicide and suggested the place to look for any likely perpetrators was in the Nixon White House. Specifically, he said to see what you could find out about the role of Chuck Colson. He was Nixon's hatchet man during that time period."

Tom straightened up. "You mean to say that my dad's death may have been orchestrated by the White House? My god, that's incredible."

Tony chimed in, "Maybe not so improbable as you might think. There were a lot of dirty tricks going on in that administration. They were autocratic and thought they could get away with anything. Morality didn't figure into their thinking."

"Jesus!" exclaimed Tom. "Holy cow. I can't believe this. Shit, my family wiped out by our fucking president or one of his henchmen. I've got to have some time to get my head around this."

∞

Tom spent many hours at one of the computers in the library looking for information about Charles Colson. He learned that he was called the "evil genius of an evil administration" by David Platz in *Slate* magazine. He found out that he was the author of Nixon's "enemy list" and organized an attack by 200 construction workers using pieces of steel re-bar against 1000 high school and college students who were protesting the Vietnam War and the killings at Kent State. He even orchestrated the event where the union leader who implemented the attack was honored at the White House. Colson had proposed firebombing the Brookings Institution in order to divert attention while his co-conspirators retrieved politically damaging documents. He received orders to "destroy the young demagogue," John Kerry, before he developed a following like Ralph Nader. He tried to smear John Ellsberg by leaking information from an FBI file on him to the press. He recruited E. Howard Hunt to find information that would prove damaging to the Democrats and he was involved in the cover-up of the Watergate crimes. Tom thought Colson certainly sounded like the kind of slimy bastard who could arrange for his dad's death if he was so inclined.

But he also learned that Colson, after serving seven months in prison, had claimed he had been "born again," becoming an Evangelical Christian. After his professed conversion, he founded an organization that worked for prison reform and wrote several books. He collected 15 honorary doctorate degrees over the years since Watergate and won a one million dollar prize for progress in religion, which he donated to his Prison Fellowship. George Bush even awarded him a Presidential Citizens Medal.

What the fuck! What kind of justice is that? And now, the sonofabitch is dead from a brain hemorrhage. Shit! I'm not going to get any revenge, no satisfaction, by following that dead-end lead. What am I going to do, go dance on the motherfucker's grave?

While Tom was struggling to let it all sink in, he developed a close bond with Cowboy and began to reveal more about himself and his experience, including the episode with the truck driver. As he related the story, Cowboy encouraged him to express his feelings and he was again overcome with the humiliation and fear he experienced at the time. And then there was the rage. Cowboy was sympathetic and supportive. Eventually, he asked Tom if he would like to obtain some justice for what had happened to him.

"Justice?" replied Tom. "What do you mean? What kind of justice are you talking about?"

"How would you like to catch this joker and hold him captive while we put him on trial in our own little courtroom? If he's found guilty, you get to do whatever you want to him?"

"Who is this 'we' you're talking about? Who is the jury? How would you find him anyway?"

"Well, I belong to this organization that believes that the usual court doesn't always get things right. Guilty defendants often get off on a technicality or damning evidence is suppressed because some smart lawyer finds a loophole someplace. So what we do is we get all the evidence and don't allow technicalities to get in the way of a fair verdict. Sometimes we have to apply a little pressure to get a confession. As for how we would be able to find him, well we have members that are very skilled at tracking people down and securing them so they can stand trial."

"It's a vigilante outfit, then?"

"Some people might call it that but we like to think of ourselves as ordinary citizens that are avengers of miscarried justice. We set the record straight, balance the scales, bring some satisfaction to those who have been wronged by the perpetrator but also by the court. I have no doubt that there is a universal force that intends for there to be a moral balance in the world. We are part of that force. In a way, we are doing God's work. We have done this many times and have no regrets. The victims of injustice that we have worked with have been grateful that someone stepped in to help them."

Tom began to imagine standing in a room with the naked truck driver bound to a chair. Vacillating between glee and trepidation, his mind devised various ways to vent his fury on the man who visited so much pain, fear, and humiliation on him when he was unable to resist. Images came to him of beating the man with a club, cutting him with his own knife, choking him as he drew him up by a rope tied round his neck, cutting his penis off.

"I've imagined what I might do if I ever met up with that bastard again. It kind of scares me what diabolic scenarios I can come up with. I want him to feel what I felt – the fear, the terror, the horror, the humiliation and mortification! The sonofabitch deserves it, for sure!"

Again weighing in on the positive side, Cowboy said, "It has given our guys a lot of satisfaction knowing that some motherfucker, some worthless, contemptible low-life has not gotten away with his crime and that righteousness has prevailed. Although most of the survivors of the perp's evil deeds don't know who we are, a lot of them have made public expressions of their gratitude to the so-called powers-that-be for leveling out the scales of justice."

"I don't know," said Tom. "It sounds dangerous and I'm sure it must be illegal. What are the chances of getting caught?"

"So far, it hasn't happened. We are very scrupulous about cleaning up any clues that we might leave at the scenes of capture, interrogation, and sentencing. We're always cautious, never do we get over-confident about how smart we are. We know the things that usually trip people up when they try to outsmart the law and we go to great lengths to avoid them."

"How would you go about it in my case? What would you do?"

"Well, first off, we'd try to locate the truck driver that did it. A couple of our members are really good with the computer, so they would locate all the records for trucking companies using that stretch of road for the period, say three months on either side of your incident. We'd narrow down this batch of possibilities further by pulling out only tanker trucks – companies that haul liquids of one sort or another such as oil, milk, liquid fertilizers, that sort of stuff. Then we'd get the employee or contractor records from those companies and sort them for any with a Texas home address. And we'd check for any that have had complaints made against them or have been arrested for any assault or sex crimes.

"All of this is going to take some time, but when we get it narrowed down to a few prime suspects, we'll see if any are using that route now or in the near future. Then one of our members will go to that restaurant where you were picked up, stake it out, and try to spot the truck and the guy from your description of him. If we get lucky and find a likely offender, we'll watch him for a while to gain more evidence that we got the right guy. We'll record his personal habits — around the truck, while he's driving, when he's in the restaurant — for later use when we want to abduct him. We'll get pictures of him and have you verify it is or is not him."

"Your people would do all this for free?" asked Tom. "That's got to involve a lot of time and effort."

"Yes, it does. We are an organization of volunteers, so money isn't a primary consideration. But we often can figure a way to get compensated for our expenses from the perp," Cowboy smiled.

"I don't know, Cowboy. I don't know. Let me think about it a while."

"Sure," said Cowboy. "Tell ya what, how about we see if we can locate the asshole and then go from there?"

"OK, I guess," Tom replied, hesitatingly.

∞

Tom asked his roommate, Tony, what he thought about getting revenge against someone.

"Well, I guess some people can forgive and forget but most of us try to get even with the person who has caused us injury or has done us wrong in some way. I'm not saying it is the right thing to do, mind you, but we mere mortals, most of us, tend to place it on the turf occupied by games or contests. We think in terms of an eye for an eye, a tooth for a tooth, tit-for-tat, payback, evening the score. That sort of thing.

"During wartime, vengeance is all over the place. There were a lot of guys in Vietnam who were inspired to fight and take risks to avenge their lost comrades. The other side, the Viet Cong, were avenging all the relatives Americans had killed and sometimes getting even for the degradation our guys visited on their women. Some guys wanted to get even with the government for having put them in that hellhole in the first place, so they stole things and disobeyed regulations, acted like old-west outlaws.

"I remember one guy who took vengeance on his platoon second lieutenant. His buddies thought this officer had caused the death of many men in their unit by setting up his Claymores pointed in the wrong direction. About half a dozen men drew straws to see who would take out the officer and this guy got the short straw. Well, he did it. He shot the LT during a skirmish and he was never found out. Later he learned that some trained soldiers position their mines that way on purpose, in preparation for the possibility that the enemy manages to get inside the wire. So then he felt miserable for possibly killing the wrong guy. Ironic, isn't it?"

"But do you think it gives you any relief, any kind of satisfaction? Does it make you feel any better? Does it help to quiet the demons that pursue you at night?" asked Tom.

"I've known some guys who were able to put their anger to rest after having settled some scores. At least that's what they claimed. 'Course they may have just been trying to justify their actions.

"The things I feel bad about weren't really in retaliation for anything. It wasn't really revenge. It was our brutality — my own cruelty — that was used to get information that we thought, or we were told, might save the lives of our guys. It still wasn't right, no matter what the higher-ups may claim. We tortured people and sometimes killed people and there is no way I can justify that. Part of me is a brute, an ogre, and that idea still haunts me."

Tom was silent, wondering how he might feel after laying waste to the life of the person responsible for his nightmares, ongoing anxiety, sense of impending doom, humiliation, and sadness. When he thought of it in the context of his own pain and suffering and allowed his anger to build without putting a lid on it, he could imagine himself being a cold-blooded avenger, the iceman who could delight in watching his victim squirm, snivel, and beg for mercy. Even when his anger subsided, he couldn't feel any empathy toward his nemesis. He was unable to conceive the monster in the tanker truck as a living being deserving of any forgiveness, leniency, forbearance, or mercy. I'm not a saint, some sage, or a guru that can just let an evil deed roll off my back, he thought. I bet I'll feel just great if I give this bastard some of his own medicine.

About a month passed before Cowboy approached Tom in an excited fashion. He had a manila folder in his hand and motioned Tom to follow him to a bench near the fish pond where they could talk without being overheard.

"Guess what," said Cowboy without waiting for an answer. "Our boys got some pictures for you to look at. We think we may have the man that did you dirty. Take a look at these and tell me what you think."

Tom took the stack of pictures and began examining the first one. It showed a tanker truck with the name Great Western painted on it and Tom looked more closely at the cab and the steel bead running above the tank. He could not make out the face of the man standing next to the truck. Flipping past the second photo which was too dark to make out any distinguishing features, Tom uncovered the third, a telephoto of a man's head. Cowboy offered him a magnifying glass and Tom inspected it closely, getting more agitated as he thought he recognized the face of the freaky Texan. He moved on to the other photos and finally to one of the devil himself sitting in a booth inside the restaurant where he had solicited the fateful ride.

"That's him," exclaimed Tom. "That's the goddamn motherfucker who terrorized me, cut me up and buried me in a fucking grave out in the middle of nowhere!"

Tom emitted a strange sound, resembling a kind of growl, as he waved the picture in front of Cowboy's face.

"God damn! God damn! You found the shit-for-brains motherfucker! Where is he? I want to kill the bastard and piss in his skull."

Cowboy grinned and put a reassuring arm around Tom's shoulder. "Just hold on there, pardner. We've still got to round him up and put him on trial. That's the way we do things. You'll get your chance soon enough, don't worry. We know where he lives, so he's not going to get away. What you've done just now is to verify that we got the right guy. Now we'll put the next stage of our operation into play. Just hold tight until I get hold of you again."

Tom could barely contain his glee when he met with Dr. Oldman for his next session. He wanted to tell him about locating the truck driver and the plans for him but knew that the doctor would disapprove. After all, he had warned Tom when he first began therapy that he would have to turn him in to the authorities if he indicated he was about to commit a crime. But the therapist noticed Tom's elevated mood and commented on it.

"You seem to have a new lease on life, Tom. Has something happened to change the way you look at things?"

"No," Tom lied. As a diversion, he reported, truthfully, "Well, I've had a good time at work lately. My boss is giving me more responsibility and says she likes my work and my attitude. And my diabetes-seizure condition has been kind of stable for a few weeks now, so that is hopeful. I'm getting to know more of the guys around here and they share some of their experiences with me. Turns out there are a lot of interesting characters that end up here. Maybe I'll write a book about it someday."

"Sounds like a good project for you, Tom. You seem to have a real appreciation for the variety in people's character, motivation and experience. Are you taking notes? It's always a good idea to take notes so you can recover your observations and bright ideas when you need them."

For several minutes, the conversation focused on ways and resources for developing Tom's literary talents while Tom tried to figure out how to get his therapist's opinion on revenge without being too obvious about his intentions. He started by nonchalantly mentioning his roommate's comments on vengeance and asking what he thought of that.

"Well he is right about a lot of things. People do seem to operate with the concept of a just world in mind. They assume people get what they deserve, that good will be rewarded and evil will be punished. There is this idea that there is, or should be, a moral equilibrium in the world and that there is some kind of universal force, like karma, that tends to keep it in balance. So we have these sayings — what goes around comes around, you reap what you sow, the chickens come home to roost. There was a lot of research on these beliefs back in the '60s and '70s, much of it focusing on blaming the victim and rationalizing injustice by the notion that one gets what he deserves rather than that the nature of an outcome can be determined by a situation."

"What was the result of the research?" asked Tom.

"There was a lot of support for the hypothesis that people do tend to blame the suffering party in calamities of various sorts — rape, illness, accidents, domestic violence — by making attributions about the character of the victim rather than the nature of the situation. They believe the person got what they deserved or should have been more careful about their behavior and avoided the situation in the first place."

"Sounds a lot like what many of the patients here feel about the way some staff treat them, like they are getting blamed for their illness."

"I'm sorry to say, that could very well be," said Dr. Oldman.

"What about people who seek revenge? They have been provoked to violence by some asshole who has harmed them. Do you think they have just cause to retaliate?"

"Sure, they have just cause to seek retribution since violence done to an innocent victim is a transgression of the social norms most people subscribe to. Some analysts think that our rapid emotional reaction to seek revenge helped early man reinforce those social norms and build stronger bonds between members of the group."

"So there may be a positive side to revenge?" Tom ventured.

"Yes, but just cause is not the same as rational justice as meted out by a court using laws and judgment by a jury or judge as the standard for establishing guilt. In other words, even though an individual may have a good reason for seeking revenge, he may not be the right person to be rendering the verdict and executing the sentence. Religions often counsel that vengeance lies in the domain of the Lord. To use a medical analogy, it's His scope of practice, not yours.

"Another thing. When a person is trying to decide what to do after being unjustly harmed, I think he should consider the consequences of his act of vengeance as well."

"What do you mean?" asked Tom.

"Well, several researchers found that people think they will feel better after getting their revenge, but follow-up studies showed that they don't. Victims actually brood more about the injustice and the perpetrator than they did before getting their payback. They mull it over even more after they exacted their revenge than before. There doesn't seem to be any universal cathartic effect for having gotten even with an attacker.

"Other research showed that people are not very good at predicting how they will feel after some future action, so that may be the reason for this effect. One study showed that women's empathy centers in the brain light up when they think about exacting revenge while in men it is the reward centers that light up, so there may be a sex difference. But women aren't the only ones that can feel empathy, so the sex difference might really be an artifact due to personality differences associated with sex. There are empathetic men too but the researchers didn't measure that in their study.

"Narcissists, self-centered individuals, tend to be more vengeful because of their thin skin when it comes to others making aspersions on their reputation. And neurotics with a problem in controlling their anger have been found to continue to seek revenge two and a half years after originally being harmed.

"You have to consider how you incorporate an act of retribution into you own identity. How are you going think of yourself after you commit this act of aggression? Will you think of yourself as a pure avenging angel or as a cruel, brutish person who has stooped to the level of your attacker? Here again, you have to remember that predicting how you feel after the fact may not be easy. You may deceive yourself, overlook or minimize some significant detail and later wish you had taken a closer look."

∞

Two weeks had passed when Cowboy caught up with Tom in the hallway on a Friday afternoon.

"Hey, man. Be at the parking lot in front of the Administration building at 8:00. Bring a change of clothes. I borrowed a car and we'll go for a little ride."

"What's up?" Tom inquired.

"I'll tell you later," Cowboy replied as he backed down the hallway. "It's a surprise. It'll be fun!"

Tom had dinner with Tony at the chow hall. Tony had a meeting of the stamp club that evening which gave Tom the opportunity to go to his room, stuff some clothes in a large shopping bag without being observed, and make his way to the parking lot. Cowboy was standing next to a nondescript older model Chrysler sedan with the driver-side door open. Spotting Tom, he waved for him to come over, got behind the wheel, and opened the passenger door, beckoning Tom to get in. Cowboy drove out the main entrance to Vetlandia and turned left.

"Where are we going?" asked Tom.

"Up to Shady Cove. Got a cabin up there alongside the river, a quiet spot where we won't be bothered. Some of our associates will be there."

"How long are we going to be there? I've got to be back at work in the library on Monday."

"Oh, it shouldn't take that long, least ways it never has taken more than a couple of days."

Tom was getting anxious. Were they going to plot how to capture the trucker? Did they already have him? Were they going to torture him? Oh my god, what do they expect me to do? He was still processing the pros and cons of vengeance and was not yet sure of his final position on the matter. Decision time might arrive much sooner than he expected.

A few miles short of Shady Cove, Cowboy took a narrow dirt road off to the left of the highway, drove about a quarter mile toward the river, and then turned left on another narrow dirt road, designated Linden Lane by an old wooden sign at the intersection, going about a half mile. The large one-story cabin with cedar shake shingles was raised on stilts to avoid the occasional floods in the area. Two cars were parked in the driveway and Cowboy snugged his vehicle up to the one on the right.

The two new arrivals climbed the stairs to the main entrance and walked in. Six men were seated around a table, drinking coffee and devouring two large pizzas. Cowboy introduced each of them to Tom by name, which Tom forgot almost immediately. They all smiled as they appraised Tom who thought they looked like friendly, ordinary middle-aged men.

"Have some pizza," one suggested as he offered paper plates and pointed at a third box yet unopened.

"Coffee or soda?" asked another.

"This here is our jury and I'm the seventh member and the foreman," said Cowboy as he sat down and took a slice of the pie. "Tom, have a seat and I'll explain our procedure.

"First, we'll have you confront the defendant, acting kind of like a prosecutor, and state the offense you are accusing him of. This is considered your opening statement. You can enter your own testimony by confirming that he is, in fact, the man who assaulted you and describing the crime he committed. Since you won't be calling any other witnesses, you can proceed to interrogate him. Ask him where he was on the date in question, if he drives such and such a rig, if he has a rope and shovel in his cab, if he uses a gel or lotion as part of his work, that sort of thing.

"Now, if the defendant denies the charges, denies that he was at the locations you mention, denies he had the specified implements, then our jury members who are familiar with the facts determined in the initial investigation are allowed to testify as to those facts and cross-examine the defendant. There is a table with various instruments they may want to use to facilitate an accurate response from the defendant. You may want to pitch in there too. Of course, a confession moves the process along more quickly.

"If the defendant does confess, then we move directly to the sentencing stage of the trial. If he continues to deny his crime or denies our legitimacy in passing judgment, the jury makes it's closing arguments and votes as to his guilt or innocence. Then we consider the penalty he should pay. The defendant's victim — you, in this case — is given the first shot at suggesting the punishment to be dispensed but other members of the committee can voice their own opinions. Finally, we all vote on the sentence and designate the persons to carry it out. I think that about covers it. Do you have any questions?"

"Do you have him here, in this building?" asked Tom.

"Yes, he is here, shackled to a bed in the back room and sedated. He has been fed and allowed to go to the bathroom. We are going to start the trial tomorrow morning."

Tom didn't sleep much that night, going over in his mind the events that transpired during the assault and rehearsing what he might say the next day. He dozed off toward daybreak, awakening to the sounds of seven men taking turns using the lone bathroom, the clatter of skillets on the stove and a refrigerator door opening and closing, and the smell of bacon and eggs frying. Staggering out to the kitchen, he poured himself a cup of coffee to help brush away the cobwebs in his head. A man brought him a plate graced with two eggs, bacon, toast, and hash browns. He put one of his eggs on the hash browns, broke the yoke, and hoped that the delicious blend of flavors would overcome the butterflies in his stomach.

It was nearly 9:30 before all the men had finished washing the dishes, had their final cups of coffee, and gone outside to smoke. Before 10:00 they had all the furniture in the large living room arranged with a steel straight-backed chair against the inside wall, facing a semicircular arrangement of chairs and a sofa. All the men wore facial masks of some sort that hid most of their features and several wore caps or hats. A table arrayed with various sharp objects, surgical knives and scissors, clamping devices, hammers, and electrical devices with wires running to alligator clips was displayed for all to see. Cowboy began the proceedings.

"Let this trial of Billy Joe Cawthorne begin. Ralph, you and Dennis bring the defendant in and secure him to the chair."

The two burly men brought the struggling captive into the room, forced him down on the chair, and bound his hands behind him and his ankles to the chair. He looked pale, his hair was disheveled, his shirt was torn, and there were bruises on his face. Tom's heart sank when he saw the incarnation of his nightmares, a momentary panic quickly assuaged by Cawthorne's fruitless attempts to move. Tom stood transfixed by the figure in front of him, focusing on the details of his facial features until Cowboy jarred him into action.

"OK, Tom. Go ahead."

Tom glanced at Cowboy and then moved closer to the ghoul from the truck stop, the fiend who haunted his daily thoughts. His plan was to overwhelm Cawthorne with his memory of details of the encounter, to paint him into a corner where he couldn't deny what he had done. If necessary, he would play the role of a crazed and vengeful maniac and imply that he was going to harm him, even though he had no intention of going that far.

"Do you remember me, shithead?" asked Tom.

"Naw. Never seen you before, you fuckin' faggot. What the hell did your goons pick me up for? Where the hell am I?"

"Are you the asshole from down Texas way that fucked his sister while your mother watched?"

"What are you talking about? My mother and sister are dead."

"Yeah, and your sister got murdered by some trick she was turning, didn't she?"

Billy Joe Cawthorne squinted at Tom through bloodshot eyes, a question on his face, but he made no sound.

"Aren't you the prick that served time for rape while claiming it was consensual, excuse me, consexual?"

"Well, it was consexual. Those jurors just wanted to make an example of me. She was a little slut, a floozy. I should never have been convicted."

"Have you ever been at the Little America truck stop in Flagstaff?"

"Yeah. That's on my regular route. Shit, thousands of truckers go through there."

"I approached you asking for a ride to Vegas at that restaurant about six months ago. You remember that, don't you?"

"I give lots of hitchhikers rides. What's wrong with that?"

"I'm not asking about a lot of hitchhikers. Do you deny that you picked me up at that truck stop?"

"I don't remember you. Why should I?"

Growing impatient with Cawthorne's evasiveness, Tom figured he had to up the ante. He walked over to the table and picked up one sharp instrument after another, bouncing them on his other hand, as if to feel the heft of them. Picking up a straight razor with a pearl handle, he unfolded it and ran the blade along the back of his left hand, shaving off a few strands of hair.

"Yeah, this will do," said Tom as he moved closer to the man in the chair. Waving the razor in front of Billy Joe's face, he inquired, "Now I'd like to know if you are going to continue to deny that you ever gave me a ride in your truck."

"What are you going to do with that thing? Get away from me." Cawthorne exclaimed as he squirmed in his chair.

Tom reached down and grabbed the sleeve of the man's shirt, holding it up and away from his arm. With a swift slashing motion, he sliced the sleeve from elbow to shoulder. Then he cut and ripped the tattered sleeve off the shirt, revealing a large tattoo of a lizard.

"You ever have a tattoo removed," asked Tom. "I know a guy who had one taken off with a laser. 'Course we don't have that kind of fancy equipment here so I guess we'll have to make do with what we've got."

Tom brought the razor blade just into contact with Cawthorne's skin. "Now, let's see, I guess I'll start here and ...," as he allowed his voice to trail off. Straightening up, he moved the blade further away, gazing into his prisoner's eyes to see if he had elicited the fear he intended.

But Cawthorne was appraising Tom too and noted a slight tremor in his hand, a tell that he took to mean that his inquisitor lacked the nerve to actually slice him up.

"Get the fuck away from me with that thing, you fucking wuss! You don't have the balls to use it anyway. I don't know what you did with that truck driver you're talking about but you're the kind of pansy that would try to set up some poor innocent sonofabitch to get your rocks off. You're the one that should be on trial here!"

Tom raised his razor hand as if to deal a deadly blow but something stopped him and, puzzled, he looked at the jury.

Ralph stood and said, "Tom, you're new at this. Here, let me show you how it's done. Taking the razor from Tom, he sliced the remainder of Cawthorne's shirt into small pieces that fell from his torso. Motioning to Dennis he said, "Help me get this bum-fucker up so we can get his pants off." That accomplished, with the prisoner as naked as a jaybird, he pushed him back down onto the chair and said, "Now let's see if we can get this piece of shit to tell us a straight story."

Ralph picked up a page of the newspaper and ran the razor over the edge of it, bending the paper and finally cutting through. "I think we need something a little sharper." Walking over to the table, he picked up a surgical knife. After finding that it could cut the paper from the edge without crumpling it, he concluded, "This should do just fine. Dennis, hold his arm still so I don't cut the fucker off while I reconfigure this here lizard. I'm going to cut his tail off, make it look like a rat instead," he laughed.

Bending over his work piece, he cut an outline around the tail of the lizard tattoo, just deep enough where it bled a little. Cawthorne screamed and struggled to pull his arm away from Dennis's strong grip. Ralph then turned the knife horizontally and began to cut away the tail section of the lizard. Blood began to ooze down Cawthorne's arm as he screamed even louder and begged Ralph to stop.

"Oh, does that hurt, Billy Joe? Here let me fix that up so it doesn't get infected." Reaching over to the table, he picked up a bottle of Vodka, poured some on a gauze bandage, and applied it to the wound. Cawthorne uttered the most wretched wail of torment as the firewater stung the debrided section of his skin.

Cawthorne's demeanor had changed considerably from the defiant stance he took with Tom. He was shivering, took furtive glances at the face of his new interrogator, and had an expression of pure terror on his face.

"Jesus Christ! You're going to skin me alive! You bastard!"

"Oh, I'm sorry. I didn't expect I'd find any red blood in your veins," said Ralph in mock disbelief. "Maybe you don't have ice water in them like I thought. Tell you what, if you give me a truthful answer to my next question, I won't have to do any more cutting on you, but if you continue to beat about the bush, I'll have to collect enough of your epidermis to make a lampshade."

"No, no, wait. What do you want? I've got money. You can take my rig. I'll get my girlfriend to give you a blow job or whatever you want. Hell, I'll give you one. Just don't do any more cutting on me. Don't kill me, please, please. I'm begging you."

"I'll ask this just once and you better not be giving me any bullshit for an answer. You gave Tom here a ride in your fucking tanker truck, didn't you, and you cut him up and raped him. Then you hit him with a shovel, threw him in a grave and left him for dead, didn't you? Spit it out, you no good motherfucker, you piece of shit!"

"Yeah, yeah. I did it. I had a bad day and I was looking for a little fun, some diversion. I'm sorry. I'm sorry. I'm a no-good sonofabitch. I have been all my life."

"You admit to tying Tom up on your truck and torturing him with a knife?"

"Yeah. I was just toying with him."

"You admit to raping Tom when he was bound up and hanging from the bead on your tanker?"

"Yeah. But I didn't hurt him. I used lots of Vaseline."

"And you admit to digging a grave, hitting Tom with a shovel, and burying him alive?"

"Yeah. But I didn't know he was alive and I really had no choice. There was a car coming down the road and I had to get out of there."

"So you plead guilty to all of the charges made against you by Mr. Tom?"

"Yeah. But I want to make amends and start a new life. I need you to forgive me, for God's sake forgive me. I can be a decent fella, just give me a chance. Let me make it up to him, to you, to all of you. I have a girlfriend and we are going to have a baby. They'd have no support if I'm not there to provide it."

"We're not in the forgiveness business, Mr. Cawthorne," said Cowboy. "There have to be consequences to your evil, depraved acts and we will move on, now that we have your confession, to determine what those will be. Your victim, Tom, will have a lot to say about what happens to you but we each get our own vote."

Motioning to Ralph and Dennis, Cowboy commanded "Take him into the back room while we deliberate his fate. Put his pants back on and get him a new shirt."

The group milled about, picked up snacks and beverages, and slowly congregated around the table. Cowboy urged the slackers to take a seat.

"OK. The slime-ball has confessed to every crime just as Tom stated it. I don't see any real remorse. That last little bit of asking for forgiveness and pleading for mercy is just more of his usual bullshit, an attempt to play on our sympathies."

"I say we kill the bastard," said Ralph. "These scum-bags are serial rapists and murderers. If we let him off, he'll just do it again and some other innocent will suffer or die. Let's stop it right here."

"Yeah, no sense in being lenient," came another voice.

"Right on!" exclaimed another.

"Does anyone see any extenuating circumstances?" asked Cowboy as he glanced at each member sitting around the table.

Silence. Then one member volunteered, "Well, he did plead guilty, if you want to consider that a mitigating factor. But he did it only after being convinced his situation could become worse."

A circle of "bullshits" echoed around the table.

"He did admit that he has always been a no-goodnick, if you want to consider mental illness is a moderating factor," suggested another.

"He's not some neurotic that can be helped by mental health workers and he's not some psychotic that didn't know what the fuck he was doing and can be treated with medications," countered another voice. "He's a fucking psychopath and the only treatment that works with them is imprisonment — or death."

"He wasn't provoked and he's not a minor, so that doesn't buy him any leniency," opined another.

"How about any aggravating conditions?" asked Cowboy.

"The whole thing is an aggravating condition," another voice put forward. "He had criminal intent. He intended to rape and murder Tom. He did him bodily harm and he used a deadly weapon."

"It may not be one of the usual aggravating conditions, but I think committing a crime against one of our disabled military men makes it especially outrageous, an abomination," maintained one of the committee.

"Here, here. I'll second that," echoed another.

"I'd like to raise another question," asked Cowboy. "Would a death sentence constitute a cruel and unusual punishment in this case?"

"How do you define that?" asked a member of the group.

"Well," said Cowboy, "The definition used by a lot of courts has four parts. First, is the severity of the punishment degrading to human dignity. Second, is it arbitrarily inflicted. Third, is the particular punishment totally rejected throughout society. And, fourth, is it clearly unnecessary. Now, I think you would be right if you think these criteria are subject to a lot of different interpretations and opinions."

"Yeah, who is to say what is degrading to society?" asked Dennis. "Is it more degrading to society to have some maniac running around raping and killing honest citizens as opposed to eliminating the maniac when you have the chance to do so?"

Ralph interjected, "Sure and if you look at the official punishments dished out by societies over the years, a nice quick and simple execution is probably one of the more humane methods. In the past and in some countries still, they have drawn and quartered, boiled to death, burned up, drowned, starved, disemboweled, crucified, crushed, dismembered, stoned, and sliced up the guilty party. Do we use the standards of our particular society or those of the rest of the world? It all seems kind of capricious to me."

A party to the left of Cowboy chimed in, "The punishment we are suggesting is not totally arbitrary either. We have considered or are considering the nature of the crime, the fact that there are virtually no extenuating circumstances and that there is a whole outhouse full of aggravating circumstances."

"What about the punishment being clearly unnecessary? I guess that means we should ask if there are any other punishments that would be better than the one that has been proposed or that would carry with it less adverse consequences?" asked Cowboy. "Anybody have any thoughts about that?"

"Well, we can't give him a life sentence because we don't have a jail," cracked a committee member. Everyone laughed.

Tom had been silent, listening to all the arguments, and now felt he should say something.

"Your arguments are all very logical. Maybe it would be better in the long run to kill him and spare potential victims from suffering or even death. He is an evil man and doesn't appear to have any redeeming qualities. I don't see any reason, including mental illness, for him to escape accountability for his crimes. But I am uncomfortable about sentencing him to death even if he deserves it."

"But Tom, this worthless scum bucket tried to kill you and damn near succeeded. He didn't have any qualms about taking your life away from you. He didn't care if you rotted in that shallow grave."

"I know, you're right about that and I'm not forgiving him. It's my conscience that's bothering me. I just don't think I can live with the fact that I took someone's life. I don't want to think of myself as being a cold-blooded killer. I know it would plague me the rest of my life."

"How about we leave Tom out of the voting so he will not be participating in something he is reluctant about. We have his input and can take that into consideration when we decide on a sentence."

Most of the members agreed but one raised the specter of Tom ratting them out. Cowboy looked directly at Tom and said, "I think Tom knows better than to do that. For now, let's call this meeting to a halt and we can resume in the morning. Let's go down to that restaurant on the river and have some drinks and a good dinner. Then we can sleep on our decision over night, maybe see if we can come up with any other options."

Cowboy drove Tom back to Vetlandia after their dinner and then returned to the cabin. Tom was relieved to be off the hook with regard to voting on a sentence but felt he had let Cowboy and the group down after they had gone to so much trouble. Nevertheless, he did not change his stance regarding the death sentence. Cowboy knew Tom felt uncomfortable and tried to ease his distress at being in a situation that pitted one form of guilt against another.

"Don't worry about the boys being mad or disappointed in you, Tom. We have all wrestled with these kinds of decisions. A man has to do what he thinks is right, no matter what other people think."

CHAPTER 10
SURVEILLANCE

It was two days before Cowboy returned to Vetlandia. He found Tom working in the library and arranged to meet him out at the fish pond later in the day. Tom was eager to hear the outcome of the sentencing and anxious about what may have happened to Billy Joe Cawthorne.

Cowboy was sitting on a bench with a fishing line and bobber in the water in front of him. Tom sat down on the bench next to him.

"Catching anything?" Tom asked, looking around to see if anyone was within voice range.

Cowboy laughed, "No and I don't think Billy Joe will be catching anything anytime soon either."

"What did you guys decide to do to him? Is he still alive?"

"Yeah, he's still alive alright," said Cowboy as he pulled out a small vial and handed it to Tom. "But he's missing some of the equipment that impelled him to make trouble for innocent travelers."

Tom held the vial up to the light and, squinting, could make out two pinkish-beige oval-shaped objects, one slightly larger than the other. He couldn't suppress the smile that spread across his face.

"Holy shit! You castrated the motherfucker. Jesus!"

"Well, we acceded to your wish not to kill him and came up with a solution that we figured would put a kink in his usual modus operandi. It's a simple operation and a couple of us that grew up on farms knew how to do it. So we did it and then dumped him off at a hospital in northern California for medical followup."

"Is there any way he can finger you, set the cops on your trail?"

"No. I don't think so. He never knew what state he was in and he couldn't identify any of us. He wouldn't want to tag you either because that would mean confessing to rape and attempted murder. So I think he will just live with it and contemplate the error of his ways."

Tom was relieved that Cowboy's vigilante group had spared the life of his tormentor so he wouldn't have to think of himself as a murderer or accomplice to murder. And he thought the sentence they imposed for the crimes Cawthorne had committed against him was fitting and might prevent the villain from perpetrating similar crimes. He could live with that. So when he next met with Dr. Oldman, he had a smile on his face and was more upbeat than he had been for several weeks.

"What's happened?" inquired Dr. Oldman. "You seem to be a lot more chipper than you have been for several weeks now."

"Oh, I've been thinking about what you said about revenge and I believe you are right. It doesn't get you anywhere and you have to consider how that gets incorporated into your idea of who you are."

"Umm, yes and...?"

"And I've decided to put my hate for the bastard that attacked me on the back burner and look to what is in my future," said Tom.

"That's probably a good idea as long as you aren't just suppressing your feelings and ignoring something important."

"Oh, don't get me wrong. I still hate the guy and what he did but I don't want to spend all my time stewing about it. He'll get his in the end, if he hasn't already," Tom said as he smiled about his private joke.

Dr. Oldman thought Tom was not giving him the whole story but decided not to challenge him further at this point, preferring to take advantage of the positive mood to make gains in Tom's planning for his life after Vetlandia.

∞

Daniel Hanson had been discharged after his physical condition had stabilized, as he had predicted. He continued to have access to outpatient treatment and attended one of Dr. Oldman's PTSD therapy groups twice a week. To pay his rent, he obtained a job as a waiter at the restaurant across the highway running in front of Vetlandia. Tom would visit him regularly at his place of employment and they frequently spent time together on weekends. Tom shared with him his experience with vigilante justice and Daniel was impressed with Tom's self-control and contentment with the outcome.

"Jesus, I think I would have slit the dip-shit's throat as soon as I saw him," he exclaimed. "You did the right thing, Tom. I think you may be more of a grown-up than I am, even though I'm a couple decades older than you. And the fact that the jury was able to come up with a suitable sentence is the topping on the cake."

Daniel's job at the restaurant brought him into contact with many vets since they served mainly guys from across the road along with the many female camp followers who were looking to cash in on lonely men likely to receive disability compensation. It was also an unending source of rumors and "did you hear about?" stories of one sort or another.

One of them that Daniel overheard was told by a man who previously claimed he was a hit man for drug runners in Riverside, California. He was now boasting to a person who appeared to be a girlfriend about having secured a job with Southside Transport to distribute drugs about the state. The man had a reputation as a braggart so Daniel didn't know if this new claim to fame was genuine or not. The man told the story to his presumed lover in hushed tones and swore her to secrecy for fear that he might be killed if his employer heard wind of his assertion. Was he telling the truth or was he just trying to impress the girl while at the same time ensuring she wouldn't check up on his story? Daniel did not know but he shared his observations with Tom who thought it might be worthwhile to walk past Southside Transport next time he was in town.

Dr. Oldman was aware of Tom's and Daniel's efforts to figure out the uneven playing field for veterans arriving at Vetlandia — the fact that some were singled out for early discharge, abuse, or neglect of one sort or another while others sailed through and were allowed, even encouraged, to take advantage of special programs or ushered into service-connected status. He had been the late Scott Parks's psychotherapist and knew the dirt that Scott had turned up on Dr. Gunnar. He and Lucas Bojorquez, the social worker, had assisted Parks in his efforts to bring Dr. Gunnar to account.

Like Parks and Tom, Oldman suspected there was something more sinister going on than a bias toward certain kinds of patients. Adding to his suspicions was the revelation by another patient, Michael Mayhew, a reformed junkie who had gone through the truck driving school and become employed at a local trucking company. When his employers tried to lure him into transporting drugs, he complied while at the same time reporting the activity to the DEA. Agents convinced him to continue playing along so they could identify all the players and their locations and routines. Michael, fantasizing himself a secret agent and being a bit of a daredevil, thought of it as an adventure and a test of his nerve.

Earlier in his stay on Section Three Tom had met and taken pity on another vet about his own age who seemed to be the most anxious person he had ever met. Gordon Sawyer was a navy vet who had just been released from prison after a conviction on numerous drug charges. Tom presumed that Gordon's experiences in prison were the reason for his anxiety. He tried to be friendly and reassuring and suggested he see Dr. Oldman, which he did. The last time Tom saw him, Gordon had calmed down considerably and was excited about being accepted into the truck driving school.

Prison life provided plenty of reasons for Gordon Sawyer to be anxious but they were not the only ones. He spent the first few years of his life in a very close-knit and loving family. Then his mother died and he was sent to live with an uncle and aunt who treated him like a slave. They resented having to care for him after being dumped on them and treated him like he was obligated to earn his keep. His aunt further humiliated him by having him lower his trousers, presumably as punishment, but she seemed to get some kind of weird sexual kick out of it as well.

Later, he returned to live with his remarried father but the father had married a wicked stepmother who all the kids hated. At one time, Gordon led a children's revolt against her, throwing a deactivated WWII hand grenade at her bedroom door where she had barricaded herself. She did not take the prank in good humor and threatened Gordon's father with a divorce if he didn't get rid of the ringleader.

So, as a young teen, Gordon Sawyer left the house and lived on the streets. He got picked up for something minor and was sent to a juvenile detention facility where he received no help but did garner a lot of abuse. Eventually recruited into the drug trade, Gordon became an independent meth "cook". By nature a kind and warmhearted individual, he felt sympathetic toward a lot of women he met who were on the fringes of the drug trade because of their social and economic circumstances. Many were unwed mothers who found it impossible to become employed. So he hired them to buy glassware and chemicals for him. In effect, he ran a little welfare agency of his own for these characters, one of the reasons he never accumulated any significant profits. Turned into the police for a reward by one of his beneficiaries, he was first imprisoned in Oregon and then transported, shackled hand and foot, via Con Air to a prison in Nevada.

Coming out of prison, Sawyer was a nervous wreck. He worked at a variety of construction jobs. Most of his employers liked his work but he always felt it was inadequate and would leave the job because he thought he was going to get fired, even though his employer would hire him right back. He at one time worked 4 different jobs in a single day.

Gordon's condition was severe enough that a VA psychologist referred him to Vetlandia. There, vocational counselors helped him to get a position sorting donations at a Goodwill Store to establish a job history so he might be able to find a better position later. However, he was constantly anxious and fidgeting.

Dr. Wolfgang Gunnar refused to give him anti-anxiety medication, rationalizing his decision by saying that giving addictive substances to druggies only encouraged their addiction. Dr. Oldman argued with him that it was appropriate in this case and less of an evil than trying to function with the patient's high anxiety level. As a result of his uncontrolled anxiety, Gordon Sawyer was fired from Goodwill.

It was at this point that his vocational counselor suggested that he might qualify for a program at Beaver State Trucking. He was told it was a training position where he would learn how to drive trucks of various types and that it would involve an agreement to pay 20% of his earnings back to the trucking firm during his first year of employment. Gordon considered himself a good driver. When he was a meth cook, he had managed to elude police many times in high-speed car chases, so he thought that truck driving might be a piece of cake. The pay he was told he would earn was enough that the 20% kickback was tolerable.

Gordon Sawyer graduated from truck driving school with flying colors, learned how to drive trucks from small panel vans to rigs with 18 wheels, passed all the licensing exams, and was hired by Beaver State when he finished. He started his employment making short hauls to various cities in the state, driving small to medium-sized vehicles.

Soon he learned that the company had an "elite" squad of drivers who hauled high-value cargo and earned substantial bonuses. When he inquired of one of these drivers, a man he knew from Vetlandia, what they were transporting and what one needed to do to join their ranks, he received evasive answers and was told to keep doing his job and perhaps he would get an invitation to join.

Gordon liked the idea of having a real job and making a lot of money but, having associated with many law-breakers in the past, he became suspicious that what they were doing might be illegal. The specter of returning to prison rekindled his anxieties and they were further heightened by his knowledge of how these guys operate. If they were running drugs or firearms and suspected that he knew and was going to rat them out, his life wouldn't be worth a plug nickel.

Tom ran into Gordon at the canteen and immediately noted his nervousness had returned.

"Jeez, I thought you were doing well, Gordon. What happened?"

"Well, I got through the school, passed all the exams, and got hired but I'm not so sure the company is on the up-and-up. I don't want to quit my job but I don't want go back to prison either."

"Have they asked you to do anything against the law?"

"No, not yet and I don't want to get to that stage either."

Tom wondered if Gordon's fears were real or were a manifestation of his paranoia. Uncertain of Gordon's mental status, Tom felt he was getting beyond his depth and suggested Gordon take his concerns to Dr. Oldman.

"What do I do, abandon my chance at making a decent living and beat it out of town or stick with it and get drawn back into a life of crime?" Gordon asked Dr. Oldman. "Who knows what they may be hauling. It's probably drugs but they might be transporting girls for prostitution or illegals for cheap labor. I may not have much of a conscience but it bothers me when people take advantage of folks that are already down and out."

"Those aren't your only two choices, Gordon, but you may need to cool it for a while, play along with what's presented to you. By the way, who was the driver you talked to at Beaver?"

"Michael Mayhew."

"OK. You don't have to worry about Michael but stay away from him or you might get *him* into trouble. I can't tell you all I know at this time, so I guess I'm going to have to ask you to just trust me on this. You won't be left hanging out there all alone. Just be very careful and don't do anything to make your employers question your loyalty to them. If you get caught in a raid or get pulled over by police, I can testify in your defense."

"You mean you know about this outfit? You know they're doing something not exactly kosher? Does the VA know? How can they go along with this?"

"I know some things but not a lot. I don't think the VA knows anything about them. Law enforcement knows and there are people trying to collect evidence. Something will happen before too long. But I can't really say much at this point. Just keep your cool, don't make anybody mad at you, go with the flow. Act as if you don't know anything and as if bending the rules doesn't bother you."

The next time Tom met with Daniel Hanson, he mentioned the conversation he had with Gordon Sawyer. Daniel reminded him of the conversation he had overheard in the restaurant.

"So now we have two instances where vets who went through the truck driving program may be involved in something shady."

"You know what? I went down to Southside Transport yesterday," said Tom, "and they are located right next door to Beaver Trucking. Isn't that an odd coincidence? Do you suppose they are one and the same company? Is Vetlandia supplying mules — couriers — for the drug trade?"

"And if they are," interjected Daniel, "who all is in on it? We need to watch that place and see if there are any other Vetlandia guys working there. Maybe see if any Vetlandia staff show up down there."

"I think we are going to need some help on this. Andrew Hammons might want to help. He seems like a decent sort of guy and has an interest in finding out what happened to his ex-roommate. He has some navy intelligence experience too. And that reminds me. My roommate is an ex-intelligence guy. He might lend us a hand. And maybe we should try to get hold of that FBI agent who visited Gene Lofgren."

"Jesus! I'm getting to feel that same sort of apprehension I felt when I was working on the drug interdiction program and stationed in Graves Registration," said Daniel. "Damn! It's a familiar feeling but it is kind of exciting too, especially if we can nail the assholes behind the patient abuse. That will make it all worthwhile for me!"

In the ensuing days, Tom recruited Andrew Hammons into the effort. Tom's roommate, Tony Napoliello, was surprised when he learned of Tom's efforts at sleuthing and impressed by his gutsiness. He agreed to participate and was excited at the prospect of working with another intelligence person from a different branch of the service. After years of depression and pessimism, he was feeling that old exhilaration he long thought was dead. He suggested a couple of other vets that he trusted and might add skills to the endeavor they were embarking upon. There was Jerry McCall, the Riverine with a missing front tooth that Tom had met on his first day at Vetlandia. And there was Ken Harper, another Riverine but with law enforcement experience, who grew up on a ranch in California. Tony said he would broach the topic with the two Riverines. They both agreed to listen to what Tom and Daniel had in mind.

As a youngster, Ken Harper had good relationships with his family and had lots of friends from participating in team sports in high school. He joined the army and was a member of the Mobile Riverine Force working the Mekong delta. He saw a lot of combat and was a ranking non-com, receiving many awards for his work. After Vietnam, he served in Germany where he was with an army group tracking down the Baader-Meinhof Gang.

He married a German woman and had three kids, staying in Germany and working for a German youth group. He was involved in a Christian church that made humanitarian truck runs carrying Bibles into the old Yugoslavia, and carrying out escapees in a hollowed-out container below the truck cab. He was caught once and tortured for a week by two women who attached electrical leads to sensitive parts of his body and turned on the juice.

One of his sons was killed by a hit-and-run driver when Ken was at a church rally. His wife blamed him for not watching the boy closely enough and got a divorce. Ken returned to the US and became a policeman in LA. During the first year, his partner was shot and killed, convincing Ken that cop life was not for him.

Ken Harper had lots of traumatic experiences in both Vietnam and Germany. He felt guilty about a soldier who killed himself in Germany, thinking he could have done something to prevent it. He came to Vetlandia very depressed and suffering from PTSD. Assigned to Section Three, he soon became a patient of Dr. Oldman.

Tom thought the six men should meet, get to know each other and develop a clear plan on how to proceed. It was agreed that they have a drive-by of Beaver Trucking and Southside Transport and then meet at a park off Springbrook Road. Traveling in two cars, they drove around the two businesses to scout out possible observation points and then congregated at one of the park tables fitted with an overhead and away from the flow of visitors.

The meeting started with some sharing of military histories and the paths that led them to Vetlandia. Tom, Daniel, and Andrew told of their revulsion at the way some veterans were treated at Vetlandia while others received special treatment. They cited the case of Scott Parks and gave examples from their own experiences. The others nodded their heads in agreement. Daniel related the conversation that he had overheard at the restaurant and Tom shared Gordon's concerns without revealing his name. All three voiced their suspicions that someone at Vetlandia was involved in the drug trade or some other kind of illegal activity. Tony and Ken, both with experience tracking criminals, conceded that it sounded very suspicious.

"What we want to find out, first of all, is if this is a real criminal enterprise or if it's just a couple of fucked up individuals that are wannabe criminals," Tony offered. "If it's a criminal enterprise, we want to know what level it's at – is it a small-time outfit with a few members or is it a full-blown hierarchy with a board of directors controlling a bunch of gangs, each with a leader, a few officers and a bunch of foot-soldiers. It's probably not a national syndicate operating out of a small city like this but it might be regional in scope. 'Course, you never know."

"Then we need to know what their product is," added Ken. "Are they trafficking in drugs, girls, weapons, illegal aliens looking for jobs, hot merchandise or other contraband, whatever."

"I don't know if we can find all that out by staking out these buildings but we might find out if they are recruiting men from Vetlandia to do something illegal and if any staff are involved in the operation," said Andrew Hammons. "How about we watch and take notes for a week or two and see where we're at then?"

"Jerry, do you still have that fancy camera with a telescopic lens?" asked Tony.

"Sure do. I can teach the rest of you how to use it before we start our surveillance."

Three of the men had cars and three didn't so they decided to pair one car owner with one hoofer for each segment of the watch. Because they had other commitments, it could not be a perfect 24-hour surveillance, but they took samples of both daytime and nighttime activities at the two businesses. They used the first week to get a feel for the routine of activities so they could concentrate their efforts at the times most likely to provide useful information.

Ken Harper, the one with the most training and experience in tracking terrorists and criminals, located vantage points for seeing both front and back entrances to the buildings. From these spots, an observer could take photos of people entering or leaving the premises. Jerry McCall was his companion on the first run and took the opportunity to best configure his camera for pictures that would reveal the identity of possible culprits.

While sitting and waiting, the two Riverines exchanged stories about their experiences in Vietnam. They had been on different types of boats, Ken on a Swiftboat and Jerry on an armored troop carrier designed to carry troops, supplies, and even a small tank upriver. Both had terrifying experiences of enemy cross-fire at a place on the Mekong River that doubled back on itself called Snoopy's Nose for its resemblance to the Peanuts cartoon character. Like other vets recalling traumatic experiences, they quickly turned to humorous events, sometimes gallows humor, to scale back the intensity of emotional response to their recollections. But the sharing of memories while they were engaged in a common task helped bond the relationship between the two veterans.

Similar bonding occurred with the other vets. Tony Napoliello and Andrew Hammons shared the different approaches to intelligence work taken in their respective services and separated by nearly a decade. Each developed an appreciation for the different kinds of challenges they experienced and respect for the other party. When Tom was paired with Jerry, they talked of their military experience but also of their shared interest in writing. They learned that their counterpart had written a story in which one of their characters resembled Dr. Oldman. They compared perceptions and exchanged different approaches to developing their characters. Each of the pairings of participants evoked different anecdotes but all of them resulted in the members becoming more attached. They were beginning to operate as a team.

During the first week of surveillance, the team identified several former Vetlandia patients as regularly employed Class A semi-truck drivers for Beaver State Trucking and car or small truck drivers for Southside Transport, which required only a Class C commercial driver's license. This was not too surprising since Vetlandia channeled vets into the "Troops to Trucks" driving program at Beaver State. However, one night who should be seen entering the back of the building but Dr. Gunnar. He emerged about 15 minutes later carrying a letter-size manila envelope.

When the team discussed it the next day, no one could think of any legitimate reason he should be visiting Beaver State Trucking, especially at night. Everyone suspected the envelope he carried was stuffed with cash. The team turned its attention to focus on nighttime visitations. What they found, over the next few weeks, was that Dr. Gunnar showed up every Monday night and executed the same routine. One of the vocational counselors at Vetlandia appeared at Southside Transport during daytime hours on Mondays, which might be expected as part of his job, but his nighttime appearance on Fridays was not so easily explained. Sometimes Dr. Whitey Green substituted for Dr. Gunnar and his toady nurse substituted for the vocational counselor at Southside Transport.

After a month of observations, the team decided to follow the Vetlandia staff members to see where they took their manila envelopes. They were disappointed when all of them seemed to just go to their residences and retire for the night. Concluding that they must transport their loot to its destination at a later time, they assigned pairs to follow them when they left home the next day. As it turned out, all of them drove directly to Vetlandia.

But each of them, carrying the envelope they obtained the previous day, made a call on the COS within a short time of their arrival. So, the team had presumptive evidence that whatever Vetlandia staff got out of their transactions with the two companies, it ended up in the hands of Mortimer Kilpatrick, the Chief of Staff.

Now, they thought, it was time to follow one of the couriers to see what they were delivering and to whom. Daniel suggested they track the braggart he overheard at the restaurant and who they had confirmed really did work at Southside, since it likely would be a relatively short trip.

Tony followed the panel truck the suspect picked up at Southside to a truck stop just off I-5 where he rendezvoused with a man standing near a semi, parked with its tail end up against a stand of trees. Tony could not see what was being exchanged and did not want to give away his position, recalling a time when he had done so, with disastrous consequences, when tracking a Russian agent from a safe house in San Francisco after the war. But the back doors of both vehicles were open and he could see legs passing between them. Then the braggart got back in his truck and quickly re-entered the freeway, heading north. Tony followed along, trying to keep one or two vehicles between him and the suspect while making sure the latter did not exit the highway without detection.

A few miles past Eugene, he turned west on Highway 20 to Newport and then north on 101 to Lincoln City, where he pulled into the Surfside Seafood Market, driving around to the service entrance in the back. Tony drove around the block and parked in the back lot of Olive Oyl's Restaurant next door, where he could view the braggart's truck. The driver had entered the market. Tony waited a few minutes until he re-emerged with someone wearing an apron splattered with the inedible remains of deceased fish. The braggart opened the back doors of his truck and both men walked up to the bumper, reaching inside. Then they both stepped back, closing the doors.

The man from the market pointed down toward the beach and gesticulated with his fingers to indicate some location. Then the braggart got back into his truck and headed west toward the ocean. Tony followed him as he found his way to the service entrance to Ocean Sands Beachfront Resort. Tony could see the braggart and another man unloading several medium-sized boxes and closing the doors to the truck. The man from the resort made a cursory inspection of their surroundings, not noticing Tony's car parked behind a fishing boat on a trailer. Then he handed the braggart a manila envelope, following which the braggart jumped back into his truck and returned to Southside, arriving just past dark. He parked the truck in the parking lot and took the envelope inside. A short time later, he drove his personal vehicle to a local bar. After an hour of waiting, Tony went inside, ordered a beer at the bar, and glanced around, spotting the braggart sitting in a booth with a woman. Tony wondered if it was the same floozy Daniel Hanson had observed in the restaurant across from Vetlandia. He memorized her facial features, hair color, and style of dress, jotting them down when he got back in his car and intending to compare notes with Daniel on their next meeting.

Tony told Tom the results of his ride to the Oregon coast when he got back to their room.

"Holy cow!" exclaimed Tom. "It sure sounds like a drug deal. We can't be sure of what they were carrying but it probably wasn't sea bass."

"Yeah," said Tony. "It is probably cocaine or marijuana. Looks like Southside is part of a distribution network. They get the stuff from someone who is one or two steps away from the manufacturers. That's the guy operating out of the semi. The guy at the Seafood place may be the kingpin for the Lincoln City market. They probably sell it to consumers staying at the resort. The folks at Vetlandia may serve as an employment service for the operation.

"I'm puzzled about how they get paid. They must not get a finders fee on a per head basis for supplying employees since they appear to get paid off on a regular basis. Maybe they get a percentage of the take somehow."

Tony told the rest of the team what he had observed and his theory of what it might indicate at their next meeting at the park. Ken, Daniel, and Andrew, the three with the most experience, concurred with Tony's conjectures. Everyone was in high spirits that they were gathering evidence that there was something malicious going on and that it involved members of the Vetlandia staff. At the same time, they were apprehensive about their ability to successfully expose the scoundrels before being found out, facing retribution or worse.

"Do you think we should go to the police," asked Tom.

"No, we don't have enough evidence yet," asserted Ken.

"They'd probably blow us off as a bunch of paranoid vets from the cuckoo factory," Tony chimed in.

Tom added, "How about we let Dr. Oldman in on what we found? He could serve as a kind of lifeline to the real world in case something goes wrong."

"Do you think he can be trusted?" asked Andrew.

"Oh, yeah. He has always shot straight with me, said Tom.

Three of the members responded in the affirmative, one of them proclaiming, "I'd trust him with my life."

When Tom mentioned what he and his companions had been up to, Dr. Oldman appeared most concerned about the welfare of the veterans.

"You know you may be dealing with some not very nice people here, don't you? I don't want you guys to get hurt for something you don't have to do."

"Yeah, yeah, doc, we know what we're getting into. Several of the guys have experience with tough guys and know how to protect themselves if it comes to that."

"OK," said Oldman. "I'm not going to suggest you stop what you are doing. I just want to be assured you won't take any unnecessary risks."

"We won't. We just want to have someone available that we know will believe us if we come across something important and need to call in the cavalry."

"I know where we can get help if we need it," said Oldman. "What I can tell you now is that there is an inside man over at Beaver State and he is connected to the DEA. We don't want to do anything to endanger him, so stick to the observation and note-taking from a distance. Any of that lone ranger stuff will just screw things up."

∞

Dr. Gunnar walked over to the office of the COS, manila envelope in hand. "Is he in?" he asked the receptionist.

"Yes, he is expecting you. Go right in."

"Good morning, Wolfgang" said Gunnar. "I see you have a delivery for me. Bring it over here."

Gunnar strode over to the huge mahogany desk and placed the envelope on it. The COS picked it up and dumped the contents — five packets of bound $100 bills — on the desk. Lifting a briefcase from the floor next to his desk, he placed the packets on top of a layer of similar bundles already contained therein and returned the briefcase to the floor.

"That should help our little organization get to the next level," said Mort.

Kirkpatrick began his criminal enterprise at Vetlandia by supplying employees to drug runners. He soon realized, by listening to seasoned lawbreakers, that there were many other goods that needed to be transported and connections that needed to be made between buyers and sellers of illicit goods. Buyers for guns stolen from cargo trains while sitting idle and unguarded in rail yards had to be found. The thieves were pressured to get rid of the guns as soon as possible because they were traceable and their recovery was high priority for a particular governmental agency.

The largest source of stolen guns, however, was from residential burglaries. The housebreakers were, for the most part, independent operators who sold small numbers to pawnshops, acquaintances and other individuals. To make the operation efficient and profitable for an intermediary, the bandits would need to be organized into gangs that pooled their efforts and sent larger volumes of their goods to fences that could distribute them. With his contacts in the militia movement, Mort would also have buyers readily available. Thus, he could envision new employment positions to be filled by veterans passing through his special Vetlandia venues, each contributing a portion of their income to the persons who made it possible.

A similar situation existed for purloiners of objects made of copper such as electrical wire, or bronze, like grave markers. Some of these metal specialists would contract to do repair work and while the homeowner was gone, tear out all the copper wire in the house and sell it to a nearby wrecking yard where it would be melted down into more transportable ingots destined for a manufacturer of metal objects. A similar fate might await the bronze remembrances of lost loved ones pilfered from nighttime raids on cemeteries. An entrepreneur like Mort could dispatch a trained agent to locate buyers, put the word out to potential thieves, arrange for transportation of the material, and take a cut of the proceeds.

And then there was the business of labor trafficking or the transportation of people desperate to find employment, such as illegal immigrants, to those businesses desperate to obtain employees for undesirable jobs, such as picking crops, working in slaughter houses, or meat packing plants. Employment in the sex industry was already under the control of organized crime so Mort did not want to run the risks associated with challenging "the mob." But there were even more buyers who offered jobs in the agricultural, hospitality, domestic service, restaurant, and some construction industries. Criminal networks had not yet staked out claims in these sectors so Mort thought it would be safe to try his hand at these markets, especially since the arrest rates were very low — employees distrusted police, and feared extradition or retaliation against themselves or their family members.

Financially, it was also attractive since parties at both ends of the transaction could be charged thousands of dollars per head for the matchmaking.

The abstract components of the organization that was forming in Mort's mind started falling into place. The goods being traded could be anything — guns, jewels, electronic devices, auto parts, metals, even people. There were buyers and sellers with a few middlemen in between — low-level fences, higher-level fences who deal only with other fences, transporters, and sometimes recruiters. At times they would need a warehouse to store goods temporarily until a buyer could be found and sometimes they would need safe houses for the parties to meet and settle arrangements. He didn't want to deal with the end user of these different products. The elements he wanted to exploit were in making deals between high volume buyers and high volume sellers, and supplying skilled employees for transportation and other aspects of the business that required persons with certain skills and flexible consciences.

The arrangement Mort developed with Beaver Trucking kept him away from the front lines of these illegal transactions. He did not deal drugs himself but only supplied drivers willing to take the risk of transporting them. He could use the people in his organization within Vetlandia to make connections with suppliers and locate potential buyers while having little personal jeopardy.

Mort Kilpatrick had had inspirations before, excitements of imagination that revealed great possibilities that could be put into action. He loved that part of the process. He loved being in charge, directing others to work together, applying pressure when needed, creating an efficient organization and, of course, profiting from his efforts. As he reflected upon his current inspiration, thinking about what would be required to make it work, and the order in which to approach it, he recalled his father's endeavors to make it big in the skills-training field after the war. He would be proud of me, he thought.

"Yeah, we can give a boost to our business as well as to the Sons of Liberty," said Gunnar. By the way, Mort, I drove over to Bend on the weekend and talked with Winifred Shepard at Evergreen Farms. She is going to need another batch of laborers for harvesting next month. I've already called Armondo down in Juarez and he says he can get about 50 ready for transport by next week. They will drive them up to our place near Twin Falls in three vans and we pick them up there. Should I set it up with our friends over at Beaver Trucking?"

"Go ahead Gunnar and keep me posted as the project proceeds. I have an appointment with our friend in the state legislature, Senator Tyler. He is up for re-election and is pushing legislation to prevent gun control, thinks it will get him votes. His opponent has supported lefty demonstrations against ownership of automatic weapons and he might want us to set up some kind of counter demonstration or protest where he can come in, act like the great mediator and get some good press."

CHAPTER 11
TURNING UP THE HEAT

Michael Mayhew, the Vetlandia patient working undercover for the DEA, had been employed by Beaver State Trucking for nearly six months and had convinced his employers that he qualified for the "elite driver" status after successfully transporting a load of copper ingots to a toy manufacturer and a load of stolen electronic equipment to the warehouse of a secondhand store. The other elites were less guarded now that he had joined their ranks and that allowed him to surreptitiously pick up bits of information about other illicit operations.

He observed that one semi-trailer had been repainted with a cornucopia overflowing with fruit, flowers, and grain on the sides topped by the banner "Evergreen Farms." A compartment was being built inside and he could see some plumbing fixtures stored nearby. On the top, workers were installing some kind of ventilation system. He surmised that the vehicle was being prepared for human transport and notified his DEA handlers. They thought the impending crime would be out of their jurisdiction if it didn't involve drugs and notified the FBI of a possible human trafficking crime. The FBI assigned a team of agents to investigate, working with Michael's "handler" from the DEA.

Meanwhile, the vets in Tom Ward's surveillance group decided to follow one of the big trucks to identify its endpoints and cargo. They, too, had observed the work being conducted on the Evergreen Farms trailer, seeing it move in and out of two of the buildings, each time altered to some degree. A visit to the preparation area by Dr. Gunnar especially piqued their interest. What possible reason could he have for inspecting one of Beaver State's trucks?

As the vets watched the progress of work on the trailer, they knew it was near completion when bottles of water and mattresses were loaded into the back. Tom and his roommate Tony Napoliello volunteered to follow the truck in Tony's Mazda RX-7. While his was a distinctive vehicle, it offered good fuel economy, speed, and maneuverability, since they had no idea how far they would be traveling and what might be needed if trouble arose.

As the truck headed north on State 62 and then east on State 140, the two vets wondered where on earth it was headed. It certainly wasn't a typical route for trucks that size. Moving across the state, they traveled through a passel of small desert towns — Silver Lake, Wagontire, Burns — finally leaving Oregon for Idaho at Ontario where they got onto Interstate 84, and headed south. There was not a lot of traffic on these back roads so they stayed well behind the truck to avoid suspicion. They stopped for gas, not having the fuel capacity of the truck, and then sped to make up the distance between them, fearing the driver might turn off someplace and they would lose him. Once on the interstate, the traffic was heavier and they could keep a few vehicles between them and their quarry. When the truck driver stopped at a truck stop in Boise, the pursuing pair pulled into a fast food establishment to resupply their bodies and relieve themselves while keeping an eye on the truck. Back on the road, the truck driver turned off the freeway at the small town of Wendell, heading south on State 46 into farm country. Turning onto a side road lined with tall corn, the truck proceeded to a large metal outbuilding with tractors and three vans parked around it. Several men and a few women were milling around the building. Tony and Tom stayed on the highway, looking down the side road, until they saw the truck's tail lights go on and it began to turn onto the property.

"Looks like we know the truck's destination," said Tom.

Tony crossed the side road and parked on a short strip of land that was a tractor entrance to the cornfield. Walking a few yards between the corn rows parallel to the road, they tried to get a better view of what was happening at the building. They could see that the back doors of the trailer were open and that a ramp had been erected up to the trailer bed. Several people were walking up the ramp and into the trailer. That was when all hell broke loose. Three black SUVs roared up the side road with sirens whining and two helicopters swooshed in with loudspeakers blaring.

"Do not move! Do not attempt to leave the property! This is the FBI and you are all being detained. Do not move or attempt to evade arrest. You cannot outrun our helicopters and you might be shot. Kneel on the ground with your hands behind your heads. Obey the orders of the officers on the ground."

Tom and Tony looked at each other and simultaneously shouted out, in pantomime, "What the fuck is going on? Where did these guys come from?" After spotting the heavily armed men with the letters FBI plastered all over their backs and vests, they quickly realized they were witnessing a raid and that someone must have tipped the authorities off to what was going down. At the same time, it dawned on them that they might be seen as involved in the operations somehow, that they could be viewed as "lookouts" or accomplices. They didn't want to have to explain to the police what they were doing in Idaho with Oregon license tags, the same as that of the truck, and why they were following the truck in the first place.

"Either we sneak back to the car and beat it out of here or we stay in this corn field all night until they are gone," said Tony.

"I vote we get the hell out of here," replied Tom.

In a crouch, they silently made their way back to the car, softly shut the doors, and backed out onto the side road. Then they made their way back to Interstate 84 and headed for Vetlandia. Tom and Tony could hardly wait to tell the rest of the surveillance team.

"Holy shit, you should have seen it," said Tom. "Black Hawks diving in blaring orders and warnings, SUVs roaring down the road filled with FBI agents. It was a sight to behold."

"They were loading the truck with migrant workers," added Tony. "From their appearance, they looked like they hailed from south of the border. They were all rounded up and forced to sit down on the ground with their hands bound behind them. The truck driver and the guys at the metal building were all arrested. We didn't stick around to see anything else."

The newspaper the following day provided the rest of the story. "FBI apprehends six in immigrant labor smuggling operation. Forty-three illegals held for deportation. Logo and name of an Oregon farm emblazoned on confiscated semi trailer intended for transportation. Investigation continues."

∞

Mort Fitzpatrick and Wolfgang Gunnar were shaken by the news and immediately started wondering who the informant was who tipped off the FBI. Was the driver that was arrested one of ours or was it someone that Beaver State hired on their own? Was it someone connected to Armondo in Mexico? How much did the FBI know? Gunnar immediately alerted his stooges to keep their ears peeled for any talk about the raid among Vetlandia residents and let him know what was said and by whom.

Winifred Shepard, owner of Evergreen Farms, was fuming mad when investigators showed up at her farm inquiring about the ownership of the semi-truck and trailer confiscated in the raid. She denied ownership of the vehicle and any knowledge of the participants. She had no idea why they would paint the name of her farm on the trailer. Yes, she sometimes hired foreign nationals but only ones with work visas. Privately, she thought about sending one of her burly lieutenants to teach Dr. Gunnar a lesson. She did call him from a phone in Portland to chew him out for the idiocy of using her farm's name on the trailer and for having allowed a leak to appear in his organization.

"I thought it would be a good disguise, that it wouldn't arouse suspicion when driving on Oregon roads," Gunnar explained.

"You're a fucking idiot," Winifred replied. "I ought to sink you to the bottom of Crater Lake, you fucking moron!"

At Beaver State Trucking everyone was suspicious of the low-level employees and some executives were even suspicious of each other. They were mad about the loss of a valuable asset and worried that the driver might reveal his employer. Arrangements were made to have a sleazy lawyer they had on retainer pay him a visit in jail to assess his backbone and ensure his silence by a veiled threat.

They weren't afraid that the truck would be traced to them since the vehicle identification number and all of the paperwork were forged and linked to a dummy owner. But the boss, Dominic Sabini, and his close associates were anxious about the leak and intended to eliminate the leaker if they could find him. Sabini started to put pressure on all of his employees to report to him any dubious comments or suspicious actions by any other employee. If one of them appeared evasive or overly anxious, they would apply a little more intimidation to get him to reveal more.

Michael Mayhew was worried that he might be betrayed out of spite by one of the other drivers that he had rubbed the wrong way, not by anything he had done since he had been very careful. He made a smart-ass quip that the man took as a derogation of his status, causing him to retaliate by challenging Michael's falsely claimed criminal exploits. Although Michael apologized and claimed he meant no disrespect, the man continued to give him long sideways glances, as if he were questioning his every move.

When Michael saw the man talking with Sabini and both of them looking in his direction, he knew he was in trouble. He figured he could bluff his way out of it by claiming his accuser was just pissed at him for having made the insulting remark.

"Jesus Christ, Dom, I already apologized to the guy! What do you expect of me?" Trying a little blame-shifting, he quipped, "How do we know he wasn't the one who tipped off the FBI?"

Sabini didn't know what to think and decided to threaten both drivers. "OK. I won't pop you fuckers right off the bat. But if I hear one word that either of you had anything to do with this fiasco, you're dead meat. You understand?"

"Yes, sir, you bet," said Michael, smiling at the other driver.

Scowling at Michael, the other driver asserted, "Yeah, boss. I didn't have anything to do with it and you can take that to the bank. But you better watch this asshole."

Although Michael had skated past the denunciation by the skin of his teeth, he worried that Sabini might do a closer check on his references than he had done previously. It might be time to beat a hasty retreat, he thought. He waited a couple of days and then told Sabini that he had to go home to another state because of a family emergency and that he would be gone for a week or more. He called Dr. Oldman and said he thought his cover may have been blown and he needed to disappear for a while. He asked his therapist to call a local DEA telephone number and tell whoever answered to relay a message to his "mother" that he was going to be out of town for an unknown period. Oldman made the call to a surprised agent who quickly said, "Oh," pause "Yeah, I'll give his mother the message."

Sabini surveyed his new truckers for a replacement for Michael. Reading over applications to truck driving school, employment records, and comments entered into his record by his supervisors at Beaver, he learned of Gordon Sawyer's time in "Stir" and his many successful evasions of pursuing drug agents when he was in business for himself. He thought he might have found the replacement he needed, someone who didn't want to get caught and would take the risks necessary to make that a reality. He called Gordon in for an interview.

"Gordon, my boy, I'm considering you for a promotion to be one of our elite drivers. In this position you would earn substantial bonuses for hauling special cargo to various locations. It is important to our clients that their names and locations not be disclosed to anyone and that you not be concerned about the nature of what you transport. If you have to go through any inspection stations, you will report only what we tell you to report and not take it on yourself to verify the contents. It is unlikely that you will confront any law enforcement agents. However, if you do, we expect you to plead ignorance and refuse to cooperate until you have legal representation, which we will provide. Do you understand?"

"Yes, sir," replied Gordon, as he fidgeted in his chair.

Surprised by Gordon's nervousness since he expected a cool character after reading about his hair-raising escapes, Sabini asked, "What's the matter with you, boy? You look like you're about to piss your pants. Don't you think you could stand up to being grilled by some government inspector or a cop?"

"No, it isn't that, boss. I know how to stonewall the cops. I've had this jumpiness ever since I went into the joint. I just don't want to go back there — too many fucking psychos in that place and you never know what they will do."

"Yeah, I know. Been there myself. Tell ya what, I don't think there's much chance of you going to prison driving a truck and we can get you out of any charges made against you if that happens, but you have to keep your trap shut and follow directions. Think you can do that?"

"Yes, sir, boss."

"You ain't got no problem with skirting the law a little bit, do you? I mean, there's a big demand out there for these products and people are willing to pay a good price for our services. So, what the hell, it's just good old American capitalism in play here."

"Yes, sir," said Gordon. "I can keep my nose clean by looking the other way, just like everybody else does."

"OK then. We'll start you out with a pick-up and delivery going to Portland from a farm out near Ashland."

∞

Gordon wasted no time telling Dr. Oldman about his new status. Feeling that he was between a rock and a hard spot, his anxiety level was high enough for him to consider a split-and-run resolution to the problem. Oldman suggested to Gordon that he might want to work with the DEA as had Michael Mayhew. Gordon didn't trust the DEA or any other government agency, for that matter, but agreed to work with them to avoid being charged with a crime if he was caught transporting illegal merchandise. He managed to get the Feds to agree that he could keep any pay and bonus he received for transporting illegal goods. He indicated to his handlers that they should be prepared for him to act out the plan proposed by his boss at Beaver

Trucking if he was apprehended in any of their raids so as not to get identified as a snitch.

Tom told Oldman about the raid by the FBI and Oldman informed Tom about Gordon's replacement for Michael. Both of them were apprehensive about future events even though they had the blessings of the DEA. There were a lot of things that could go wrong and people they cared about could get hurt if events spun out of control.

Andrew Hammons managed to track down the FBI friend of his old roommate, Gene Lofgren. The agent reported that Gene was still alive but in ill health, thanks to his premature discharge from Vetlandia. Andrew filled him in on what had inspired their formation of a group to investigate patient abuse at Vetlandia, how it came to pass that they began watching the activities at Beaver Trucking, and what they had found out about possible staff involvement in illegal activities. The agent agreed it sounded suspicious and expressed worry about the inside man working with the DEA. He cautioned the group members to be careful and not take any impulsive action. Andrew reassured him that their group contained a couple of men experienced in intelligence work and law enforcement and that they were not any kind of fanatical organization. The agent said he would like some time to confer with Gene and his regional office before he got back to them with a plan of action.

∞

Over on the administrative side, tensions were also rising. The Director of Vetlandia, Alfred Horton, was interviewed by the FBI about the death of Scott Parks. The autopsy results finally came back and suggested that he likely was the victim of foul play. Did Horton know of anyone who would have a reason for killing him? What were the deceased's relations like with other veterans at the facility? Had he filed any complaints or been subject to any disciplinary action? While he responded to the investigator's questions using data and interpretations provided to him by Mort Kilpatrick, Alfred began to feel uneasy because some of the questions he was asked raised doubts about the version of events provided by the COS. He confronted Mort, asking him how certain he was that his information was correct. Not convinced by the answers he received, he still trusted the COS enough to give him the benefit of the doubt, at least for the time being.

But, a short time later, federal investigators, informed by Gene Lofgren's FBI friend, began inquiring about his case too. They mentioned allegations of patient abuse and questioned Vetlandia's contracts for training veterans with Beaver Trucking. Horton's doubts about the stories Mort was telling him returned to haunt him, driving him to distraction and dithering on important decisions.

The Director was contemplating various ways he might determine if Mort was lying to him and if he was involved in anything sinister. He could just confront him directly and force him to explain himself. But if Mort was innocent it might adversely affect their subsequent relationship and he knew he would need help running the place in the future. He struggled to remember what he had been taught in the VA management classes about exposing deception in the workplace. What was it the training consultants had said — keep your cool and don't accuse the employee of anything. Try to get the suspect to contradict himself or make mistakes by encouraging him to provide more details. Throw in some unexpected questions to see if that throws him off. Yeah, that's the way to go, he thought. Of course, I'll have to remember to pay attention to mismatched movements and inappropriate grooming behaviors. Does he ask questions before answering? Does he make gestures to dismiss further inquiry? Does he display tell-tale movements designed to hide an emotion?

Uncertain of himself, as usual, Horton called Mort to his office for a "little chat about the FBI inquiry." When Mort arrived, Horton followed the prescribed practice of putting the employee at ease before subjecting him to questioning.

"Would you like a cup of coffee, Mort?"

"Thanks," said the COS, searching with his eyes for any indication of what Horton was up to.

"Mort, the FBI agent asked some detailed questions I didn't have the answers to. I'd like for you to give me some more details about Scott Parks. What was he protesting and what did you do to address his complaints?"

"I told you before, Parks was a born troublemaker. He was accusing Dr. Gunnar of malpractice and patient abuse. He was a liar and a provocateur. He had done the same thing when he was in the service, accusing his superiors of war crimes. This was just another instance of his radical agenda to get even with authorities who had caught him misrepresenting the facts. Parks had mental problems that Gunnar identified and he didn't like it. He was out to get a service connection and he didn't care who he libeled to do it."

"What about his death? The feds claim he was the victim of foul play. Did you look into that at all?"

"Yes, we looked into it. The guy was an alcoholic and a drug addict. There's no way they can rule out the possibility that he got drunk and overdosed while fucking around over on that island. Did they show you any evidence of foul play?"

"No, but they claimed there was such evidence. They told me Parks had filed official complaints with regional office and with the Secretary about Gunnar and about you. They said Parks had all sorts of court documents implicating Gunnar. Did you know that?"

"Those documents don't prove a thing, believe me! Gunnar is a board-certified psychiatrist. Do you think he would do anything to jeopardize his reputation? I think not! There is nothing there. It is all a fabrication and the feds are dumb enough to fall for it!"

"What about this Gene Lofgren case? The last investigator they sent was a friend of this guy. Did you know that? He said that Lofgren was prematurely discharged from this facility and is recovering in a Veteran's Home in California. Is that true? Was he discharged without just cause and consideration for his medical condition?"

"No, that's absurd! Lofgren was not complying with the requirements of our medical staff. He was using outside medical facilities to thwart the efforts of one of our doctors. There was nothing wrong with him when he was discharged."

"They said he suffered from PTSD and cardiac problems when he was sent from here to Roseburg. They said you had him on some kind of Don't Readmit List when he returned. That is illegal, you must know that. Do you maintain that kind of list at this facility?"

"No, no, you've got it all wrong, Mr. Horton. We just try to keep from admitting and readmitting the same old scheming patients who have no need to be here. You know me. I wouldn't do anything to break the law or harm patients. I'm one of the good guys, don't you see?"

"Hmm! I don't know, Mortimer. I don't know! I'm going to give you the benefit of the doubt but there are just too many questions, too many suspicions raised by those investigators. I'll let the matter drop for now but I want to get a clearer understanding of what's been going on around here and I'll get it, one way or another."

Although he had temporarily let Kilpatrick off the hook, Horton was even more suspicious of Mort than he had been. Mort had simply reiterated the same old explanations he had provided before. He didn't add any new detail and he avoided answering the more probing questions. In some cases, he had denied facts that could be proven from the records of disciplinary boards and the patient representative. Horton wanted to check that out by having one of his aides read the records and report back to him. Mort also acted offended that he was even being questioned but the Director had the feeling that it was all an act, not a genuine expression of a wounded ego. He would have to get some other sources of information, maybe interview some of the other staff.

∞

Mort felt anxious and angry when he left Horton's office. He was surprised by the Director's unusually aggressive approach, thinking that maybe that sonofabitch wasn't as dumb as he had thought. He walked over to Wolfgang Gunnar's office. The psychiatrist's scheduled appointment had not shown up, a frequent occurrence, so Mort asked him to go for a walk with him.

"I just got out of the Director's office, Wolfgang. A couple of FBI agents paid him visits that have him shitting in his pants and asking too many questions. They asked him about Parks, told him they had evidence of foul play and now he wants to know about those complaints the bastard filed with Regional Office and the Secretary. One of the agents was that friend of Gene Lofgren, so we aren't going to get any break if he listens to him and finds out how we ushered that old drug sniffing dog out the door. And now they're asking about our contracts with Beaver Trucking. We've got to be prepared for some heat coming our way. Alert Whitey Green, that nurse, what's her name — Diane — and Carole Harding to keep low profiles 'till we see where this is headed."

"OK, boss. I've got my boys out with their ears tuned to the scuttlebutt around here. If the leak is someone at Vetlandia, they should be able to round up some suspects."

Indeed, Gunnar had ordered Georgie Cramden and Herb Sims to work together, try to eavesdrop on conversations at the canteen, the mess hall, and all the day rooms for any clues as to who might be collaborating with the FBI. They listened for any references to law enforcement and paid attention to any newly formed groups who expressed any criticism of the COS or Dr. Gunnar. They pretended to have a gripe about the facility and asked who they should go to for help. Most patients ignored them, their reputation as scumbags having preceded them, but several innocents mentioned the patient rep and Dr. Oldman. A few mentioned Tom Ward and Daniel Hanson for their protests at the Infirmary and they had both been seen in the company of someone named Andrew.

CHAPTER 12
PLAYING DEAD

Gordon Sawyer received his first assignment as an elite driver. The task was to deliver a shipment of stolen electronic devices from a repair shop in Roseburg to a warehouse in Portland. Again, the DEA did not see it as within their jurisdiction but passed the information on to the state police. Gordon feared that he might be stopped by police along the way to his destination. If he was arrested, he would have to convince them that he was working undercover for the DEA; if they let him go he would likely be suspected of being a snitch by Sabini. Luckily, the authorities involved decided to wait a week to see where the merchandise would be moved to from the warehouse before they made any arrests. As it turned out, the TVs, radios, and music systems were being retailed over the Internet. So when the police raided the business, the news did not arouse suspicions at Beaver Trucking. They just assumed it was one of the warehouse's employees who was careless in his communications with friends.

"Hey, you, what's yer name?"

The man who Michael believed fingered him to Sabini, Pete Donovan, approached Gordon one day and began to quiz him about Mayhew's whereabouts.

"Gordon."

"Yeah, Gordon, you knew Michael Mayhew, didn't you?"

"I talked to him once, if that's what you mean by knowing him," Gordon said, hoping to throw off his inquisitor.

"You both came out of Vetlandia, didn't you?"

"Yeah, I guess. Why do you ask?"

"Oh, I was just wondering if you knew what happened to him. He hasn't been around here for several days. He said he had some kind of family emergency. You don't know where they live do you?"

"Oh, no. I never talked with him about his family. Could be in Timbuktu for all I know."

"Well, we'd like to get hold of him. You don't suppose you could go over to Vetlandia and find out where his family lives, do you?"

"I don't think they are allowed to give out that information to non-family members."

"No, not from his medical record. I mean just ask around to people that knew him, his friends. Someone must know where he went."

"Well, I...." Gordon stammered.

"It would put you in good with the boss, you know. Don't want to have him wondering about your loyalty do you?"

"No, no. I guess I can ask around. But don't expect me to pull off any miracles. People come and go every day out there. The biggest share of the population turns over damn near every year."

Gordon was pretty sure that Donovan had tagged Michael for being the rat that tipped off the feds about the truck that was to be used to carry farm workers. He suspected the guy wanted to show his boss that he was right about Michael all along, thereby achieving a measure of revenge. Gordon worried about getting exposed as an informant for the DEA but hoped that the agency might be able to supply him with a phony address that he could use to placate Sabini and his minions. Maybe they could even have a plant send Sabini's goons off on a wild goose chase, buying more time for himself as well as Michael. He arranged to meet his handler at a coffee shop in town and asked him if the agency could accomplish what he was proposing.

"Gordon, we don't have the budget to set up a phony apartment and assign an agent to it just to keep these goons off Michael's tail. About all we can do is give you a phony address but as soon as they find out there is no such place, they'd be back after you, asking why you sent them to a nonexistent address.

You'd be better off just telling them you couldn't find anyone who knew where Michael came from."

"Shit, that's not going to do me any good. If I don't come up with something, they're going to think I am protecting the guy. Maybe I should just tell them I found out that he was working for the DEA."

"No, no, no. You can't do that or they'll know we are on to them and scatter to the four winds. Keep your damn mouth shut. If they try to rough you up, we'll come to the rescue."

"Yeah, I'll bet," Gordon taunted. Fucking feds, he thought. About what I expected of the bastards. They god-damn use you and don't give a shit if the really bad guys knock you off. You're just an expendable prop to them. He headed over to Vetlandia to see if he could get some help from Dr. Oldman or Tom Ward. When he got there, Dr. Oldman was in session so he went over to the library to see if he could find Tom.

Walking up to the Help Desk, where Tom was working, Gordon pretended to be looking for a book. He passed a note to Tom that said *How to Disappear Completely and Never Be Found* and underneath a comment saying Gordon needed to meet with him.

Tom said, "Hmm. I think the author of that book was a guy named Richmond." Playing along with the charade, he added, "Let me check the card file. Oh, yes. It's been checked out. From the looks of the number of readers, there seems to be a lot of demand for it around here. Let me write on your note when it is expected to be back. You can try again then."

Tom wrote, "1 hour – Dr. O's office. I have an appointment."

Dr. Oldman was surprised to see the two men waiting as he returned from one of his PTSD groups which was held in a different building. Since the door to his Department Chief's office, was open, Tom rose to make his request to be seen together with Gordon appear natural.

"We got in kind of a tussle the other day and was wondering if you could help us work through it?"

"Sure, I'm always up to resolving a conflict in a reasonable way. Let's give it a try," said Dr. Oldman, knowing that the meeting must have something to do with the surveillance project.

Dr. James Holbrook, Chief of Psychology, took note of the comments with a raised eyebrow, but shrugged, thinking it was just another one of Dr. O's offbeat approaches to treatment, and returned to his paperwork.

Once in the room with the door closed, Tom, in hushed tones, said, "Gordon has a problem over at Beaver. They're pushing him hard to find out where Michael Mayhew has gone. The DEA isn't providing any real help, just thinks he should tell them he couldn't find out. Sabini won't buy that. What should we do?"

"How about telling them that Michael is dead," suggested Dr. Oldman. "Gordon, you'd have to stall them for a few days until we can put an obit in the local newspaper. We could say that a local veteran, identified as Michael Mayhew from documents found on the body, died in a one-person automobile crash in another state and no next of kin could be found. Then, as long as Michael doesn't show up, we're in the clear, for a while at least."

"That might work," said Tom. "Do you think they would try to find the funeral home to check out the story?"

"I don't know. They might but I kind of doubt it. We could have the funeral home say that final arrangements were pending."

"Is there any chance that Michael could come back here?" asked Gordon.

"He seemed to be pretty fearful of that gang over at Beaver, so I don't think so. At least not before it is public knowledge that the feds have closed down their operation. Gordon, it's your life that's on the line here, so you should have veto power over whether or not we go ahead with it."

"I... I don't know," said Gordon in a faltering voice. "I know they won't lay off me if I don't come back to them with something. They'll use some muscle. And the feds aren't going to come to my rescue in time if at all. So I guess this is the best option. I'm just worried they will want some more proof besides an article in a newspaper." After a pregnant pause, "Oh, hell, let's go with it."

Tom and Dr. Oldman exchanged glances and then studied Gordon's demeanor.

"OK," said Dr. Oldman. "I'll write up the obit and contact the DEA to see if they will help us pull off the ruse. It's probably illegal but I think I can persuade them to go along with it rather than see their inside man bite the dust. They'll have no risk and they might be able to help us pull it off. Maybe they can find a cooperative mortician who will lend his business as a backup source where it can be claimed that the body has already been cremated. If there is no body, no identification is possible."

∞

Herb Sims and Georgie Cramden, Dr. Gunnar's tattletales, decided that Tom Ward and Daniel Hanson were suspects that deserved closer scrutiny. After all, they had put up a big fuss over at the infirmary and made the staff mad at them. They were the kind that would cause trouble. One day, Herb would hang out in the library to observe Tom while Georgie frequented the restaurant across the street to spy on Daniel Hanson. Then they would switch locations the next day. When their prey would leave their usual locations, they would try as best they could to follow them without being noticed. Their first few days as amateur detectives yielded no significant results but on day four they both followed their quarry to the restaurant where they observed them having coffee and talking with someone they addressed as Andrew. Herb Sims followed Tom to Dr. Oldman's office and saw Tom and Gordon enter the office together. When the receptionist asked if she could help him, Herb asked if he could make an appointment for biofeedback. She explained that he would have to arrange that with his section psychologist. Knowing that would be the answer, he said he would do so and then beat a hasty retreat to the canteen where he met with his collaborator.

"Well, we've connected those two with each other and with this guy named Andrew and Gordon Sawyer. That's a start. We know Tom shows up most days at the canteen for lunch with his roommate, Tony Napoliello. Maybe we should hang out here and see if anyone joins them."

"Good idea," responded Georgie. "Do you think we should wear disguises?"

Nonplussed, Herb looked at his associate and asked, sarcastically, "You mean like mustaches and dark glasses, maybe a trench coat? You gotta be kidding me."

Embarrassed by his naivete, Georgie looked down at the table and said, "Naw. I guess that's a bad idea."

"On second thought," said Herb, "why don't we continue watching Hanson and Ward — see if they have any other friends of interest. "

A few days later Herb spotted Tom having lunch with his roommate, Tony Napoliello, and two vets that he presumed were also from the Vietnam era. He asked the guy in line at the food counter if he knew who they were.

"Them? Oh, that's Jerry McCall and Ken Harper. They're a couple of old Brown-water Navy guys — Riverines. I know them because we are all members of Dr. Oldman's weekday PTSD group. Nice guys. You want to meet them?"

"No, just curious what they are doing associating with the young guy. Seems strange he is hanging out with them rather than guys his own age."

"I don't know. I've seen the young guy working over at the library. Seems like a decent kid to me. Maybe he doesn't have any prejudice against the older generation. Maybe you young guys can learn something from us old farts."

"Yeah," replied Herb with a smirk, "maybe I can."

Later, Herb and Georgie reported their suspicions to Wolfgang Gunnar.

"So, you saw Tom Ward associating with Daniel Hanson, a guy named Andrew, and Gordon Sawyer and you think two or three Vietnam veterans might be part of the group too? That's not a lot to go on but let me check it out. In the meantime, keep nosing around to see if you can turn up anything specific."

On his computer, Gunnar looked up the records of the men his stooges had identified. All but Andrew Hammons were patients of Dr. Oldman. That's interesting, he thought. And Andrew was the roommate of Gene Lofgren, the drug-sniffing dude we ran out of here. Hmm! Patients don't get to choose their roommates but it is interesting that Napoliello was in army intelligence and what is this? The mysterious "Andrew" was in navy intelligence and Ken Harper chased the Baader-Meinhof gang in Germany? I better tell Mort about this. Maybe it's just chance but this group has the brain power and experience to cause us some trouble, if they want.

As Gunnar relayed to Mort what he had learned of the backgrounds of the patients who were associating with each other and appeared to have grievances toward them and other members of their little ring of malefactors, Mort became increasingly agitated, chewing his nicotine gum at a rapid rate and bouncing his right foot as if he were marking the tempo of a jazz band.

"Jesus Christ, Wolfgang! We've got a troop of fucking left-wing do-gooders trying to infiltrate our business and take us down. I never expected that much gumption from a bunch of broken-down veterans. Do you suppose they know about our arrangement with Beaver Trucking and Southside Transport? Could they be the ones who tipped off the Feds' raid?"

"Could be, Mort. That damn Oldman is probably involved in this somehow. Ward and Hanson appear to be the ring leaders. We've got to get rid of them or break them up so they can't expose us any further. What do you think we should do?"

"Well, at this late stage, we can't simply kill the lot of them, although I'd like to. There are too many of them and the law would be down on everyone connected with Vetlandia for sure. We could plant dope on them and kick them out of the facility for violating the rules. But then I suppose they are smart enough to appeal to the Director. That would take time and the Director is getting pretty suspicious of me now too. I don't know about Oldman. Maybe we could get a patient to accuse him of some ethical violation, and get him worried about getting sued and losing his license.

"This might be the time to get the militia involved. Senator Tyler, our friend in the state legislature, has been pushing me to stage a protest where he could get some TV and press coverage. Maybe we can kill two birds with one stone – distract the Director and take care of the snoopers at the same time. Let me think about this for a while. In the meantime, why don't you find some way to arrange an accident for Tom Ward? Don't kill him, just get him sent off to a hospital and out of the way for a while.

∞

Dr. Oldman managed to convince Gordon's DEA handlers that it would not look good for them if a volunteer for their agency, a military veteran no less, was murdered and they did not lift a finger to try to prevent it. He indicated that the press would surely track down all leads in the case and eventually ask them to confirm or deny that Gordon was working for them. A "no comment" response would simply be taken as evasiveness and the reporters would assume the truth was in the affirmative. A better approach, he suggested, would be if they helped Dr. Oldman and Gordon persuade Sabini and his gang that Michael was dead. All they would have to do would be to coax a funeral home director that he would be doing a valuable public service by responding to all inquiries about a certain individual said to be residing at his facility with a scripted answer – that the individual had died in an automobile accident, that unrecognizable remains of his body had already been cremated and that they were looking for any surviving relatives. And, of course, that they would not be prosecuted in any way for telling the fib. The DEA went along with the plan and found a funeral home director in northern California who would regard it as a privilege to do his civic duty.

Gordon Sawyer didn't want to give the impression that it was easy to find out information about the missing truck driver or his family, so he parried questions from Michael's pursuer, Pete Donovan, with "I haven't been able to find anyone who knows anything yet," and then "I think I have a lead." Finally, the day came to present the story of Michael's death.

"Did ya find anything about Michael yet, Gordon? The boss is getting worried that you're just playing him along and not really trying to find out what happened to that son of a bitch, ya know?"

Gordon pulled out a wrinkled newspaper clipping and handed it to his inquisitor. "Michael's dead. Got killed in a fiery one car accident. Looks like his ashes are in a funeral home down in California. See there," as he pointed at the article. "They're looking for relatives."

"Well, I'll be damned," Donovan said as he took the article from Gordon's hand. "How do they know it is him? I better check on that before I tell the boss."

Donovan called the funeral home and got the prepared speech. When he asked how they knew it was Michael, he was told that the victim was identified by his VIN, which had survived the fire. They simply searched for the registered owner of the vehicle and assumed that was who was driving. Since the remaining body parts were consistent with those of a 35-year-old male and they had no evidence to think otherwise, they assumed it was Michael.

Donovan showed the newspaper article that Michael was killed in an auto accident to Sabini. As he explained the circumstances and what he had learned from the funeral home, they both acknowledged that not having an identifiable body left doubt in their minds. But the story the funeral home director related seemed perfectly reasonable and what reason would he have to make up such a tale?

Gordon thought he was in the clear since Donovan and Sabini ceased confronting him and scheduled him for new pick-ups and deliveries. But then the Great Random Number Generator in the Sky grabbed an item from the area under the normal curve three-standard deviations from the mean. The unexpected happened — the "dead" Michael returned.

Sabini learned from another employee that Michael was seen at a local bar. It seems that he had a girlfriend the existence of whom he had not confided to anyone including Dr. Oldman. Michael maintained contact with her while on his leave of absence and, when she turned up pregnant, he returned to "do the right thing" by spiriting his love away with him. Mistakenly, he had allowed her to lure him into a nightspot so she could bid adieu to her bar-tender sister. And that was where one of Sabini's men spotted him.

Sabini dispatched Donovan to try to locate and dispose of Michael. Raging mad, he and a couple of henchmen called Gordon into a back room at the company headquarters and confronted him with his lies about Michael's death.

"I didn't know, boss, honest," Gordon whimpered. "Someone over at Vetlandia gave me the newspaper clipping and I thought it was true. I didn't know he had a girlfriend and no one I asked about Michael ever mentioned it, I swear!"

Sabini shoved Gordon down on a chair and his two goons tied the frightened captive's hands behind him.

"Bullshit!" yelled the red-faced Sabini just inches from Gordon's nose. "Who do you and Michael work for? What have you two been up to?"

"I don't know anything about Michael but I work for you, boss. I've been loyal. I just do what I'm told. I'm not involved in any plot to get you."

"Plot to get me? Is that it?"

Sabini punched Gordon in the jaw, drawing a drizzle of blood as his cheek was forced into his teeth.

"Are you assholes working for the mob? Huh, huh, trying to take over my operation, are you? Or are you working for the cops? That's even worse. Am I going to have to beat it out of you, you little turd!"

Gordon again protested his innocence. Sabini went over to a rack of equipment next to the wall and unraveled a pair of electrodes, attaching one to Gordon's left ear and another to his right index finger.

"Now, I'm just going to give you a taste of how electricity feels, Gordon. I can change the locations of these electrodes to include your... well, you know. And I can increase the amount of juice I feed into them to be more persuasive, you know? So why not fess up to what you been doing?"

"I don't know nothing boss. I've been tricked by whoever is behind this thing with Michael too. I'm a victim, just like you. I didn't rat you out. Please believe me, please!"

Sabini pressed a button on a controller for a rheostat that he held in his hand and Gordon went into convulsions, unable to even scream in pain until after the current was turned off with the release of the button. Then he let out an unearthly groaning sound followed by a series of whimpers. Sabini grabbed him by his shirt collar and again yelled in his face.

"You worthless piece of shit! Spit it out! What have you been up to?"

Gordon did not respond, either out of shock or in an attempt to look like it. Sabini ordered his stooges to remove Gordon's pants and change one of the leads to his scrotum. Gordon screamed and flailed his legs as the two beefy assistants carried out the order.

"Alright then. Let's see if this will change your mind, you motherfucker!"

In a fit of rage, Sabini shook the rheostat in front of Gordon's eyes and turned it to its maximum setting, pressing the button down longer than before.

"How do you like that, jerkwad? That get your attention? Huh? Huh?"

After the initial convulsion, Gordon didn't move, his head hanging down on his chest, his arms and legs limp as overcooked pasta. The assistants moved up to him, pushed his shoulders, and kicked his legs. Nothing. No response.

"I think you killed him, boss."

Sabini's jaw dropped, a brief moment of regret. He felt for a pulse in Gordon's carotid and, finding none, dropped his hand. Then he threw up both arms and said, "You saw me. I gave him a chance. He made the choice to clam up. He killed himself, the dumb sonofabitch. Nothing anyone can do about it now. Alright, get the fucking body out of here. Go dump it near Table Rock and they'll think he died hiking. Better yet, put it in Bear Creek Park and they'll think some homeless dude did him in."

∞

Donovan went to the last known location of the elusive Michael Mayhew, the bar where his girlfriend's sister, Marie, worked. Starting with the tale that he was an old friend of Michael, he inquired of the buxom blond where he might find him.

"I haven't seen him in many weeks," she responded. "I think he might be in California. He had some family problems to take care of."

"Now look here, sister, I know for a fact that he was seen in this here bar just two days ago with your sister. If you don't cough up his whereabouts, things could get troublesome for her and for you too."

Unruffled, Marie gave her interrogator a long "are you sure you want to do this?" glance before saying, "Maybe you should talk with my boss about this. Hey, Reuben," she yelled out, "I got a customer that says he's going to make trouble for us if we don't tell him where Julie and Michael are. You want to come out here and clarify matters for him?"

Donovan gulped as he saw Rueben, a muscular six-and-a-half-foot gentleman who was removing his apron and wadding it up as he ducked when coming through the doorway to the kitchen in back.

"So you think you can come in here and threaten my employees?" said the bald giant as he strode forward, red-faced with the veins in his neck and head visibly pulsating.

"No, no! I was just asking," Donovan backpedaled. "I didn't mean no offense, really, I just need to find this guy."

Reuben reached over with his baseball mitt-sized hand, grabbing Donovan by the shirt collar and lifting him off the ground with one arm. "I'm going to say this just once and you better listen real careful, you understand? I don't want you showing up here again *ever* or I'll break you in half, you fucking scumbag! And if you have any friends that want to give me some trouble, the same fate will be waiting for them." With that, he dragged the intruder over to the door and threw him out on the sidewalk.

Donovan was shaken. He didn't want to tangle with that bastard again, not without shooting him first and he wasn't sure even that would stop him. Now what kind of excuse could he make up for Sabini? Maybe he'd just spend some time chasing around town, pretending to look for Michael until Sabini was preoccupied with other things.

∞

Gunnar wracked his brain trying to find some way to get rid of the threat posed by Tom Ward, Dan Hanson, and Dr. Oldman without bringing federal investigators down on the criminal enterprise they had going. Maybe he could arrange for Tom to have another seizure and send him off to Portland for an evaluation. He would have to get Tom to ingest a placebo rather than Dilantin or get him to take a medication that would increase the likelihood of seizure. That would require that Gunnar inject himself into the route from the dispensary to the patient or force Tom to take his meds on the pill line. That would, in turn, require a collaborator to make the switch in medications. Nope, too complicated and prone to error, he thought. And besides, the evaluation in Portland would probably only take a few days, not keeping the target out of action for a substantial period. He considered several other "medical" methods to get him out of the way but they all had some potential flaw.

Finally, he decided on the simple direct approach — have Tom meet with an accident, not one that would kill him but one severe enough to require hospitalization for an extended period. What he would do is get one of his militia veterans who had been assigned to the Golf Course Grounds-keeping Program, a man with a violent history who had been paroled from prison, to "mistakenly" run him over with one of the carts they used to carry materials and equipment. According to the plan, the cart driver would get from Georgie and Herb the routes Tom regularly took from one building to another and position himself on one of those routes, pretending to work on some project,

211

while awaiting his victim. Then, when Tom was close enough, he would "inadvertently" lurch forward or backward in his cart, running over Tom in the process.

The trap was set — the driver waited in his Kubota utility vehicle alongside the sidewalk leading from the canteen to the library, motor running, with a chain attached to a juniper bush that was to be removed. The chain was attached to a clasp encircling the bush in such a way that it would give way at a slight tug. As Tom walked by, the driver would gun the engine, the chain would break free, and the vehicle would lurch forward at a rapid rate, hitting the unsuspecting victim. The driver would get out of the vehicle and render first aid while claiming that he was surprised by the chain breaking, his loss of control, and accidentally striking Tom.

That was the plan. However, the chain did not give way as anticipated and the driver had to make a second attempt to break it free and run down his prey. This time he revved the engine so much that the chain built up a tremendous amount of force before it broke loose, sending it swirling into the cab of the Kubota and striking the driver in the face. Hearing the commotion, Tom turned about and rushed to render aid to the unconscious driver while at the same time yelling for a passing veteran to get help. The driver was taken to the infirmary, revived, and patched up enough for him to be sent to the nearest VA hospital.

The director hailed Tom as a hero of the moment for his quick thinking and provision of first aid, issuing him a Special Contribution Award at the first opportunity. When Gunnar heard from Georgie what had happened, he couldn't believe it.

"What the fuck? Does this guy have some sort of guardian angel floating overhead?"

∞

Gordon's body was found in Bear Creek Parkway by a homeless person who summoned the police. The discovery was reported in the local newspaper the next day and it quickly spread throughout Vetlandia. Dr. Oldman was shaken by the news. Did he coax Gordon into continuing in the surveillance when he should have advised him to quit Beaver Trucking and find a legitimate job? Were the rest of the members of the surveillance group in danger? How much about them did the conspirators in the Vetlandia staff know? He called the DEA agent who was Gordon's handler and asked if he had heard what happened.

"Yeah, we heard. Too bad, he was a pretty decent guy even if he had been a meth cook. But he must have gotten careless and dropped a hint they picked up on. He knew what he was getting into but that's the way it goes sometimes. We'll get them sooner or later."

Sooner or later? Dr. Oldman was disgusted by the DEA response. Gordon deserved better protection than that. These were his guys and he felt responsible for allowing them, even encouraging them, to continue their surveillance operation. He felt he should have told them to stay out of it and let the authorities handle it. Now another brave soul had been silenced.

Tom was shaken too. Were they onto us? Are they planning to get rid of all of us like they did Gordon and old Scott Parks? He walked over to consult Dan in the restaurant

Dan Hanson had been rattled by the news too, rekindling feelings he had in Vietnam when he believed the drug runners had identified him as an informer for the government in Nixon's drug interdiction program.

"These are the same kind of bastards I ran into before. They don't give a shit if they kill you or your family. They don't have any kind of conscience. If they think they need to do it in order to protect their income, they'll do it."

"Let's get our guys together and see what they think," said Tom. "I'll drop by his office and see if Dr. Oldman can be there too. At the park about 7:00."

Tom and Tony arrived in Tony's Mazda. Andrew and Jerry arrived in Andrew's modified mail truck and Dan and Ken Harper rode up on Ken's vintage Harley-Davidson. All eyes were on the brown Vanagon as it slowly made its way to their location. Everyone heaved a sigh of relief when Dr. Oldman stepped out and made his way to the table.

"Are you guys alright?" asked Dr. Oldman.

"Yeah," said one.

"More or less," said another.

"A little anxious," voiced another.

"I'm mad as hell at the fuckers that killed Gordon and Scott," said Jerry McCall.

"Let's take the bastards on," said Ken Harper. "We've dealt with this kind of scum before and we can do it again."

"I'm thinking that way too," said Tony Napoliello.

Andrew Hammons gave his assent and added, "We need a plan."

"A self-defense plan and a plan to take these assholes down," Ken chimed in.

Tom, now looked to as the leader of the surveillance team, was inspired by the camaraderie and aggressive stance taken by his friends who had much more experience than he in confronting evil doers. He tossed an inquisitive glance at the rebellious Daniel who smiled and shouted out, "Right on! We've had enough of this shit. Let's toss a little their way."

Dr. Oldman urged them to think it through and discover all the implications before committing themselves to any particular course of action.

"Yeah, Doc, don't worry," Tony interjected. "We've all been in deep do-do before and survived that. We can survive this too."

"So what can we do to protect ourselves?" asked Tom.

"First off, we should never travel alone, even here at Vetlandia," said Ken. "Then we could all use some kind of weapon. Since we are on government property, we can't use firearms or serious knives like the old K-bar. But we can use pepper spray, get a collapsible baton, carry some kind of noise-maker, carry a pen knife or defensive key chain. And we need to brush up on our defensive moves — gun takeaways, getting out of a choke hold, using your palm to break a nose, eye strikes, knee strikes, using our elbows. We got to keep tabs on our environment, avoid dark places without an escape route, that sort of thing. Maybe we can practice down at the gym."

"I agree, those are all good ideas," said Dan, "but we don't want to raise too much suspicion and some of us are getting a little too old and frayed around the edges for that physical stuff except when really pushed to it. Besides, bringing the battle to them might throw them into a defensive posture. I think we need to forget about the truckers for the time being and concentrate our efforts at home, do some more investigating right here at Vetlandia. I think we also need to recruit some more guys to our cause."

Pondering Dan's words, Tony tried to focus the group by summing up what they knew. "We have evidence that Kilpatrick is getting payoffs from Beaver Trucking for recruiting employees to run drugs, cheap labor, and stolen equipment. And we know Dr. Gunnar and Carole Harding are up to their eyeballs assisting in this thing. I'll bet Dr. Greene is involved too but we don't have any evidence other than that he is an asshole to patients. We certainly could use some help to figure out how this whole operation works. And we could use more members for our security as well.

CHAPTER 13
SILVIA

Thinking he needed a less agile target, Gunnar next considered taking action against Daniel Hanson. His not-so-undercover agents, Cramden and Sims, found that Hanson left his work at about two o'clock every Wednesday crossing the highway to attend a psychotherapy session with Dr. Magnuson. An hour later, more or less, he again crossed the heavily used highway to return to his job at the restaurant. Wouldn't it be convenient, he thought, if Mr. Hanson were to be hit by one of the huge logging trucks traversing this route?

The stop light at the intersection with the main entrance to Vetlandia was often filled with vehicles waiting to get into the facility and those looking to get out onto the highway to go into town. The light was slow to change and impatient pedestrians would often try to cross while the light was green. The short yellow light might catch disabled veterans halfway across, forcing them to bid a hasty retreat or take their chances and rush forward. Several times a logging truck or some other vehicle whose visibility was obscured by an overloaded logging truck had struck hapless veterans, sometimes dragging their walkers or wheelchairs and bodies nearly down to The 909 before they could stop. The logging company usually avoided liability by claiming the veteran was drunk, had committed suicide, or was recklessly disregarding the law.

Veterans and other concerned citizens had protested that the speed limit was too high for the area and that logging trucks were often overloaded and lacked proper maintenance. They wanted speed limits to be reduced by a half mile on each side of the entrance to Vetlandia, for the yellow light to be on longer to allow pedestrians to get out of the street, for loads on the trucks to be limited, and for logging trucks to be inspected every year to make sure they complied with safety standards. They made proposals to that effect to the county commission. The logging industry objected to what they called unnecessary regulations that would adversely affect their ability to deliver products on time and, of course, their profitability.

Gunnar figured he could find and induce someone to drive a logging truck or a partner vehicle over Mr. Hanson as he crossed the road. However, coordinating the timing presented a problem. Logging trucks are not like automobiles that can get up to killing speed very quickly. They take a considerable distance to attain sufficient velocity, causing a coordination problem. Simplify, simplify Gunnar told himself. Just get someone to push Daniel out in front of a truck or vehicle, or trip him so he can't get away in time. Cramden and Simms were probably not up to the task. He'd have to call in one of his heavy hitters to do the deed.

It so happened that Dr. Gunnar's favorite hit-man was none other than, Jimmy Fasick, the man Daniel had spotted in the restaurant bragging to his lady friend about his new job with Southside Transport. After negotiating a price for his services, Jimmy watched Daniel for a couple of days, noting the limp in his quarry's right leg, and recording his habits when crossing the road.

Jimmy was waiting at the stoplight with a couple of other vets on Wednesday when Daniel limped up to return to work. The light turned yellow and Jimmy grabbed Daniel by the arm and stepped onto the roadway.

"Come on, we can make it, let's go," yelled Jimmy, pulling at Daniel's arm. Once out nearly to the center of the road, he kicked Daniel's right leg in the back of the knee, causing Tom's friend to go down in a heap. Glancing at the oncoming traffic rushing toward him, Jimmy ran to safety on the restaurant side of the road, figuring for sure that Daniel would be hit by the panel truck barreling down on him. He made his escape in a car driven by his girlfriend.

But Jimmy had not counted on Daniel's over-learned military skills. Daniel had tucked both arms close to his body, swung his head and shoulders vigorously toward the entrance to Vetlandia, and rolled quickly to the edge of the road as the panel truck screeched to a halt where he had previously fallen.

Waiting vets had run to help the man who was struggling to get up and sent emissaries to Vetlandia to get medical help. Tom got word of the incident and rushed over to help his friend.

"That dirty sonofabitch suckered me!" screamed Daniel. "I know who he is, that fucker we identified who works for Southside. God dammit, I'm going to get that asshole one way or another."

"How about we let the cops take care of this one," said Tom. "It's clear that it was an attempted assassination. You've got other vets that witnessed the whole thing. I'll get their names and room numbers. If the cops don't do anything, then we can give him a little Cowboy justice."

When Gunnar learned that Daniel was living and mad as hell, he exclaimed, "Shit, what the fuck? Fate has turned against me! I can't even kill a fucking gimp crossing the street!"

∞

Gunnar turned his attention to Dr. Oldman. How was he going to get rid of this "pain-in-the-ass," as Whitey Greene called him? Mort's idea of having someone accuse him of ethical improprieties sounded like the best bet, but what could they use? After all, the administration had given him several awards for outstanding performance. He even got the Hearts and Hands Award for his "professional expertise and devotion to providing quality healthcare" from the Secretary of the VA. He decided to consult Carole Harding, the fake psychologist Mort got hired by the Psychology Service. She might have more personal information that could be used against Oldman. He called her and arranged a meeting after work at a restaurant in town.

"Carole, we've got to get rid of Dr. Oldman before he gets the feds in here investigating our operation. Do you know of anything we could use against him? It doesn't have to be true, but it has to be something that will tie him up for a while fighting the accusation."

"Hmm… let me see. Actually, he has been pretty straight-laced around here and he had exceptional recommendations when he was hired. He has taken his turn giving presentations to the psychology staff, even did some research on the MMPI and the MBTI. Patients seem to like him and he even does one-to-one psychotherapy with a lot of them. He is married and I haven't heard of him making any passes at anyone. He gets along with everyone on the staff and has collaborated with Dr. Anderson in doing some research and getting it published. It's going to be pretty hard to accuse him of anything that will stick."

"Oh, come on Carole. There's got to be something we can use!"

"Wait a minute…. There is something but we'd have to get another person to go along with cooking something up and I don't know if she will do it."

"What's that?"

"Well, you have probably seen that new young intern strutting around here in skin tight blouses and pants taught enough to see the dimples in her ass. Silvia Knox is her name. She wears high pointy heels and shows a good deal of ankle."

"Oh, yeah. I've seen her. I hear she gives all the patients hard-ons, even some of the old guys from WWII."

"Yeah, well she heard from the other interns about how well Dr. Oldman's PTSD groups were received by the vets so she asked him if she could sit in on one as part of her training. He voiced some reservations about it in our staff meeting but we convinced him he'd be seen as a sexist if he didn't let her participate, so he agreed to do it."

"So what are you thinking? How can we use her to nail Oldman?

"Well, if we could get her to say that Dr. Oldman did something inappropriate, something sexual, in her presence…"

"Like touching her boobs, putting his hand on her ass."

"Yeah, something like that. We'd have to see what she is willing to put in writing or say in front of witnesses.

"You think she'd go along with it? We could provide her some incentive, like offering her a job when she is finished with her internship, send her off to some exotic place for a conference, give her some extra time off."

"That would probably help. We'll also have to cook up some story that will make her doubt that Oldman is on the up and up. Maybe we can get the COS to confide in her that other women have been coaxed into sexual relationships with Oldman and, when he was through with them, he has unceremoniously dumped them, causing them great mental anguish."

"That sounds good. Then we can have the director order the police to put Oldman in cuffs and march him off the premises. Can you approach her and see if she will go along with the plan?"

"I'll see her tomorrow, see if she'll buy into it."

Silvia Knox grew up the only child in a well-off family who paved her way through private schools and college even though she was endowed with only mediocre talents. They wanted her to have a respectable but not too challenging occupation that would impress their friends or at least not embarrass them. After consulting with career counselors, they encouraged her to pursue a PsyD degree from a mostly online university.

Silvia had always been rather slight in build with plain facial features and shy in disposition. In high school, she had a growth spurt and turned into a lanky specimen, not fully formed in the feminine way, who excelled at soccer but had difficulty attracting the interest of boys. It was not until her junior year in college that she discovered how to maximize her native gifts to get young men to pay attention to her. Wearing an uplift bra and the thinnest of panties, she adorned herself with colorful, very tight-fitting garments that emphasized her long, slender legs and firm buttocks. She learned to take long, assertive strides in spike heels when she walked and perfected many provocative poses that elicited the attention of the testosterone set. While she discovered that many advantages accrued to her from this newfound self, she still had not developed the inner confidence that onlookers believed she possessed.

Silvia had been supervised by Carole Harding for the first part of her internship. Carole, not having attended graduate school, didn't comprehend what her role should be in helping an aspirant to join the ranks of the psychology profession.

Consequently, she did not mentor Silvia in psychotherapy nor tutor her in the nuances and pitfalls of psychological testing. Instead, she assigned her to attend the group sessions conducted by the substance abuse counselor and the one run by the COS. She directed her to carry out a certain number of each of the common tests used at the facility and write up reports on them. She met with her once a week to assess her progress in completing her assignments. This was in considerable contrast to the approach of Dr. Oldman who had one-to-one sessions with his interns to coach and criticize their progress in psychotherapy sessions with specific patients and had interns give tests and interpret them but then assess the validity of said interpretations from the patient's behavioral data. So Silvia learned little from Carole but looked forward to the gains other interns claimed to have achieved from their work with Dr. Oldman.

Carole knew it would be a hard sell to convince Silvia that it would be a good idea to tell a lie about Dr. Oldman. Her strategy was to first create doubts in her intern's mind about her competence as a budding psychologist by criticizing her abilities in test interpretation and telling her that the substance abuse counselor found her less than effective as a co-therapist, even though that discussion never occurred. Then she started to create doubts that Dr. Oldman was what he appeared to be by suggesting that Silvia was naive and implying that she and the COS knew "facts" about him that would change her mind if she could only reveal them. Finally, the coup de grace: telling her, in confidence because she feared that Dr. Oldman would get revenge on her, that he had had sexual affairs with other interns and then dumped them when a more attractive replacement came along.

"I find that hard to believe, Dr. Harding. He has always been very professional with me and I've never heard any of the other interns suggest that he is promiscuous — a Lothario, a seducer, no way."

"Oh, my child, you are so wet behind the ears, so immature. Why do you think a guy with his credentials came to this backwater place to practice? For the mountains and the forests, for the good fishing? No, it was because he got in trouble where he worked before. He figured he could get away with his wanton ways out here in the sticks."

"I don't know. How can you be so convinced that is true and not just a rumor that someone made up?"

"Would you believe it if the COS told you it was true?"

"Well, I suppose, but the picture you are painting is not consistent with what I know personally."

Carole arranged an appointment between the COS and Silvia to discuss the matter. Mort welcomed her into his plush office and offered her a coffee or soft drink and a bonbon. He put on his most gracious manner.

"Silvia, my dear, this is a very sensitive matter. What Carole told you is true and we need your help. We need some statement from an offended party in order to rid Vetlandia of this scoundrel. If you could tell us that he has approached you in some inappropriate manner, we could file charges that would cause him to lose his license to practice in this state."

"But he hasn't done anything to me, personally."

"Yes, I know, but you wouldn't want other women to be damaged, psychologically, by his depredations, would you? You would be doing a great service to our facility and to the women who work here, to future female interns, if you could tell of some sexually suggestive behavior on his part."

"I haven't seen any. Maybe he isn't attracted to me."

"No, no, my dear. You are very attractive and I'm sure he is waiting his chance to make a move on you. What we want to do is to stop his depredation before something lethal happens, before a young woman commits suicide because of him."

"What will he do to me if he finds out I am the one who turned him in? Will he harm me? Will he make trouble for my career plans?"

"He won't find out, I can guarantee you that." Thinking it was time for a little carrot to provide incentive, Mort added, "By the way, we can be helpful to you in your career if you help us with this."

"Like how? What can you do for me?"

"Well, we can do a lot. We can offer you a job after you complete your internship. We can send you to San Francisco or New York City, all expenses paid, to attend a conference of your choosing. You could take in a play while you were there and eat at the best restaurants. We can give you time off to prepare for your licensing exams."

"Can I have some time to think about it? I mean, this is a big step for me."

"Sure," Mort replied. "Just remember, the longer we wait, the greater the risk of someone being hurt by this pervert. I'll set up an appointment for you a week from now when we can discuss your decision."

After she left, Mort called Carole and told her to keep working on Silvia, that she was close to doing their bidding. Carole dutifully complied, reminding Silvia every day that the clock was ticking and she might never get an opportunity like this one to stand up for women's rights.

Finally, Silvia gave in and looked for some bit of behavior that she could construe in the direction Carole and Mort desired. She found her "suggestive" behavior during a presentation Dr. Oldman was giving to the five interns in attendance. Dr. Oldman had just risen from a seated position and was having a problem with his shorts riding up, causing discomfort in his crotch. He absentmindedly adjusted his pants to relieve his annoyance before returning to his lecture.

That's it! Now I can tell the Chief what he wants to know, Silvia thought while Dr. Oldman answered questions from the others present who were unaware of the tantalizing action. She told Carole she had "seen something" and Carole immediately phoned Mort to announce they had achieved their goal and she was bringing Silvia to his office to fill out the appropriate forms. When Silvia hesitated before affixing her signature to the document proclaiming that Dr. Oldman had acted in a sexually provocative manner in her presence, Mort reassured her, saying it would be alright and asking where she would like to go for her conference.

Once he had the accusation in hand, Mort made haste to the Director's Office to get authorization to have the facility police relieve Dr. Oldman of his duties and escort him in handcuffs off the facility property. Mr. Horton asked why they had to rush into action and Mort told him that they could all be held liable if they hesitated after they had been informed there was a sexual predator in their midst and the culprit offended again. Four policemen, including the rotund Chief, descended on Dr. Oldman as he was seeing a patient, Tom Ward. As they handcuffed the bewildered doctor, they told him he had been accused of sexual impropriety and was ordered off the premises. They instructed Tom, mouth agape, to leave the office, that he would learn the details soon enough.

Dr. Oldman said to Tom, "Don't worry. I can handle this. Someone's getting afraid. It is all a set-up. Tell your friends I can be reached at home."

Oldman told his wife what had happened as soon as he got home and she laughed. "You gotta be kidding. You were sexually provocative during a lecture to interns? Wish I could have seen it. You must have really pissed someone off this time."

"Yeah, it's a set-up. Somebody thinks we are getting too close to finding out what is going on at Vetlandia. I've got to call my attorney right away."

"What evidence do they have?" asked Walt Hancock, the attorney.

"They have an affidavit signed by a female intern that says I made a sexually provocative act while teaching a class."

Walt asked, "Do they have any corroborating witnesses?"

"I don't think so. There were five interns there. I doubt any of them will verify her claim. I mentioned to you my suspicions about certain people at Vetlandia back when I asked you about suing them for patient abuse."

"Yeah, I remember that. I asked you if you were hurt in any tangible way and you said probably not so then I told you that you wouldn't have any standing in court if you weren't harmed by their actions. Then you brought up the possibility that you might be forced to resign for ethical reasons and I agreed that was an interesting point but it might be expensive making it in court and they could delay and delay until you ran out of money."

"Yeah, that was the case then but now they have deprived me of my livelihood and threaten my whole career."

"We can work with that. Let me get to work on getting an injunction to stop what they are doing and work out some details for a lawsuit for libel against them. It will take a few days. In the meantime, write down what you know about details of the incident so you don't forget."

Oldman knew he couldn't do anything on his own to fight the federal government without a lawyer in his corner. But others were not constrained by legal issues. The other interns, after hearing about the claimed incident, were in disbelief and said none of them had seen what Silvia had seen. They gathered at the office of the Chief of Psychology to register their belief that Silvia was simply misperceiving the situation or, worse still, was just lying for some reason.

Tom notified all the members of the surveillance team of what he had observed and each did his part to spread the word to all the patients in Section Three. It took a couple of days before about 60 of Dr. Oldman's patients mounted a protest in front of the Director's Office demanding that Dr. Oldman be reinstated and threatening to take it to the Central Office in Washington, DC.

Looking out the window at the angry mob carrying signs to free Dr. Oldman, Director Horton said to his secretary, "Oh, God. What has Mortimer gotten me into this time?"

Figuring he should try to quell an impending riot, Mr. Alfred Horton went down to face the protesters.

"Now, now boys. I don't know what all the facts are but I think we can get this thing resolved and give Dr. Oldman a fair hearing. Just calm down and go back to your rooms. Let the administration take care of it."

"Fair hearing, my ass!" said one of the protesters. You signed the order to get rid of one of the best people at this facility. You assholes shit on all the good people working here and reward all the goof-offs. Time for a change in administration, if you ask me!"

A chorus of "Yeah"s and "Right-on"s arose from the protesters.

Horton didn't know how to respond and beat it back to the safety of his office, hoping the police would be able to handle the situation before he got called on the carpet by the folks at the Regional Office. He phoned Kilpatrick but got no reply. He told his secretary to keep calling and sent an aide to hunt down the slippery COS.

About that time, the Director was served with a subpoena to show cause for the action taken against Dr. Oldman and notification of a lawsuit against all administrators involved in the amount of two million dollars. Oh, crap, he thought. I'm in deep shit now. I'm going to have to defend myself from the goons upstairs and probably in court too. I'll probably lose my job, get fined, and be blacklisted for any position in the VA after this. Where is that fucking Mortimer? I'm going to have him pay for this debacle with his hide.

For his part, Mortimer Kilpatrick thought the commotion going on in front of the Director's Office could be another one of those opportunities he could use to his advantage.

He had been thinking about how he might pay off a financial debt to Senator Tyler for having solicited donations for "the cause" and get rid of Horton at the same time. Tyler's son, Randy, was being investigated for his role in proffering bribes to influence legislation and rulings affecting the timber industry. If he could raise questions in the public's mind about the legitimacy of the investigation and show popular support for the senator's son, the senator would be in his debt rather than the other way around. And if, at the same time, he could distract the Director and have him incapacitated, he could avoid any meddling in his affairs by representatives of the upper VA administration. Time to call out the militia!

CHAPTER 14
THE INCURSION

Wolfgang Gunnar reluctantly reported to Mort the failures of his efforts to throw fear into the minds of the surveillance group.

"I don't know what it is Mort. Here recently everything I've tried has turned to shit! Am I getting too old, am I losing my grip? I don't get it."

"Don't worry about that now, Wolfgang. We've got bigger fish to fry. I want you to call out the militia and get them ready to take over Vetlandia. We're going to create enough confusion around here that they won't have any time to look into our personal affairs. We're going to kidnap the Director and hold him incommunicado, scaring the shit out of him and keeping his mind off the lies I told him and his concerns about how I run things here. And we're going to get the TV cameras out here and show them what we want them to see — that our militia is a righteous force for good in society, supported by our veterans and the public. We'll use the investigation of Randy Tyler, the senator's son, to show that left-wing radicals with uncontrolled power are using it as a political tool to cover up their lack of patriotism and regard for one of the biggest industries in our state."

"Holy shit, Mortimer!" Gunnar responded, his mouth wide open, dumbfounded by Mort's audacious announcement. His mind jumped back and forth from inspiration to fear, from images of the militia triumphantly invading Vetlandia to images of the police, the feds, or National Guard troops descending on them in force and arresting them all.

Seeing the astonishment on Gunnar's face, Mort declared, "You think this is too arrogant, too high-handed, don't you? Well, I think we can pull it off and not serve a day in jail. Actually, we won't even be suspects. Here's the thing — we'll get that ambitious young officer in the militia, Clarence Youngblood, to be our front man. He'll take all the flack and it will seem like we are just victims, held captive like all the rest, when, in fact, we are pulling the strings behind the scenes. But we have to plan it all out. We don't want any surprises. Let's call a meeting of the militia executive committee and Youngblood and start to plot this all out."

At the meeting, Mort, outlining his vision, stated "We'll stage a blitzkrieg attack, secure all the entrances, disable the facility police force, and establish control over all employees and patients. We'll need five squads to take over each residence building to keep the vets in line and we'll need other teams to round up employees and confine them, for a time, to the auditorium. We'll tell the patients involved in food service and maintenance to continue with their usual activities with the exception that no one will be allowed to enter or leave the premises. Another squad will take control of the director's office, and take Horton into custody. The militia command center will be set up in the COS's residence, ostensibly taking me and Gunnar in custody but actually taking orders from us. Signs will be posted telling the public that Vetlandia is temporarily under control of the militia in order to protest the unjust investigation of Senator Tyler's son."

Mort continued, "Two communication centers will be established. The first will handle our public propaganda announcements to radio and TV stations and also try to recruit resident vets to our cause, get some of them to endorse our views during public interviews. The second will handle negotiations with authorities for the length and conditions of the occupation and the militia's eventual safe departure. I expect that police will demand we vacate the premises immediately but we'll respond with demands of our own, emphasizing the danger of harming innocent victims if the authorities attempt to take the encampment by storm."

"How are we going to justify taking these steps?" a member of the committee asked.

"We will claim that the purpose of the occupation of Vetlandia is to protest the Tyler investigation. But the militia will then have a platform to make our arguments and dispense our own propaganda about how liberal leaning officials are weakening our country and how we are important for saving a democratic society from the foolish ideas of liberal leaders."

"I like the idea of making a statement in a big way but how are we going to get out of there without being arrested?" asked another member.

"I think we can count on the authorities making a deal with us to vacate the premises without any arrests in order to avoid bloodshed. We'll have the senator act as the mediator. That's a position that will give him great significance and a substantial amount of camera time."

With little resistance from those present, Mort began to ask for volunteers to provide oversight of the required tasks. Clarence Youngblood jumped at the chance to lead the invasion and immediately began to plot how it would unfold and who would lead each team needed to secure the facility. He asked for time to evaluate the entrances and routines at Vetlandia and practice the assault at their camp near Grants Pass. Other members volunteered to create propaganda materials, write press releases, obtain information about the capabilities of local and federal authorities, and carry out other tasks necessary for the success of the operation. Several subsequent meetings evaluated the readiness of the militia for the takeover.

Finally, D-day and H-hour arrived. The decision was made to go in with 200 troops at night on Friday after most employees had left for the weekend since fewer troops would be required to secure the premises. Four men in a van were dispatched to kidnap Director Horton as he drove home and take him to a secure location until the takeover was complete and he could be returned to Vetlandia.

Commander Youngblood had managed to assemble a convoy of rehabilitated military vehicles and improvised troop transports to carry the militia into the facility. Leading the assault were two vintage M1151 Enhanced Armament Carriers (Humvees) followed by a variety of pickup trucks with machine guns mounted on the back and crammed with militiamen in camouflage clothing. Vehicles gathered on either side of the three entrances, out of sight and awaiting the signal to proceed, each vehicle having a prearranged destination. Once the signal was given, the convoy entered and used barricades to close off the entrances to traffic. A machine-gun-mounted truck was stationed a few yards back from each entrance. "Do not enter" signs were posted that indicated the facility was being occupied by the Sons of Liberty.

The first Humvee drove directly to the Administration Building where the Station Police were located. The three officers on duty, seeing they were out-manned and out-gunned, immediately surrendered their weapons and were placed in restraints.

Five squads took over each residence hall, descending on the section offices, astonishing the nighttime patient Incentive Therapy employees. Several laughed uproariously until they realized the invasion was not an elaborate prank. The troops reassured the IT workers they had nothing to fear as long as they complied with the orders of the occupying force and didn't do anything stupid. They encouraged them, as patriots, to help keep the other patients in the section calm when they awakened and even suggested they join the militia.

A communications center was established in the Director's office on the second floor of the administration building making use of his telecommunication devices. Early Saturday morning, local TV and radio stations were contacted and told that Vetlandia had been taken over to protest the investigation of Senator Tyler's son, the lack of true patriotism, and the ill effects of liberalism. They were told that no one would be harmed if the authorities maintained their distance and the militia's demands were met. The next press release would be the following day.

The kidnapped Director was returned to Vetlandia, chained to the floor in a dark windowless room in an old building used for vehicle maintenance, deprived of food and water, and intimidated through blustering, domineering, and threatening behavior on the part of his captors. The command center for the militia was set up in the COS's residence. It would be announced at the first press release that COS Kilpatrick and Chief of Psychiatry, Wolfgang Gunnar, who was supposedly visiting because the two of them planned on going fishing the next day, had been taken into custody. In fact, the militia were taking orders from them.

Early Saturday morning, when the food service workers showed up at the mess hall to make breakfast for the residents, they learned that if they carried out their duties as usual, they wouldn't be harmed but if they resisted, they would be forcibly restrained and suffer deprivations throughout the occupation. When patients awoke and began arriving for breakfast, the room buzzed with questions: What's going on? Who are these guys with guns and why are they here? What do they want? As the men sat down in their usual cliques, rumors circulated rapidly: The government had fallen. We've been invaded by China, or Russia, or drug cartels from Mexico, or aliens from outer space. It's all a big stunt for some motion picture. It's a test of our ability to adapt to an invasion or an occupation run by the CIA. Finally, one of the masked gunmen stood on a table and addressed the assembly.

"You men are not the target of this occupation. We don't want to hurt any of you if it can be prevented. In fact, we would like to invite you to join us as true patriots in our quest for justice. We are taking this action to protest the political persecution of a family member of one of our duly elected senators, a good man who is the scapegoat for the negligence and irresponsibility of a sinister group of men who want to see the destruction of our country and the American way of life. You will be allowed to go about your usual activities here at Vetlandia as long as you respect our authority and do not try to escape to the world outside. I have issued an order to collect all of your cell phones before you leave this room. You will be able to retrieve them once the occupation is over. If you choose to resist, you can expect to lose your freedom and have a hard time of it during the remainder of the occupation. You will each be issued an arm-band color-coded to indicate your section membership. Wear your arm-band at all times so you do not get restrained or shot as an enemy infiltrator."

Most of the patients were still uncertain about what was taking place and chose to bide their time until they knew more about what was happening. A few recognized the conciliatory, mollifying statements for what they were and cried out "Bullshit." Members of the militia soon descended upon such rabble-rousers, dragging them out of the room by force, binding their hands, and placing them under guard in the music room. Overt resistance ceased although there were many grimaces and knowing glances exchanged.

Tom Ward was sitting with Tony Napoliello and Jerry McCall. They were as flummoxed as the rest. Tom whispered, "We've got to meet!"

"Where, they've got men with guns everywhere?" asked Tony.

"In the tunnels. I'll show you where to get in," said Jerry.

The tunnels were utility tunnels constructed for servicing the heating, sewer, electrical, and plumbing systems in the facility. Jerry, used to working in claustrophobic spaces from when he refurbished submarines on Mare Island, had deduced their existence soon after his arrival at Vetlandia and quickly discovered there were entrances in most buildings by watching the travels of repairmen when there was some kind of failure in function, such as a clogged drain or a failure of heating for the building. Repairmen would arrive and suddenly disappear when walking down a hallway. Most patients were preoccupied with other things and paid no attention to such matters. But, for the curious few, a little more snooping revealed the small door leading into the tunnels, from which the repairmen would emerge when the problem was solved. At times, after "lights-out," Jerry would make his way into the tunnels and find other patients hiding out there for one reason or another. One WWII vet was seeking shelter from bombers that appeared in his dreams, replicas of those he experienced for real on a US airfield in China. Others found it a good place to enjoy a joint or store alcohol for later use. Some were "regulars" that developed a bit of camaraderie among themselves while others just checked it out as a resource for disappearing if needed at some time in the future.

The three men arranged to rendezvous in the tunnel under their section building in an hour, their arrivals staggered by five minutes. Jerry arrived first and signaled his location by flashing a penlight when he saw the door open as each of the others entered the dark passageway cramped by pipes and electrical circuitry on both sides.

"It's a zoo up there," said Tom as he leaned against an electrical circuit box. "Rumors are going around that they have the Director stashed somewhere and plan to use him as a hostage. Someone claimed he saw a bunch of militiamen dragging equipment over to the COS's residence. One of the IT workers for the police say the officers are all trussed up over in the auditorium. There's lots of hearsay about what is happening and the know-it-alls are pontificating about who's behind it and what it all means. Some of the PTSD guys are freaking out, some are mad as hell and want to fight, and some are planning an escape. Others are falling for the crap those militia bozos are spouting and offering to help them out. We've got to find out what they are up to and what they plan to do."

"And some of those guys in the militia used to be patients here at Vetlandia," said Jerry. "The guys who have been here a while recognize them. Some of them know their way around here and are familiar with our routines."

"That's interesting," said Tom. "Makes you wonder just who is involved in this thing."

"We need some intel," said Tony, "and we've got to have a plan. We need to get the rest of our guys together and recruit some of the food service workers, grounds keepers and maintenance men to help us find out without tipping off the invaders. Jerry, do you know where all these tunnels go? Can we get to any building from here"

"Maybe not all of them," said Jerry, "but probably most of them. The camp was built with a central power plant in mind and they had to lay out the tunnel system along with the foundations before they could start putting up buildings."

The conspirators agreed to meet again in a few hours. The other members of the surveillance group were to be notified except for Daniel Hanson, who had been working at the cafe across the road when the occupation began. Tom said he would figure out a way to contact Daniel. Jerry was dispatched to the leather-work shop to enlist the help of Terry Wells and the other guys there in creating imitation armbands so they could avoid detection when traveling in a foreign section. He also was to construct a map of the tunnels leading to the other buildings. Tony was to try to recruit the food service workers and other maintenance IT workers in Section Three as spies to gather intelligence on the invaders and get them to spread the word to their comrades in other sections when they had contact with them. Everyone expressed fear of the possibility of getting turned in by someone abetting the occupiers and promised to be discreet.

∞

The municipal police were the first authorities to learn of the occupation of Vetlandia after passersby notified them of strange goings on at the facility. Officers were dispatched to investigate after no response could be elicited from the Vetlandia Police Department. Reporters from local TV stations called to ask the police to verify reports that Vetlandia had been occupied by the Sons of Liberty Militia. When officers arrived on the scene and saw the barricades and machine guns mounted on pickup trucks at the entrances, they immediately retreated to a safe distance, called for backup, and suggested the chief might want to notify the state police and National Guard. The chief reminded them that they had no authority on federal property and told them to ensure the safety of citizens in the area and remain watchful while he notified the FBI of a possible terrorist event. The FBI sent some men from the Portland Office down to assess the situation and figure out what was needed to deal with it.

When the total Surveillance Group met, Ken Harper revealed that he had stashed a cell phone in a holster taped to his leg. Reception was poor from within the tunnels so Tom had Ken call both Daniel and Dr. Oldman, appraising them of what the group knew once he got above ground, and urging him to be careful not to be discovered. He also asked Ken to find out if the men on the other end of the call could find out what was the status of any plans the law enforcement authorities had for ending the occupation.

Several residents of Vetlandia had observed that the militia had conspicuously marched the COS and Dr. Gunnar into the COS residence, a one story structure with a parade field on one side near the middle entrance, with hands tied behind their backs, and posted many heavily armed members to surround the building. The group thought it a priority that they find out what was happening there. The small tunnel extension to the COS residence allowed traversing by only one person at a time, so Jerry McCall and Andrew Hammons took turns lying under the house, trying to make out the conversations taking place overhead.

Clarence Youngblood had just entered the living room above where Jerry was positioned. Mort poured a glass of champagne and held it out to the young man wearing the insignia of a colonel. Wolfgang already had a glass in hand and the two of them toasted Youngblood for having masterfully pulled off a coup détat.

"Very professional," said Wolfgang.

"Spectacular," gushed Mort. "Now we've got to get ready for a challenge from the law. They always try to test your mettle to see if you mean business. Then they'll want to negotiate. So be prepared for an assault on our periphery. I'll leave it to you as to how you respond but we want them to know we are not going to be a pushover and that we mean business. I'd also like you to track down Daniel Hanson and Tom Ward, take them into custody and rough them up a bit. Put them in the building where we are holding the Director. We don't want any resistance from these fucking trouble-makers. Maybe they'll be collateral damage before we leave, I haven't decided yet. After you get that taken care of, send your communications person over so we can set up the message we want to send to the public."

Jerry had been lying there for close to two hours, nearly falling asleep, when he was roused by excited talking above, the clinking of glasses, and the laughing. Focusing on the voices, he was able to recognize that of Mort Kilpatrick and Wolfgang Gunnar but not that of a third person. The third person addressed one of the others as "sir" and appeared to be taking orders rather than dispensing them. When Jerry heard the names Daniel Hanson and Tom Ward being bandied about, he said to himself, "Oh, oh, this is not good."

Crawling back out of the tunnel, he encountered Tony and asked, "Where is Tom? The COS and Dr. Gunnar are directing this whole thing. I think they've sent some goons to capture Tom and work him over. We've got to warn him."

"I don't know where he is right now. He was going to see if he could find someone on the cleaning crew to break into the pharmacy and then he was going to talk with a couple of food service workers on Section Three."

The pair emerged from the tunnel into the Section Three dormitory. Splitting up to cover the building quickly, they walked the halls, avoiding any militia members but asking residents they met if they had seen Tom. Finally, they learned from Buster Rollins that Tom had been apprehended and taken off by two militiamen. Buster said that Bennie Foster, the IT worker in physical therapy, was following them at a discrete distance to see where they went. Buster promised to relay the message to Bennie to contact them when he returned.

∞

Vladimir Kumar was assigned to the Vetlandia disturbance by the Portland FBI office. Vlad (sometimes called "The Impaler") had been with the Bureau for 10 years and had distinguished himself by swiftly crushing a student uprising to protest Desert Storm at the Federal Building in Corvallis but with many casualties in the process. He didn't like to "fool around negotiating" with lawbreakers and believed that rapid application of overwhelming force was the most effective method. When he arrived on the scene at Vetlandia, it did not take him long to determine what he thought was the weak point in the occupier's defense, the entrance on the north end of the property. Since the situation could become urgent at any moment and it would take a few days to get all the men and equipment he needed from federal sources, he decided to request that he be allowed to federalize local law enforcement and National Guard troops and commandeer the necessary equipment. Although local National Guard units were immediately alerted to the possibility they would be called up, obtaining clearances from the various levels involved — adjutant general, governor, president — took most of the day. It was after dusk before the personnel and equipment started to accumulate on the highway outside Vetlandia and the disparate leaders worked out a modus operandi for them to work together to quell the ruckus taking place behind the high-fenced compound.

The National Guardsmen and the local police officers and sheriff's deputies were doing a lot of nervous joking around, not sure if this was going to be a real physical confrontation or just a lark, a harmless prank that would end in capitulation by the invaders. It didn't occur to Vlad that one of the men on his side of the fence might also be a member of the Sons of Liberty. But, indeed, Roscoe Robinson, a National Guard sergeant, was that man and he was in regular communication with Clarence Youngblood, the commander on the inside. He did his best to get within earshot of the guy who was tossing out orders left and right, Vlad Kumar, to discern his plans so he could relay them to Youngblood. Robinson observed three men come up to Kumar, who placed a hand on the shoulder of each man in turn, then pointing to each of the three entrances, wherefore they departed to the areas across from those entrances. After about a half hour, the men returned and gave their reports to the FBI man. Kumar then began to concentrate his attention and forces on the second, the northern entrance to Vetlandia. About an hour later, an armored vehicle, a Cadillac Gage Ranger, appeared on the scene and Kumar approached it for a powwow with the driver.

Robinson reported these actions to Youngblood and offered his opinion that Kumar intended to try to breach the northern entrance. Youngblood thanked him and told him to call again with any new developments such as assembling troops behind the Ranger. Summoning his lieutenants, he issued orders to prepare for an attempt to crash a vehicle through the barricades at the designated entrance. The ranking National Guard officer, surmising what Kumar had in mind, approached him to try to talk him out of any direct assault on Vetlandia.

"You can't just go barging in there with guns blazing like some hot-dog looking to make a name for himself. You could get a lot of innocent people killed. Why not wait a while, let the negotiators get here and have a shot at talking them down before you resort to that sort of thing? It's not like we have some sort of deadline to get these terrorists out of there. We've got time and they'll find it hard to sustain themselves for long without supplies from the outside."

"I'm the one in charge here, Colonel. The longer we wait, the more they'll think they can get away with everything — murder, mayhem, even rape — You know they've got women in there don't you?"

"Yes, but..."

"No yes but, Colonel. This is just some rinky-dink outfit that's playing a big bluff. They don't have any real fire-power. Their small arms fire will just bounce off the Caddy. Getting through those barricades will be like cutting butter with a hot knife. We'll just wait until it's daylight, then drive in there, lay down a little machine gun fire and some smoke and they'll be tossing their weapons on the ground, putting their arms in the air!"

"They're gathering troops behind the Ranger, putting a few guys inside with rifles and there's a guy on top manning the machine gun," reported Robinson to Youngblood. "Better get ready. I think they're fixing to attack at dawn."

As the rising sun began to cast long shadows westward from the buildings of Vetlandia, the Cadillac Ranger fired up its engine and began to move toward the northern gate. The men behind it peered around the vehicle to see if they could make out any resistance. Once the vehicle crossed the middle of the highway, the machine gunner on top began to spray the area with short bursts of fire. As it smashed into the barricade, there was a large explosion emanating from the ground, and the vehicle tilted to one side. An exploding Rocket Propelled Grenade further tilted the Cadillac until it was on its side. The men inside the vehicle crawled out and dashed back to the relative safety on the other side of the road along with those who were following behind the vehicle.

"Holy shit!" exclaimed Kumar. Addressing the colonel, he said, "I guess I underestimated this outfit. They've got some real fire-power. We need better equipment and more men. We need a tank and maybe some mortars. Think you could get that for us from the National Guard?"

As word spread of Kumar's failure, there was a lot of grumbling among the conscripts, who didn't relish the idea of dying for no good reason. The National Guard colonel knew enough about dealing with superiors with inflated egos to restrain himself from saying, "I told you so." But he did make a call to the governor's office to appraise her of the situation and request a negotiator.

"He's on the way, Colonel," said the governor. "Should get there by noon. Is there any way you can keep that hothead from the FBI to back off and wait until he gets there?"

"Well, I can slow-walk his requests for equipment and men. I think he's chastened enough to wait until he has an overwhelming force. You could help by giving his superiors at the Portland FBI office a heads-up and suggest they talk some sense into him."

Roscoe Robinson reported to Youngblood that the FBI initiative had been halted and that Kumar was now requesting reinforcements from the National Guard. Youngblood was pleased with the way he and his men handled the attempted incursion. While it was still dark, he had a man plant an Improvised Explosive Device of sufficient power to disable but not destroy a small armored vehicle in the driveway of the northern entrance. The RPG was a backup in case the mine didn't do the job. He intended to dissuade the opposition but not incur so many casualties that the other side would mount a major retaliation before a negotiated withdrawal could be implemented. And rounding up the resources that Kumar wanted from the Guard would buy them some time.

Mort and Wolfgang were discombobulated by the gunfire and explosions and summoned Commander Youngblood to find out what had happened. They were reassured by his report but had a sense of urgency about getting a negotiation channel opened up. While Wolfgang wanted to make contact with the authorities right away, Mort counseled that their negotiating position would be strengthened if they waited until they were contacted. In the meantime, they could set up a press conference, making sure to explain to the public that the occupation of Vetlandia is a "protest" and not an "insurrection."

"I've got my best PR man working on it right now," said Youngblood. "He has invited reporters from the local TV stations to show up for a Q and A session with me and the two residents suggested by Dr. Gunnar — George Cramden and Herbert Sims — are being prepped for the cameras right now to say that they are being well-treated and that they concur with our views. We're also trying to get one of the women residents to confirm that there is no hanky-panky going on with the ladies."

"That's right, Clarence, make sure to cast the militia in a positive light and indicate that our motives are benevolent, that we just want justice to be done with regard to Senator Tyler's son. Get in some digs against the liberals that are ruining our country and play up our traditional conservative values."

"I've got it," responded Youngblood. "It should all be ready for the evening news."

The reporters received an armed escort to the second floor of the administration building where facility cameras were already set up. It was explained to them that videotaping of the session would be carried out by militia members and they would be provided a copy at the end of the session for rebroadcast on their networks. Primarily, they did not want cameramen from the news stations to zoom in on any untoward facial reactions or views of militia that could be used for prosecution after the siege was over.

Youngblood, wearing a hat and facial mask, was well-prepared for the interview. He indicated to his inquisitors that the group he represented considered the prosecution of Senator Taylor's son to be unjustified and merely a political stunt to try to detract from the senator's good works and popularity. He read off a laundry list of examples of excessive use of, or grabs for, power by liberal opponents of the senator as well as indiscretions on their part that brought their motives into question. He asked the reporters, rhetorically, "Are these the actions of decent and reliable men? Do they care about our republic and our traditions?" When asked when the occupation would end, he responded that it would depend on actions taken in good faith to halt the prosecution and persecution of Randy Taylor. Asked about the explosions that occurred earlier in the day, he indicated that theirs was a dedicated group and they would stand up against abuse of power wherever and however it occurred.

After Youngblood's interview, Cramden and Sims were paraded out for the reporters to ask them questions. Both patients sang praises of the militia and how they represented the best in America, true patriots, who stood for right, justice, and the American Way. They indicated that they had not been harmed by the invaders and continued to be fed and cared for by resident IT workers. A female resident joined them at the end to assert that none of the female residents had been abused or harassed by members of the militia.

∞

Daniel Hanson was working at the restaurant across from Vetlandia that the FBI had converted into a quasi-command center. Watching the activities taking place outside and overhearing comments of those directing the activities as well as those from agents who would come inside to get coffee or a snack, he would try to determine the status of the men outside and the intentions of their leaders, all the while performing his duties as waiter and dishwasher. He had seen the early morning attempted penetration of Vetlandia and the explosions that upended the armored vehicle. Concerned that the authorities would escalate the conflict into a bloodbath, he was anxious to learn of the welfare of his friends inside the compound. He was relieved by the first phone call from Ken, who reported that the surveillance group was well and meeting in the tunnels, trying to find out what the militia was doing — and trying to do —with their occupation of the facility. Ken asked Daniel to contact Dr. Oldman to see if he could influence the authorities in their actions if they were able to provide intelligence from the inside. Dr. Oldman agreed to get closer to the action by taking up residence at The 909 but indicated that he did not want to divulge the existence of their group just yet, being wary of how the Feds might use the information. Daniel agreed and said he would keep him appraised of any new developments.

Meanwhile, Tony, alarmed by the kidnapping of his roommate Tom and determined to find where he had been taken, tracked down Bennie Foster and escorted him to the tunnels for a meeting with Jerry, Andrew, and Ken. Bennie, eager to take action to right a wrong, revealed that he had tracked the kidnappers to one of the white buildings near the rear of the VA property that was used as a repair shop for facility vehicles. He said he had a friend, Claude Pitts, who had an IT job in the repair shop and, befriended by the regular employees, worked on his truck there. Claude could tell them the layout of the building and where they might find equipment to use in a rescue operation. He was in his room now because the militia had declared the repair shop and all storage buildings to be off-limits during the occupation.

Directing his question to Bennie, Tony asked, "Can you go get Claude and bring him here so we can develop a plan of action?"

"Sure. Claude's a stand-up guy but he has had a lot of hard knocks so he is quite distrustful of people. It may take a while to get him to participate."

While in the Navy, Claude was positioned at deck level on an aircraft carrier to "set the ball" for aircraft coming in for a landing. Oftentimes, the planes would drop their unexpended rockets or bombs as they landed, the ordnance hurling right down toward him and giving him quite a fright. Claude was on a journey searching for his mother when he checked into Vetlandia. He characterized her as "either a spy or prostitute" when he was a child because she had placed him in the care of relatives who owned an orchard and one of the workers there sexually abused him. This early experience and his on-again-off-again relationship with his mother crushed his natural desire to care about others and fostered a belief that he was inferior, inadequate, and not of any value to anyone. He was a profoundly unhappy person, intending to commit suicide once he had found his mother. Resentful and distrusting others, he feared being disappointed if he held any positive expectations, and became guarded, with a gruff exterior that many interpreted as hostility.

Although a muscular and towering figure at six feet four inches, Claude thought of himself as "just a simple man" who couldn't understand people, especially the slick talkers who operated with hidden motives. He preferred working with animals rather than people and got a training position at a wildlife refuge nearby, one that was supposed to turn into a full-time job. However, the owner was just exploiting the government-funded program, which paid for Claude's expenses in going there every day, and the job never materialized. His feeling that the world was no damn good was reinforced by instances of disrespect shown to him by several other employers as well as by Drs. Greene and Gunnar at Vetlandia.

Claude was initially suspicious when Bennie approached him, but when he heard that it was Tom Ward who was in danger, he jumped at the chance to help.

"Tom was the first one to show me some kindness and respect when I got here. He showed me around and clued me in on who couldn't be trusted. He's one of the good guys around here — him and Dr. Oldman. You think he's down in the vehicle shop? I can help you with that."

Back down in the tunnels, the rest of the crew welcomed the new additions and expressed their appreciation for their help. Claude drew out the layout of the building housing the vehicle shop, pointing out where tools were stored that could be used as weapons or to gain entry to locked rooms. Jerry volunteered that there was a tunnel going to that building and suggested that they first send a couple of people down to see if any guards were stationed there and, if so, how many. Ken volunteered to be on the reconnaissance party and Claude said he would tag along to get some equipment that might be useful in the future.

Ken's penlight threw strange shadows on the walls as he and Claude wended their way down the long tunnel to the vehicle shop. Working on a worthwhile mission together rekindled the sense of excitement and camaraderie they had during their time in the service. Both turned out to have an appreciation for gallows humor as they joked about what could go wrong once they arrived at their destination. When the entrance to the building appeared in the dim light, Ken held up a hand and slowly approached, listening to silence for several minutes before cracking the door. The door opened into the back of an open bay pit used for changing oil and doing work on the underside of facility vehicles. Claude's old Dodge truck was parked over the pit, providing a degree of cover for the pair as they moved toward the stairs at the opposite end of the trench. Light poured in from an open overhead door at the far side of the building, landing ten feet from the rear end of the truck. They could smell cigarette smoke and hear laughing voices coming from the outside. Claude whispered the locations of various parts of the room above to his companion, who cautiously poked his head up under the truck far enough to be able to see where the voices were coming from. Two men in militia uniforms with rifles were outside the building, smoking, drinking sodas, and telling tall tales to each other. A card table with two chairs sat near the wall next to the open door. Ken pulled himself up by the front bumper of the truck and rolled out of sight of the open door. Claude followed suit and swiftly moved to a tool chest where he extracted a large bolt cutter. Ken pointed to a door with a large steel bar piercing a latch on the door, preventing it from being opened from the inside. By hand gestures, he indicated to Claude that he should keep an eye on the guards while he removed the steel bar and quietly placed it on the floor. Peering inside, he saw two bloody and immobile bodies lying on the floor — Tom and the director, Mr. Horton. Rather than trying to rouse them, he closed the door, replaced the steel bar, and motioned for Claude to join him in the pit.

Whispering to Claude, Ken said, "The director is in there too along with Tom. I think they are too injured to try to move now. We would be bound to make noise and alert the guards. What we need to do is go back and get more help for an assault on this place at night. We need four men to help the two prisoners and we need a couple of men or more to take out the guards if they discover us."

CHAPTER 15
FIGHTING BACK

Back at their tunnel meeting place, Ken explained what they had found and what would be required to extract the prisoners. He indicated that they might need some medical supplies to administer first aid, if necessary, and maybe stretchers to transport the victims back to safety in the tunnel. Claude Pitts suggested taking them to the back fence area where he could cut an opening with his bolt cutters so they could escape to the outside. All agreed they would make that decision once they determined the status of the prisoners. They considered obtaining a firearm by overpowering a member of the militia but decided against making a commotion and alerting the others. Andrew said he could probably obtain some Oriental fighting weapons — nunchucks, throwing stars and spikes, knives — from a Hawaiian vet he knew. Jerry McCall said he had a hunting slingshot stashed in his belongings. Ken and Claude said other weapons could be improvised from tools in the vehicle shop but stealth and surprise would have to be their major weapons.

It took a few hours to round up the supplies they needed before the six men started down the tunnel to the vehicle shop. Once they were all at the entrance to the service pit, they halted while Ken determined the location of the guards. They were both at the card table, playing cards and smoking with their rifles leaning against the wall. He asked if Jerry could hit a target with his slingshot from 30 feet.

"No sweat," Jerry replied. His was not your average wooden Y slingshot but a high-tech wonder from Japan with a laser sight, round rubber bands, double springs, and wrist support that could shoot steel balls 165 feet at 100 meters per second.

Andrew Hammons prepared to pull himself up from the front of the truck and throw spikes at the second guard while Claude readied himself to throw a crowbar at whichever guard was still standing. The other men prepared to climb the stairs out of the pit as soon as Jerry launched his missile.

Jerry inched his way up to the front of the pit where he could get off a shot. Placing the red laser dot between the eyes of the guard to the right of the table, he let fly with a barely noticeable whooshing sound. His target suddenly raised both hands to his face as blood gushed between his fingers. The other guard jumped up from his chair and reached for his rifle as a spike lodged in his side while Claude's crowbar struck him on the side of his face, knocking him to the ground. The rest of the men quickly descended on the hapless guards who were both losing consciousness. Trussing them up, the men dragged them up to the door where the prisoners were being held.

Removing the steel bar and opening the door, Tony rushed into the room to assess the condition of the two men inside. Bruises and dried blood indicated both men had been beaten. Tom may have had a seizure and likely had been deprived of his anti-seizure medications. Tony administered glucose IV and gave Tom a capsule of Dilantin obtained from the medications in his room. The director was conscious but had a hard time breathing and winced with pain if touched in his abdomen, suggesting a broken rib, possibly penetrating a lung. Tony decided the director needed urgent professional treatment and should be escorted to the back fence by Claude. He asked Tom if he wanted to go along with the director.

"No. Take me back with the others. I need to help get these bastards and keep this fucking militia from blowing up the damn place. I can make it, just give me some food and a little time to recover. I don't think I have anything broken, just a bunch of bruises and shit in my pants."

"OK, then. Claude, you and Andrew take Mr. Horton to the back fence and get him into the hands of the authorities. The rest of you, help me get these guards into this room to take the place of our guys. Jerry, you and Bennie help Tom back to our meeting place and let him regain his strength. I'll carry the weapons back. We may need them in the next few days."

The men dragged the two bound and unconscious guards into the room, closed the door, and replaced the steel bar. Claude Pitts and Andrew helped the director out the back door and moved toward the fence. A militiaman on guard duty intercepted them and held them at gunpoint, asking what they were doing in a restricted area. Claude bent over to lessen his imposing stature and simulated a fawning, hillbilly pose.

"We all are just trying to help this drunken sot back to his dormitory, sir. We're meaning no disrespect to you fine fellas of the militia."

The militiaman dropped his guard and drew his rifle up to his chest, thinking this was just some lamebrain who was trying to help out an inebriated friend. About that time, Claude rose to his full height and slammed his bolt cutters alongside the head of the militiaman, rendering him unconscious if not dead.

Proceeding to the fence, Claude cut an opening sufficient for the three of them to exit. He and Andrew each grabbed an arm of the dazed director and pulled him through the fence. Once on the other side, Claude hoisted the director on his back and made his way north of Vetlandia and then back to the highway until they encountered National Guard troops. Andrew wanted to rejoin his friends to fight the militia so he made his way back to the vehicle repair shop where he reentered the tunnel and made his way back to his compatriots.

Alfred Horton explained to federal authorities that he was the director of Vetlandia and that they had just escaped from the facility. A nearby ambulance was summoned to carry him to the nearest hospital. Claude was taken to the diner headquarters of the FBI for interrogation. Afterward, he was asked to stay in case they had other questions to ask him. As Claude wandered about the diner, the waiter, Daniel Hanson, approached him, offered him a cup of coffee and a cherry-filled turnover, and directed him to a table toward the back side of the restaurant. Daniel whispered in his ear that he had received a call from Ken Harper and would like to have a few words with him about the situation inside so he could relay it to Dr. Oldman.

∞

The hostage negotiating team had finally arrived from the Critical Incident Response Group in Washington, the situation at Vetlandia being considered too sensitive and complicated for agents from the Field Office in Portland. Mark Lindahl took command of the operation, at least temporarily displacing Vlad The Impaler. Vlad filled him in on what Claude had revealed about there being a resistance group within the veteran's community that managed to free the director and was gathering intelligence about the invaders.

Mark was a tall man, mustachioed with a receding hairline and craggy face. He grew up in Minnesota and had been with the Bureau for over 20 years, most of it in hostage negotiation and in training the craft to recruits. He thought this might be his final field assignment as retirement in Santa Fe with his wife and two dogs was beckoning.

"Anyone establish a communication channel with the invaders?" he asked as he strode into the command center in the diner. No one answered as Vlad's men looked at each other hoping someone could reply in the affirmative. Vlad volunteered that the militia had taken over the switchboard and were not accepting any calls at present.

"OK then. I want you to make up three cardboard signs large enough to be seen from across the road asking whoever is in command to call this number: 202-341-0009. That's my cell phone number. I want you to go out and display those signs in front of the gates right away. What do we know about this Sons of Liberty outfit? Do we know what they want?"

"They're some local militia that claims Senator Tyler's son, Randy, is being unfairly prosecuted by liberal Democrats. That's what they said on TV, anyway, and they were spouting a bunch of other bullshit about how the country is going to hell in a hand-basket. They're even claiming that the vets inside are supporting their cause."

"Yeah, well our first step is getting them to talk to us. We have to let them know we are ready to listen and aren't going to escalate the conflict by threatening them with use of force.

That's just the wrong thing to do at this stage. That was already tried and look at how that turned out."

Roscoe Robinson overheard Mark's comments and went outside, presumably to have a cigarette, but actually so he could call Commander Youngblood to let him know that the feds wanted to negotiate. Youngblood, buying some time so he could get over to Mort and Wolfgang for instructions, indicated that there would be a delay in responding to the fed's request.

"We'll let them stew a while, Roscoe. It'll work in our favor."

After Youngblood reported to his superiors, Mort said, "Clarence, I'll coach you on how to handle this. Now, the first thing they'll try to do is build rapport and we want them to think they have succeeded. They'll try to get you to tell your view of the situation, and they won't interrupt or argue with you about it." Handing two typewritten pages to Youngblood, he continued, "Here is the script that I have made up for you to read off when they ask that question. Expect them to sympathize and say 'uh-huh' or 'I see'. They'll repeat back what you just said and they'll ask questions in order to show you they've been paying attention. You just play along, say how disappointed you are in our government and play up the virtues of Senator Tyler. Say you would like the senator to come to Vetlandia to negotiate directly with us. Be vague about what we want. We'll deal with that down the line some."

Mark Lindahl was pacing around in front of the restaurant, anxiously awaiting a call from inside the compound as three pairs of men each held a cardboard sign with his number on it, occasionally hoisting it above their heads and shaking it in an attempt to gain some attention from those across the highway. An hour passed before Mark's phone came to life.

"Who am I talking with?" he asked the voice on the other end.

"This is the mission commander of the Sons of Liberty."

"I see," said Mark. "What have we got going here, my friend? What makes you want to take over Vetlandia?"

"We are protesting the prosecution of Senator Tyler's son by those liberal commies. It is all a political stunt, trying to throw dirt on the good senator so he won't get re-elected. We are a group of patriots that want to see fair play and justice in this matter." He rambled off several instances where he expressed the belief that the left-wing government had seized power, disregarding the interests of ordinary citizens and threatening the economic welfare of a state that is dependent on the timber industry.

"We're sick and tired of being pushed around while the fat cats in the legislature get away with murder. The honest hard-working people we represent are being harmed by all of this game-playing."

Mark responded, "You sound pretty hurt about being left out of the decision-making process. It doesn't seem fair, does it?"

"It isn't fair and we have lost all trust in the government, except for Senator Tyler, who has always stood by us and tried to do the right thing. That's why we'd like to have him come down here so we can explain what we need, so we can end this occupation without bloodshed."

"So you'd like Senator Tyler to act as your go-between, to help negotiate an end to this situation. Is that correct?"

"Yes, sir. That is what we would like," said Youngblood. "And we don't want any more attempts to storm in here by force. You do that again and there will be a lot of dead veterans you will have to explain to your superiors and to the public!"

"Whoa, whoa, there partner. We don't want that to happen and we don't want to have pick up a lot of militia members bodies either. We appreciate it that you didn't kill anyone when you stopped that armored vehicle from entering Vetlandia. Now I know you want to get justice and so do I. Just keep your cool while I see if I can get Senator Tyler down here to help out. I know you want to find a solution to this situation. We all do. Do you have a number where we can call you?"

"Just call into the switchboard. They will be directed to forward your call to me wherever I am at the moment."

Mark bounced his cell phone on the palm of his left hand, as he thought about what had transpired. It was implied that the commander was moving about the facility. He thought the commander's statement sounded like it had been rehearsed. I wonder if he is getting directions from someone else lurking in the background. Hmm, I'll have to see if I can learn more about that next time.

Summoning his second in command, he asked, "Find out the whereabouts of Senator Tyler and let him know that the FBI would like to talk with him, pronto. Then see what you can find out about the senator and why his son is being prosecuted. I need to know what the issues are if we are going to negotiate a settlement. That is, assuming that is what this is really about and there aren't any hidden agendas."

∞

Back in the tunnel, Tom's cuts and bruises were being patched up by Bennie Foster, the PT aide, who had training in emergency medical care while in the Coast Guard. A vet who was on the cleaning crew had responded in the positive to Tom's inquiry about breaking into the dispensary and obtaining a large number of downer drugs – benzos, Benadryl, Ambien, Lunesta, even anti-psychotics and anti-depressives. The plan was to inject the drugs into meals prepared for the militia, rendering them somnolent or at least drowsy and unprepared to respond to rebellious patients. The kitchen worker who had smuggled a ration of soup down to help Tom recover was asked if he thought they could pull it off and if he had any idea of how much it would take.

"I don't know for sure but we can experiment. I suggest we use Cramden and Sims, the traitorous little bastards who have been singing the praises of the militia on TV, as our guinea pigs. We'll try it out on their next meal — see how they respond. If they don't nod off within an hour, we'll up the dose for their next meal, keep on doing it until they crash or drop dead."

"May your experiments meet with great success. Let me know how it goes so we can plan how to put it on the menu for the rest of our militia friends. We have to get the timing down so we can take out a bunch of them, get them trussed up and stored away before they have a chance to warn the others."

It took only two trials for the saboteurs in the kitchen to have favorable results, getting both experimental subjects to head for bed or doze off on a sofa within an hour. Even when they were awakened by other vets, they were dizzy, disoriented, and had short-term memory problems.

Tom then planned an assault on three of the guards for Section Three after the rebel kitchen help had applied the medicinal remedy to their evening meals. For the most part, the operation went off without a hitch, the veterans absconding with the guards' weapons and uniforms after they succumbed to the effects of the potion in their consumables. The hands and feet of two somnolent guards were bound, their mouths covered with duct tape, and they were dragged to a storage room with a door that could be locked. One guard did not eat the regular meal and, as he watched his comrades stumble about and fall to the floor, was about to sound the alarm when Ken and Tony overpowered him.

"You're amateur soldiering days are over, young man," said Tony as he ripped off a strip of duct tape from the roll and pasted it over the guard's mouth. "Best you go along quietly and you will live to see your loved ones. If not, Vetlandia may be your final resting place."

When Tom learned of the success of the mission, he felt confident in the methods employed and considered extending them to the other sections and the militia units manning the entrances. Everything would have to come off perfectly for the scheme to work. First, he would get the food service workers to poison the food of the guards in each residence building using drugs stolen from the pharmacy. Once they succumbed to the effects of the drugs, a group of volunteers from the section would overpower and capture them, take their weapons, and stash their bound bodies in locations where they wouldn't be discovered. They would cut power and water to various parts of the facility and, under cover of darkness, another group would sabotage the invader vehicles so they couldn't escape. Once they had accumulated sufficient arms and manpower, if the food service workers could induce the gate guards to partake of the doctored foodstuffs, the insurgents could attempt the most dangerous task: to capture the pickup trucks at the gates and allow the police to enter the facility.

Tom figured there would be a sufficient number of veterans capable of physical altercations with the militia on each section but there were also many patients who were severely impaired, mentally or physically, who would be unable to participate and could be harmed in the process. Those in the infirmary probably couldn't be moved at all. Maybe before launching a full-scale assault on the militia, they should first try to get these less capable veterans out of harm's way, a few at a time so as not to be easily noticed.

Tom sent word to representatives of each section, through those who had recently joined the resistance, to identify impaired vets who needed to be removed from the facility before any fighting broke out. He asked that a priority list be made up of those in the section who needed to be evacuated, excluding those patients who were so impaired they couldn't be moved at all. Then, using a "pathfinder" process as was done at Normandy, cohorts of impaired vets were led by a few capable vets through the tunnels to the old storage buildings near the back fence where bolt cutters were again used to cut openings large enough for several people to exit at one time. The pathfinders then led the handicapped veterans across the river and back toward a safe location near The 909, thereby depleting the number of veterans in the residency halls. To reduce the chances of discovery, the empty beds were stuffed with clothing and pillows to simulate sleeping bodies.

∞

Mark Lindahl, learning that the man who rescued the director, Claude Pitts, was still in the diner building, asked a subordinate to fetch him so they could talk. He wanted to know more about the resistance group within Vetlandia and see if they could help end the occupation.

"Mr. Pitts, can you tell me more about the group you were working with that rescued the director and the other man being held captive?"

"The other man was Tom Ward. He is a young guy, at least compared to the others in the group. He works in the library and was the one who got a few guys together to try to figure out strange things going on in Vetlandia, things that harmed patients. A lot of them are Vietnam vets and a few from Desert Storm. They kind of look to him as their leader insofar as they have a leader. He isn't some kind of hotshot who wants to boss people around. The older guys in the group contribute a lot of ideas and suggestions so it is more like a team effort with men taking the lead in areas where they have the expertise. I got to know the other guys only after this militia thing happened, when we had meetings down in the tunnels."

"How many are in the group?"

"Well, there was about half a dozen to begin with but after this occupation started, guys have been offering to help right and left. There must be at least 30 different guys that I have seen down in the tunnels. And there are some of the employees that have worked with them too – Dr. Oldman especially. I just learned that he is down at The 909, a bar about half a mile away. He knows most of the guys and they trust him."

Lindahl asked one of his aides to go down to The 909 and bring Dr. Oldman back to the diner.

"What are they trying to do? Do you know their game plan?"

"No, not exactly. They were trying to collect intel on what the militia is doing in the camp. Tom got picked up by some militia goons and taken down to the vehicle shop and worked over. Someone must have told them he was a trouble maker. Bennie Foster followed them and reported back where they had taken him. When the others learned about that, they called me in for the rescue effort because I knew the layout of the shop and they thought I'd be helpful if it came to a fight. When we got down there, we found the director tied up in the same room with Tom. He was in pretty bad shape and we decided he needed to be taken to a hospital. So I volunteered to haul him back here."

Mark's aide returned with Dr. Oldman in tow. He acknowledged Claude's glance with a smile but said nothing. Mark said, "Thank you for coming, Dr. Oldman. I understand you know a lot of the members of the resistance group inside Vetlandia."

"I do and I think they are a great group of guys, guys who try to do the right thing and don't cower when they are threatened or, in Tom's case, beaten all to hell."

"Are you in communication with them?"

"Sort of. Reception is poor down in the tunnels so I get a call when one of them can get above ground and take the chance, hoping not to be discovered. Latest word I have is that they have captured three guards on Section Three, taken their weapons, tied them up and sequestered them in a locked room."

"No shit," said Lindahl as a smile slowly graced his face. "That is really something! How did they do it?"

"I wouldn't know," Oldman lied. "But they are a resourceful bunch. I think it would be a good idea to coordinate with them before you make any drastic moves."

"Yeah, we can do that," said Lindahl as he wondered just how resourceful a bunch of disabled vets could be. Could they significantly weaken the defenses of the militia? He ordered Dr. Oldman and Claude to stay in the area in case they were needed. An assistant brought Senator Tyler to agent Lindahl and introduced them.

Mark initiated the conversation. "I'm told these guys are protesting the prosecution of your son, is that right?"

"That's what I heard on TV. My son is unjustly being prosecuted. That is true, but I didn't ask the militia to invade Vetlandia. I have been sympathetic to the stance they take on many issues and to a lot of their beliefs but I don't endorse the use of violence, you have to believe that. They trust me because I stand up to the outrages that liberals try to get away with and I don't let them belittle the militia's conservative values. I would be proud to help bring this ruckus to a peaceful end for both sides."

"OK, senator. Are you willing to go over there and find out what it is they want in order to call off this seizure of government property? I can't guarantee your safety but we can give you a white flag and let those in charge know it is you who is coming to palaver with them."

Signaling the TV crew that accompanied him to start recording, the senator replied with transparent puffery, "I'll do it for my son and for my country."

Lindahl rolled his eyes in disbelief. Another ass-wipe politician grandstanding to win a few votes, he thought, and I suppose he will. But right now he's the only chance we can keep this thing from escalating into a nightmare. He called the switchboard at Vetlandia and asked to speak with the mission commander telling Youngblood that Senator Tyler was on his way over at the main gate carrying a white flag.

∞

Once inside the gate, two militiamen quickly shepherded Tyler to the COS residence, the ostensible headquarters for the occupying militia. Having planned and discussed this meeting beforehand, Mort and Senator Tyler broke into wide grins as they hoisted glasses of champagne to toast the successful unfolding of their plan. Mort sat down in his big easy chair and propped his feet on an ottoman.

"Now all we have to do is sit here for a couple of hours. Then you can go back over to the feds and tell them our demands for vacating the premises – stop prosecuting your son and guarantee the safe passage of the militia out of Vetlandia without charging the members with any offense. They probably won't like those terms, so then you tell them we are prepared to start blowing up buildings until they do."

It wasn't long before Youngblood appeared at the door to the COS residence, blurting out in an agitated fashion that the prisoners, Tom and the director, had escaped and that three members of the militia were missing.

"What's going on, Clarence?" Mort demanded. "Who did you have guarding the prisoners, some grade school kids? Can't you keep your troops in line? Are you a bunch of bum-fuck rubes who don't know what the hell they are doing? Jesus Christ

Clarence! You better get your act together before this whole thing begins to unravel!"

Commander Youngblood was distraught. "I'm checking everything, sir. I've got guys looking through all the residences, room by room. We'll find them, for sure. Just give me a little time. We're looking at the records of the guys who disappeared. I don't think they deserted. I think there is something strange going on here."

"Well, you better fix it or you're toast, my friend. Did you put explosives in all those buildings I told you to? We'll need a distraction so we can escape if this effort goes south. Do you have a vehicle we can use if we need to?"

"Yes, sir. We have C4 charges in all the major buildings, including the residences, and they can all be set off by remote control. We can make this place look like a Roman Candle if we need to."

"OK then," Mort continued. "Now go throw the fear of God into those men of yours! Find those prisoners and the missing guards. Use some muscle on the IT workers to get them to reveal their whereabouts. I'm sure that there are some of them that know what's going on. We've got to stop fucking around and get some results. Take Gunnar here with you. He knows how to convince the reluctant how to sing for their own good."

"Yes sir. I'm sorry sir," said Youngblood apologetically as he left the room with Gunnar trailing behind.

Addressing Senator Tyler, Mort remarked, "Looks like we don't have time to waste. You better get back across the street and make our offer to that fed bastard who's running the show over there. We've gone over the script before, so just stick to it and don't let him con you into anything."

Senator Tyler picked up his white flag and crossed the highway to the diner. Lindahl was waiting for him as he walked in the door and quickly ushered him into a back room.

"So what do they want, senator? What are their terms for vacating the premises?"

"They want you to persuade the state to drop the criminal action against my son. They want you to guarantee safe passage for the demonstrators out of Vetlandia and promise, publicly, not to subsequently bring charges against any members of the militia."

"Nothing else? That's all they want?" asked Lindahl, thinking there must be more to this hullabaloo than to vacate the charges against young Tyler and let the "demonstrators" off Scott-free.

"Yes, agent Lindahl. That's the deal."

"I don't know if I can do that," replied Lindahl. "Your son is facing criminal charges and hasn't had a trial yet. And members of the militia are not just 'demonstrators' as you call them. They have violated federal law by forcibly occupying federal land and taking veterans hostage. We won't know what other crimes they may have committed until we get into the facility and question the residents."

Senator Tyler hesitated before divulging the threat, "They have explosives planted all over the facility. If their demands are not met, they say they will start blowing up buildings, first empty ones and then those containing veteran patients. I certainly don't condone their methods. I tried to talk them out of it but they wouldn't listen to me. They think theirs is a just cause and that they are in the right. Now, they may just be bluffing but if it were me making the decision, I wouldn't want to have to answer for a big mistake in judgment."

Mark Lindahl was silent for several seconds, thinking about his alternatives and their respective consequences. Finally, he said, "I see, senator. Let me consult with my superiors to see if they can accommodate any of the demands of the people you are representing. Stay here and don't talk with anybody about this. I'll return as soon as I can."

Immediately, upon leaving the senator, Mark beckoned an aide and instructed him to fetch Dr. Oldman. Upon the latter's arrival, he asked, "Can you get hold of the resistance group inside? I have to know what their status is and what they can do to help us."

"Yes, of course," said Oldman. "We may have to wait until dark because the guy with the phone, Ken Harper, doesn't like to surface until then for fear of discovery."

CHAPTER 16
BLOW THE FUCKER UP!

Below ground Andrew Hammons was listening as Mort, Gunnar, and Youngblood discussed their plans. Upon hearing Mort ask about the placement of the explosives and say that he would blow up Vetlandia buildings to cover his escape if things turned sour, Andrew quickly backed out of the section of the tunnel leading to the COS residence and made his way to Tom's location under Building 205. Tony Napoliello took his place at the listening post.

"Tom, they're planning on blowing up buildings to cover their escape if they don't get what they want from the feds. What do you think we should do?"

Tom fired back, "I think we need to contact Daniel Hanson or Dr. Oldman and find out what is going on across the street. I wonder if they know about the plan to blow up the place? Hunt down Ken Harper and have him make a call. Have him tell the feds what we know and indicate to them that we have a lightly armed group of vets that are willing to take some action. We need to know what we can count on from the feds. Then have him come down here and we'll cook something up that we can do. Find Jerry McCall, Terry Wells, and Hank Burns and get them over here."

Ken called Daniel Hanson who happened to be with Dr. Oldman at the time. When he learned of the threat to blow up buildings in Vetlandia, Dr. Oldman quickly asked one of the FBI agents if he could talk to Mark Lindahl, the hostage negotiator, on an important matter. Anticipating the content of Oldman's comments, Lindahl asked if he had talked with the defiant veterans inside.

"Yes," Oldman replied. "They learned that the Chief of Staff of Vetlandia is not really being held captive and is, in fact, behind

263

this whole occupation. He's the one who is directing the negotiations. Dr. Gunnar and the senator are in league with him too. Senator Tyler knew about this thing before he ever showed up on the scene. The vets have gained possession of a few rifles and a couple of hand grenades and they have several men ready to make some kind of an assault on the occupiers. They think they need to take some action before Mort Kilpatrick starts blowing up buildings and killing veterans. They want to know what they can expect from you if they take some action."

"Yes, I just learned about the explosives from Senator Tyler. What kind of action are they planning? We don't want them to set off a melee and get themselves shot, god forbid! Let me take another shot at deescalating this thing with the senator. Now that we know who is behind this thing, maybe we can put some pressure on the bastards and get them to give up."

Signaling one of his assistants, Lindahl ordered him to retrieve Senator Tyler.

"OK, senator. We know Mort Kilpatrick is behind all this bullshit and that you are in cahoots with him. You're going to spend some time in the gray-bar hotel before this is all over. Maybe, if you're lucky, you'll get a cell next to your son. Now, I want you to go over and tell that fucked-up Chief of Staff that the jig is up. He better have his militia lay down their arms and come out with their hands up. And if he starts blowing anything up and hurting vets, there are going to be murder charges added on to those already prepared for him. You got that? And don't try any funny stuff once you get over there or you'll never see the light of day."

"But Mr. Lindahl — Mark — you have to believe that I have been taken in, just like you. I didn't know that Mort was planning this take over. I would never try to deceive you or the authorities. I wouldn't want to tarnish my reputation. I've got a family to take care of. I..., I...," he stammered.

"Tell it to someone who cares, senator! Now get you ass over there and get those idiots to give themselves up before we have some serious bloodshed."

Tyler picked up his white flag and made his way back to the COS residence. Speaking to Mort, he tearfully related that the feds knew everything and were demanding that everyone put down their arms and march out with their hands up.

"Bullshit! I'm not going to prison for one second," exclaimed Mort. We've got to show them we mean business." Gesturing to a guard, he continued, "Go find Youngblood and bring him here right away. We'll see who has the upper hand here, by god!"

Mort walked into an adjoining room to make a phone call that wouldn't be overheard. Then he ordered another guard to fetch all of the cash stashed away in his office, place it in a suitcase, and bring it to him.

When Youngblood arrived, Mort ordered him to ready an armored vehicle that could get the two of them and Gunnar out of the place by going overland through the fence bounding the north side of the property. Then he ordered Youngblood to go to one of the white storage buildings on the southeast side of the VA campus.

"Blow the fucker up!" shouted Mort. "Then have a list of cell phone numbers ready to activate explosives in other buildings if we need more cover to make our escape. I'll show them who's in control here, goddammit."

Youngblood hesitated. "Don't you think that is a pretty drastic step to take, Dr. Kilpatrick? That may just force the feds to take action, to come in here with guns blazing."

"I don't think they will do it, Clarence. They'll probably do anything to avoid an indiscriminate slaughter— a massacre where a lot of innocent vets get killed. They know the newspapers and the politicians will ask why they didn't wait and take a more measured approach. No, Clarence, they don't want to ruin their careers by being hasty. In the meantime, we'll make it out of here and get to that little landing strip up by Grants Pass. I've already arranged for a small plane and pilot to be there to whisk us off to Armondo's place in Mexico where we can lay low for a while."

Tony, hearing the latest update to Mort's plans, decided it was important enough that Tom know about it immediately. As he extricated himself from the passageway to Mort's residence, he heard and felt the explosive report of a bomb going off a few hundred yards from his location.

"Holy shit! They've started it already," he said to those members of the resistance standing around.

He rushed to Tom's hideout below Building 205. Tom, Jerry McCall, Terry Wells, Ken Harper, and Hank Burns were discussing the recent explosion and plans for an armed uprising of Vetlandia residents as Tony burst in, excitedly proclaiming that Mort was readying himself to escape in an armored car imminently with Gunnar and Youngblood and that they planned to divert attention from themselves by blowing up buildings housing veterans.

"We've got to do something right away or the bastards are going to kill a bunch of our guys and fucking get away with it!"

"OK," said Tom. "I know what we can do. We'll just do a more focused version of what we have just been talking about. The guys with the muscle and skills that I think can pull it off are here right now. We've got three captured militia outfits and some rifles that we can use. The rest of you can don dark outfits and pose like interrogators or undercover militia. What you'll do is drag me over to the COS residence and proclaim that you have caught the head of the veteran resistance and need to see the commander right away. Once we have the COS within our grasp, we take out the guards and take their place outside the door. We've got to capture the commander of the militia as well or he could initiate action without passing it by the COS. Time is of the essence — let's get going."

The six men dressed themselves for their expected roles. Tom put on the clothes he had been wearing when he was first captured and applied food coloring to simulate bruises and cuts supposedly inflicted during his apprehension. Three men dressed themselves in militia uniforms and carried rifles they had captured. Two men, Terry Wells and Hank Burns, found ski masks to complement their dark "enforcer" clothing.

"Ken, you give Oldman a call to let the feds know what we are doing. Tell them that we will call them once we have accomplished our mission. If they don't hear from us, they can assume we didn't make it. I think that they should take out the machine gunners at whichever gate appears to have the weakest defense. They can then send a small force to come rescue our little band and take the COS and whoever else we manage to disable into custody."

As they emerged into the darkness from Building 205, Jerry, Ken, and Tony marched directly toward the door to the COS residence with rifles held across their chests at the ready position. Behind them, Terry and Hank each grasped one of Tom's arms and dragged him along, his feet splayed out in simulated non-functional status.

When they got close enough to the COS residence to be noticed, a guard yelled out, "Halt. Who goes there? Identify yourself!"

"It is I, Sergeant York," said Tony. We have found the head of the veteran resistance group and need to bring him to the commander at once."

"The commander isn't here right now." Beckoning another guard, he said, "I'll send someone to retrieve him. Stay where you are."

Once the messenger was out of sight, there were only three guards on duty. Tom signaled it was time to act by groaning and dropping to the ground, feigning loss of consciousness. The guard in charge came closer and asked what was wrong with their prisoner.

"I guess we worked him over a little too much before we brought him over here. Could you help us get him into a chair. We don't want to kill the sonofabitch before they have a chance to find out what he knows."

The guard leaned his rifle against the building and brought a white plastic yard chair over to Tom. At that point, Terry and Hank overpowered him while Jerry, Ken, and Tony subdued the other two guards. Each of the guards was bound hand and foot, had their mouths taped shut, and were dragged to the garage adjoining the residence. Terry and Hank confiscated their weapons and embellished themselves with militia shirts and headgear. Tom now sported a rifle of his own. He motioned Jerry to open the door to the residence.

"Who's there?" Mort yelled out. Senator Tyler began to shake in fear.

Tom poked his head into the living room and pointed his rifle at the COS. "I hear you been looking to talk to me, Mr. Kilpatrick."

"Who the hell are you? I never seen you before."

"It's Tom Ward, doctor. Don't you remember sending your goon boys after me, beating the shit out of me and throwing me in a dungeon with your boss, Mr. Horton? Don't you remember sending your thugs to arrange for me to have a fatal accident? Don't you remember sending your lackey, Gunnar, to hunt me down and silence me?"

"Oh, *that* Tom Ward! Jesus, man, I never meant to harm you. My boys just got a little carried away trying to please me. And you know what Gunnar is like. Why, I can make you rich right now if you let me go free. I see that you're a bright kid. You could work for me and you could really get rich."

"Sorry Mort. Your grifting days are over. The feds are going to put you away for so long you will leave on a slab. Gunnar and all your minions are going with you. No more recruiting drivers for criminal enterprises and taking a cut of the profits from your truck company pals. No more phony veteran compensation awards. No more kooky militia bullshit. You're finished Mort!"

Jerry McCall pushed Gunnar into the room at the point of his rifle.

"Well, if it isn't the good psychiatrist paying his respects," observed Tom. How are you Dr. Gunnar?"

Not waiting for a reply, Tom, Jerry, and Ken trussed up the errant physicians and pushed them down on a sofa alongside Senator Tyler.

Youngblood, notified that his men had captured the head of the veteran's resistance, soon appeared on the scene. Taking a close look at the sham guards and becoming suspicious, Youngblood asked, "Where are the guards that were here a half hour ago? What unit do you belong to?"

"We are replacements, sir," answered Hank. We were asked to come over here by Dr. Gunnar, who is inside interrogating the prisoner. The other guards took a break once we arrived. They will be back shortly."

Youngblood backed away, at the same time reaching for his revolver. Rather than shooting him and drawing attention to their presence at the COS residence, Terry rushed in and performed a karate kick on the surprised militia commander, catching him in his groin. Relieving him of his sidearm, Terry quickly ushered him into the living room where Youngblood was astonished by the scene before him.

"Join the party, commander," joked Tom as Youngblood was bound and gagged.

Ken Harper called Dr. Oldman and told him they had completed their mission. Dr. Kilpatrick, Dr. Gunnar, Senator Tyler, and Clarence Youngblood, the militia commander, were all in custody. He asked if the feds could send help to get them out of the compound.

"No worries," said Lindahl. "Help is on the way! Good job boys!"

After he had learned of Tom's impending effort to capture the COS, Lindahl had arranged a rescue plan which he now executed. Two Rocket Propelled Grenades were fired at the truck hosting a dual 60-caliber machine gun at the south entrance. Seeing their comrades go up in smoke and fire, the attendant militia members freaked out, threw down their arms, and fled the scene. Federal agents swooped in and headed to the COS residence with only minor resistance, dropping off men along the way to ensure their safe egress.

Seeing the federal agents approaching, Terry and Hank laid down their arms and raised their hands, announcing that they were with the resistance and not the militia. Two agents continued to train their weapons on the pair while another four agents entered the building and assessed the situation inside.

"Wow!" said one of the agents. "You guys have got things under control and all the major culprits are ready to deliver to our boss. Lindahl is going to love this. Everybody is going to call you heroes for what you have done. It's not going to be like the last time you served your country, that's for sure."

When the veterans were safely across the highway and the prisoners stowed in a paddy wagon under heavy guard, Lindahl had loudspeakers blare the news across the street that the leaders of the occupation had been arrested and that all participants should throw down their arms, surrender and walk out the front gates with their arms in the air. Within short order, some 20 militia members complied and then it became a total capitulation with participants exiting from all three entrances. The few holdouts were persuaded to follow suit when three of their members were shot and killed. Police raided the farm near Grants Pass used as a training ground for the militia and confiscated all armaments and supplies stored there.

Once things were going the way Lindahl wanted, he got together with Tom and the other participants for a debriefing. He wanted to know everything about how they first became suspicious of Gunnar and Kilpatrick, how they managed to observe activities at the trucking company and work with guys on the inside who answered to the DEA. He wanted to know all about their road trips, surveillance activities, and how they tracked the money trail to Mort's office.

"I've got to hand it to you. You boys broke this case wide open and captured all the bad guys before they could inflict more suffering on your fellow veterans and get away with fraud, supplying fences with the objects of their trade, drug-running, human trafficking, and god knows what other crimes. You all deserve medals and a huge reward and you'll get them if I have anything to say about it."

∞

The next few days were a whirlwind of newspaper and TV interviews for Tom and his squad. Tom maintained that the impetus for his activism was instances of cruel and improper treatment of patients and that those events led to the discovery of the network of participating staff members and their other nefarious activities. Modestly, he downplayed his role and credited the intelligence, courage, and willingness to take risks and get involved in the project by his comrades at Vetlandia.

"We've all had difficult times since our military service. In spite of the handicaps we all suffer from, these guys have chosen to fight for what is right, have taken a courageous stand against all odds. And we shouldn't forget that some employees stuck their necks out to help too. They resisted considerable threats and peer pressure to keep quiet and hide in the background."

Newspapers, magazines, and talking heads on TV picked up on various aspects of the evolving story of what happened at Vetlandia. One headline read *Band of disabled veterans capture masterminds of militia takeover of VA facility* with a detailed description of the activities of Tom's surveillance group in exposing the criminal activities of the COS and his henchmen and their marshaling of resources to capture the main culprits in the scheme. Reporters were impressed with the acumen of the veterans, their courage and their bravery in carrying out their mission. Some contrasted the jaundiced image of down-and-out, alcoholic, and drug-addicted veterans held by the public and even many employees of the facility with their obviously patriotic and heroic actions in the theater of war known as Vetlandia.

There were articles on militias, two-thirds of whose members tend to be white supremacists and the reasons for their emergence. The rise in power of doctors Kilpatrick, Gunnar, and Greene was dissected as to possible traits and motives and the failure of oversight in the system to catch them before they could do any damage. Other writers focused on the ill-treatment of patients, the practice of presumptive medicine, PTSD, and the other factors that brought veterans into the VA system in the first place.

All of the veterans who participated in the resistance were required to remain available for testimony in the trials of Mort and his gang. Additional defendants, such as Carole Harding — the phony psychologist — were exposed by informers and government investigations of the extent of Mort's network. The two transportation companies were closed down and their tentacles were traced to other criminal enterprises which were also investigated and raided. Prosecutors had enough business to occupy them for years.

The President of the United States lauded Tom for spearheading the veteran's efforts and invited him to Washington to have a chat and receive the Medal of Freedom.

The head of the Department of Veterans Affairs traveled to Vetlandia to present awards to all the veterans who actively participated in exposing the corruption at its no longer "best-kept secret in the VA system." Of course, he did not acknowledge his complicity in burying the documents Scott Parks had sent to his office, but when the president learned of it, he asked for his resignation within a few months. All of the veterans who took part in uncovering the depravity of the Kilpatrick regime had their service connections reviewed and upgraded where appropriate. For those who still wanted to join the workforce, their opportunities for education and training in fields of their choice were expedited. Dr. Oldman and Mr. Horton were both given awards of merit with a financial bonus as well.

Vetlandia would itself experience a renaissance and face lift to many of its WWII-era buildings as a result of congressional investigations and new guilt-induced appropriations for which politicians of all stripes were willing to take credit. Many buildings were closed down as asbestos was removed from them while others were completely leveled and replaced with one-story structures that looked a lot like motel buildings one might see along the highway.

After Tom had a few interviews with reporters, he complained to Dr. Oldman, "They keep going on about how I am some kind of hero. I'm not a hero. I don't want any glory. I shouldn't be singled out for praise. The rest of our group took just as many risks as I did. I just did what was necessary under the circumstances. I saw the needs and responded to them the only way I knew how. So did the rest of the guys. The thing that drove me to continue investigating Gunnar and the others was my outrage at how some patients were being treated here. That really puzzled me and pissed me off. I've got just as many faults as anyone else. Jeez, some of those reporters think a movie should be made about it. Can you believe that?"

"Yes, I can, Tom. I have seen many people who have been hailed as heroes and have medals to prove it. Yet they don't feel like they are anything special. Heroism is not a feeling or a character trait. The hero is something — a projection, a concept, a myth, — that a community creates for itself, an affirmation of their better values and aspirations. They need to have a concrete exemplar of those values for the good of the community because things go more smoothly when those values are manifested by its members. They celebrate a hero in order to promote adherence to those values, to show how obstacles can be overcome to realize them, and, it is believed, change an ordinary person who gets labeled as a hero in the process. In celebrating their hero, they give others a goal to aspire to and they celebrate themselves for holding such values."

"I guess I have changed from when I first came in here. I'm not the scared little epileptic that drifted in here after being taken advantage of by some dumb sister-fucking hillbilly on the road. Working with these other guys on a project that is worthwhile and solving the damn problem has given me a lot more confidence. I know what I regard as important, mostly, and I know I have enough smarts to get what I want. I can trust my judgment in important matters. And a shout out to you for helping me navigate these waters!"

"Sure, Tom. Glad to be of assistance."

Tom thought more about what Oldman had said. Then he ventured "You mean I am just a tool for promoting cultural values, a character in a cultural drama?"

"In a way, yes," said Dr. Oldman. "That is your burden and your reward for participating in community life."

"I don't know if I want to play that role or even *how* to play that role," Tom proffered. "I feel kind of like a phony pretending to be something I'm not. I'd be scared all the time that someone would catch me and expose me as a fraud."

"You don't have to play a role, Tom. All you have to do is be yourself. Recognize any overblown complements for what they are and brush them off as attempts to win your favor for whatever purpose the other person may have in mind. Don't let your head be turned by offers of riches and popularity. Remember what is important to you and to those you care about. And remember that this, too, shall pass, that public attention will be turned elsewhere and in a little while you will just be Tom Ward making his way in the world."

"Yeah, I guess I know that's true, deep down."

A month after the liberation of Vetlandia most of the vets who took part in it met for a reunion and celebration. Daniel Hanson had merged several smaller tables into one large one covered with checkered tablecloths and chairs all around. He had arranged for beverages and snacks before a formal dinner. When Tom walked in everyone else stood, clapped, and cheered for the man who spearheaded the surveillance group and resistance. Tom turned crimson with embarrassment.

"That means a lot to me," said Tom. "I love all you guys that stuck your necks out to help a whacked-out inexperienced newbie who, for all you knew, might just be tilting at windmills. No matter what brought you to Vetlandia, you each played your parts in this little drama, contributed your unique talents to figure out what was happening here and helped set it right. I am proud to be a member of such an upstanding group. You all came to my aid when I really needed it and for that I am thankful. And I'm thankful for you remembering the training you got in the military too. It certainly came in handy when we had to work as a team to defeat the goofballs that took over Vetlandia."

Another round of applause. Then the men began talking with their neighbors at the table about how pumped up they were during the siege and how they felt "alive again" when they began to work on their military-like mission to rid Vetlandia of the invaders.

"It brought back the feeling I had when we were on a large air assault with hundreds of helicopters hopscotching up the countryside to take out the enemy. That was one of the times over there that things went right!"

"Amid a thousand that went wrong," joked the man across the table.

"When the militia took over, I had that same anxiety, that fear, we had when we were about to get overrun," said another. "I thought for sure those idiots were going to panic and start shooting us in our beds at any moment."

Andrew volunteered, "I got to feeling claustrophobic in those tunnels and especially that one under the COS residence. It was dark and damp and stunk to high heaven. I felt like the damn thing was going to collapse on top of me at any minute."

"Yeah," said Tony, "There were lots of ways the whole thing could have gone sideways. The vets that worked for the trucking outfits could have ratted us out to save their own asses and their goons could have come looking for us just like they did with Michael Mayhew. Just think of what happened to poor old Gordon Sawyer. Here's a toast to one who didn't make it through," as he raised his cup of coffee.

"Don't forget that Tom and Mr. Horton both got the shit pounded out of them and thrown in that vehicle repair building to rot." Raising his glass, Daniel exclaimed, "Here's to the rescue crew!"

"And the cops could have come in shooting and got us all killed. Thank God Mark Lindahl had a cool head and thought things through before he acted," voiced another.

Ken Harper commented, "I was proud of the way we worked together once we knew what was happening. Everybody was able to keep their shit together in spite of being scared and we didn't have any hotshots going off on their own, thinking they knew better than everybody else. I think Tom did a great job of picking people out for different tasks and he played a damn good beat-up prisoner." Tom laughed.

"Any time I need someone who can throw a wrench 20 feet and hit an asshole in the head, I'm going to call on Claude," joked another. Everyone laughed.

There were many memories of events during the surveillance operation and the militia occupation that triggered recollections of military experiences as the night went on. The group seemed to progress toward greater closeness as a result of sharing common experiences in wartime as well as in their efforts at Vetlandia.

CHAPTER 17

Epilogue

At the trial of Mort Kilpatrick, his attorney argued for a reduced sentence due to his client's alcoholism and depression. The judge was unimpressed with that argument and gave him the maximum sentence, 20 years without possibility of parole. Dr. Gunnar received a 15-year sentence and both physicians lost their licenses to practice medicine ever again. Commander Youngblood was sentenced to ten years for his part in the violent occupation of government property and, as a convicted felon, he could never own a firearm again. Senator Tyler was stripped of his position in state government by a vote of his peers in the state senate.

Mort Kilpatrick developed prostate cancer and died in prison. Dr. Gunnar was unable to keep his snide remarks about other prisoners to himself and was rewarded with a shiv in the ribs, from which he did not recover, during a courtyard encounter. Whitey Greene, the incompetent staff physician and militia member, served 10 years in prison, got religion (or so he claimed), and became a fundamentalist proselytizer. His conversion, however, did not hold at bay the temptation of easy riches and he was convicted of fraudulently absconding with the life savings of one of his elderly parishioners. He spent his remaining years behind bars, grumbling about the unfairness of life.

Dominic Sabini, owner of Beaver Trucking, was imprisoned for life as a career criminal. In prison, he continued to have a small coterie of convicts who looked up to him as a master criminal. He persuaded some of his followers to help him escape prison by making their way through heating and air conditioning duct-work. The vacancy in his cell was discovered and the police mounted a major manhunt, assuming that he had somehow made his way to the outside. It was several months later when the smell of death began permeating the prison, that his body and those of his accomplices were found stuck and rotting in a cold-air return.

Carole Harding, the phony psychologist, served 6 years in prison after which she moved into the rural house owned by her spinster sister. She became a potter, selling her wares on the side of the road along with sweetcorn she grew in in her backyard.

Herb Sims, one of Gunnar's informants, tattled on his cohort, Georgie Cramden, for selling child porn on the Internet. Georgie received a 20-year sentence and was required to register on the sex offenders database.

Roscoe Robinson's connection with the militia was discovered during the investigation following the occupation. He was fired from his job with the local police force.

Silvia Knox, the tightly clad psychology intern, was ostracized by her fellow interns and experienced a great deal of humiliation when it was revealed that she had conspired with Carole Harding and Mort Kilpatrick in trying to frame Dr. Oldman with a sexual offense. She dropped out of the internship program and hid out with her mother for two years before trying her hand at another career. She gained over 100 pounds and began to wear dowdy clothes, abandoning any hope of finding a suitable romantic partner. Her mother paid for her psychotherapy for 10 years and consented to funding a small used clothing business for her.

Peter Steele (Cowboy) and his wife Lois retired to the family ranch where they lived out their days in relative comfort. They continued to plan and organize livestock drives but hired younger folks to carry out the actual herding. Peter resumed flying in a Cessna 182 Skylane and attended a reunion of several of the Ravens who managed to survive the war.

Bennie Foster, the former Coast Guardsman and physical therapy aide, became a TV salesman, hawking various household products such as pots and pans, air fryers, and sealants. Hugely successful due to his humorous presentations, he built a mansion on the coast in Washington State where he could enjoy the ocean and entertain other veterans. His good fortune caused him to laugh all the way to the bank.

Terry Wells, the fighting leather-worker, went to culinary arts school in Coos Bay, Oregon, and became famous for his seafood entrees. He started a chic restaurant in San Francisco but it failed when his wife of one year absconded with all the funds in their joint bank account. He resumed drinking and fighting at any provocation, supporting himself as a short-order cook in a string of run-down bars and nightclubs.

Andrew Hammons, Gene Lofgren's roommate at Vetlandia, moved to Portland and worked for a veterans organization. He wrote a book about the ill-fated Iran hostage rescue operation, illustrated by his pencil sketches, which was well-received by military historians. He married late in life.

FBI agent Frank Celeberti tracked down Gene Lofgren, who had been living on the streets in Berkeley, and helped him gain employment in a halfway house for addicts. They continued their friendship until Gene died from a heart attack at work. Frank notified Andrew of Gene's demise. They were the only ones who knew of and appreciated Gene's heroic efforts to fight the drug pushers and help those suffering from addiction.

Ken Harper, the surveillance group member, torture victim, and former tracker of the Baader-Meinhof Gang, returned to his hometown in California where he worked as a security guard for many years. That career ended when he was forced to shoot back at an intruder on one of the properties he guarded. A morally devout person, he was so re-traumatized by the experience that he vowed never to touch a gun again. He spent the remainder of his life in the state veterans home in Chula Vista, California.

Daniel Hanson, Tom's long-time partner at Vetlandia, continued in one of Dr. Oldman's PTSD groups and eventually got his condition under control. Returning to Minnesota, he became a veterans crisis counselor working for the state in rural areas. His children liked the new stable father figure Daniel had become and welcomed him to family gatherings.

Claude Pitts, the big lug who carried the director out of Vetlandia during the siege, developed many friends as a result of his participation in the rescue operation. "I never thought I'd be able to trust another human being," he said. "I'm amazed that these guys can see me for what I am – a simple man." Claude purchased an old school bus, parked it on a friend's property, and transformed it into a comfortable place to live on his newly received disability award.

Michael Mayhew, the would-be DEA spy, stayed away from Oregon for several years to avoid any retribution from drug dealers he had betrayed. He lived under an assumed name with his loving wife. His former "mother" at the DEA helped him get a job with the National Park Service. He called Dr. Oldman once to let him know that he was still alive.

Doc Oldman continued to treat veterans at Vetlandia until his retirement. He won an award for the publication of a paper on the treatment of PTSD and was recognized for his numerous research articles involving Psychological Type. He maintained correspondence with the vets of the surveillance group for many years.

Jan Burke, the outreach social worker, continued to walk the streets of the local community searching for homeless veterans in need of medical, occupational, and/or psychological help despite her advanced age. Respected by veterans but neglected by the administration, she and her husband bought Doctor Oldman's Vanagon when he retired and used it for camping trips around the state. Some of her "rescues" got together and presented her with an award for her caring and doggedness in helping down-and-out veterans.

Fred Bojorquez, a frequent ally of Dr. Oldman in his battles with physicians and administrative personnel, took a medical retirement due to MS and rode his BMW motorcycle off into the sunset.

Thanks to demonstrations by Hmong refugees and the intervention of his many political friends in California, Minnesota, and Wisconsin as well as congressional supporters in

Washington, DC, and, importantly, his indebted CIA friends, all of the federal charges against Vang Pao and his group were summarily dropped in 2007. He continued to provide leadership in community building and setting up viable Laotian and Hmong communities in the US. He founded the non-profit Lao Family Community, in Orange County, California, which supplied social services to many Hmong communities. He founded a Hmong grocery wholesale cooperative and a Hmong credit union. He originated the Hmong 18 Clans Council in Fresno, which strove to maintain traditional Hmong cultural ways of solving problems such as the wise elders' council forum for dispute resolution. He promoted education and urged Hmong youngsters to be studious, excel in their endeavors, and return to help their people thrive. He mined new opportunities for Hmong people by working with local, state, and federal government officials. He fostered entrepreneurship and public service and actively participated in local veterans affairs, creating the Lao Veterans of America and the Special Guerrilla Units Veterans and Families of USA, Inc. He worked with diplomats and Hmong Americans to stop the United Nations-sponsored repatriation back to Laos of thousands of Hmong refugees living in Thailand with its consequent persecution by the communists. Involvement in the affair for which he was arrested was simply part of his dream that someday the Laotians living in foreign lands would be able to return to a democratic Laos.

Vang Pao was braving the weather to celebrate the 2011 Hmong International New Year in Fresno, California when he contracted pneumonia and did not recover. In the words of his firstborn grandchild, Pacyinz Lyfoung, "Like a true soldier and devoted leader, General Vang Pao worked for his Lao-Hmong People until his last breath and his last step."

General Vang Pao was survived by two ex-wives, twenty-five children, sixty-eight grandchildren, and seventeen great-grandchildren. He also had an extended family comprising many children and several hundred orphans whom he raised as his own. All of the 18 Hmong clans mourned him as a Father.

Mark Lindahl received a promotion at the FBI and served as District Director of the Portland Field Office until his retirement.

He moved to Santa Fe and became involved in state politics, often consulting with state agencies about strategies to combat juvenile crime and reduce unnecessary police violence.

A neurologist who was an expert on the peculiarities of patients who took both Dilantin and insulin volunteered his services when he read a newspaper account describing Tom's medical history. He was able to adjust Tom's medications so that adverse side effects were dramatically reduced which delighted the patient tremendously.

Mark Lindahl tried to recruit Tom into the FBI Critical Incident Negotiation Unit but Tom was turned off when he contemplated the amount of education required first to become eligible for employment at the FBI, then becoming trained as a special agent, followed by even more training as a negotiator. He did not want to put his life on hold while getting ready to live it. Instead, Tom moved to Las Vegas where he worked in various areas of the gambling trade: slots floor-person, table games dealer, camera surveillance operator, cage cashier, VIP Lounge representative, human resources manager, and, finally, general manager of a casino. He became known for his creativity in calmly defusing conflicts that arose on the floor between certain unruly patrons and casino employees. He instinctively knew when to offer incentives and when to call for the application of force. His superiors recognized that Tom had developed discerning skills for assessing both employees and patrons and promoted him to management positions for that reason. Tom got married to the daughter of a casino owner and raised two children. The family frequently made trips to Oregon where Tom was known to give inspirational speeches to the new occupants of Vetlandia.

His roommate, Tony, and friend, Jerry the Riverine, moved to English-speaking Belize and were part of the expatriate Vietnam Veteran community there. They enjoyed the balmy weather, palm trees and jungle, the sea with a protective reef, and the relaxed lifestyle as well as the low cost of living. They would take a two-hour flight back to a VA facility in Texas for health care, as needed. Unfortunately, Jerry developed asbestosis from his work on ships at Mare Island and died before realizing his dream of building and living on his own boat. Tony returned to California where he received training in computer security, eventually joining a software company that specialized in tracking ransomware. After many years of separation, his daughter helped him reconnect with his former wife and they moved in together.

ABOUT THE AUTHOR

Gerald D. Otis

Gerald D. Otis was born in Northfield, Minnesota, graduated from Northfield High School, attended St. Olaf College for two years, and graduated from the University of Minnesota. He earned his Ph.D. in Psychology from the University of Arizona in 1966. After completing a clinical internship at the Veterans Administration Hospital in Palo Alto, California he joined the University of New Mexico School of Medicine leading a research team in a longitudinal study of the career decision-making process of medical students and physicians, taught classes, and maintained a clinical practice. For 10 years after Dr. Otis left the University, he maintained a private clinical practice while designing and constructing sculptural furniture and developing computer programs for statistical analysis. During his years as a psychologist, he published results of research on incidental learning, the interaction of stress and personality, family psychotherapy, physician career choice, psychological type and the Myers-Briggs Type Indicator, post-traumatic stress disorder, and trends in violent death. He received two awards from the Association for Psychological Type and several awards for his efforts at fine woodworking. Following 16 years working for the Veterans Administration in Medford, Oregon, where he specialized in the treatment of post-traumatic stress disorder, Dr. Otis retired from clinical practice and now lives in Las Cruces, New Mexico with his wife Connie. He has authored six books: Joseph Lee Heywood: His Life and Tragic Death (2012), Paroxysm: Love, Murder, and Justice in Post-Civil War Washington, DC. (2013), Presumed Crazy: A Fisherman Gets Entangled in the Mental Health Gulag (2014), Physician Career Choice and Satisfaction (2019 with Naomi L. Quenk), Down the Cannon (2020), and the current Vetlandia (2024).

www.ingramcontent.com/pod-product-compliance
Lightning Source LLC
Chambersburg PA
CBHW071305170626
46809CB00001B/338